GRANT US MERCY

A POST-APOCALYPTIC SERIAL NOVEL:
PART ONE
INSTALLMENTS 1-5

DC LITTLE

This is a work of fiction. Names, characters, organizations, places, events, and incidents are either products of the author's imaginations or are used fictitiously.

Copyright © 2019, 2020, 2021 DC Little, Little Publishing

All rights reserved.

No part of this book may be reproduced, or stored in a retrieval system, or transmitted in any form or by any means, electronic, mechanical, photocopying, recording, or otherwise, without express written permission of the publisher.

DEDICATION

To my Mountain MacGyver who inspires me every day and my special boy who sees things others only wish they could.

ACKNOWLEDGMENTS

Wow! What a journey this has been! I have to say my first thank you to the wonderful lady, talented author, fierce mama, and supportive friend, Heather Yates, for encouraging me to go forth with my dream of writing Post-Apocalyptic even though it is so different from the genre I found my success in.

Of course, I need to thank my writer's group, Women Writers of the Well. Without all of your support and encouragement I still would be writing stories for my eyes only. It's been fun sharing this series with you every step along the way!

A heart-felt thank you to my fantastic editors, Dianne McCleery and Joan Simpson. Without your guidance and keen eye, my books wouldn't be near as clean and consistent! And my ARC readers whose encouragement feeds me during those dry spells.

Thanks to my mom for her unwavering support and encouragement. And a special thanks for my Sis, whose namesake will be making a special star appearance later on in the series.

And of course, where would I be without the two main men in my life! Thank you, My Love, for helping me with all the nuances of natural disasters and survival thinking. Your support in this project keeps me going strong. Thank you, My Little Love, for understanding how important Mommy's writing time is and being excited whenever I receive one of my books in the mail.

INSTALLMENT ONE

~1~

DATE: October 10   19:03

Blake Chantry wiped the sweat from his brow. His knees creaked as he covertly shifted his position behind the bushes. If they caught him, the consequence would be the end of his career and probably his life, not to mention negate the reason for his eavesdropping in the first place. Yet, the threat of death came with every assignment, so steadying his heart rate came easily as he patiently waited.

The heavy night air felt more like August than October. It clung to him like a cloak as he hid behind a thick stand of manzanita bushes. He wiped at his brow again as he searched the sky for signs of the moon. It shouldn't rise for another few hours, and the tall pines gave him enough cover with only the light from the stars.

He settled back in to continue his surveillance of the bunker hidden less than ten yards away. It could only be seen because he knew exactly where it lay veiled underground. An impressive formation of rock outcropping shielded the entrance from anyone who didn't know exactly where to look. He nodded to himself. He had accomplished his task well. No one could complain about the placement of this safety house.

This last op left him uneasy and restless. The sense of urgency spoke with every command uttered.

Something was going down. He clenched his teeth. He had to unearth the truth in order to safeguard his family.

His thumb rubbed the empty indentation around his left ring finger. It had been a year since he had gone undercover for this assignment, but the indentation remained a constant reminder of what he had left behind. If he allowed himself the freedom, his heart would ache with longing. He couldn't undo the time he had spent away, but maybe he could protect his family from whatever threat caused such panic in the higher-ups—if he could find out the intel.

Spying on his superiors didn't sit well with Blake. In fact, it made the bile in his gut churn, but the thought of something happening to his family when he had a chance at finding out how to protect them far outweighed the discomfort.

Finally, someone stirred at the hidden entrance. Governor Dutton ducked out of the bunker. Blake froze, his palms sweating. This could be the moment he had been waiting for.

Blake had enjoyed working for the governor for the last several years. The guy would make a reliable president if he won this next election like people predicted. If Blake hadn't promised his family that this assignment would be his last, he would have thrived continuing his service protecting the new president.

Dutton ran a hand down his haggard face before staring up at the sky as if he would never see it again.

Blake hungered to talk with him—one-on-one. He knew that the Governor would be direct with him. Sweeping the landscape once more, he began to stand. Before his shadow had left the brush, an exasperated sigh came from someone else exiting the bunker. Blake slowly squatted, resuming his stealth position.

Simmons wormed out from the bunker to stand beside Governor Dutton. The small man's beady eyes and frantic movements unsettled Blake.

"I know this is hard to take in, sir. It has to be done, and done soon." Simmons glanced furtively in quick succession all around him.

Did the man feel Blake's eyes on him?

"The attack is imminent." Simmons' words shot out in rapid fire.

Attack? Blake held his breath. This was the intel he had been waiting for. He had watched people of interest changing funds and stockpiling supplies, like ammunition and food. Blake and other coverts like him had been instructed to find secure locations for bunkers such as this one. He focused, intent on every word he could glean.

"What about our families and our men? I have some men that have been with me since the beginning. We can't just let them..." The governor's voice trailed off as he scanned the brush.

The dark night hid Blake well, of that he was certain. Yet, he had the uncanny feeling that Dutton knew he was there, listening.

"My men are on their way to pick up your family as we speak." Simmons moved like a weasel, a weasel who was about to snatch another animal's food. "No one can know of our locations. A few of our men will stay on as guards, but most will be dispatched."

Dispatched? The hairs stood up on the back of Blake's neck.

Dutton seemed to stare right at Blake. "What if

those men run?"

Blake tensed. Was Dutton trying to tell him to go AWOL?

"Run? They have no idea of our intentions, but if some evade us, we don't have the manpower to chase after them. The time is at hand." Simmons shrugged. "We'll have to assume those men, and their information, will get lost in the aftermath."

The aftermath—the words echoed in Blake's mind. He had heard the projections about how the country's civilians would deteriorate after a catastrophic event. No wonder Simmons didn't seem too concerned about leaky intel.

"And if not?" Dutton asked.

"Well, we'll hope they respect the fact that we are doing what has to be done to keep our country's leaders alive and not try to harass us for supplies. If they do, we'll have no choice but to destroy them. That's why we had different teams. Not one squad will know all of our defenses."

Blake leaned forward. He remembered separate teams coming in as his squad had been relocated and had wondered what those armored trucks were doing at this bunker. His eyes quickly darted around. Where had the cameras been hidden and the remote artilleries? He knew they had them.

"Hmm. Do I get to choose the men I want to keep?" Dutton's voice brought Blake's attention back to the conversation. The governor's hands squeezed and opened at his sides.

Blake understood. Tension coursed through him as well.

"No, sir, the director has chosen the ones we know are loyal to our cause." Simmons took a step back toward the bunker entrance.

Loyal to what cause? Blake quieted the urge to strangle the information from the weasel.

"I see." Governor Dutton made a signal against his thigh as he turned.

Blake knew the signal even in the dim starlight. He knew what the governor ordered. *Leave. Now. Disappear.*

"Sir, are you ready to go back inside and finalize the preparations?" Simmons asked, halfway behind the rock outcropping already.

Blake wanted to laugh. The little man was probably scared of the dark.

"I'm going to miss these stars." The governor raised his eyes to the night sky once more.

"Yes, well, our task is to survive this so we can see them again." Simmons shifted his weight and glanced at the bunker door.

"You go back in. I'm going to call my wife so she can prepare."

"Sir…"

Governor Dutton dismissed the smaller man with a hard stare.

"Yes, sir." Simmons scurried back inside, the bunker door closing behind him with a resounding clank.

The governor may be next in line for presidency, and he may be in politics now, but he once served his country as a respected general. He knew how to command men, and he knew how to work the system to protect the ones he cared for.

Blake drew in a breath and let it out soundlessly. He didn't know if the attack would be of natural causes or come by nuke, electromagnetic pulse, or what, or who would be behind it. His guess was China, though North Korea and ISIS would be a close second. Yet, there had been many discussions of the increase of solar activity. A tendril of fear tingled down his spine. Could their demise really stem from a natural disaster?

"You know the protocol," Dutton said, the phone to his ear.

Blake thought the governor talked to his wife, yet his superior had taken a step or two closer toward Blake, seeming to meet his eyes.

"You must leave now," he commanded. "Avoid the cities. I hope to see you after the chaos has settled and order is once again restored. It is then I will need your service more than ever."

Blake scanned his surroundings. Nothing else stirred except himself and the governor. He slowly stood, a dark shadow in the brush. "It's been an honor, sir."

"The honor has been mine. Now disappear and stay alive." Dutton's eyes lowered. "Yes, dear, I'm here. Yes, I'm okay. Remember what I've been preparing you for? You need to remain calm and remember the emergency plan. Agents should be arriving any minute to bring you and the kids to my location."

With one last look at the governor as he spoke to his wife, Blake silently stepped behind a tree and disappeared into the night.

~*~

Kris sighed as she picked up the Cheerios off the carpet for the third time this morning. You would think that by six, the boy would know how to keep the cereal in his bowl.

"Tucker, please put down that magazine and get your clothes on. We're going to be late for school again." She took the boy's now empty bowl and tossed it into the overflowing sink. If she was late again, her principal was sure to give her another long-torturing reprimand. Even tenure couldn't save her from that.

"Mommy, did you know that this knife can saw, screw, spark a fire, and be used like a regular knife." Tucker held the picture in the survival magazine against her nose.

She pulled it back and looked at the cruel-looking knife—something she didn't want to think of her first-grader wielding. "That's great, Sweetie, but can it help us get to school on time?"

"Well, no, but I will go lightning speed. Watch!" The boy zoomed towards his room in a flurry of movement that sent papers flying. A couple of Cheerios that had stuck to his pajamas fell to the floor, leaving a trail behind.

She wished her absent husband wouldn't send those magazines, like they were any sort of replacement for his actual presence. As if to mock her, his piercing green eyes watched her from their wedding photo. She slammed the frame down on the top of the bookcase where it stood. No matter how many times she had put it away, Tucker had always found it and put it back up. For his sake, she left it there now, even though most of the time she would rather not see the man's smiling face.

Kris stuffed their sandwiches into their lunch bags and took them to the door where Tucker hastily slammed his feet into his shoes. He had put his shirt on backwards and wore ripped jeans, but he had dressed himself. Some days she had to choose her battles and feel grateful for the little things.

They clambered into the car and pulled down the long driveway through their well-maintained forest. No brush grew beneath the tall pines, spruces, and firs, and each tree's dead branches had been cut off to leave only healthy trees and bare ground. In this dry year, it just might save their house from a wildfire. After her husband had completed all the initial work, he insisted on having a grounds keeper come out to ensure the forest stayed maintained. Too bad she had to let the hired man go two months ago. Luckily, there hadn't been much growth since then due to the lack of rain.

At the end of the drive, she slowed the car to wait for the gate to open automatically. Besides the large piece of property and the grounds keeper, her husband also had insisted upon this gate. As the automatic gate closed behind them, she looked at the clock and sighed with relief. They would get to school before the second bell. Her shoulders eased, and a few breaths later, her white-knuckled grip loosened.

"Mommy, can I go over to Vinny's house today?"

"You know why I don't like you going over there." She pursed her lips.

"But Dad says those games are good for my skills, that one day I will need to know how to shoot."

"Shooting zombies on a video game is nothing like shooting a real gun toward something living, Tuck." She did her best to soften her tone. He wanted to grow up so fast, and all she wanted was him to be her sweet little boy for a little longer. It wasn't too much to ask, was it?

The long standing fight between her and her husband warred within her as she kept the one-sided conversation going even in his absence.

He needs to be prepared, he would say.

Why would a six-year-old need to know how to survive on his own or defend himself? That's why he had parents, and though her husband might leave them for months at a time, *she* never left their son. With a sigh, Kris realized she was the one keeping this fight going, for she hadn't heard from her husband in close to a year.

A year of no contact. Her knuckles turned white on the steering wheel, fury causing her muscles to go rigid. Not one single call. Nothing. Then two months ago his checks stopped being automatically deposited. What did that mean? He promised to always return. Rage consumed her until a torrent of fear washed through it. What if he had died? How could she keep up the life they had created for Tuck without him? Her chest squeezed tight, making it difficult to breathe.

"Well, can Vinny come to our house then?"

Kris blinked her eyes. She didn't need to waste her time thinking about that reckless, selfish man right now. Tuck was her everything, and she had a classroom of fourth-graders waiting for her.

"We'll see, Sweetie." She glanced at him in the mirror.

"I want to show him my new survival magazine."

"I'm sure he would love it." Vinny, though a sweet and respectful kid, loved anything to do with weapons, and his parents seemed to encourage his interest with all the war-type video games they bought for him.

Kris pulled into a parking space in the staff lot just as the first bell rang. As soon as the car shut off, Tucker scrambled out of his booster seat and kissed her on the cheek. His green eyes and the sandy brown hair she tousled reminded her so much of his father.

"I love you, Mommy."

"I love you, too, Tuck" She squeezed him tightly. He may get his looks from his dad, but his sweetness, she knew, he got from her. "Have a good day. Be nice to Mrs. Robins."

"I always am. I'll wave to you at lunch!"

"I'll be looking for it." She grabbed her purse and bag, slinging them over her shoulder.

"We always return to each other," Tuck said as he did every time they parted.

"We always return to each other." She blew him a kiss as he threw his backpack over a shoulder and ran towards his classroom.

That saying meant a lot to her, and though her husband left without notice for months at a time, he did always return. This time she would ask him not to. A year with no contact besides a few magazines was too much to let go.

~2~

"Are you sure you don't mind, Sara? It shouldn't be longer than an hour," Kris asked while watching Tucker play with Vinny on the school's playground.

"Of course, it's no trouble at all. Vinny will be ecstatic. You know, I could just take him to our house instead of having them play here the whole time. Vinny has a new game he's been wanting to show off."

A rock sat heavy in Kris's belly. She didn't approve of the video games Tucker played at their house, but she couldn't take her son to the last-minute, emergency staff meeting. Kris cringed, but did her best to cover it up.

"Don't worry, this one doesn't have any zombies." Sara laughed lightly.

"Oh, that's nice, but it really shouldn't take that long." Kris continued to watched her son playing. Was it wrong that she wanted him to stay innocent for a little while longer?

"It's not that far. I could get them a snack. Besides, it's really hot today."

Kris had rolled up the sleeves on her shirt. The sun beat down on them, which was unusual for October. Another teacher called Kris and motioned for her to hurry. She trusted Sara to keep Tucker safe, even if she did allow things that Kris wasn't quite comfortable with, and if they didn't play the zombie game... "Okay, if that would be easiest on you." She didn't like going back on her word, but she also was told no children were allowed at this meeting. Times like now it sure would be nice to have a husband to call for help.

"Great. We'll see you when you get there." Sara smiled.

"Thank you." Kris turned toward the field and called Tucker over.

"Yeah, Mommy?" He panted as he arrived.

"Sweetie, they called a quick staff meeting that I have to go to."

"It's not Monday, though."

"I know. It's a special meeting, but Vinny's mom said you could hang out at their house until I'm finished."

"Yes!" He turned to his friend who still made his way from the field. "Vinny, I get to come over!"

"I'll see you soon." She kissed her son on the head. "You be good for Sara."

"I will. We always return to each other."

"We always return to each other."

The other teachers already had assembled. They whispered together in little groups while everyone waited for their principal. He had been new this year and was not a favorite among the staff. Mrs. Robbins, Tucker's teacher, called her over to an empty seat next to her.

"Do you know what this is all about?" Kris asked, a fluttering making her hands shake.

"Nope. Probably some budget meeting or something." She shrugged. "Have you thought any more about what I suggested?"

"In truth, no," she said, unable to meet the woman's eyes. "My husband and I want him to stay with his peers."

"He's so bright, though, Kris. He's going to be bored, and you know what happens to children who aren't challenged enough."

"I appreciate your concern. We supplement quite a bit at home." Kris did her best to smile. Mrs. Robbins had been on her case all year to request Tucker skip a grade. Kris had known he was intelligent from an early age, and she and her husband had agreed they wanted him to stay with his peers at school.

"How long has your husband been gone this time? What does he do again?"

Luckily, the principal walked in right then, and with the whole room going silent, Kris didn't have to skate around that question. She let out a breath, but sucked it back in when she saw her boss. The man's face had no color, his eyes glared red, and he moved as if he had aged fifty years.

"Thank you all for coming." The principal spoke barely louder than a whisper.

It seemed as if the whole room, Kris included, held their breaths.

"I wish I didn't have to share this news with you." He hung his head for a moment. When he lifted it, his Adam's apple bobbed rapidly. "I'm sure all of you have been following the government shutdown."

Many nodded their heads and murmured assents. Kris, though, only knew tidbits she had picked up in the staff break room. She didn't follow the news or politics. The depressing state of their country only added stress onto an already stressful life. Besides, she feared learning of her husband's death through the news or finding out whatever it was he actually did for a living.

She knew the government had a shutdown, but didn't quite know the extent or how it might affect her. It could affect her husband's checks, which may be why they hadn't been depositing in their account over the last couple months. Yet who knew which branch of government paid him...or if it was government at all. Still, it was easier thinking the loss of income was due to a shutdown rather than the alternative.

"Today things got worse." He swallowed and looked down at his hands twisting in front of him. "You will not be receiving your checks tomorrow, and as it looks now, schools will begin closing in the coming weeks, if not days."

The uproar in the room deafened Kris. No check? She had been pinching pennies the last couple of weeks. After her husband's monthly deposits had stopped, she had to dip into their joint savings. Affording the mortgage payment for the house and big chunk of property that he had insisted on buying quickly sapped up the meager amount and that was with letting go of things like the grounds keeper, cable, and other non-necessities.

She knew they had some in IRAs and other money market accounts, but had hoped she would make it without pulling them out. Now, it looked like she would have to go to the bank and pay the monstrous fees to do so. Otherwise, without money coming in, she wouldn't have enough to last the rest of the month.

The room closed in around her, the chaos darkening into a muted background as her own dilemma sucked her in. How would she feed Tucker? How long could she stay in the house without making payments before they kicked them out?

Kris wanted to flee this doomsday meeting, but the questions kept coming no matter how many times her principal answered with *I don't know*. Panic lined everyone's voices.

Maybe her husband had been right all along. Kris struggled to keep in the tears, and her throat seized up.

The meeting carried on for over an hour with just as many unanswered questions. Her head pounded and swirled with what all this meant, not only for her immediate situation, but for life as they knew it. Snippets of long-ago conversations with her husband filtered in.

She had used to love talking about what they would do in the aftermath of disaster. To her, it had been a game that passed the time, not something they seriously needed to consider. After having Tucker, she had more than enough to preoccupy her, and the constant doomsday planning her husband fixated on got on her nerves. Maybe she should have listened more.

When the meeting finally dispersed, she drove the two minutes from school to pick up Tucker. Yet she sat in the driveway for several minutes, watching her hands shake on the steering wheel and feeling her heart flutter with so much force she felt out of breath. Where was her husband when she needed him the most?

She sat there long enough that Tucker came out of the house and toward the car himself. Sara waved from the door. Kris lifted a hand in acknowledgement, thankful she wouldn't have to answer any questions. She took a few deep breaths and plastered on a smile as Tucker climbed into his seat.

"Hey, Sweetie. Did you have a good time?"

"Yeah, Vinny got a new game. Don't worry, it doesn't have zombies." Excitement bubbled from him.

"That's good." How she wished she could just revel in this moment of her son's sweet innocence rather than consciously forcing herself to focus on the conversation.

"Yeah, it was so lifelike, like the animals were alive. We had to hunt to provide food for our people."

Kris bit her cheeks. At this point, maybe zombies would have been better.

"Speaking of food, we have to stop by the grocery store." If her husband was right, soon they would be closing, too. She hated the panicked feeling flooding her. Knowing that she based her decisions on her husband's nonsense made it even worse. Thinking that he might actually be right scared the pants off of her.

"Can we get some ice cream?"

"Not tonight, Sweetie." She heard his disappointed groan, but she would have to pay close attention to how much she spent and only buy things that she could extend out as much as possible.

In the store, she scanned the rows of food, building sustaining menus in her mind. "Mommy, why are you getting such big bags of rice and beans? Are you replenishing Daddy's barrels?"

His innocent question made her laugh. She had forgotten about all the barrels of freeze-dried food they had stored in the bunker. The once hated and despised underground shelter now filled her with joy.

With that food alone, she and Tucker could eat for a year or more.

She kissed her son on the head. "Thank you, Tuck. On second thought, let's get that ice cream."

"Mommy, are you okay?" He raised his small hand to her head. "You're acting kind of strange."

"I'll be all right. Everything will be okay."

~*~

Blake watched headquarters through his night-vision binoculars. He had seen two of his team go in, and in over four hours, they had not come back out. Normally his team would go there sporadically and only long enough to be debriefed and released.

In his locker, he had extra clothes, his civilian ID, ammunition, and, most importantly, his wedding ring. He needed those things. Yet, with what he had overheard earlier in the night, an uneasy feeling settled in his stomach, and he hesitated to strut into a place he had once thought as safe.

With all the hours staying hidden, his mind had wrapped around more skills he needed to teach his son. Time became of the essence, and he had been gone too long. The little black book he kept in his cargo pants' pocket felt tattered as he pulled it out. He flipped past the full pages of the book to the few empty pages left. Feeling for the pen in his pocket and trying to write by night-vision goggles, he scribbled his words across the page. Hopefully, his handwriting still made sense.

Movement at the back entrance caught his attention. Blake quickly and quietly stored the book and pen. A truck backed up to the door, and shortly after, the door opened. Three men deposited two hefty bags into the back of the vehicle. Adrenaline pricked his chest. The two bags looked an awful lot like body bags.

Blake's heart thundered as his mind raced. He felt as if he had been hit with a sledge hammer, sucking in air through a collapsed straw. He knew those bodies being thrown into the back of that truck were the men from his squad. He knew it as much as he knew he had to disappear this instant.

An animal scurried by, probably a rabbit by its speed and the flash of white that streaked into the brush in front of him. Blake's fists squeezed into tight balls as he held his breath. The sound and movement had alerted the men at the truck.

Blake froze as the men watched where he sat hidden behind the brush. He didn't want to end up like his friends. He couldn't. The survival of his son and wife depended on it. Clenching his teeth, he steeled himself to do what had to be done to get home to them. He didn't enjoy killing, but desperate times called for desperate measures.

The men spoke, but the words faded into unintelligible sounds by the time they reached his ears. Flashlights lit the area around Blake, but he had hidden well. When the sound of a nine-millimeter cocking echoed, a primal urgency rushed through Blake. He had overstayed his welcome.

The men spread out and began methodically making their way into the forest. After the next sweep of light passed him, Blake disappeared into the night.

With quiet, practiced feet, he crept out of ear shot and sight of headquarters. Once in the clear, he picked up his pace and jogged through the trees. A weight lifted off his shoulders, something that seemed ironic when the world was about to end…or at least how the human race knew it. Yet, knowing that his life of working for the government was finished for now let him breathe in the fresh mountain air a little deeper.

A wry grin pulled at the corners of his mouth, and the sensation left an awkward feeling in him. How long had it been since he had smiled?

Too long. Probably since he last saw his son. For a five-year-old, he had quite the knack for picking up skills. Wait, not five any more. He had missed a birthday a few months back. Blake's smile faltered. He had missed another birthday.

He quickened his pace in grim determination. He would not miss another one. The promise repeated over and over as the sound of his heart thundered in his ears.

At the edge of a clearing, Blake stopped and craned his neck to listen for any pursuit. The only sound he heard was the blood pumping through him. Adjusting his night-vision goggles, he scanned the perimeter. Once he deemed himself alone, he made his way to where he had hidden his Jeep in a thick stand of manzanita trees.

He had no idea how long he had to make it the couple hundred miles south he needed, and he sure didn't want to get trapped in a city between here and there. He pulled out a map and double-checked the route he had mentally planned out on the jog over. It would take him a full day to drive there. He pulled the night-vision goggles off his head and rubbed the spots where the elastic had squeezed.

A faint glow grew over the mountains to the east.

He had an hour until sunrise. The Jeep started with a rumble, and a quickening vibrated through him. The event he had been preparing for was upon them, and he was ready…well, almost. He needed to get to his family before the attack, from wherever it may arrive.

~*~

Kris rinsed off the last dish in the sink and set it in the rack. She wiped her hands on the dish towel and then scanned her home. Everything sparkled. The house felt eerily quiet, and for about the tenth time, she regretted telling Tucker he could stay the night at Vinny's.

He had been so excited for his first-ever sleep over, so she had swallowed her own trepidation. She couldn't allow her fear to hamper the natural progression of her son's social growth. Yet, she found herself too distracted for her normal lazy evening with a good book. What would Tuck do if he had a nightmare like he did so often?

Her fretting continued, keeping the need to stay busy a must. Since his father had left this last time, Tucker had crawled into bed with her on a nightly basis. What would he do when he woke up at Vinny's and she wasn't there?

She grabbed the cleaning rag and spray and headed to the bathroom. Maybe she hadn't cleaned all the way around the toilet.

The abrupt sound of a knock at the door made her jump and cover her mouth to squelch a scream. She wasn't a screamer, but someone at her front door was the last thing she expected. How had someone gotten past the gate?

Only Tucker and she knew the code to open it. About six months ago, she had all the locks changed and entered a new code. Her anger at her absent husband had spurred the actions on.

She slipped along the walls toward the front door and wrapped her hand around the bat she kept there. Her thoughts immediately flew to the pistol her husband had made her keep, even though she detested guns. Fear pricked her chest. The solid wood of the bat felt reassuring enough in her hand as she stood on tippy-toes to look through the peephole.

Darkness greeted her. The automatic light hadn't turned on. Fear surged through her as the hair on the back of her neck stood on end.

The sound of a second knock from the other side of the door had her swallowing another scream. She couldn't see a dang thing out there. For a moment she thought about acting as if she wasn't home, and then the knob started to turn. Slowly at first, and then frantically as if the intruder was frustrated it hadn't opened.

Kris threw herself against the wall and gulped for breath. The porch lights. Maybe if she flickered the lights, they would go away. She reached a tentative hand across the door and flipped on the switch, but nothing happened. Of course, the bulb had burnt out, hence the light not turning on automatically.

Again she thought of the gun as the intruder began fiddling with the lock. It was too far to the bedroom and too time-consuming to open the safe to get the gun and then find the bullets in the hidden compartment in her closet. As her heart pounded and lips trembled, she sent up a silent prayer of gratitude that Tucker wasn't there.

Gripping the bat tighter, she scanned her entry way for a better weapon as the clicking in the door produced sounds like the lock giving way to the intruder's picking. Her purse caught her eye. The Taser.

The door handle clicked as the lock gave way and a satisfied sigh sounded from the intruder. Kris acted fast, reached across for her purse, and in one swift movement grabbed the Taser as the door opened slowly, carefully.

A short-haired head emerged out of the crack in the doorway. The man moved cautiously. Just another inch or two and his vulnerable neck would show.

Kris's hands shook as she grasped the Taser in a white-knuckled grip. She licked her lips and slowly, soundlessly, let the air out of her lungs.

Right as the intruder's neck appeared, she thrust the Taser into the sensitive skin and pulled the trigger.

"Agh!" the man snarled as he dropped to the ground.

Kris raised her arm with the bat and aimed at the man's head when something about the pained voice broke through her all-consuming fear. Yet the bat had its momentum as it swung down towards the sandy-haired man.

At the last moment, a massive hand shot out and caught the bat before it hit his head.

Kris's eyes shot wide open as she froze.

The man moved his hand to lower the bat, revealing a steel-cold green gaze.

"Blake?" she whispered.

~*~

Blake's neck burned and his hand ached from stopping the bat before it smashed his head in. Kris had quite the power behind that swing. His blood pumped and pulsed as he fought the urge to return the attack. Letting out a shaking breath, he met the eyes of the one woman who meant everything to him.

"Hello, Kris," he rasped out.

Her blue eyes opened wide in surprise. The pulse in her neck throbbed rapidly. She still held the other end of the bat in one hand and the Taser in the other. A small smile tugged at the corner of his mouth. She had done well.

After a few blinks, her eyes softened, as did her grip on the weapons. The bat now hung limp at her side, and she thumbed the Taser to the off position. Blake watched her every movement and yet never let go of her gaze.

"That's quite the welcome home," he said as he forced a chuckle out. Truth be told, he had no idea what to expect, yet it surely wasn't this.

He saw the emotions warring in her eyes. She had told him before he left this time that if he went, he might as well not return. Her words had been said in anger, but he knew he had surpassed her limits. His only hope now was that she would be calm enough to listen to reason.

As her eyes turned darker and stormier, he knew he had no such luck.

"What kind of welcome did you expect breaking into *my* home?"

"*Your* home?" He rocked back onto his heels. "You had the code and the locks changed. What else should I have done?" Indignation came to a boil in his gut. It wasn't like he had been traipsing around and partying. He had worked hard this past year.

"Umm, let's see, a phone call perhaps? Since we're on that conversation, you never thought to call even once during the last year? Never once wanted to make sure your family was okay or let us know you were still alive? Oh, yeah, and maybe a heads up your checks wouldn't be coming in? Then you tramp back here expecting everything to be like it was as if you had only been gone a day!"

Blake swallowed the reaction he wanted to spit at her. His fists clenched and unclenched as he watched her pace and flail the bat and Taser around. Then, as if everything dawned on him, he realized he had heard no trace of Tucker.

"Where's my son?" He shot to his feet and strode straight to the boy's room. The walls were lined full of pictures from the survival magazines Blake had sent him. Tucker's hammock hung between the walls, empty. It swung back and forth as Blake searched his room for any sign of his son. They had a protocol should someone unwanted enter the home, but he wasn't in any of his hiding spots.

Blake strode out of the room, a rage building inside him. He almost ran into Kris, who stood there, arms crossed across her slight chest and her eyes cold and unyielding.

"He's at a friend's." Her voice held the same coldness her eyes did.

"At ten o'clock at night! I told you to never let him be that far away from you. Why don't you ever listen to what I say?" Frustration pounded in him, pushing out reason. He noticed his fury and consciously let his hands hang by his sides while he internally counted.

Kris rolled her eyes and walked away. "Always the

pessimist. Besides, you lost the right to demand what I do or don't do when you left for a year and didn't even have enough consideration to contact us—at all!"

"You know how it is. You know I can't just pick up a phone and call you. When I'm undercover, anything I do could be linked back to you and Tucker. I can't chance that." He ran his hand through his short hair, his heart aching with need to see his son, to make sure he was alive and well, to make sure he didn't hate him like his mother obviously did.

Her eyes followed his hand. "Just like you can't chance wearing your wedding ring?"

If she could breathe fire, Blake had a feeling she would be right now. Jealousy flared in her eyes as well as distrust and pure livid rage. A rage as red as her long hair.

"I can't wear it on assignment, and I couldn't get back into headquarters to retrieve it." A flash of the two body bags passed through his mind once again. He shook off the goosebumps that rippled through him. Somehow, he needed to get her to listen.

"Sure, headquarters." She turned her back to him and walked out into the living room.

"Look, Krista, Baby, you've got to listen to me." He followed her, watching helplessly while she slumped into their couch. "Something is going down, and soon. I barely escaped."

Her eyes met his sharply. They bore into him as if she dug for the truth in his words. Her lips pursed tight, but he had her attention.

"They started dispatching my squad. All the top officials are heading toward their bunkers if they aren't already there. I came back as fast as I could, but now we have to get our son and get into our bunker. I don't know when the attack will hit."

Kris watched him, her gaze hard and dark. Then she did the last thing he expected. She laughed. Not the belly-full-of-joy laugh that he longed to hear, but a merciless laugh devoid of mirth.

"You're gone a year, without a word to us, then come home out of nowhere and expect me to allow you to lock us into that stinking bunker with you?"

"I sent you the contact I could."

"A magazine?! Really?"

"Yes, and the messages in them…"

Kris's phone rang from near her purse where it still lay on the floor, contents strewn about. She ran to the device as if her life depended on it.

"Is everything okay?" She hastily exhaled, her eyes frantic and the knuckles holding the phone white. "Of course, it's his first attempt. I'm sure it will. Yes, I'll be down there in about ten minutes. Let him know I'm on my way."

She ended the call and turned toward Blake.

"I'm leaving to get Tucker now." Her eyes flickered across his, but wouldn't stay.

"I'm going with you." He stood and took a step toward the door.

"The hell you are. You are going to be gone by the time we get back. He doesn't need you traipsing in and out of his life, and neither do I." Even with fists shoved into her hips and fire in her eyes, a deep wanting filled him. He loved her tenacity, though he didn't necessarily desire it directed at him.

"You can't do that." His words were simple and direct. The fight had left him. He knew she had no choice but to listen. It would only be a matter of time.

"You can go fight it in court, but right now, you need to leave, or I'll have to call the cops." Her bottom lip quivered as she said the words.

"You don't get it, Kris. Very soon there will be no courts, there will be no cops, there will only be survival…and you will need me." He had hoped she would be easier to convince, but the fact was it would come down to this…to survival.

"Right now I *need* you to leave." With that, she stuffed the contents back into her purse and walked out the door.

If he didn't know her as well as he did and situations weren't so dire, he would think it was over. No more marriage, no more love. Yet, as she had said the last words and cleaned up, her bottom lip had trembled and her watery eyes wouldn't meet his. She was hurt and angry, and in truth she had no reason to trust him.

He could grant her a reprieve, let her win this fight. He knew the war would be upon them soon, and he would not let them fight through this disaster alone.

After her tail lights faded, he went through his hidden compartments in the house, collecting guns, ammunition, and other gear. He wouldn't leave, but he would prepare. He hoisted the items in the pack on his back and hiked out to the fence-line and their bunker. It wasn't nearly as luxurious as the ones he had found placements for, but it would be enough for him and his family. Kris would see how much she needed him. She would come around. He knew it, he knew it as much as he knew that disaster would strike at any moment, and he had to be ready.

~3~

Kris let her tears fall unbidden on the drive to pick up Tucker. The road blurred, making it difficult to see. She swiped at her eyes and sniffled. How dare Blake appear out of nowhere and start demanding ludicrous expectations!

Through her anger, her memory of his green eyes blazed. How had she forgotten how handsome he was? Her anger at his absence was so deep because of the depth of her love. She knew that. When you loved someone that much, the pain that he could cause you ran deeper than the Grand Canyon and just as wild as the river that made it.

Her fingers dug into the steering wheel. Love or not, he had been gone without a word for over a year. How could she excuse that kind of behavior? It wasn't just her anymore.

Her thoughts focused on her little boy. He worshiped his dad. It had taken Tucker months of moping around after Blake left this time before he settled into his absence. She couldn't have her boy's heart subjected to that type of abuse. It wasn't fair to him or her.

A flash of color streamed across the sky. Kris took her foot off the gas and leaned forward for a better look, but the color had disappeared. Only the bright moonlight filled the sky. Maybe it had only been a weird reflection. She shook her head. Blake's paranoia fuddled her thinking. That was the last thing she needed.

As she turned into the housing development where Sara lived, she took deep, long breaths. Her son needed her right now. He was scared and probably embarrassed. She needed to be fully present with him, not lost in some doomsday future her husband had created. Though with all the things happening, doomsday thoughts nagged on her mind.

She pulled up to the house, and her heart squeezed with love for her son. Tucker's face was squished against the living room window. As soon as he saw her, the curtain dropped, and a moment later the front door ripped open. She quickly climbed out of the car and onto the sidewalk where he ran into her open arms.

"Mommy!" He nestled into her neck and squeezed her like he hadn't seen her for a week.

"Oh, Sweetie. You okay?" She knelt down and looked into his green eyes so much like the ones she had just ordered to disappear out of their lives.

"Yeah." He looked down and scuffed his shoe on the ground. He had put his shoes on over his footie pajamas, and Kris had to suppress the smile at the innocent image. "My thoughts just wouldn't stop. If a big catastrophe happens, I want to be with you."

"Oh, Tuck," she said as she brought him back in her arms. A ripple of anger at her husband traveled through her like fire through a pile of straw. If Blake hadn't planted all this crazy survival stuff in the boy's head, Tucker wouldn't have so many fears and nightmares.

"I just wanna come home."

"Of course." She stood and held his hand as they walked to the still flung-open front door.

Sara met them there with Tucker's bag and a smile. "I'm sorry."

"Please don't be. He was brave to try," Kris said as she took the bag and squeezed Tucker against her.

"Yes, he was, and he's welcome to try again any time." Sara reached out and tussled Tucker's hair. "Vinny's already asleep. He'll be excited to see you at school on Monday."

"Thank you, Ms. Sara." He hid against his mom's legs.

"Thank you, Sara. See you Monday."

They waved goodbye and walked hand-in-hand to the car. Tucker yawned as Kris helped him with his seat belt.

"I'm tired."

"I bet. It's way past your bedtime." She kissed him on the tip of his nose, shut his door, and then climbed into the driver's seat.

Back on the road, she sensed an eerie silence. How long had it been since she drove on their mountain roads this late at night? The woods loomed alongside the highway in the darkness. She flicked her high beams on and kept a good look out for any deer or other wildlife. She had hit a raccoon once, and it nearly broke her heart.

On the way down to pick Tucker up, her anger had consumed her thoughts so much she hadn't noticed the deserted roads. Now, with her scared son in the back seat, the realization hit her with a slight flutter. Camping season had ended, though it was still warm enough, and ski season hadn't started. The only traffic they had were locals, and even on a Saturday night that didn't account for much.

"Mommy?"

"Yeah, Tuck?"

"What are those strange lights in the sky?"

Kris leaned forward to look out the windshield better. Sure enough, wavering colors lit the sky, like pictures she had seen showing the northern lights. Yet, that couldn't be...they were in central California.

She slowed to a crawl while watching the lights. Their beauty only slightly mollified the crazy, unsettled quivering traveling through her.

"They're auroras, right? I didn't think we could see them this far south." Hearing those big words from her son's mouth caused her to shake her head in wonder.

"You're right, Sweetie. We usually can't see them here."

"You don't think it's a sign of a solar storm, do you?" Tuck's voice quivered. "Solar storms can be really bad, a real catastrophe."

Kris's heart began beating at a quicker pace. "I'm not sure, but let's get home and search Google, okay?"

"Okay. I feel safer at home anyway. We have all of our survival gear there."

Kris sat back in her seat, her hands gripping the steering wheel until they ached. Her six-year-old shouldn't have to be worried about natural disasters and needing survival gear to feel safe. Clenching her teeth, she pressed down on the gas to get home as fast as possible. Blake had better be gone. By the time she got there, she wasn't sure if she could control her rage.

The car sputtered. She glanced down at her gas gauge. It read over half-full. *What in the world?*

She pressed the gas harder, but the car kept

sputtering and lurching. The lights in the dash flickered, and the radio turned channels like a seek sensor with too much caffeine. Pressing the off button repeatedly did nothing to stop the blaring sound.

"Mommy?" Tuck's voice held every ounce of fear that dripped through her system.

She glanced at him in the mirror.

His wide eyes brimmed with tears and his lip quivered.

"It's going to be alright, Sweetie. The car is just having issues."

Deep breaths. Her heart hammered loudly, adding a rhythmic base to the frantic sounds of the radio. She maneuvered the car over to a turnout on the side of the deserted highway just as wires began crackling in the dashboard. Smoke tendrils rose from the gauges and radio. The flickering headlights went dark and the radio faded out, leaving an eerie silence.

The pungent smell of electrical burning drove her to action. "Let's get out of the car. Quickly." She turned to Tucker and helped him unfasten his belt.

"Wait! My survival magazine!" He crawled back to his bag and yanked it with him as Kris pulled him from the car with her.

"We have to hurry," Kris urged him. She didn't know why the frantic feeling coursed through her, but she had learned to listen to her intuition. Her instincts told her she had to get him away from the car.

She wrapped an arm around his shoulder tightly, pulling him as fast as his little legs could go. Behind them she heard a sizzling whoosh, like a big balloon had sprung a leak. Tucker dug his heels in and turned. Flames reflected in his eyes. Kris didn't take time to look back. She picked up her son and ran towards the forest to duck behind a wall of large evergreens.

She had just shoved Tucker behind the biggest spruce and covered him with her body when she heard explosions from everywhere around her. All the transformers on the power poles sparked and fizzed. A blast of hot air whipped past them. Her ears thrummed with the deep vibrations. Tucker didn't scream. He just clung to her as tightly as his little arms could squeeze.

After the last explosions blasted, she peeked out to see the car crackle in flames. Kris's mind cleared enough to wonder what in the world could have happened to make her car catch on fire and transformers to explode.

She looked towards the aurora-filled skies, tears streaming down her face. She internally screamed at the heavens, asking for help.

Her answer didn't come with mercy. It came with explosions and havoc. The few houses in the stretch of forest between her home and the town of Forest Glen where Sara lived threw sparks in the air. Not enough to catch them on fire, but enough that their lights flickered off and billows of smoke reflected the colored lights in the sky.

Towards town more explosions sputtered, muted in the distance. The electricity lines sparked and crackled loudly at the smaller transformers.

"What's happening, Mommy?"

"I don't know." Kris pulled Tucker tighter to her. With the dry summer and fall they had, she worried about all of those sparks starting wildfires. A shiver coursed through her as she clutched her son.

"Dad will find us. He will. He said he would!"

Kris pulled back to look him in the eyes. She opened her mouth, but she couldn't form any words. How could she tell him that she had just told his dad never to return?

Was this what Blake had been talking about? The attack? What kind of attack could cause cars and electrical panels to spark and blow up?

Tucker had a good point. Maybe she should call Blake. Even if she was angry with him, he would know what to do. She reached for her cell phone only to realize she had left it in her purse, which now was surely ablaze along with everything else in her car. So much for the survival bag Blake had stashed in there.

"Come on, Tuck. We need to keep moving. It's not too far to walk home. It will be like a night hike." She stood up and pulled him up with her. "We can do this. We will do it together."

Her brave son nodded, readjusted his backpack, and squeezed her hand back as if his life depended on it, and it just might. Kris bit her cheeks and blinked rapidly. She didn't have time to think about what was happening. She only had one goal: get her boy home and safe.

~*~

Blake had just finished dumping another load into the bunker and crawled out the door when he heard the crackling in the power lines back at the house. He shielded his eyes as the small transformer blew, sending sparks spraying into the air like fireworks.

It's happening.

Adrenaline surged through him as he threw the bunker door shut and sprinted towards the house.

Kris's car was still missing. His heart raced, and more fear coursed through him than ever did on any of his assignments. Clenching his fists, he lifted his head and let out a roar. He had let her go without him, against all of his instincts.

The rock of guilt in his gut weighed him down, but he didn't let it slow him as he ran into the house. Flinging open the closet door, he saw the emergency pack right where he had stashed it years ago. Thank goodness Kris had enough sense to let that one stay.

His hand instinctively felt his belt for the reassuring weight of his pistol in its holster and the rounds of bullets. Slinging the backpack over his shoulder as he checked the locks on the house, he jogged down the long driveway to where he had left his Jeep.

With the way the sparks showered from the transformer, he was sure the electricity had surged, probably from an electromagnetic pulse. Who had set off the EMP? He wondered how powerful it had been. Had it taken out vehicles, too? He didn't know if his Jeep would run or not, but he had to try. It would get him to his family quicker if it did.

He scrambled over the gate, swearing again. Why did she have to go and change the code? His Jeep lay hidden at the end of the private road. Sticking the key in the ignition, he asked for a granting of mercy, but only silence answered him. Not even a click sounded.

His head fell against the steering wheel while he allowed himself a short moment of panic. Then, with determination, he scrambled out of the vehicle, threw the backpack back on, cinched up the straps, and took off at jog down their private road with only the moonlight to guide him.

He didn't know where Tucker had been and thus had no direction. The rock in his stomach twisted, almost causing him to retch. How much had he missed of his son's life?

Ten minutes. The words repeated in his head, pulling his thoughts back to the mission. Kris said she would be down there in ten minutes. Down. Tucker's friend must live in Forest Glen. Immediately, maps spread out in his mind. If he cut through the properties west of the highway, he might shave off a good mile or two. Yet, what if he missed them?

He ground his teeth and would have growled, but he needed his all his breath at this moment as he ran down their private road. Once he hit the main road he turned left to travel down to the highway. He couldn't take the chance of passing them. He hoped that Kris would stick to the highway. Knowing her fear of the dark, he could assume she wouldn't push into the gloomy forests unless she had to.

As he came into view of the more populated neighborhoods, he realized how difficult it might actually be to make it through to them. People shouted, asking their neighbors if they knew what was going on. *You don't want to know.* Better they don't. Mass hysteria would only make it more difficult for him to reach his family.

"Hey! Hey!" A man ran out to the road, shouting at him. "Do you know what the hell's going on?"

Blake kept his pace and shrugged, feeling the reassuring weight of his pistol hugging him as he jogged.

"Why are you running? What's going on?" Anger filled the man's voice. Blake knew that was the fear talking.

He needed to get to Tucker and Kris. Stopping would ruin his pace.

"I'm going to check. It's probably just a power surge." He did his best to keep his voice calm and reassuring.

"Oh, great. Another week without power, just what we need." The man lifted a hand before grumbling his way back towards his house. "It's probably going to start another wildfire, too."

Sweat beaded on Blake's forehead. He swiped at it before it slipped into his eyes and glanced back once to make sure the man had gone back to his home. Hopefully, he would spread the word and ease the fears of the others. As much as he didn't like to lie, delaying the mass panic would benefit everyone. Besides, it hadn't been a full falsehood. A power surge definitely caused the transformers to blow and their power to go out. At this point, they didn't need to know that there was something bigger behind that surge.

The rhythm of his feet pounding the pavement soon gave way to the almost meditative state that overcame him on long runs. His mind used the time to decipher the clues of what the cause actually was. If it had been a nuclear attack, there would be other signs and death.

Blake shook his head. He couldn't go there. Power surges. Exploding transformers. Cars out of commission. Must be an EMP, a dreaded device that would take out a country's electrical grid and other electrical components as well. What was the game plan, though? Would the attackers come out right away, or would they wait until most of the population died off in the struggle and then take advantage?

Simmons' words echoed in him: *get lost in the aftermath*. Blake shivered. Why hadn't the country's leaders done more to prepare their citizens?

He turned off the tree-lined road and right down the highway. The skies opened up in a clearing, and the colors filling them shocked him so much he almost stopped running...almost.

It wasn't an attack from another country but from the earth itself, a natural disaster. Not an EMP, a CME. Coronal Mass Ejection, the scientist he had guarded during the last global safety meeting had told him. He knew about these solar storms from shows on the Science Channel, but this scientist had even more doomsday information. For once, things were actually worse than what the TV shows portrayed.

CMEs were like a nature-made EMP. There was a massive one recorded back in the eighteen-hundreds that took out all the telegraph lines, electrocuting the operators and starting fires across the country. The scientist's prediction of a similar CME attack hitting the electrically-dependent nation today was almost too horrifying to believe. Pretty much anything electrical would no longer function, or worse would explode, affecting the population in such a way that even after the immediate threat would leave them without power, water, and food. Civilization would break down, leaving people grasping onto life and fighting each other for the chance of survival on meager resources.

A softness entered his heart as he thought of watching the documentary with Tucker nestled against him on the couch. That boy loved watching natural disaster and survival shows almost as much as he did. It was probably unnatural for a five-year-old to be interested in such things, but Blake saw it as a good thing and used his interest to prepare him for what he knew would eventually come.

Tucker had looked over at Blake with wide eyes, which had made Blake feel like he looked into a mirror. "What if that mega solar storm happens, Dad?"

"We'll be prepared, Tuck."

"But what if you're on one of your assignments?" His bottom lip had trembled, making Blake wish he had chosen a different profession. Yet, he had one more assignment, just one.

"Son, let me tell you something. No matter where you are or what happens, I will move heaven and earth to find you."

"Promise?"

"I promise." He had made his voice as grave as he could, wanting to make the boy understand he would do anything to keep him safe. "We always return to each other."

"We always return to each other." Tuck had thrown his arms around his neck then.

Longing filled Blake with the memory. What he wouldn't give to feel those little arms around his neck right now. He evened his breath and then pushed his legs faster. He would keep his promise. Nothing would stop him from finding his family.

~4~

The night became silent the farther from town they traveled. Kris held her son's hand, encouraging him to keep moving. The colorful auroras and almost full moon lit the road, but the darkness loomed beyond the highway into the forests.

Kris focused her eyes on the road as far as she could see ahead. She did her best not to look into the blackness and wonder what lurked in there. No matter how much time she had spent camping in the woods, she never outgrew her fear of the all-consuming darkness that could be found in them. Of course, when Blake stood by her side, fear didn't enter into the equation. She had always felt safe with him.

A flash of anger fueled her. How could she still long to have him protect her when he had deserted them for so long without a word?

"Mommy, I'm tired." Tucker pulled on her hand as his steps slowed, and he dragged his feet.

If it wasn't for the fact that she felt they were running for their lives, she would be amused by the situation, her dragging her son down the highway an hour before midnight in his footie pajamas. She stopped walking and knelt down to his level, allowing him a momentary break.

"I know, Sweetie. This isn't easy, and it's way past your bedtime. You are being so tough." She kissed his forehead as she slipped the backpack off his shoulders. "Do you have any water or snacks in here?"

"You know I always carry those and that multi-tool Daddy gave me. Though I have to hide that from my teachers. They aren't allowed at school."

"You bring your multi-tool to school?" A lecture formed on her tongue, but the look in her son's eyes stopped the words. This was not the time. She sifted through his backpack, and pulled out a water and a protein bar. "You are a very prepared boy, you know that?"

He nodded. "It always pays to be prepared." He mimicked his dad's words.

"You definitely saved us." She made a catalog of all that filled his pack: clothes, a few more snacks, a small first aid kit, a whistle, another bottle of water, an emergency blanket, a small wind-up flashlight, and his multi-tool. "Are you warm enough? Do you want to put on some of your clothes?"

He shook his head. "I just want to go home."

"I know, Sweetie. Just a few more miles." Though, as she calculated in her head, it was more like six and all up hill. Their house was a good fifteen hundred feet higher than Forest Glen, and the further up they traveled, the colder the air. "Eat a few bites of bar to get a little boost of energy."

He methodically did as he was told, but she assumed his exhaustion overran his fear of the position they were in. "Dad will find us, won't he?"

Kris thought about her response. She warred with the idea herself. Part of her hoped every shadow she saw in the distance would be Blake running toward them. The other part jutted her chin out and told her that they didn't need someone who might abandon them at any moment.

"We're going to be okay, Sweetie. We'll be home before you know it. How about we sing the Ants Go Marching while we walk to help distract us?"

"Okay." He rewrapped the bar with only a couple bites out of it and handed it to her.

She stuffed it into her pants pocket, gave him a drink from the water bottle, took one herself, and then put that into the backpack before slinging the pack over her shoulder.

Tucker reached for her hand and started singing the first verse of the song. She forced herself to sing along with him, pretending they were on a night hike.

When Blake had been home, he had made it a tradition to go on a night hike every full moon. It had become a family outing that they all looked forward to. She had done her best to continue the tradition, but it pushed her limits. The hikes had become much shorter and designated to out their long driveway and back.

She tried to keep her mind busy as they walked up the highway. Every shadow that flickered sent her heart hammering. Blake had all sorts of ideas of the mayhem society would turn into after a catastrophe like this. He expected everyone to go crazy right away, to riot and attack their fellow men. It had been a fun discussion with them sitting on opposite sides.

Yet, right now, alone on a deserted highway in the dead of night, his ominous view-point threatened her peace of mind.

"Mommy, you stopped singing."

"Sorry, Sweetie. What number are we on?" She focused on Tucker again.

"Never mind. I'm too tired to sing anymore

anyway."

Kris watched her young son, so wise and knowledgeable beyond his years. Maybe she shouldn't have given Blake such a difficult time about preparing him.

Her feet ached. When rushing out to get Tucker, she had shoved her feet into slip-on shoes, and the soles felt worn through already. She shifted the backpack on her shoulders as her son dragged his feet once again.

"Come here, Tuck. I'll carry you for a while."

She hefted him up as he hugged her like a little koala. He had grown so much over this last year. Weighing over fifty pounds now, his body pushed on her hips and back. She wouldn't be able to carry him for long, but for now, she soaked in the feeling of his arms around her and his sweet-smelling head lying on her shoulder.

Each step up the steep hill took more out of her until finally she felt like she couldn't carry him one more step.

"Okay, Sweetie, I have to put you down now."

"No," he murmured, and she realized he had fallen asleep.

Her chest squeezed. She wished she could carry him the whole way home, but her back screamed in protest and her legs refused to move.

"I'm sorry, I have to." She squatted to put him down, but he only wrapped around her tighter. "Tucker, please." She looked across the distance, fighting back the tears. She just wanted to be cuddling at home in their warm beds, not forcing him to walk in the middle of the night with who-knows-what going on.

Her blurry eyes caught a glow further up the highway. She blinked several times until the glow focused into a fire...a car fire. Someone else's car caught on fire?

Adrenaline spiked within her. She pushed her body up, with Tuck still clinging to her, until she stood and moved her feet towards the burning vehicle. Where were the occupants? Just then, she saw a lone woman rocking back and forth on the opposite side of the road watching her car slowly burn.

"Tucker, someone needs our help. We need to see if she's hurt. Can you help me?"

Finally, his little arms loosened, and he slipped to the ground. "Is she burnt? I have my first aid kit." Even groggy, he showed compassion.

She kissed her sweet son on his head and grasped his hand. "Let's go see." They walked a few more yards before she called out to the lady. "Hello! Are you okay?"

The lady lifted her head and looked around until her eyes found Kris and Tucker.

She's just a kid! Kris picked up her pace, Tucker following only a step behind.

The girl shot up onto her feet and ran to meet them. "I don't know what I did wrong! It just started stuttering and then smoking, and then flames came out of the hood! I barely got out before it consumed the whole thing."

"You didn't do anything wrong. I'm Kris. This is Tucker. What's your name?"

"Hannah." She looked down the road where they had come from. "Wait...why are you walking down the highway?" She took a step back, her face paling even further.

"Our car caught fire, too, just outside of Forest Glen."

"Really?" She looked up into the sky and jabbed a finger towards the aurora. "Do those have anything to do with this?"

"It's probably a solar storm." Tucker nodded. "It can make all things electrical explode."

"Are you for real?" Hannah gave Tucker an unsure glance.

"Yes, he is." Kris looked the girl over. "You hurt at all?"

"My hand is a little burnt. I tried to get back in for my phone…" She showed them her open hand where an angry red welt sliced across her palm.

Tucker pulled at the backpack on Kris's shoulders. "I've got a first aid kit. I'll patch that right up."

"He's a pretty incredible kid," the teenager said while Tucker search the bag for his kit.

"Yes, he is. I'm pretty lucky." Kris's heart warmed as she watched her son.

"Yeah, I've got a cousin about his age and he isn't near as cool."

"Where were you headed, Hannah?" Kris asked.

"Home. My dad's going to be pissed." She watched as Tucker spread out the contents of the first aid kit, sounding out what the tubes said.

"Burn cream!"

Kris smiled at her son as she took the cream and gingerly covered Hannah's burns.

"Your dad won't care about the car or anything else once he sees you're okay."

"Maybe," she said with a wince as Kris covered her burn with the gauze Tucker handed her.

"You make a great medical assistant, Tuck. Once

again, your preparedness has saved us." Kris kissed his cheek, handing him the medical tape back.

Tucker smiled and then dug in his pack again. "Water?" he asked as he handed Hannah an unopened bottle.

"Thanks." She took the bottle with her left hand and guzzled about half of it. "My throat's raw. I screamed for help for like twenty minutes."

"Not many houses around here," Kris said as she scanned the forest around them.

"Why didn't you start walking?" Tucker asked.

Hannah's eyes flickered over to the dark woods beyond her burning car. "You're not scared of the dark, Tucker?"

"Nope." He shook his head.

Kris knew different. He acted brave, but that was why the night walks started: to get him accustomed to the dark. He acted brave during them, but every night he ran screaming to her bed because of darkness.

"I don't blame you for not wanting to walk alone. Want to join us?" Kris nodded her head towards the direction they had been traveling.

"You don't mind?" Hannah bit her lip.

"Of course not. I wouldn't leave you here all by yourself. Where do you live?"

"Just past Thirteen Corners, across from the post office."

Kris nodded. She knew exactly where she meant. There was a housing development up the road across from their town's post office.

"Do you think there will be people at the gas station?" Hannah asked, hope lining her voice.

Kris shook her head. The only station between Forest Glen and her town of Cedar Ridge was an older gas station, but it closed at nine.

"Don't worry. My daddy's going to find us." Tucker puffed his chest out as he said the words.

Kris's heart lurched at the pride and hope filling Tucker's eyes. She opened her mouth to say something and thought better of it. Hope might be the only thing that kept them going. She packed the bag back up, held her hand out for Tucker's, and headed past Hannah's burning car into the darkness.

Thirteen Corners was just past the gas station. The winding road was aptly named for the thirteen sharp turns in the creek canyon. That stretch of highway was overgrown with wild forest on both sides. The tall pines and firs would black out the moon and aurora-lit sky. A shiver coursed through her with the thought of the eerie almost-alive silence.

Hannah talked nonstop while they made their way up the highway. The wired teen told her all about coming from her boyfriend's and the fight with her dad for staying out past her curfew. She talked about her classes in high school and asked Tucker about his school. She talked as if it would save her from insanity.

The constant chatter taxed Kris. She couldn't think or plan with the constant need to reply. When the teen suddenly stopped mid-sentence, Kris looked up quickly.

The gas station's neon sign still sparked, throwing embers into the night. All other lights were out. She sniffed the air, relieved when she couldn't smell gasoline. She didn't know if the old-school pumps had saved it or if there were failsafe to make sure the tanks and pumps would not be affected. Either way, gratefulness filled her.

Still, the hairs on the back of her neck stood on end. Lingering here was not a good idea.

"Let's keep going," she said, urging the others on.

"Why are the lights off? What's wrong with that sign?" Hannah asked.

"The solar storm," Tucker said like a wise old man.

The girl nodded and followed Kris past the desolate store and into the beginning of Thirteen Corners. The few other places of business lay dark and ominous, nestled in the woods at the edge of road.

Hannah looked around with wide eyes. "This is really eerie."

"Yes, it is," Kris said as she squeezed Tuck's hand, and he moved closer to brush against her leg.

As they entered the darkened turns, Kris pushed herself not to show the fear coursing through her. She had to act at ease for Tucker and this girl they had picked up along the way. As they wound their way up into the darkness, an orange glow showed itself around the next turn.

She stopped walking, and the others mimicked her stillness. A crackling roar sounded from ahead.

"Another car on fire?" Hannah asked.

Kris shook her head. This was larger. "Stay here." She squatted to look her son in the eyes. "Tuck, stay with Hannah. I'm going to run ahead for just a moment."

"Mommy, no! I want to go with you."

"You're right, Sweetie. We need to stay together." She kissed his nose and took his hand. She looked at Hannah. "Stay close. We'll go only as far as needed to see what's going on."

They only walked a few hundred yards around the next bend in order to see what was needed. The picture made her knees wobble and threaten to buckle.

A hay truck had jackknifed in the big turn. When it ignited, it must have set its load ablaze. It probably hadn't taken long for the surrounding trees to catch.

The heat seared Kris's face. She stood in front of Tucker, and held her hand in front of her for protection. She wondered if the driver had escaped in time. Then the reality of what this meant hit her. She had her son, and now this girl, to protect and no road to follow home.

As mad as she was at Blake, she found herself hoping along with her son. *Come on, Blake. For once keep a promise.*

~*~

A surge of urgency shot through Blake, and he picked up his pace. He had just passed the post office, ignoring the yells from the housing development up the road. He didn't have time to make sure strangers were safe. He had to get to his family.

That urgency thrummed inside of him, prickling his skin with anxiety. The feeling was new to him and quite uncomfortable. He shook his hands out trying to dispel the sensation, yet it only increased. The road straightened now for a good half-mile or more until it came to the tree-lined Thirteen Corners—the rite of passage between Forest Glen and Cedar Ridge.

He sniffed the air. A pungent, unmistakable scent filled his nostrils: fire. Not just any kind of fire. Forest fire. His legs pumped of their own accord, carrying him towards the inevitable. He rounded the first two corners before he saw it.

The heat seared his cheeks as the flames ripped up the underbrush, towering into the pines and crackling in anger. He stopped in his tracks, gasping to breathe, the smoky air burning his throat and lungs. Throwing his head back at the trees covering the moon, he roared at the top of his lungs, "Tucker!"

~*~

"Did you hear that?" Tucker tilted his head.

"It's the fire, Sweetie. We need to go back the way we came." Kris pulled on his arm, but the boy planted his feet firmly.

"No, it was Dad. He called my name."

Kris's throat tightened. "Tuck, I wish that were true…"

"It is true." He struggled out of her grasp, ran a few yards toward the fire, stopped, put his hands to his mouth, and yelled louder than she had ever heard him. "Daddy!"

The call echoed in her soul, breaking the hold she had on sanity. Tears streamed down her face as she scooped her protesting son into her arms and traveled away from the increasing threat.

~*~

Blake hung his head, self-contempt pulverizing him. Then he heard it. He easily could have passed it off as his imagination except for that fact that the sound of his name being called on his son's lips caused the hairs on his arms to stand on end.

His family was just on the other side of the fire. He had to get to them. Puffing out a few breaths and calming his heart, he scanned his surroundings.

The fire had spread from a hay truck to both sides of the highway. On the left, the blaze was eating up the mountain, hungrily devouring the underbrush. He knew that hillside was lost. You couldn't stop a fire going up a steep-sided mountain, especially as dry and overgrown as it was. It hit him then. There would be no one to stop it. No fire trucks. No firemen. No airplanes or helicopters with retardant.

Panic fueled him. He needed to get to his family now. This fire could destroy the whole of Cedar Ridge. The right side of the road burned, but the flames had not traveled down into the creek canyon yet. He had no idea how long that would last, but it didn't matter. He was already making his way through the underbrush down to the big boulders in the creek.

The ground was treacherous. Hardly any light traveled down into the little canyon. By the time he tripped over an unseen root or rock a third time, he decided it would be worth stopping to find the headlamp he hoped was still stashed in the pack. It was, as was a water. He downed a third of it before putting it back.

With the headlamp, he could see his footing, and travel was much faster. *I'm coming, Tuck. I'm coming.*

He kept the chant up in his head while shoving through underbrush, scrambling over the large boulders, splashing through the creek, and fighting as fast as he could to his family.

Glancing at the fire a hundred feet above him propelled him to move even faster. He scrambled, using his hands to help speed him farther along in the canyon. Would Tucker remember what he had taught him? Would Kris? He held the hope in his heart as he growled and shoved through the brush that kept him from his son.

~*~

Kris pulled at her son, panic flooding her. The wind could turn the fire upon them at any moment.

"Please, Tuck! We have to get out of the fire's path!"

"No! Dad's out there! I heard him!"

Kris stopped struggling with him. Her strength had waned from the fight. It had taken her what felt like an eternity to get him even a hundred yards away from the imminent danger of the forest fire. Luckily, Tucker didn't run back but stayed put, his eyes frantically searching the canyon.

"Tucker, why are you so sure he's coming?"

"Why wouldn't he be?" Hannah asked.

Kris had forgotten the girl was there because she had been so intent on getting her son away from the flames.

"Just because he's been gone on assignment doesn't mean he won't keep his promise." He folded his arms across his chest. "Besides, he told me he would be home soon."

"What do you mean he told you?" Kris took him by the shoulders, her world falling apart around her.

"He's coming, and I heard him!" His defiance shocked Kris, shocked her enough to make her second-guess her actions.

"Okay, Tuck." She nodded, releasing her ego. "What should we do?"

Tucker looked at her, his eyes wide and wild. "We have to stay in one place. That's what he's always told us. Stay in one place and blow the whistle three times in a row."

Kris glanced towards the fire. It seemed to be moving away from them, but she feared it could turn at any moment. "Wouldn't he want us to stay in one place where it was safe?"

Tucker cocked his head.

"That forest fire is very dangerous. You know how they can change direction without notice. If the wind starts blowing towards us, we'll be in danger." She did her best to keep her voice calm.

"We're downhill. Fires don't move downhill fast."

"Let's compromise. One more corner and closer to the creek in the big clearing. We can stop there and blow the whistle unless the fire changes."

Tucker nodded. "We have to hurry. He's going to be listening for the whistle."

Kris followed Tucker as he ran down the hill. Hannah stepped up next to her.

"Is he losing it, or is your husband out there?"

"I don't know, but I need time to come up with a plan anyway."

Kris and Hannah caught up with the boy, and he yanked at the backpack on her back, soon coming up with his emergency whistle. He took in a lung-full of air and blew as loud as he could. Then he took in another breath and repeated the call two more times.

His brows furrowed as he whispered-counted to one hundred. Kris wanted to bring him into her arms, hold him, comfort him, but she saw her husband in him right now. He had to act. That's how he would make it through this, but how would she?

Once Tucker whispered one hundred, he repeated the call. Three piercing whistles that would wake the heavens themselves. While he continued his procedure, Kris hoped her son was right. She hoped that he had heard Blake call him and that he was on his way. Watching her son's heart break was not something she could stand right now.

Just in case, she had to prepare for their next steps. She thought of all the possible routes to get back to their house. The easiest, though longest, would be to follow the road next to the gas station to the cut-off road that wound around Thirteen Corners. A calculated look at the fire, and she knew that would be risky. The fire was traveling in that direction, and they might just be trapped like they are now, except with no place to go than to try to outrun the inferno.

There weren't any roads on the other side. The creek canyon grew into a deeper gorge that would be a perilous and dangerous hike through an overgrown forest. With the addition of the fire, which might follow them and rip through the steep terrain, it wasn't an option.

Her heart raced with indecision as Tucker began his call for the fourth time. She held her hands over her ears. If it wasn't for her adamant and resilient son, she would probably just give up. As it was, she saw no other choice than to go back down to Sara's. As much as Kris wanted to be back home where they had provisions and safety and beds, she didn't know how to get them there safely.

Kris sat on the gravel pull-out and brought her son down into her lap after he finished his last round of whistles. Thankfully the talkative teen had become silent, wide eyes watching the smoke billowing up in the forest.

"Mommy, I have to count." He struggled in her arms.

"Sweetie, we can't stay here. We have to go back to Forest Glen. The fire is blocking our way home."

"Dad's coming. Can't you feel it? We have to stay in one place."

Kris hung her head. "I'll give you five more minutes, and then we have to move." She kissed him on the temple before letting go.

She wished she had his tenacity. She wished she still believed in her husband that way. What if he had listened to her? What if he left like she had wanted? He had wanted to come with her. Things would have been so different if she had let him. The weight of her decision sat heavy on her shoulders.

In the midst of a whistle, a baritone voice traveled from the canyon.

"Stop," she told Tucker.

"But Dad…"

"Shhh. Listen."

When they heard the sound again, Tucker met her gaze. Hers held disbelief and relief, and his, affirmation and dedication.

"I told you," he said smugly before running towards the canyon. "Daddy! We're here!"

"Tucker! I'm coming! I'm coming, son!" Blake's voice held more emotion than Kris had heard from him since the day Tucker was born.

"He came!" Hannah clapped.

"He came," Kris repeated, a slight smile bending her lips as she felt a weight lifting off her.

"Daddy!" Tucker ran into the shadow that appeared from the canyon.

"Oh, Tuck!" Blake grabbed his son in a bear hug, the boy practically disappearing. "I found you!"

"I knew you would. I never gave up. We always return to each other."

"We always return to each other." Blake tightened his arms around Tuck. "You remembered the whistle." Pride filled his voice.

Kris understood. She was quite proud of her son right now, too. He had saved them.

"And I made Mommy stay in one place. I have water, too. Are you thirsty?"

"You have grown so much, my boy." He gave him one more squeeze before setting him down and stepping back to look at him. "Look how tall you are!"

"I'm six now and in first grade."

"I'm sorry I've been gone so long."

"You've been on assignment," he said with a nod.

"The last one. Now, it's just you."

Kris turned abruptly to watch Blake. *Last assignment?* He hadn't said anything about that to her. Regret sat heavy within her. She hadn't given him the chance.

"And Mommy," Tucker added.

"Yes," Blake said meeting her shocked gaze. A sheen of emotion reflected in his eyes. "And Mommy."

"Me too?" Hannah spoke up timidly.

Blake's gaze shot to the teenager and then back to Kris.

"This is Hannah. That's her car burning down there. She lives off Mountain View." Kris took a step closer to the girl, wanting her to feel supported.

"We'll get you home to your parents, Hannah,"

Blake said with a nod.

"How, Dad? How do we get past this fire?"

"Which way does a fire travel the easiest, Tuck?" he asked while adjusting the backpack on his shoulders.

"Uphill, of course. That's why I told Mommy not to worry."

"Don't forget the wind," she said gently.

"Well, of course the wind, but it's night, so the wind is traveling up the canyon." Tucker turned back to Blake as if asking for confirmation.

"How did you get to be so smart?" Blake picked the boy up and squeezed him again.

"You and Mommy," he said with a shrug and then buried himself in his dad's neck.

"So, with that information, what would you suggest we do?" Blake asked him.

Tucker, pulled back, squeezed his eyebrows together, and put a finger on his lips as he thought. "Go up the creek where you just came out of?"

Blake looked up into the trees, back toward the fire, and then down into the canyon. "I think that's our best option if we want to make it home."

Kris looked down into the black expanse where she knew the creek flowed through a rocky little gorge. A shudder ran through her body. She sensed Blake watching her, so she met his concerned gaze. A softness filled his eyes and a promise. He would protect them.

"Won't we be going right past the fire?" Hannah asked, her hands twisting in front of her, careful of the bandage.

"Yes, Hannah, we will. It takes a lot to move a fire downhill, including wind. Right now, the wind is on our side. It's pushing up the other side, away from the creek. If we hurry, we should be able to get past it before it turns...if it does."

"Why did that sound so ominous?" the girl asked.

"If the fire does make it down into the canyon and the wind picks up...it won't stop."

"The firefighters will come put it out, Dad. We have the best firefighters." Tucker smiled proudly.

Kris knew he thought about the field trip he had just taken to the fire station with his class. He had spoken about it nonstop for the rest of the week and said if he decided not to do assignments like Daddy, he wanted to be a firefighter.

Blake knelt down in front of Tucker. "Tuck, there won't be any firefighters coming to stop this fire." The serious and factual way he said it caused a shiver to run down Kris's spine.

"What?" Hannah shrieked.

"Why, Daddy?"

"Think about what happened to Hannah's car."

"Ours too, Dad. Mommy's car exploded like on Mythbusters."

Blake squeezed his eyes shut. When he opened them, Kris swore she saw moisture wetting his eyelashes.

"I'm so glad you got out in time."

"Mommy did it. She rushed us out, and we hid behind a big tree."

Blake met Kris's eyes. His gaze told her everything she wanted to know, and she felt the hardening of her heart begin to lessen.

"So, you're saying every car has exploded?" Hannah asked, her face paling.

"Not necessarily exploded, but most will no longer

function." Blake stood, eyes scanning the fire.

Hannah abruptly lowered herself into a plop on the asphalt. She hung her head between her knees as her body shook.

Kris squatted next to her and rested a hand on her back. Words did not come. What could you say to cheer up a girl at the start of her life when the world collapsed around her?

Blake shifted from foot to foot. She immediately felt anxiety course through her, pushing her to action. He had never kept still well, and emotions, well, they never made him comfortable.

"We've got to get moving," Blake spoke as he dug through Tucker's backpack and then placed it on the boy's back. He pulled out the flashlight, and after zipping the bag back up, wound it with ferocity as if winding it would dispel the fear that coursed through him…at least that's how Kris saw it. She almost wished she could have a go at it right now, too.

"I also have an emergency blanket," Tucker said, pushing his little chest out in pride.

"You have done well, son. Better than I could have ever hoped for."

Tucker's beaming smile almost made Kris forget the predicament they were in. She took the flashlight Blake handed her, grabbed the girl's hand, and stood up.

The girl followed, wiping at her eyes and breathing shakily.

"My dad's here, just like I said, Hannah. He's going to get us home." Tucker touched the girl's arm before turning toward the creek.

"He's very brave," she whispered to Kris.

"Yes, he is," she said, squeezing the girl's hand

before letting it go.

"We'll stay in pairs. I've got Tuck. You okay with Hannah?"

"We'll be fine," Kris said to the girl with a nod. Yet a trembling began within, and she hoped it wouldn't cause the flashlight to waver and show her weakness.

"Then let's head out. Stay close."

Kris couldn't help but feel as if she were just a member of Blake's team, rather than his wife. But isn't a marriage supposed to be the best team? She sighed. She had never had the chance to find out. He had been gone too much to know what that would be like. Would he stay now, when they needed him the most?

~5~

Blake fought against the emotions that kept trying to surface. He had his family. They were alive, and now it was his responsibility to get them home safe. Once they were there, he had no concerns. The bunker would feed them for a year if needed, and they could survive whatever chaos the sun might throw at them…or the demise of humanity in their neighbors.

He gripped his son's hand tightly, trying not to hurt the boy. He had grown so much over the last year it had knocked the breath out of him. The boy's face had leaned out and his top adult teeth were just growing in. His eyes may look like his, but Kris's smile filled their son's face, that beautiful smile he hoped would return to her.

He calculated the fire's movements again. It had crept another five feet towards the creek than it had when he went through the first time. It would be cutting it close at the end. The bank on their left rose in sheer granite cliffs. No scaling that without rope. He had a roll in the backpack he carried, but not enough to get them up that height.

They had no choice but to push through if they wanted to get home. They needed to be home. This fire was only a minor obstacle in the big picture. The world wouldn't be the same after this, at least not for many years. He clenched his teeth, berating himself for not leaving for home a long time ago.

Duty.

That word had been ingrained in him since he enlisted at seventeen. Duty for his country. Duty for his officers. Duty for the elected officials he had sworn to protect.

He glanced back to see how Kris and Hannah were scrambling through the overgrown creek canyon. Then he met the eyes of his son, so trusting. Duty.

This was where his duty lay. Duty to his family.

Blake boosted Tucker up a large boulder and then shimmied up himself. He positioned in a way to grab first Hannah's arm and then Kris's to help pull them up onto the mossy rock. Kris didn't immediately let go of his hand once on top, and he clung to it as a call line of hope.

She had always been his grounding rod. That woman had kept him on his toes since the moment they met. She challenged his conspiracy theories and laughed at his preparations, but she worked alongside him to prepare. He always thought she did so to indulge him. Kris never really fully believed this type of event would happen.

Playing around with the idea, researching survival techniques, practicing them in nature had bonded them together. He knew she didn't take it seriously, but every time he had to leave her, a small fulfillment eased his heart. At least she would have the skills she needed.

After Tuck had been born, things changed. She no longer wanted to pretend the world could end at any moment. He didn't blame her. The thought of his child having to suffer through a post-apocalyptic event made him want to retch. Which was why, even as Kris backed away from it, he pushed even harder to prepare.

He had even more reasons to live and protect the ones he loved.

The small sense of satisfaction that played inside him was easily overwhelmed by the heaviness of the situation. So much rested on his shoulders, but he would do it. He would make sure his wife and son survived, whatever the cost.

A blast of hot wind hit him in the face, drawing him back to the present. He froze. The wind had shifted. Damn it. He dropped Kris's hand, hopped off the rock and peered into the distance. The fire slowly edged its way down into the canyon.

"Tucker, pull off your pack and unwrap that emergency blanket." Blake shrugged out of his and did the same. "Quickly!"

Tucker spurred his movement, hastily finding the packaged shiny blanket.

Kris shot Blake a disgruntled glance before helping their son open the package and put his backpack back on.

He knew the look, but now was not a time for niceties. It was time for action. Life and death could hang in the seconds it took to think of feelings.

"Got it!" Tucker held up the opened blanket.

"Good. Give it to your mom and come here." Blake lowered him from the rock and then helped the girls down.

"What do we do with this?" Kris asked curtly.

"Wrap it around yourself and Hannah. Move as fast as possible. Stubbed toes or not, do not stop." He picked up his son, his weight reassuring in his arms, and then wrapped both them up in his blanket.

The crinkling sound distracted Blake. He couldn't

hear the rush of the fire or the trickle of the creek or the girls behind him. He turned to see their progress. They fiddled with the blanket, trying to get it around them both, tucking it into places and moving much too slowly.

"What are you two doing? Just move!" Panic burned through his veins. The fire rapidly crawled down the bank on their right side. "Cross the creek and don't stop."

He ushered them in front of him, urging them to move faster, pick up their feet, and stop crying.

He assumed the sobs escaped from the girl. Kris had learned long ago not to cry when their lives were held in suspension. He had many times brought them to places they had no business going. They had stared down death and lived to tell about their adventures. This would just be another to add to the list. There was no doubt. They would make it. Even if he had to pick up the lot of them.

At the bend in the creek, the fire had already made it halfway down the bank. He could feel the heat as he lowered the blanket to assess the situation. The boulders on the opposite side of the canyon allowed no escape.

He turned to look behind him. Just before the creek escaped into darkness, he saw flames lapping on the overgrowth at the edge of the water. They couldn't go back even if he wanted.

"Hold that blanket around you tight. Breathe as shallowly as possible. Pick up your feet and run. Our lives depend upon it." He barked the orders, ignoring the girl's sucking, sobbing breaths.

This transition would be hard on Hannah, but she would learn. She would have to.

He pulled Tucker tighter to him. The boy had not made a peep. He just clung to him like a baby chimpanzee. The boy had good sense. It eased the heavy weight of responsibility on him. All those fights with Kris had been worth it. Tucker probably had saved them all.

"Tuck, I need to use my hands. Can you hold on without my help?"

"Yes," he said, his young voice serious and determined.

"Hang tight." Blake held the blanket in a way that would keep any direct heat off his son. It left his knuckles exposed, and they burned as he ran, picking his way through watermelon-sized rocks in the bottom of the creek bed. His boots splashed in the water, causing droplets to sizzle on the shiny blanket surrounding them.

Tucker squeezed his neck and wrapped his legs around his waist, hanging on with grunts each time Blake landed hard. He felt his son's grips loosening. The slight boy began to slip down. He didn't make a sound beyond the grunts of exertion.

Blake dropped the blanket in order to hoist Tucker back in place. The heat seared the side of his face, and he felt Tucker's hand pull in away from the blast. Once his son was secured, he grabbed at the blanket and yanked it back over them. His face burned, and his throat felt on fire from the heat.

Tucker coughed a little and took in small, light breaths. The boy sure knew how to follow directions.

They soon caught back up to the women.

"You've got to hurry. I know it hurts like hell, but it will get worse if we don't get out of here now!"

The bright blanket reflected the orange glow of the

fire that sped through the creek in front of him. He could see the girls' feet stumble and catch themselves, but thank goodness it didn't stop their momentum.

The roar of the fire made it past the crinkling of the blanket and he knew they had made it to the worst spot. If they could push through this they would make it. A quick glance revealed the road lay only a hundred yards away.

One of the girls fell. He reached out an arm that seared without the protection of the blanket and pulled Hannah back on her feet. He could hear Kris's whispered words of encouragement. She had always been great at that sort of thing. His heart softened with thoughts of her gentle words cheering him on in some of his darkest days.

A fire lit within him. He would make sure they got through this.

"You're almost there! The road is just ahead. You got this." His attempt at encouraging was rewarded with a pace he hadn't seen yet. The girls scrambled across the boulders and then up the far bank and onto the road.

The fire crackled behind them, still threatening close and yet a safe distance for the moment.

No one spoke. Everyone drew in deep, painful, and labored breaths. Blake's throat seared. He knew everyone's did. Tears streaked through the grime on Hannah's face. Even Kris's had a few trails.

Kneeling down, he took Tucker by the shoulders and looked deeply into his son's eyes. "Are you okay?"

Tucker nodded. His lower lip trembled, but he stood tall.

"You are so brave, so very brave." He brought the

boy into his arms, feeling a sting when he rested his face against his son's hair. It sent him inhaling sharply, and Tucker immediately pulled back.

"You're hurt, Dad! I have burn cream!"

Blake felt the smile pull at the corners of his mouth. "Thanks, Tuck. Let's get farther from this fire before we stop long enough for that." He looked at the two girls, who seemed to be staring at hell. "You two did well."

Kris nodded her head, and Hannah released a fresh stream of tears.

"I didn't think we were going to make it," the girl barely whispered.

"Yet, you pushed forward." Blake softened his tone.

"Thanks to Kris," she said, granting Kris a brief flash of a smile in gratitude.

"She's good at that." He nodded, taking a moment to look into his wife's eyes. "Let's stash these blankets back into the packs and head farther away from this inferno." He glanced at the sky.

The aurora had become muted by what looked like roiling colored clouds. Please let that be rain. It would be the only chance against the fire consuming their town. Would God have that kind of mercy for them?

~*~

Kris's mind warred while she clung to Tucker. With each step the boy became heavier and heavier. Her son was tired, and she couldn't just put him in his comfy bed. In fact, they still had a few miles to go before she could…if she could even then. Longer than that depending on how far up Mountain View

Hannah lived.

She glanced at the girl who had sobbed her way through the creek canyon. Kris understood. She wanted to cry, too. Sucking in a deep breath, she took another step. Just one more step. The words became her motto even as the now limp Tucker slipped with each movement she made. Her arms screamed and her back spasmed, but she didn't want to let go of her son.

It had been pure torture not to have him in her arms through the canyon. Even though she knew Blake would do anything to keep their son safe, she longed to feel his breath and know that he was okay. She longed to reassure him and comfort him. That was not Blake's strong point.

Blake had pushed and yelled and forced them through. She had never really understood his tendency to become short and demanding during intense danger. Kris always thought kindness would go much farther. Yet, when they clambered over the rocky terrain, Hannah only moved when Blake raised his voice. Kris soothed her as they traveled, but her soothings couldn't motivate the girl like Blake's forceful commands.

Maybe there was a happier middle ground?

Her back spasmed so hard it made her suck in a breath and freeze. Strong hands rubbed down her back and then around her to take Tucker from her arms. She pulled back for a moment before the spasm doubled her over.

"He's gotten heavy." Blake watched her, his brows knitted together.

"A lot happens in a year." She stretched down to relieve the tension in her back. A few deep breaths later it faded. She stood to look her husband in his eyes. The darkness shaded them, yet she felt their penetrating stare.

"Kris, I...give me time to explain?"

"Well, it looks like you'll have plenty of time." She swept her hand to the disaster that lay around them.

The fire a mile or more behind them lit the sky in an eerie glow. As they slowly made their way to the housing around Mountain View Drive, no light emitted from the neighborhoods. Everything seemed eerie and filled with doom.

Kris took a deep breath in as she stretched, but ended up coughing, her lungs rebelling at the smoke that filled them. Once she caught her breath, she glanced with worry at Blake. White flakes fell on Tucker in his arms.

"Ash." The simple word escaping her mouth seemed to seal their fate.

"The wind has changed." Blake hoisted Tucker into a different position, causing the boy to murmur in his sleep. "We have to hurry."

"Where on Mountain View do you live, Hannah?" Kris asked.

"At the end," she said, her voice hoarse from sobbing.

"That's two miles round trip out of our way." Kris hadn't meant to say it aloud. She looked back at the fire now heading toward them, toward their house, toward the whole town.

"We'll make it." Blake reached out a hand while holding Tucker against him with the other. "We're going to be okay, Kris."

She wanted to believe him, but the odds were against them. Her gaze caressed her son as tears filled her eyes.

"I...I can make it from here by myself..." Hannah's lower lip trembled, but she jutted her chin out in defiance of the emotions that consumed her.

"Not going to happen. We'll get you home to your parents." Blake started up Mountain View Drive.

"It's just me and my dad," Hannah barely whispered.

Kris knew he wouldn't leave the girl behind. Doing something that cold wasn't in his nature. He protected out of a sense of self, not duty or training, just innate nature. That part of him was one of many she had fallen in love with. She didn't want to leave the girl to fend for herself either, but as she looked over her shoulder while following Blake, she wondered if that choice would cost them their lives.

As they trudged up the steep road, houses became closer together with each lot an acre or a half-acre rather than tens of acres. This had been the neighborhood she had pictured her children growing up in. A community that watched their kids ride bikes on the low-populated streets and held neighborhood barbeques.

It hadn't been Blake's vision. He wanted autonomy. He wanted privacy and to sit smack dab in the middle of nowhere with only many acres surrounding them on all sides. There had definitely been a peace in living so far from others, but she felt sad that Tucker didn't have neighborhood kids to play with, something she had enjoyed immensely in her childhood.

Low voices met them as they arrived at the heaviest populated part of the neighborhood. People gathered in small groups, panic lining their voices as they pointed toward the glowing orange sky.

Blake slowed until she and Hannah were even with him. "Stay close."

"They're just my neighbors." Hannah shrugged, her slight form lit by the weirdly-illuminated sky.

"Events like this can change people. Be on guard." Blake continued on, ensuring he kept them close to him.

Kris watched him check his ankle holster and side holster. She knew he had packed his guns. Part of it reassured her, the other part felt that normal annoyance. He always had such a negative outlook on humanity. When talking survival, he planned alone. He had no thought to work with a community of people. To him, others couldn't be trusted during disaster. Dog-eat-dog was his motto.

Yet, as they leveled out on the street, their motion set off a couple dogs. The groups walked onto the road blocking their path, and she had a fleeting thought that Blake might be right. Unconsciously, she moved closer to Blake, seeking security in his nearness.

"What's going on here?" One man stood in front of the others. The tall, buff guy wearing a flannel with cut-off sleeves crossed his arms, causing his large biceps to reflect the eerie orange glow. "Where'd you guys come from?"

"Jake, it's Hannah. Have you seen my dad?"

"Yeah, girl, he's going stir-crazy over you. Just headed home to pack a bag and go looking for you. None of our cars work."

"Yeah, mine's burning down the highway in Forest Glen."

"Who's this with you?" The guy looked Blake

over, his jaw clenching.

"They saved me. There's a fire in Thirteen Corners. It's coming this way."

"I'm Kris. This is my husband Blake and our son." Kris took a tentative step forward and held out her hand.

"Jake." He shook her hand, his grip squeezing her fingers. "We were just talking about what to do. The phones aren't working. Cars aren't working. Nothing's working."

Blake shifted next to her, and she heard his teeth grind before he blew a quiet breath out.

"If it continues this way, there'll be no stopping it. The forest between here and there is overgrown and dry. I'd pack up what you can carry and get as far north as possible," Blake said as if a command.

"You serious, man? We have families, no cars, nowhere to go. You expect us just to hike out of here?"

Blake tensed. "I don't expect anything from you. Just sharing my two cents that could save you and your family's hide before we travel on our way. Let's get you to your father, Hannah."

Kris followed Blake as the group in front of them slowly parted to let them through. The hairs on the back of her neck stiffened. Had Blake just made enemies for them? Yet, he was right. That fire would tear through that forest and could be here in a few hours depending on the wind. A soft gust blew her hair and chilled the back of her neck even more.

A young man ran past them toward the group. "Another fire! Southeast near town. We're going to be surrounded."

Blake didn't say a thing, but Kris had to push her

tired legs to keep up with his quickened pace. She glanced back at Hannah, who looked from the group to them, and back and forth.

"We'll get you to your dad, Hannah. He'll let you know what you guys should do," Kris assured her.

"He will. My dad is really smart, like rocket-science smart."

"Hannah!" A tall, lanky man ran toward them as if he hadn't run in years and forgot where to put his long arms.

"Dad!" Hannah bolted to meet him, letting her dad wrap her in a hug as she sobbed. "I'm sorry about the car, Dad. I didn't do anything. It just sputtered and lit on fire. I swear I didn't do anything."

"Shh, it's okay, Sweetie. It wasn't your fault." He looked up at them and met Kris's eyes and then Blake's. "You brought my girl home. I will forever be in your debt."

"No debt. Though if you have an idea of what is really going on..." Blake looked toward the sky where the smoke and clouds covered the aurora and back to the man. "And I think you do. You should get out of here."

Hannah's dad kissed her on the head and pulled himself partly away, though he kept a protective arm around the girl. He reached out a hand. "Arland Walters."

"Blake Chantry."

Surprise filled Kris. Blake didn't often give much information away. Something about Hannah's dad must have impressed him.

"Kris." She shook his hand, noting its smoothness and gentle grip.

"And this is Tucker, Dad. He's the smartest little

guy I have ever met." Hannah motioned to the boy stirring in Blake's arms.

"Are we home?" Tucker's voice tugged at Kris's heart.

"Not yet, Sweetie. Soon," Kris soothed, brushing his hair back.

"Here, buddy. Why don't you stretch your legs a bit while Mr. Walters and I have a quick chat?"

Kris looked up at the sky and the ash that gently fell around them. They didn't have time to talk, yet she had to trust Blake. He wouldn't put them in unnecessary danger.

"Why don't you guys come to my house and at least refill your waters before you have to go on? It's just right there." Hannah pointed to a house just down the road.

"We won't be staying long, but a refill would be a good idea." Blake turned to Arland. "Water's still working?"

"For now. I think there's still pressure left over."

Blake nodded. "Kris, go ahead and take Tucker in to refill those waters, but don't dawdle."

Kris wanted to chirp back a snide *yes sir,* but she just turned to do as he bade. Now was not the time to make little digs. As much as she didn't want to admit it, she and Tucker needed him to get home safely. She glanced back to see Blake leaning close to the lanky man, his voice serious and earnest.

~*~

Blake immediately felt a need to warn Arland of the dangers that lay in their future. Something about the man made him realize the survival of the people in this neighborhood would lie in hands of men like him. Arland didn't shout "leader quality," but it lay hidden just under the surface of his nerdy, scientisty exterior.

"You know what's going on, don't you?" Blake asked.

"My bets are on a CME, like in 1859."

"Yeah, like that, except these days our lives are structured around all that has just failed."

"I don't understand. I thought they had warning systems." Arland pinched the bridge of his nose.

"They're limited, but yeah. I don't know why they didn't use them, at least here. Who knows what it's like down in the cities."

"Thank goodness for that. You and I both know the chaos this would do with that density of population."

"Exactly." Blake nodded his head, the respect for this man growing with their conversation. "What are your plans?"

"I may be a scientist, Blake, but I'm no survival expert. I've been running the numbers and coming up with the same answer—run."

"Unfortunately, that would be my advice, too."

"North?"

"Yeah, and settle near a creek where you have a good view point within easy access that is up out of the smoke." He looked up into the smoky sky. "All this will settle in the low spots. Bring as much water as you can and a pan to boil it once you run out. Blankets. Food. Anything you have to hunt with. It's not going to be easy, Arland. Morals sometimes have to flee when you are fighting for the survival of your family."

Arland's gaze shifted back towards his house as Hannah led Kris and Tucker back out. "Thank you."

"There's more..." Blake continued to give him a quick version of Survival 101 while Kris watched from a distance. He saw the worry on her face and did his best to impart all he could as precious time ticked by.

"I appreciate you sharing all of this. I'm not sure why you are, or why you picked me, but thank you." Arland shook his hand.

"You just keep that girl safe. She's tough, but she needs you right now." Blake nodded to Kris, who took Tucker's hand and met him. "Say goodbye to Hannah, son. We have to get going before we can't make it back."

"Would you want to stay?" Arland asked as he shifted his weight and gripped his hands tightly in front of him.

"Thanks, but we need to be home."

"Yeah, we have..." Tuck began.

"It's where we belong, right, Tuck?" Blake cut off his son before he could give away vital information.

Tucker's eyes widened, and he nodded his head. "Yeah, we belong at home."

Kris gave Hannah a hug and whispered something in the girl's ears that made her smile and nod. Then she shook Arland's hand. "You have quite the daughter. I wish you both the best of luck."

Arland wrapped his arm around his daughter. "Together, we can make it through anything, right?"

"Right," Hannah said as she leaned against her dad for support. Her face was still covered in soot and exhaustion dulled her eyes, but Blake knew that girl would not go down without a fight. She might cry through it, but she'd keep pushing. "Thank you, all of you, for getting me home."

"Of course, may we see you again." Blake nodded, reached back for Tucker's hand and walked down the road.

"Will we make it in time?" Kris whispered before looking up at the orange sky, blinking back the ash.

"If we cut through the forest and across the gully. You up for it?" He slowed so he didn't drag his son.

"I'm up for it," Tucker said with a yawn.

"Whatever will get us home safely." Kris met his eyes briefly before ruffing up Tucker's hair. "You've been such a trooper."

"Yes, you have." Blake scooped the boy up and put him on his shoulders. They only protested the added weight a little. With his family now by his side, he felt unstoppable.

The group still stood around in the distance. Blake squeezed his fists. He didn't trust a group of people in situations like this. Chaos was sure to follow, especially when they realized just how serious this event was.

An empty lot opened up next to them. Quickly and quietly, he took Kris's hand and pulled her into the safety of the trees. Once behind the screen of trees, he stopped and put Tucker back on his feet.

"I'm going to need you to walk for a while. It's too dangerous to carry you on my shoulders in the dark."

"Because a tree branch could knock me off?"

"That's right, Tuck." He looked toward his wife, who scanned the darkness around them. He knew she feared the woods at night, and with a fire chasing them down, who could blame her. "We're going to head east through the forest and down into the gully.

Once there, if we follow the creek, it will take us right to our property."

"Why are you telling me this?" Her voice quivered, making him want to take her in his arms.

"It's just precautionary, Kris." He reached out a tentative hand to brush the soot from her cheek. "We're going to make it."

She bit her lip and nodded. He always had been able to count on her to keep her resolve in dangerous situations. It was one of the many things he fell in love with. She had an inner strength that most couldn't even fathom. In fact, he drew on that strength now. Hoping to be the man she needed him to be. Hoping to win a place back by her side and in her heart.

"It's just like a night hike, Tuck." She clasped the boy's hand and started walking through the trees.

"Except it's more survival-like, for real, with a fire chasing us down!"

Blake did his best to restrain the smile trying to force its way out. He had to hand it to the kid for his excitement and making the best of the situation. Yet, this was no game, and true survival was on the line. He glanced at Kris. The hard line of her lips let him know she didn't like Tucker making this into a game. She was smart though, and what she said next only solidified his high opinion of her.

"And we're the survivalists having to storm through the woods, jump over fallen logs, avoid other people, and make it back to base camp."

"Yeah, and if we see any game on our way, we should hunt it for food. I wish I had my bow." He put his arms in archery position and released pretend arrows with whooshes at imaginary creatures hiding in the dark.

"You've kept up your practice?"

"Almost every day!"

Delight filled Blake, even with danger rushing toward them and no idea what lay in store for them, or the world for that matter. He enjoyed being back with his family. A rightness filled him. He would make sure they survived. In fact, he would make sure they thrived.

~6~

Kris watched her son shoot at imaginary game and bad guys as they made their way as quickly as possible through the dense forest. She knew that it would open up slightly soon, but then they would be in another creek canyon. Thankfully, this one was wider and less steep than the one they barely made it through just an hour or so before.

The smoke in the air burned her already parched throat. Without stopping, she hoisted the backpack she had taken from Tucker and brought out the water bottle. She took a slow drink, allowing the water to cool her mouth and throat. Less than half of the bottle sloshed around when she stopped, and she still wished for more. With a few quick steps, she sidled up to Tucker and handed him the bottle.

"Thanks, Mommy. My throat feels all rough."

"It's from the smoke, Sweetie. It should feel better tomorrow." She watched as he almost finished off the bottle.

"Sorry, I almost drank it all before asking Daddy if he wants some." His kindness burned at her heart.

Knowing that he had his dad to rely on again, for a while at least, warmed her even more. Who knew when Blake would leave again. Though, he had said he was done…

She watched Blake's reaction to their son offering him the last bit of their water. He took the bottle reverently but then handed it back. "It's okay, Tuck. I have a few more bottles in my pack. You go ahead."

Kris bent down and kissed him on the cheek. "You are very thoughtful to think of others."

"You sure?" Tucker questioned.

"Yep," Blake said as he shifted his bag around and dug out another bottle. "See?"

"Okay." The word had hardly left his mouth before he had downed the rest of the water.

Kris's mouth watered at the thought of more, but she didn't know how much they might still need. She swallowed painfully, took the empty bottle from Tuck, and shoved it into the pack before readjusting it to her back.

"Here." Blake's voice had softened as he handed her the bottle. "There are two more in here, and we're almost back."

"Thank you," she whispered, taking the bottle and swallowing two large drinks.

"You still have that aloe plant at home?"

"Yeah," she said, thinking of how big it had grown since he had left.

"Good. We can mix some with water and drink it once we get back. It will help our throats, and the filtered air will help our lungs."

"And your face, Dad."

"You really expect us to go into that bunker?"

"Wouldn't you rather not sleep in fear of the fire tearing down our house in the middle of the night?"

"Hmmphf." Kris didn't like it when he was right. A night in the bunker wouldn't be too bad, except there was only the one large bed plus a hammock for Tucker. Maybe she could convince Blake to sleep in the hammock. An inner laugh shook her with the image of Blake's massive body hanging out all sides of the child's hammock.

They had several slumber parties in there after Blake installed the bunker. The whole idea wowed Tucker. Staying underground and all of them in one room made a fun adventure for the boy. Now, though, the thought of being trapped in such small quarters with her husband who had been gone for a year…well, let's just say it wasn't a comfortable thought.

She squeezed her arms around her just as her foot caught on an unseen stump. She threw her hands out to catch her fall as she crashed onto the forest floor. A piercing worse than anything she had ever felt slashed into her palm. She gasped and pulled her hand to her chest as she rolled to her back.

"Mommy!" Tucker ran over to her.

"It's okay, Tuck." She did her best to reassure him, but her voice sounded strained and breathless even to her.

"You're hurt." Blake stood over her and then squatted, his hands roaming her body.

"Stop. I'll be fine. Just stuck my hand with something." Kris bit her cheeks, both from the pain and from the crazy emotions rolling through her from his hands all over her.

Blake turned on his headlamp, which he had said they should keep off in order to not draw any attention to themselves. He shined it on the hand she still clutched to her chest. It throbbed and burned. The last thing she wanted to do was open it.

"Let me see." His demand held no room for argument, and grudgingly she brought her hand into the light.

Seeing it might have been worse than the pain. A

pencil-sized splinter of wood stuck out of her palm. The crazy thing was, no blood dripped from the wound.

"We have to get that out."

She nodded, the thought making her face go numb as the blood drained from it.

"Can you make it another hundred yards down to the creek?"

"Yes," she said as she took his hand with her uninjured one and stood. A wash of dizziness rolled through her.

Blake steadied her, grasping her elbow and steering her toward the sound of a gentle brook. This creek didn't have much in it, a sure sign of the hot drought they were in and another reason the fire would be raging toward them. She glanced back at the orange-lit horizon. How close was it? Did they have time for this stop?

"We have to make time to do this. If we don't, it will be worse once we get home."

"Does it hurt, Mommy?" Tucker laid a gentle hand on her arm.

"Yes, but Daddy will make it better."

"He's great at wilderness medicine, huh?"

"Well, I've taken some classes at least." Blake laughed, a tight-squeezed sound that didn't seem full of confidence.

He led her to a low rock at the creek's edge and instructed her to let her hand soak while he filtered through the emergency medical kit. He laid out tweezers, bandages, antibiotic ointment, and some gauze on the rock beside her and then squatted next to her.

"Okay, I would suggest you look away." He took

in a large breath and breathed it out. For someone good in emergency situations, medical things and blood did not come easy to him.

Kris opened her hand for him, seeing the crooked way the splinter stuck in her palm. She feared the worst and looked away as he suggested.

"Take a deep breath in. Okay, blow it out now."

Kris did as instructed and felt a searing pain as he withdrew the splinter. She bit back the cuss word that wanted to spew from her lips and looked sharply at her hand. Blood burst from the wound like a plugged pipe that had been set free. When Blake pressed the wad of gauze into the gaping hole, she almost passed out from the pain.

Blake cursed under his breath as he readjusted the gauze and then poked around. "There's still a piece inside." The doom in his voice flooded her veins with fiery panic.

"What does that mean, Daddy? Can't you get it out? Will Mommy be okay?" The boy who had been brave during this whole ordeal now had tears streaming down his face. His lips trembled, and he took in shaky breaths.

"I won't let anything happen to Mommy." Blake reached up and cupped the boy's chin. "Do you remember that moss we saw on the survival show?"

"Yeah, it stopped bleeding."

"That's right. I saw some just back in the forest. Could you be brave enough to take the other flashlight and get some?"

"Yes," he said with determination in his little voice. It made Kris's heart ache almost as much as her hand.

"I don't want him going out there by himself," she

said shakily.

"I can do it, Mommy. I'm doing it for you." He stood tall before rummaging in the pack for the flashlight. He gave her a little kiss on the cheek. "We always return to each other."

"We always return to each other," Kris and Blake said at the same time.

"I'll get that moss." Then he turned and strode into the dark woods.

"I don't like this." Panic flooded her system.

"I'll be able to see his light the whole time. He doesn't need to see this." He took in a shaky breath. "It's going to hurt like hell, Kris."

"I'll try not to pass out on you."

He rinsed a stick in the creek. "I'll try not to as well." He offered a small smile. "Bite on the stick. It helps."

Kris bit down hard on the stick, fear making her stomach churn and threaten to heave.

"Okay, here we go."

The pain bit into her palm like a searing flame. She clenched down on the stick, reminding herself she had been through labor, she could do anything. Sucking in air through her nose, she did her best to breathe and force herself to stay present. Rather than focusing on the searing pain that threatened to push her out of consciousness, she turned her entire concentration to listening for Tucker's movements in the forest behind her.

Blake cursed a few times, his panting breath doing nothing to reassure her.

With one final blaze of pain, his movement stopped. Her hand throbbed, and her teeth and jaw ached. She spat out the stick. "You done?" she said in a raspy, haggard voice.

"Yes, tough lady." He pressed a wad of gauze over the even bigger hole and then brought his head to hers, wrapping a hand around the back of her neck to lean her forehead against his own. His sheen of perspiration mingled with the drops of hers as they breathed each other's breaths. "You're amazing."

"Thank you," she whispered, wishing that things were different, wishing that he hadn't been gone for a year, wishing that the world wasn't ending as they knew it, and wishing she hadn't fallen on her hand. She knew what this could mean with no hospitals or doctors able to administer medication or stitches or whatever may be needed.

She heard rushed steps in the leaves and pine needles. Relief washed through her, almost enough that she wanted just to close her eyes and sleep. Surely this all had to be a dream, or rather a nightmare.

"I got it!" Tucker said triumphantly.

"I'm so proud of you, Sweetie!" Kris leaned back from Blake and reached her uninjured hand to her son. "You are so brave and courageous putting your life in danger to help me."

Tucker smiled and looked to Blake.

"That's a sign of a good man right there," he said as he ruffed up Tuck's hair. "Wash that moss off in the creek, and we'll pound it with this rock."

"Then we put it on Mommy's owie, right?"

"Yep, and wrap it up."

Kris watched her boys work together. Maybe she had been too hard on Blake. All the skills he had insisted Tucker learn were actually paying off. In fact, it had saved them or at least brought them back together.

A warm wind whipped up her hair. The blast caused prickles of fear to pierce her chest. She turned and saw the orange brighter than it had been and even a few flames licking the sky a distance away.

"Blake?" She turned to catch his eyes and saw him staring at the same scene.

"Almost done, Buddy? We've got to get this on mom and move."

"Got it." Tucker picked up a wad of the green goo, looked up at her, and with her nod, he gently placed it on her wound.

Blake wrapped it in place and then stuck everything back in the packs. He held down a hand to Kris and pulled her up. The world spun slightly, but she widened her stance and set her jaw.

"You got this, tough girl," Blake reassured her, using the term he called her when they first met. He kissed her on the forehead and then reached for Tucker's hand. "Okay, a mile to go and we're home, safe and sound."

"Let's do this!" Tucker cheered.

Despite the danger racing them down, the situation the world was in, and the way her hand throbbed, a warmth spread through her. She had her family back together, and her little miracle made that happen.

~7~

Blake pushed down the fear that raced up his spine. He didn't have time for it. He needed to be ready and completely focused in order to get his family to safety. Mapping out their route, he made sure not to go too close to any neighbors' houses. Another delay could cost them everything.

As they charged up the little gorge, a cooler gust hit them from the opposite direction of the fire. On the wind he smelled the most delicious scent. Rain.

Kris must have smelled it, too, because her eyes swiftly met his, hope glowing within…overpowering the orange reflection of the sky.

"Is it too much to hope for some mercy?" she asked.

"Oh, I'm hoping with every ounce of my being, not only for us…but everyone." The truth hit him hard. He knew he could have helped all those people back there when they dropped off Hannah. He knew he could help his neighbors, but it may be at the cost of losing his loved ones. You just can't trust a group of humans. He had seen it too many times.

"All those people…" Kris's voice faded off.

He knew she would rescue each and every one of them. They didn't have the supplies for that. As it was, they would have to figure out how to survive without amenities soon enough. At least, they had enough to get through this first winter and the bunker to keep them safe through it as well.

Another gust brought a spattering of wetness.

"Rain!" Tucker shouted.

Both Blake and Kris shushed him. Not that he shouldn't be excited about the rain. It was a Godsend, but they came up to the neighbor's property line. The one with the aggressive dogs. The last thing they needed was to be run down by one of them.

"It's raining, though. We haven't had rain in like a year, and isn't this good for the fire?"

"Yes, it is, Tuck. It's very good. We just have to be stealthy to get home right now. Can you be sneaky through Mr. Smither's property?" Blake redirected him.

"Oh, like a ninja on a mission?"

"Yeah, like that."

They ninjaed their way through the property until they hit their fence line. Blake saw the fence and his shoulders relaxed. They had made it. Their house lay just on the other side of the fence and their bunker, too. A year's supply of food, water, and everything else they needed. He looked at Kris clutching her hand to her chest—even antibiotics if needed.

They walked the fence line to the gate, and Tucker ran up to it, punching in the code. Blake watched closely. He pressed each number carefully, his birthday. Why hadn't Blake thought of that when he tried to get in earlier? The gate, of course, didn't budge.

"Why isn't the gate opening?" Tucker tried the combination again. "Oh, that's right…no power."

"We'll hop it," Blake said, taking a step toward it.

"Hey look, it's your Jeep."

"Yeah, it doesn't work anymore, though."

"We should still push it onto our property. Maybe

we could fix it."

"There's always that possibility, I guess, but not tonight." Blake picked him up and set him as high on the fence as he could. Then he clambered up to the top and lowered the boy down the other side. Then he jumped back off to help Kris over. With her injured hand, the clambering was a bit awkward, and she fell more than landed on the other side.

"You okay, Mommy?"

"Yeah, Sweetie. I'm okay."

Her voice caused worry to grow inside Blake. She was exhausted. They were so close.

"Can we have a sleepover in the bunker tonight?"

"Absolutely, Tuck. I think that's a great idea." The boy had read his mind. He stole a glance at Kris as they walked down their long driveway.

"I just need to grab a few things from the house, and then I'll join you." Kris moved toward the house while Tucker took off into the forest where the bunker lay hidden.

"I can get whatever you need. You should go rest."

"No, I know where everything is. I'll be fine."

"Oh, Mommy! Would you get my survival magazines?"

"Sure, Sweetie. Go with Daddy, and I'll be right there."

Blake handed her his headlamp, although he wished she would listen to reason. He wanted to make her go to the bunker, but he knew her too well and didn't want to start their time with an argument. Reluctantly, he took up Tucker and traveled through their maintained forest to the pile of boulders the entrance hid behind.

The sky began to lighten on the horizon, and in the faint glow he could see the healthy, cleared forest. He was happy that Kris had allowed the grounds keeper he hired to continue his work to keep their property fire-safe. It cost a pretty penny, but one that might just save their house tonight.

~*~

Kris watched them head off toward the bunker. They had made it. The fire still raged and roared toward them, but they had made it back to their property, to their home. The rain had only produced a few showers, barely enough to wet their clothes, but the air still hung heavy with expectancy. A storm brewed, hopefully a storm of mercy.

The house was dark and cold. She clicked on the headlamp. It wasn't like it was the first time she wandered around her house with a flashlight. Power outages were normal upcountry and even more so since the big fires. The electrical company would shut it off if there was any threat of fire whatsoever. Well, they couldn't have prevented this one.

Kris emptied a tub of toys onto Tucker's floor so she could use the box to load what they needed. A tear rolled down her cheek while she scanned his room. Tuck would be so heartbroken if the fire burned up his adventure room and all his toys. She threw a few treasured toys, his stuffed animal, and favorite blanket into the tub.

She then sifted through his closet to find the memento box that held his footprints from the day he was born, a lock of hair from his first haircut, his four baby teeth, and a few other special things. She left the room and came back with an arm-load of photo albums, a few books and pictures, and other keepsakes.

Pushing the tub to the door as best she could with her injured hand, she couldn't stop the feeling that she forgot something. His survival magazines!

She walked back into his room and tried to grab them with her uninjured hand. They slipped from her grasp and spread out on the floor. She knelt to pick them back up, noticing slips of white paper sticking out of most of them.

Knowing she didn't have much time but not able to stop her curiosity, she pulled one out. Scrawled in Tucker's wavering handwriting, which must have been from earlier that year because his penmanship had improved dramatically with the start of first grade, were numbers and letters underneath them. She focused a little more, mentally adding spaces between words. *We Always Return to Each Other.*

Her heart hammered in her chest. She pulled out another one. *Don't forget to store extra water.* Another: *I love you. Tell your Mommy I love her too.* And then another from the top of the stack: *I'll be home soon!*

Kris's eyes blurred with tears. Blake had sent messages.

The door slammed open. "Kris, are you okay?" Blake's voice sounded from the living room and then closer. "What are you doing? We have to go…" His voice ended right next to her.

She looked up at him, the tears now flowing freely. "You sent messages…"

"Yes," he said, squatting next to her. "You didn't know?"

She shook her head, emotions rushing through

her. Why didn't Tucker tell her about these messages? Then, shame filled her with the hot coals of knowing. She hadn't want to hear anything about Blake. Her anger had pushed her boy away from her. His fear kept these hidden.

Blake touched her face gently. "I did everything I could, and I know it wasn't enough." His thumb wiped at the tears streaming down. "I promise I will never leave you two like that again."

Kris sucked in a sob and allowed him to wrap her up in an embrace.

Warmth filled her. The warmth of his large, protective body, the warmth of feeling safe, and the warmth of love. When he pulled her to her feet, he planted a lingering kiss on her forehead.

"Please give me the chance to rebuild your trust in me."

She looked up into his green eyes, so full of love and adoration. How could she say no? Besides, where would she be without him right now as the world crumbled, or rather burned, around them?

She nodded, and he bent to pick up the magazines and all the messages Tucker had scrawled out. She fought the pain that her son had done such a thing without her help or even her knowing. That kid was smart, almost too smart.

Blake set the magazines in the tub. "Anything else."

She walked to the picture of their wedding day that she had slammed down the day before and placed it in the tub Blake now carried. With a sigh of longing, she looked around her home. It was a place filled with memories of their wedding night, of laying on the couch while feeling Tucker rolling around in her belly, the carpet where Tucker took his first steps, the bed he crawled in to sleep with her every night, the pictures of their life lining the walls.

Thinking that all this may burn and this might be the last time she saw it all, created a hole in her heart much larger than the one that throbbed in her palm.

"I wish we could take it all," she whispered as he led her out the door and turned the key. With the tub under one arm, he took her hand in his.

"I know, but we have each other, and that is all that matters." He pulled her close into him as she felt a few more drops of rain splash on her face.

"Maybe God will grant us mercy and let this rain come down in a torrent."

"I pray that He does," Blake said in the same reverent tone.

Tucker met them at the entrance to the bunker. His enthusiasm for the adventure filled her heart with love. How she wished she could have the eyes of a child. As she watched him sift through the tub to find his special things, she remembered Blake's words. Yes, they had each other. With that, they could get through anything.

****

INSTALLMENT TWO

~1~

DATE: October 14   11:37

Silence filled the bunker, the type of silence Kris thought would exist in a tomb. Empty. Void of life. She looked up at the ceiling knowing yards of dirt separated her from the life that still forged on up there.

She couldn't hear the crickets chirping, nor wind singing through the trees. She didn't understand the absoluteness of silence until spending time in the bunker. Moving closer to her son's body wrapped around her, she took solace in hearing the slight whisper of his breath.

The urge to open a window and look out about drove her mad. Had the rain come with enough ferocity to douse the raging fire? Or were those flames right now devouring her land, her home, and her memories?

She untangled herself from Tucker who had refused to sleep alone in the hammock and quietly sat on the edge of the thin mattress. Her son rustled in the bed, snuggling into the warm spot she had just vacated. The air tensed, and though she couldn't see her hand in front of her, she knew her movement had awoken Blake on the other side of the bed.

Kris froze. The last thing she wanted was a conversation with him. There was too much to say, too many emotions living behind those words to be useful. She needed space.

Her gaze roamed the pitch black, closed-in box holding her family. She couldn't see the restricting walls, but she could feel their cold metal presence. The only thing she didn't have right now was space.

The darkness enveloped her, and she hoped Blake would fall back asleep. Her breath came silently, long and deep. The air tasted stale and dense. What she wouldn't give to go outside and breathe the pine-scented breeze.

To her dismay the sheet rustled, and the unmistakable pure manly scent of her husband came on waves of air caused by his movement. Her body reacted, and an instant need to be in his arms and comforted washed over her.

Her mind though, reinforced the invisible wall between them, a wall as dark as the space surrounding them. She wanted to focus on anything besides him and settled on the throbbing of her injured hand.

His presence invaded her barriers, overwhelming her with the heat of his torso moving to rest on the squeaky mattress next to her. He turned on the dim, red light on the wall next to the bed. It illuminated his naked, sculpted chest in a soft glow. Why did he have to sleep in his underwear? Couldn't he at least have worn a shirt?

Her mind swirled. Here she was worried about her husband sitting inches away from her when outside the world was burning. People were probably dying or fleeing their homes with nowhere to go. The quandary almost caused her to let out a cynical laugh, but she caught herself just in time.

"Can't sleep?" Blake's gravely voice broke the eerie silence. He set the light on his lap and rubbed his face and short hair with large, thick hands.

Where had he been for the last year? She noticed a few new scars, still puckered pink on his arms and chest. Desire to know everything about his time away flooded her, but she dammed up the rush. So much time had passed. She had accustomed herself to the life of a single mom. It would take time readjusting to his constant presence—if he remained as he had promised.

"I'm worried about my parents, and my brother." The statement wasn't a lie. She had been thinking of them, among many other things.

"They're prepared. They'll make it." He yawned and stretched.

"Maybe the CME didn't affect them?" Hoped lined her voice, but with one look of Blake's resigned features glowing in the red light, she knew the hope was false.

"I'm not sure, but with auroras like that, I would surmise this to be a national event, if not global."

She hung her head. Her family still lived in the rurals of Idaho where she left them when she had gone off to college in California. Who knew she would meet a crazy, military survivalist and fall in love? She had always planned on returning.

"Your brother knows what he's doing. Remember? Last Christmas they talked about their rendezvous plan so he could get your parents to his land."

"You weren't here last Christmas," she said. Her words held no bite, only exhaustion and acceptance.

She reminded herself that he had sent contact. Her eyes instinctively went to the tub in the dark corner. Its outline was barely visible in the soft red glow. The tub contained the secret coded messages Blake had sent over the last year, the messages her six year old boy decoded himself and didn't share with her, out of fear she was certain.

"I'm sorry." He hung his head. "The Christmas before that. Any word of change to their plan?"

"No, I'm sure they saw it all as a game they played with their crazy son-in-law."

"Game or not, it will save them."

Kris nodded. It probably would. She knew her brother and his wife had started living off the land as much as possible, not because they feared an apocalyptic event, but because they liked the idea of the freedom of being off-grid. Her heart squeezed. Would she ever get to see them all again?

"What about your dad?" she asked and tensed. She never knew what his reaction would be when mentioning his dad. There was no love lost between them. His mom had passed away when he was a teenager. Hate and anger filled the house after her loss, which spurred Blake to enlist as soon as he was of age.

"I've shared all he allowed me. His survival is now up to him. Not much I can do about it anymore." His voice was devoid of emotion as he said it, but his lips twitched ever so slightly.

He rose off the bed, taking the glowing light with him. His muscular back faced her, a specimen that most men in their forties would not have. She craved to reach out and touch him, to allow him to enfold her in his strong arms, and pretend that they were just playing the game again. Man, did she wish that the world as she knew it was not burning up this very instant.

Blake cocked his ear toward the vent in the ceiling.

He touched the air ventilation system in the corner of the room. With a few rapid cranks of a handle, the soft hum of the system echoed in the small space. Kris knew many people who used white noise to sleep every night. She never could understand how a constant drone could help a person sleep.

Blake's steps barely made a sound besides a soft sticky suction of bare feet on the linoleum as he walked silently back to the vent. For such a large man, she had no idea how he walked so quietly. She assumed his occupation had required that level of stealth though, otherwise he might not be with them now. A shudder ran through her.

Kris held her breath as her husband stood silently below the outtake. That vent, the door, and secret crawl space were the only passages out into life. Her heart hammered with the thought of being stuck in this ten by twenty box for more than just a night.

"Can you hear anything?" she asked.

"No," he shook his head, and then stretched, his hands flat on the ceiling. He paced the floor, his barefooted steps sounding like walking on a sticky kitchen floor. It hadn't even been half a day and he already acted like a caged animal. He turned his eyes back on her, their depths blackened by the lack of light. She knew that look and didn't want to go there.

"What happens if the fire makes it here?" she quickly asked, wanting to delay the words almost spilling from his mouth.

"It will burn through the duff. Since you have kept the grounds so clean, the house should be fine."

Kris's shoulders relaxed. "There's still so much in there that I don't want to see gone. What about the bunker. Will it just go right over the top of us?"

"If it has enough fuel to do that. It might not make it much into our property at all."

"If it does go over us," Tucker's little voice said from the bed behind her, "will the smoke come down the air pipe?"

"No, Tuck. You don't have to worry about that. This air filtration system is top-of-the-art. No particles or gas can get through it," Blake reassured.

"Good. My throat hurts from all that smoke." His voice sounded deep and raspy.

Kris grabbed a water bottle with her uninjured hand and handed it to him. "We'll put some aloe in it in the morning."

"It's actually almost noon." Blake said after looking at a cell phone, the glow illuminating his face.

"It still works?" she asked, hope lining her voice.

"No reception. The cell towers fried just like the power lines. The bunker acts as a faraday cage so…"

"I made one, Dad!" Tucker sat up in bed, his little voice hoarse and raw. "It's in the house. I have the radio in it, just like you instructed." He threw his hands over his mouth, and his eyes went wide as he looked at his mother.

"It's okay, Tuck. I know about the messages." Kris brought him into her lap. "I'm sorry you felt like you couldn't share them with me."

"You were just so mad at Daddy." The defeat in his words squeezed her heart.

Her gaze shot to Blake's before hiding from his intense gaze. "I know, Sweetie. I'm sorry."

Blake blew out his breath, and then sat next to them. "It's my fault, Tuck. A man shouldn't leave his family."

Kris met Blake's eyes over Tucker's head.

"I've learned that now. I won't be leaving you two again." Even in the red glow, she swore she could see the earnestness alive in his green eyes.

"I know. We're together now, as a family." Tucker wiggled and squirmed next to Kris.

"Sweetie, do you need to use the bathroom?"

"Yeah, but that composting toilet is weird, and it's so small in there, and it's so...dark." His voice had lowered to a whisper. He had been exceptionally brave last night, but he was still just a boy, a boy afraid of the dark.

"Something's going on with the DC power system. I'll have to go and check. You can take this." Blake handed Tucker the cell phone after turning on flashlight mode.

Kris slid to her feet. The cold floor seeped through her skin, and she wished she had pushed to get better flooring in here. Not that she had ever believed they would be using it for real.

"There's a lantern in here..." She rummaged through a small storage compartment next to the bed. There were several storage places stashed throughout the small quarters. "Here." She pulled out the battery operated lantern and turned it on.

The small room lit up, but it still felt like night. It would always feel like night this far underground. How long would they have to stay here?

"Much better," Tucker said with a smile. "Could I still leave the door open?"

"Of course, let's get you all set up." Kris held out her hand, and they took the five steps to the bathroom together.

Blake grunted as he fiddled with the battery compartment next to the bathroom. He muttered under his breath and then rested his head against the wall. Kris knew better than to interrupt with a question, so she just watched him out of the corner of her eye while she ensured Tucker had everything he needed.

"I've got to go up top." Blake ground his teeth. She could hear them grating even five feet away.

"Is that safe?" she asked, keeping her voice low.

"I don't know yet, but it has to be done." He shoved his feet into his pants, tugged on a shirt over his washboard abs, and then donned a holster.

The click-click of him checking his gun before slipping it into the holster sent a shiver down Kris's spine.

"You expecting trouble?"

"Expect the—"

"The unexpected and prepare for everything in between," Tucker finished for him as he stood from the toilet and pulled up his pants.

"That's right my boy." Blake's goofy grin made him seem so boyish that Kris had to work hard to hide her smile. He pulled out another handgun and held it out for Kris, handle first. "I know you don't like them, but you need it…just in case."

"Can't you just put it on the table? I'll grab it if something crazy happens."

"Don't be ridiculous, Krista." Blake shook his head as he flicked the safety on and slipped the gun into her pants pocket.

The weight and cold steel sent chills throughout Kris. She glared at her husband. She had gotten accustomed to making her own decisions. Having him dictate her life again would take some getting used to.

~2~

Blake avoided the glare Kris sent him. He didn't need her anger. There was enough to worry about without crazy notions about firearms. The power in the bunker had kicked on last night. Why had it gone out? He tapped the battery packs one more time and checked the camera screen out of habit only to find it still unnervingly dark.

Would he open the door to flames, foe, or a rabid wild bear? Being blind did not suit him. He walked to the door, set his hand on the cold steel, unsure of what he could feel through the thick metal.

"Dad, I got your back." Tucker's voice had grown so much over the last year, and he could hear the pride in it.

Blake turned toward his son, a smile warming his face when he saw the boy holding his bow and a quiver of arrows. "Well, I believe you would, son." He took a step toward him and lowered to a knee. "I have an even more important job for you." He glanced at Kris and then looked deep into Tuckers eyes. In a whisper he said, "I need you to protect Mom."

Tucker eyed him, glanced at his mom who conveniently busied herself in the food cupboards, and then nodded. "Okay. I'll protect Mommy."

"Thanks, Buddy. I knew I could count on you." He leaned forward and touched foreheads with his son. "We always return to each other."

"We always return to each other." Tucker's voice held reverence, and then he squeezed him tight. "Keep your eyes open."

"Will do, son." Blake rested a hand on his little champ's head. The last thing he wanted to do was leave his side again.

They needed power though. Without power there would be no air filtration system, no heat, no lights, no comfort to keep them from going crazy locked underground. He checked his artillery again and then pushed his shoulders back.

"Keep it locked tight. Don't open it until you hear my knock." He turned to ensure Kris listened.

Kris sat on her haunches, a look of resignation in her eyes. For a moment he actually wished to have that fire in there instead, even if it was directed at him. With her long red hair pulled up into a messy bun, flashes of earlier years filtered through him, times when he would have scooped her up in his arms and forgotten the world.

He shifted his weight, shoving the longing down as he had for a year now. "You remember the pattern?"

Kris nodded, but it was Tucker that pounded the rhythmic knock on the table.

"How do you remember all of this?" Blake asked, shaking his head in awe.

"It's important."

"Yes, it is," Blake said in a whisper. "I'll be back as soon as possible. If I don't return, do not come looking for me. Understood?" He looked at both his wife and son while swallowing the tightness that had stuck in his throat. It wasn't like he was leaving them. He was only going out to check the lines to the solar panels. Why did his heart act like it ran a marathon?

"I'll see you in a few minutes, Dad." Tucker's confidence settled his pounding heart. Nothing would keep him away from his family again.

"See you in a few. Looking forward to some good freeze-dried breakfast when I get back." He winked at Kris who rolled her eyes. "Hey, I haven't eaten a home-cooked meal in a year. Give a man a break." He laughed, albeit forcefully, but it still felt good.

"I'm hungry too." Tucker rubbed his belly.

"Family breakfast when I get back then." Blake smiled at Tucker before turning the handle on the door. If he didn't leave now, he never would.

The handle creaked as if it wanted to let the world know it opened. Blake pulled out his handgun and covertly scrutinized the open area at the bottom of the stairs. Nothing stirred. No movement. No sounds. Just the hollow echo of his breath.

He glanced back in the bunker, met his son's eyes, and nodded before closing the door behind him. The stairs took off the left side of the door, giving it a ninety degree turn. How that would stop radiation from getting into the bunker, he didn't understand, but it was what the builder had told him.

He stepped lightly on the grated stairs, careful not to let them echo and announce his ascent. At the bunker door that would open in the midst of a group of granite boulders, he laid his hand on the cold steel. Listening closely he heard the patter of rain bouncing off the reinforced door.

Blake pulled his hood up, took three steadying breaths, and pushed up the door just far enough to peer out. Once he assessed the area was clear, he quickly squirmed through and shut the hatch quietly. The coded lock clicked. Thank goodness Kris hadn't changed this lock during her tirade.

From the protection of the boulders, Blake scanned the area. Nothing stirred besides the rain crashing down. The house lay three hundred yards to the west and the solar panels, at an angle, lay in between. With his right arm holding the gun out and his left supporting it, he eased into the cleared woods and into the opening between them and the house.

His first idea of potential problems was the converter. Had it fried during the CME and the batteries had just enough charge to get them through the night? He could fix most things, but electricity did not sit easy with him.

As he approached the solar panels, something about the converter box caught his attention. A few steps closer, and he realized it stood open, the connector hanging limply from it. The hair on the back of his neck rose. His senses heightened even more. He quickly studied the area further, but he could not detect any evidence of another's presence.

Filing through his memories he checked and double checked that he had closed that box door, that he had hooked that connector securely.

In front of the box now, he knelt while staying aware of every single movement around him. He hooked the connecter back up, wiggled it to ensure it held tight, and then shut the door, twisting the tab to lock it. The actions felt familiar, and it made him look warily around him once more.

His gaze fell to the wet ground around him. No grass grew due to the extended summer. Only pine needles and madrone leaves carpeted the otherwise clean landscape. As his hand brushed the ground, looking for broken brittle leaves, the rain eased and then stopped.

Blake stood and pulled his hood back, constantly watching the tree line and edges around the house and trunks of the trees. That prickly, uneasy feeling coursed through him as he battled with returning to the bunker and his family or checking the perimeter.

Habit took precedence, and he eased his way into a perimeter check, starting with the house. He couldn't shake the feeling that someone had been there and tampered with the solar panels. The idea of him being careless enough to have forgotten such a vital component did not sit well with him. Not well at all.

Each new room he entered in the house left him more stressed. There was no sign of entry by anyone, and yet it felt off. Different somehow. He grabbed a few last minute items from the house and checked the lock three times before covertly making his way to the outskirts of the property.

The fire's presence made itself known with that wet, smoky scent that only wildfires smelled like after a rain, or when he wetted a burn pile while he cleaned up the property. He missed that work. Seeing the wild forest become tame and yet still natural, and hard work that made him sweat from exertion and not stress, made him feel like all was right in the world. He craved that feeling right now.

Just as he had suspected, the fire had made its way only a few feet into their property before smoldering out. Satisfaction made his chest puff out. His insistence at hiring the landscaper, and clearing it in the first place, paid off. He would try not to rub it in the fiery face of his wife though. A small smile tilted his lips and eased his nerves.

That brief reprieve almost sent him into a heart

attack when he heard the distant gunshots. They came from the south, from the direction of the highway. Instinctually he started at a run toward the altercation, but stopped at the end of the private road.

His family waited for him in the bunker. They had everything they needed to live for six months to a year if they rationed. He didn't need to go play hero. Besides, who would he be protecting? It was life for life now. People, even neighbors they had known for the last ten years, could no longer be trusted. They fought for survival. Everyone did.

Distant shouts traveled on the breeze only to be silenced by two more gunshots. That settled it. He would return to the bunker and hope that in a few months the rioting would have settled and it would be safe to exit once again.

The fire would no longer be a threat. The destroyed power grid would not stop him and his family from surviving, but now the real danger they faced would come. The danger of their fellow man.

He jogged to the solar panels once again and double-checked the locks. Uneasiness sent a chill down his spine while he scanned his surroundings one last time before slipping into the group of boulders.

With what may be the last lungful of fresh air for the next several months, Blake said goodbye to the sky and slipped into the bunker, latching and locking the door above him.

~3~

Kris breathed in a sigh of relief when she heard the rhythmic tapping on the bunker door. She shook out her hands, barely registering the bandage that still wrapped one, as she took the few steps to let Blake in.

"Daddy!" Tucker shouted, bouncing up and down. He had been pacing the room like a miniature version of his father for the last half hour.

Turning the lock and opening the crank as the door groaned inward sent chills up her spine. She wanted to go out there, breathe the fresh air and see the expansive sky. It hadn't even been a full twenty-four hours, and she already felt closed in.

When Blake's head came through the opening, his eyes met hers. The unguarded contact left her knees week and heart pounding. His hand lifted as if he would reach out and caress her cheek like he used to. Before he made contact, Tucker ran into his legs and wrapped his arms around them.

"I knew you'd come back."

"Of course. I'm not going anywhere Champ." He picked the boy up into his arms and hung him upside down.

Tucker squealed in delight and the moment had passed, leaving Kris questioning if it had even happened. He carried the boy upside to the battery box. After setting Tucker down, he focused on connecting cords and flipping switches. Sure enough the air filtration kicked back on with a hum, and then he flicked the overhead lights on. Blake beamed a smile towards her before erupting in a tickle fest with their son.

Kris shook her head and went back to finish cooking breakfast: freeze-dried eggs and bacon cooked over the alcohol burner. It took a little getting used to, but the couple times they had been persuaded to have sleepovers in the bunker, she had also been urged to try out the cooking. As she stirred the mixture that looked and smelled pretty close to the real thing, she realized that knowing how everything worked had relieved what could have been one more added stress to an already overly stressful situation.

She groaned, hating that Blake had been right again.

"You okay?" Blake's voice vibrated behind her so close his breath teased the tendrils of hair on her neck.

"Yep, breakfast is just about done. Grab the plates?" She purposefully kept her eyes on the eggs.

"Sure." He bent down to sort through cupboards and drawers, loudly closing each one and banging stuff around.

"Don't get in a tizzy. They're up here." She pointed to the cupboard to the left of the sink. He had packed this place. How did he not know where everything was?

"I'm not in a tizzy." He smiled.

Maybe she just didn't remember how loud he was. The slamming and jamming noises seemed angry and loud to her. Yet, being in such close quarters with noises that echoed off metal walls could definitely be attributing to that.

She carried the scrambled eggs with bacon to the small table that Blake folded off the wall. Blake set out the plates, and she dished everyone a good sized portion.

Blake eyed the plates and then her.

"What?" Kris asked, all too familiar with the look he gave her.

"We're going to have to ration better."

"We expended a lot of energy yesterday. We need to refuel." She tightened her lips in a hard line.

Blake opened his mouth, but closed it without saying anything.

Kris nodded. At least he knew when to keep his mouth shut. Later today she would have to do a closer inventory of exactly how much they had stored. Right now the bucketed freeze-dried food seemed endless. She swallowed her first bite, pleased with the flavor. Yet, it would all depend on how long they would be stuck down here.

"What was it like out there, Daddy?"

Kris was thankful Tucker asked the question. She wanted to know too, but anger at being lectured over cooking too much had kept her lips sealed.

"Wet. It smells like a campfire after we douse it with water."

Tucker closed his eyes. "I remember that smell."

"What about the fire and our house?" Kris couldn't stop the question that shot out.

Blake met her eyes. "Our house is untouched. The fire barely made the edges of our property, at least out front. I didn't go to the back forty. The most important acres are cleared out though. We'll be safe."

"So we can leave?" Kris's fork froze halfway to her

mouth. Hope rose in her chest. The thought of leaving relieved the weight that seemed to cramp down on her temples.

That hope fell in a crashing heap, heavy in her belly when Blake shook his head.

"There's too much unrest. Gunshots and yelling fill the streets."

Kris immediately looked at Tucker. The boy's eyes went wide and his face paled. She glared at her husband. "Blake," she hissed.

"He needs to know what we're up against just as much as we do." He straightened in his seat, the broad expanse of him seeming to fill the entire bunker.

Heat traveled from the pit of her stomach up into her neck and cheeks. She squinted her eyes at Blake. The old argument came to surface with a roiling boil as if it had never dissipated. Tucker didn't need to hear the harsh truth of this world yet.

"It's okay, Mommy." Tucker laid his little hand on hers. "I got this. I can take it."

Her eyes misted as she watched her six-year-old son swallow his fear and put on a brave face. "How long until people start behaving again, Dad?"

"Interesting way to put it, Tuck," Blake said with a hint of a chuckle. "People are scared, and they're trying to get what they need to survive. Most of them won't stop for anything. I'm not sure how long it will take for people to work together again, if they ever can. I think a few months though should at least reduce the occurrences and let most of the people disperse or…." Luckily, he stopped there.

"A few months?!" Kris blanched. Her gaze shot to the small two hundred square feet of space they were in. A few months in this small box with a rambunctious child and a loud husband? She shoved her half-eaten plate towards Blake, no longer feeling hungry.

Blake watched her silently, his face expressionless. It made her feel like an experiment being observed by a calculating scientist.

She closed her eyes and took in a deep breath.

"Uh-oh," Tucker whispered. "You better just be quiet for a while."

Tucker's words squeezed her heart, but the fear overrode her ability to stay calm. She needed space, but the walls closed her in. She needed time to transition and to wrap her mind around their new life. A few months of living in the bunker, and it was only the first day.

She opened her eyes and stood, almost methodically pushed her chair in, walked two steps to the tiny bathroom, and shut the door.

Sitting on the lidded toilet with the wall just inches from her face did not help her demeanor at all. In fact, it only made it worse. She squeezed her eyes shut, took in a deep breath, and tried to calm the crazy whirring in her mind.

The walls of the tiny bathroom closed in on her though, even with her eyes shut. She could feel the oppression. She stood awkwardly in the tiny space, opened the cupboards that occupied most of the wall space, and found a bottle of cleaning wipes. She tore one out and slammed the bottle back where it came from. Scrubbing each and every nook and cranny with her uninjured hand, she did her best to focus on the moment, to forget where she was and what was happening. Yet, every time she moved her elbow, shoulder, or knee hit something. She couldn't even move without bumping into an object.

With an exasperated sigh, she slid open the tiny door and walked back out into the room. After throwing what was left of the disposable cloth in the trash, she took a breath and looked at the two watching her from the table.

Blake shoveled the last bite of his food into his mouth, and Tucker followed suit. The pan sat empty. She walked over and took the handle. Blake's hand landed gently on hers.

"I'll take care of it. Why don't you try finishing your plate?"

"Not hungry. You two eat it." She resisted the overpowering urge to fling his hand off her. Instead, with her mind buzzing, she gently pulled her hand away. Just being touched made her skin crawl, not because she was angry, but because anxiety buzzed within her, feeling like an angry hive under her skin.

"Why don't you rest for a bit? I stashed some books for you in the bedside table," Blake urged her, nodding toward the bed.

Kris glanced at him, her eyes knitted. Was this really her husband? Offering to clean up after a meal? Thinking of her relaxation needs? Dazed, she shuffled to the bed on the far side of the bunker, not that you could call anything far in the ten by twenty space.

In the storage next to the bed she sifted through the half-dozen or so books he acquired for her. A smirk tweaked her mouth as she read the titles: Survival Gardening, Life in a Bunker, Outdoors Woman, and a selection of other non-fiction survival type books. Of course, he had brought books she could learn from. No rest for the weary.

She settled with the gardening book. Maybe seeing pictures of life and plants and skies would help her feel a bit better.

Blake cleaned up at the sink. She should be grateful for one less chore, and for the running water and electricity. When Blake had insisted hooking the well up to the bunker, she had blanched at the price the second pump would cost. Now, though, with the water and the solar-powered battery system, they could almost live as normal. A shiver ran through her.

She rested the book on her knees and hugged her freezing hands under her arms. Being underground meant a constant temperature, but almost twenty degrees colder than her perfect seventy-five degrees.

Dishes knocked around with loud bangs. Each clatter sent a shockwave through Kris. The constant noise of her son zooming a car back and forth on all the walls and cupboards expounded the effect. She trembled with cold, sensory overload, emotion, and underlying anxiety that built up with every sound. The noises pounded into Kris's mind, shattering the desperate hold she had on a semblance of sanity.

Her mind rebelled against any attempt to quell the anxiety building up to an inferno inside of her. The book dropped from her lap as she covered her ears and squeezed her eyes shut, yet the barrage kept attacking her.

Her heart raced, its pulsing adding to the roar inside of her head. She blew out a breath and sucked it back in, feeling like the thick air couldn't get into her lungs.

The gentle touch on her arm sent her jumping and then repelling away from the intruder.

"Krista, breathe." Blake's voice muddled into her

consciousness, but she couldn't hold on to it.

The panic rose. She opened her eyes to find her vision still black as her body began to shut down. Her face tingled in that numb sort of way, and she knew she was on the verge of passing out. She quickly squeezed her eyes shut again. Sucking in another lungful of dense air, she gulped it down, frantic to get oxygen.

"Not now, Tuck. Go read a book at the table for a few minutes." His words fumbled into her subconscious, but she couldn't figure them out.

Large hands covered hers still over her ears. She didn't flee from the touch this time. She clung to it as the only thread to sanity she had. The warmth seeping in combatted the crazy sensations coursing through her body.

"Krista. Breathe. Breathe in one, two, three, four." Blake loudly sucked in air. "Breathe out, one, two, three, four." He audibly pushed his breath out. He continued this pattern in a gentle yet firm tone.

About the fifth time through, Kris found herself following his breath. Her heart beat eased. The whirring in her head lessened. She dropped her hands from her ears, Blake's hands following hers. His warmth seeped into her, easing the racing of her heart, breath, and mind. His voice soothed her frayed nerves and slowly brought her back to the room. To him.

"There you go. You got this, tough girl."

She slowly opened her eyes to find his green gaze holding onto her as if he would never let go. Emotions swept through her as tears streamed down her face and throat clenched. She had missed her husband.

He took her in his arms then, wrapping her in his protective embrace. She sunk into the one place she had always felt safe, the one place she could relax and know that everything would be okay.

~*~

Blake held his wife, and even with the craziness raging twenty feet above them, the world finally felt right.

Kris's tears soaked his shirt, and her nails dug into his arms where she gripped him as if he alone could give her solace. He just pulled her closer into him and soothed her with calm, whispered words of love, of apology, of all the things he had wanted to say to her for the last year.

It took several minutes before Kris relaxed, the tension leaving her body as she melted into his lap. He brushed back her hair then, a rhythmic soothing motion that calmed his own nerves. Yet, he held the greatest elixir for peace in his arms. He had dreamed of this every night while away, of holding her, loving her, and reminding her how much he needed her.

Tucker rustled at the table. Blake turned his gaze toward the boy, watching him watch them from the corner of his eyes while pretending to read a book he held upside down.

Kris stirred in his arms, not pulling away, but readjusting.

"Better now?" He kissed the top of her head nestled in his neck.

She nodded and murmured.

"Mommy?" Tucker had slipped so silently from the table that Blake wouldn't have known he had moved except for years of observing even the slightest motion.

Blake held one arm out to the boy, and he hurried into a family hug.

"I'm okay, Tuck," Kris whispered and wrapped her arm around their son too. "I'm sorry."

Blake heard the words choke in her throat. He knew guilt would be overrunning her now. She expected herself to be perfect for their son. He kissed her head and hoped that one day she would realize that having occasional imperfections would create an even deeper bond with Tucker. At least, it had with his own mom.

He shoved the memories down as he held his family in his arms. They were together. The rest they would get through.

"Maybe a nice, hot shower would help?" He leaned back a ways to read her expression.

She blinked, her blue eyes red, swollen, and bright. Her smooth forehead creased. "*Hot* shower?"

"Yep, I installed a tankless automatic water heater last year. Since we're on the well, you can take a long hot shower if needed."

She hid her head in his neck again. "I'm sorry."

"Don't apologize. Even the hardcore men on my team have panic attacks when enclosed in small spaces."

"Really?" Tucker asked.

He nodded at the boy. Tucker needed to know that being brave had nothing to do with not being scared. It was acting despite the fear.

"I meant," Kris said, as she glanced back up at him, her brow furrowed. "I meant, I'm sorry for not trusting you."

"Oh," Blake said with a chuckle. He knew admitting that had cost her. His tough girl did not admit defeat easily. "I only wanted us to be safe."

"I understand that now." Kris reached up and laid her hand on the stubble that had started growing on his face.

"Does that mean you're not mad at Daddy anymore?" Tucker asked starting to bounce next to them on the bed.

"Calm down, Buckaroo. Your mom needs us to be calm for a while."

Kris hadn't answered. In fact, Blake was almost scared she would. He would rather believe the trust and love that shone in her eyes. He of all people knew that words were sometimes difficult to allow. He would rather she showed him anyway.

"Come on, Tuck. Let's get this hot water heater working for Mom." Blake grabbed up his son and carried him to the automatic water heater attached high on the wall.

He explained the process to Tucker while he heard Kris sorting through compartments to find the clothes they had stashed here years ago. Luckily, she was the same size she had always been…small, yet strong.

"Wow," Tucker exclaimed while pulling his hand back from the steaming water spraying out the shower head. "It's really hot!"

"Yep, and just what the doctor ordered for your mom."

Blake noticed a sudden shift in Tucker. After shutting off the water, he set him on the floor and then bent to look in his eyes. "What's the matter?"

"What about doctors, Dad? What if we get sick or

hurt?" Tucker's forehead scrunched in the same worried pattern that his mother's did.

Blake reached out and smoothed the wrinkles. "We have supplies, and we'll do the best we can. We even have some books to help."

"And your daddy has training." Kris squatted next to him. She held open her bandaged palm.

Guilt shot through him as he realized he hadn't checked her wound since they had arrived at the bunker. "Speaking of that, let's take a look."

Blake gently pulled away the bandage.

The wound was angry, red and swollen. No pus oozed out, and the blood had stopped, but it worried him. He ground his teeth. How could he have forgotten to check this last night as soon as they made it to the bunker? He gingerly touched the red skin. It was warm to the touch.

"I'll make a solution while you are taking a shower. We need to remember to clean it several times a day." He left the consequences unsaid, but the flicker of fear that passed through Kris's eyes let him know she understood what could happen if her hand became infected.

"Can I help?" Tucker asked. His son had been enthralled with each move he had made, watching his hands, reading his face. Blake could see his little mind working.

"Of course. Now, let's give your mom some time to relax in the shower." He stood, and brought Kris up with him. Without preamble he brought her into his arms and sighed. He couldn't do this without her. He wouldn't want to.

"Thank you," Kris said, and he felt a small kiss on the side of his neck.

The contact of her lips on him set his body ablaze. He pulled back and looked longingly in her eyes. He wouldn't kiss her, as much as he wanted to. He would wait, give her time, and let her come to him.

"Have a good shower, Mommy!"

"Thanks, Sweetie." She bent down and kissed Tucker on the cheek. Her bottom lip quivered, and Blake knew he had made the right choice...in giving her time.

Once she was in the shower, Blake sifted through all the containers of food until he found the ten pound bucket of salt. Kris had laughed at him at first, saying they would die from high blood pressure before consuming that much.

He had just smiled. She had no idea of all the uses for salt. Not only to season food, but cure meat, which as soon as they left the bunker he would need to hunt. The food rations here would help get them by for a while, but without supplementing their stock, they wouldn't last much longer than a year.

A ripple of fear coursed down his spine. The bunkers he helped prepare had at least ten years of rations. Would those officials leave the bunkers before then, or wait until most of the civilians had died off? Would they ever be able to restore order?

His mind had become distracted, but as he pulled out the tub of salt, he remembered his son who stood peering over his shoulder.

"That's a lot of salt." Tucker peeked into the bucket.

"Yep. We need to salt to live. If we don't eat salt, we won't make it."

"Then why are we using it to wash out Mommy's wound?"

"It has many uses, son." He went on to explain them. "A saline solution, which is salt and water, could mean the difference between a deadly infection and a healing wound."

"Like Mom's?" His green eyes widened and face paled.

"Don't worry, Champ. Mom's going to be just fine. We're going to take care of her, and she's a great healer."

Tucker nodded. "What else is salt good for?"

Blake suppressed a smile. He knew the drill. Tucker changed the subject in order not to think those scary thoughts. He did the same thing. "Well, for curing meat."

"Curing meat? Like if it's sick?"

Blake laughed and squeezed the boy to his side. "Curing meat is something you do to help it last longer. Salt dries out the meat so it doesn't spoil."

"Like beef jerky?"

"Something like that." Blake took a bottle of water and dumped a third of it out into a glass. Then he poured salt into the bottle.

Tucker watched him closely. "Will you teach me how to cure meat, too?"

"Of course. As soon as it is safe to leave the bunker, I'll go hunting and you can help me cure the meat when I come back."

"I want to go hunting too! I can shoot my bow real good now."

"I bet you can, Tuck. We will definitely go hunting together, just maybe not yet. I need to make sure it's safe." He tousled the boy's sandy hair. "For now, why don't you hunt down a pack of cards, and we'll play some games."

Tucker smiled his toothless smile and scrambled to the cupboard where they kept the games. One of the things Blake had learned, not only in the service, but while preparing for the officials' survivals, people needed mental stimulus and entertainment in order to thrive. He had made certain to install a TV with movies for both adults and children, as well as books, games, cards, and puzzle books. He wanted his family to be as comfortable as possible.

He scanned the bunker and peered at the steel ceiling as if he could see through to the yards of dirt above them. Pushing down the trepidation that he was making the right decision, he eased his stress by telling himself he had prepared the best he could. And he had.

~4~

If Kris closed her eyes while letting the hot water roll off her back, she almost felt like she was home in her own bathroom. Well, as long as she didn't move in the tiny space. She was glad that Blake had chosen the option with a separate shower. Even as tight as it was, it was better than having to shower with a toilet at her feet.

The soothing shower replenished her. Her heart rate slowed, her breathing deepened, and her mind almost felt clear.

A taste of hope tantalized her. She would pull it together for Tucker. The worried expression on his face still gutted her. Whatever had to be done to keep him safe and as stress-free as possible, she could withstand it. She would be brave for him.

Reluctantly she shut off the hot water. The tiny bathroom had steamed up so thick she could hardly see, and she liked it that way. She could pretend a little longer.

Blake really had accomplished so much that would not only ensure their survival, but brought in as much comfort as possible. A warmth of appreciation spread through her. The memory of his eyes and soothing voice pulling her out of the panic attack clutched at her heart.

She ached to be in his arms again and battled with whether she could or should allow herself that comfort.

After she dried and dressed in the cramped space, she wrung her hair up in the towel, took a deep breath, and re-entered the bunker life.

Blake and Tucker sat at the little table playing with a deck of cards. A smile played at the edges of her lips. Tucker had craved this time with his dad for the last year. Now he had him, and had him for a long and close duration. Blake didn't have any idea what he was in for.

"Mommy! How did the shower do?"

"It did wonderfully." She bent to kiss him on the forehead. "How are you doing?"

"Great. Daddy and I are playing Go Fish. He didn't know I was so good." Tucker laughed.

"He's grown a lot," Blake said in admiration.

"It happened fast." She pulled a chair up at the end of the table. "Deal me in?"

"First we need to wash out that wound." Blake stood and waited by the sink for her where he had a small water bottle with murky looking liquid, bandages, and antibiotic ointment.

Her hand throbbed in expectation. She couldn't imagine salt water feeling great on her open wound. Even the shower had stung the hole in her palm. Unfortunately he was right again, and she knew she couldn't refuse.

Tucker ran over to the sink to watch the ordeal, so she put on a straight face doing her best to not grimace as Blake squirted the water into her wound. The pain didn't last long. Soon he had gooped up her palm and placed bandages around it once again.

"Did that moss do a good job, Dad?"

"Well, there's no sign of infection so I'm hoping so."

"It'll be fine. Now let's get to that game," Kris said as she sat back down at the table. She looked forward to time with her family. If she could keep the feeling of adventure and of gratitude for being with the two people she loved the most, she could get through this.

The day sped by with card games, taking inventory of their stock, and the boys taking showers. She had made a quick and easy add-water stew, in smaller portions, and they ate dinner while watching a cartoon movie.

When Blake had shown them the TV that swiveled toward them and a CD case full of DVDs, Tucker's eyes lit up and Kris sighed in relief. She marveled how the table folded in and the chairs swiveled to turn into a small couch. It was a tight fit, but Tucker stretched out over both of their laps and currently breathed heavy in sleep.

The credits rolled as she met eyes with her husband. He had done so much to see to their comfort during this catastrophic event. His foresight, which she had fought at every turn the last six years, had saved them. Her heart warmed looking at him, and once again she ached to be in his arms.

"Want to help me get him in his hammock?" she asked.

He raised his eyebrows, but then effortlessly picked their son up and situated him in the hammock above the bed. When Blake had first brought up the idea, Tucker squealed in delight. He got to sleep in a hammock, and he would be right above them, so he had the best of both worlds.

Blake watched the boy sleep, and Kris met him there, a blanket in her hands. She tucked it around their son.

"He looks so peaceful," Blake whispered.

"About the only time." She laughed. "He won't sleep all night in there, but it's a start."

"When did he start sleeping with you again?"

"The night you left." Kris leaned in and gave Tucker a kiss. "Good night, Sweet Boy."

She heard Blake clench his jaw, and she turned to look at him.

"I'm sorry I was gone so long."

Kris took his hand and led him back to the couch. "Tell me about it."

He sat down, and she settled against him, letting his arms wrap around her.

"It didn't start out as mayhem." He paused, and she held her breath. He had never talked about his assignments before. "You know I protect people in high places in the government."

"The Secret Service?"

"Exactly. Except I belong to a covert team in the Secret Service."

Kris nodded, afraid to say anything that would stop him from sharing.

"During this assignment, one thing led to another until I found secure locations for bunkers that would house elite government officials. I've done things like that before, but from the start this felt different."

Kris settled further into him and trailed her finger along his rough, thick hands.

"The higher-ups acted strange, stressed. Panic flooded their hushed conversations. They outfitted these bunkers with more heavy artillery and a larger inventory of food and other supplies, enough to last ten years or more. At the end though, I knew with certainty that something was happening, and soon."

Kris's fingers stopped. Hearing a touch of fear in Blake's voice started her heart racing.

"I overheard a conversation saying the attack was coming. They didn't go into detail, so I didn't know the source of the attack or what to expect. My immediate thought was of you and Tuck. During that conversation I also overheard them say they would be dispatching my entire team."

Kris sucked in a breath. She had heard him use that word before and the finality of it caused fear to surge through her.

"The governor, the one I had been assigned to, told me to run. So I did. I rushed back to headquarters to collect my things and race home, but something told me to hide out. Luckily I did. Two of my team went in, and when they came back out, they were in body bags."

The thought of Blake being one of his team members in a body bag caused a rush of emotion to overtake her. She clung to the man she promised to live the rest of her life with. The man who had saved them from almost certain doom.

"I barely escaped with my life, and now that all this has happened, I don't know what to expect. I doubt they would come looking for me. They wouldn't have the resources."

Kris gripped his hand. She knew that his position was dangerous, she just didn't know how involved in things he had been or how close to death. His behavior when he first showed up made more sense now. Guilt sat heavy in the pit of her stomach, but she ignored it as she sat up.

"I'm glad you made it back. Your timing was impeccable." She let her hand cup his day growth's stubble.

"I would have died trying. I'm sorry I left you alone for so long. I promise," he leaned forward, close enough she could feel his breath, "I promise I will never leave you like that again."

"I'm holding you to that, Hero." Her mouth quirked into a smile as her eyes left his and trailed down to his lips.

She closed her eyes and breathed in his freshly washed, manly scent. She had worn his t-shirt to bed for a month after he had first left just to have his scent close to her. It made her feel safe and closer to him. Now, with the living, breathing warmth of her husband so close, she had no choice but to act upon it.

Parting her lips, heart pounding, she edged closer, letting her lips touch his, tantalizingly slow. Then a ferocity overtook her husband. He deepened their kiss, threading his fingers through her long hair around the back of her neck and pulling her closer and even deeper. Kris could feel his need as a living thing, something more than physical but an emotional inferno bringing them from one body into one being.

Her breath came in gasps as he broke contact only to plant fiery kisses down her neck. All else faded. The walls that had been oppressive disappeared along with the past hurt. The only thing that mattered was her being right where she belonged, in her husband's arms. She wrapped her arms around him, and he wrapped his around and under her, lifting her off the couch and to the bed.

~5~

The next few days they fell into a routine. Before breakfast they would work out in some form or another. Tucker had come up with the idea of taking turns leading the exercises. Kris had led them in yoga. Blake, of course, had some military/combat exercises, and Tucker, well, he had silly poses and lots of jumping. Luckily, Blake had put in the linoleum-covered wood floor so the echoing wasn't near as bad as it could have been.

After breakfast they had quiet time, whether it was reading books, playing solitaire, drawing, or school workbooks that Kris had insisted be brought to the bunker. Before lunch they would play a game together. The rest of the day hadn't become too routine yet, but it felt like a good transition into their new way of living for the next few months.

Blake spent a good portion of time staring at the security cameras he had set up. Another expense that Kris had been upset about before the world had come crashing down around them. She didn't ask much about them, though every once in a while she would watch them too, just to remind herself that life still continued. Birds still flew. Squirrels still collected nuts for the coming winter. The sun still shined.

Kris was too absorbed in having her husband near her again to become lost in another panic attack. She felt as if they were honeymooning, only with a special little boy stopping romantic moments. Yet, he brought his own warmth to her mood. He was the true reason she held it together. She would do anything for her child.

Any time she began feeling closed in, she would reset by taking a nap, nothing she had ever done before. Or she would clean, read a book, journal, or something else semi-quiet and non-overwhelming. Blake had been vigilant and thoughtful, reading her moods almost better than she did herself. He would involve Tucker in a quiet card game, read books with him, or let him watch a movie with headphones whenever Kris began to act anxious.

If Kris imagined things just right, she could pretend they were in a fancy RV on vacation. Only this RV never stopped, and it didn't have any windows to look out at the scenery.

She marked another day off the calendar that had been stored down there. Today was day five in the bunker, five days since the world had changed. For a moment she became preoccupied with thoughts of how others fared. Did Sara and Vinny get to a safe place? Did her parents make it to her brother's? How were her students faring?

She swallowed some guilt knowing that many of her students could be suffering right now. If Blake's statistics were correct, most would not survive this catastrophe. A shudder shot through her as their faces popped up in her mind.

A deep cough pulled her from her thoughts. Blake and Tucker were curled up on the bed while Tucker read a chapter book aloud. She squinted, watching them until the cough happened again.

Tucker covered his mouth with his elbow while a hoarse cough bellowed out. Where had that come from?

Blake's gaze raised to hers, two little lines forming between his eyebrows.

Kris's heart pounded as she counted five coughs in three minutes. Forcing herself to move slow and act nonchalant, she sat on the edge of the bed pretending to listen to Tucker finish the chapter. When he did, he covered his mouth and coughed again.

"That was great reading, Sweetie." She laid a hand on his forehead, her face falling as soon as she touched his burning skin.

"It's a two point nine level." He looked at his dad. "That's the end of second grade."

"Very impressive, Tuck."

Tucker beamed as he sat back against his dad.

"You feeling okay?" Kris asked, though the glassy look of his eyes told her everything she needed to know.

"I think I caught the cough from Vinny. That's why he went to bed early during our sleepover."

Kris bit her cheek. Why hadn't Sara told her that?

"Do you think he's okay? He doesn't have a bunker." Tucker's brow wrinkled.

"His parent's had a plan should things like this happen. They didn't share in detail, but I know they were prepared."

"Just like we are," Blake said as Tucker coughed again. "Even for things like that cough."

Kris caught his meaning. She headed to the cupboard that held their medical supplies. She shifted through the different over-the-counter medicines and a few different bottles of antibiotics. Finding a thermometer and a children's cough and cold formula, she pulled them out. Yet, looking further, she saw there was only one bottle.

She set the bottle on the counter and sat by Tucker's side with the thermometer. He only complained slightly when she had him open his mouth and stick the device under his tongue.

Her heart raced as she saw the numbers steadily climb. Even Blake's eyes went wide. They stopped around one hundred two when it finally beeped. She reached for his head again, placing her cool hands on his fiery hot skin.

"I'm tired, Mommy." Tucker snuggled deeper into the bed.

"Rest, Sweetie."

"Rest is best," he murmured as he fell asleep.

Once she was sure he was sleeping, she rose and walked a few steps away. She heard Blake untangle himself from their son and reach her.

"Why didn't you give him the medicine?" Blake rubbed her shoulders and brought her into his arms, showing her he wasn't mad, just curious.

"There's only one bottle. This is the beginning. It will get worse. Remember when he caught bronchitis?"

"He was so small then."

"It was terrifying. What if..." Her voice quivered as she looked at her peaceful son. "What if it's bad like that again?"

"He's going to be okay." Blake's words held hope, but Kris heard the unsaid fears just the same.

She leaned into his strong chest and let herself feel the fear pulsating through her. For once she allowed herself to freely feel and her body shook with the release.

~*~

Blake once again held his wife while she cried. She had been through quite a bit this last week, but his nerves were fried. Every time she lost it emotionally, he felt like a failure. He couldn't even keep his wife from crying, and now Tucker was sick.

He hoped that it would just be a quick cold that they always took care of at home anyway, but Kris's fears echoed within him. What if it was worse?

Once she had calmed, Blake went into action. He pulled out the disinfecting wipes and then dug into the medicine kit. They had stashed some vitamins in there as well as that syrup that Kris said built up the immune system. What was it again? He nodded as he pulled out a bottle reading, elderberry syrup, and set it on the counter too.

Kris had already grabbed the wipes and started cleaning. He knew she cleaned when stressed, and this time it was needed desperately. He and Kris had to stay healthy. They couldn't catch whatever bug Tucker had.

That night, Tucker's cough kept them awake a good portion of the time until Blake finally convinced Kris to give him some medicine. Twenty minutes later, Tucker fell into a quiet slumber. Within moments, Blake fell asleep as well.

By the time they woke up, Tucker's fever had spiked again. He was listless and not really responsive. Fear pulsated in Blake. He clenched his jaw as he paced the small room.

"Stop pacing and make yourself useful." Kris tossed him a medical manual before returning to place a cool cloth on Tucker's forehead.

Blake released a low growl before plopping into a chair at the table and scanning the table of contents until he reached cough. He read the few pages dedicated to coughing sicknesses and then set it aside to watch Kris.

She stuffed more pillows under Tucker's head. Elevate head, the book had said. Well, she knew that. Then she rubbed some white lotion on his chest and a minty smell wafted towards him. Use a menthol, peppermint, or eucalyptus rub, the book had instructed. Check, but didn't it say to put it on the feet too? He watched as Kris moved to do just that, and he wondered if she could read his mind.

Why did she have him read the book if she already knew it all. The only thing she hadn't done was take him into the steamy bathroom, but he knew she knew about that one because he found them in there many nights when Tucker was younger and had the croup. Even last night she had talked about it, but after the medicine it wasn't needed.

They had exhausted all of their resources. Now they could only hope and pray for mercy.

~*~

Kris bit her cheeks and closed her eyes. If Blake didn't stop pacing she was going to tie him to a chair. She wet the cloth and laid it on Tucker's forehead. His body racked with coughs. It pained her every time to hear it, but she kept her voice soft and soothing.

"Let's sit you up a little more, Sweetie." She added a few more pillows behind his head so he almost sat upright.

"Thanks, Mommy," he whispered weakly before

letting his head fall to the side and closing his eyes once again.

Once she heard his deep breathing, she eased herself away from him to rummage through their supplies. They had to have something more to help him.

She squatted near the storage compartment under the bed and looked up at Blake in his umpteenth lap of the small space.

"Do we happen to have a humidifier?" she asked him.

"A what? No. See this is why you should have been more involved in the preparations, but no, you thought I was crazy. You tired of playing the *game*." Blake's eyes seemed to flame as his nostrils flared and sweat beaded on his forehead despite the cool temperature.

Kris watched him with wide eyes as she inwardly went through a plethora of emotions and reactions. Before she could reply, Tucker went into another coughing fit. She turned her back on her fuming husband and soothed her son.

Tucker's coughing eased as she caressed his head with the cool cloth and spoke calmly to him. She hummed a little song she had sung to him since he was a baby. Soon his breathing calmed and he fell back into slumber.

When she turned back toward Blake, she found him sitting with his head in his hands. Empathy filled her as she made her way to her husband. She sat next to him and leaned into his tough body.

"I'm scared, too." She concentrated on keeping her words light, unrestricted by his earlier outburst.

"I'm sorry. I just..." His voice trailed off into a

growl.

"I know. It's like being trapped in a cage of our own making with no way to help our son feel better."

He looked at her then. His tortured eyes pleading into hers. "Could you do anything different if we were on the surface?"

"I could make him some pine needle tea. It's an expectorant."

Blake squeezed his lips together, seeming to hide the smile trying to ruin the serious moment.

"What?" Kris asked in mock shock. "I listened to some of those foraging videos you had me watch."

"I just…" He shook his head. "Would having that make a big difference for Tucker?"

"The tea could keep it from going to into pneumonia." Kris squeezed her hands together, trying to not get her hopes up. "It wouldn't take me long to get them, only a few minutes."

The idea of even a minute of fresh air filled her with euphoria, besides the hope of having something to help keep Tucker's lungs from turning into something dangerous.

"I'm sorry," Blake said, resting a hand on her arm. "I can't let you go out there without me, and we can't leave Tucker alone."

Kris's shoulders dropped right along with her heart. She turned her eyes toward Tucker moaning in his sleep. After a moment, she steeled herself, narrowed her eyes, and met Blake's again.

"Will you go then?" All that mattered was her son.

She could read the appreciation in Blake's eyes as he met hers and nodded his head. He rose to prepare, which meant holstering guns all over his body along with a wicked looking knife strapped to his thigh. He peered at the camera screens for a good ten minutes before he handed her the dreaded pistol.

"The area appears secure. Come here." He held a hand out to her.

When she grasped it, warmth flooded through her as he guided her to the screens. In front of them, he wrapped his arms around her as he pointed to each one.

"This one shows the area around the gate. This one the house. And this one the land on the other side of the bunker. These monitors here have no video but if one of them beeps and flashes red it means the perimeter has been breached."

Kris's heart pounded. No wonder he had stood over here for hours every day.

"Here's a radio." He set down a walkie-talkie on the shelf by all the screens. "I have the other one." He tugged on the black device stuck in his shirt pocket. "If you see any movement or hear any alarms, relay the location at once. Whisper, don't yell."

Kris nodded her head. "No one has come here in the last week. Why would they now?"

"You just never know, Kris. Always be—"

"Prepared," Tucker choked out before going into another coughing fit.

Both Kris and Blake swiftly made their way to his side. When he could breathe once again, he looked straight at Blake.

"Don't go out, Daddy."

"I won't be gone long, son. Less than ten minutes. I need to get something to help you feel better." Blake reached out and touched Tucker's cheek. A look of panic filled her husband's eyes as he came in contact with their son's flaming hot skin. "I better go now." He leaned over and kissed Tucker's head and then kissed Kris's cheek.

"No, Daddy! There are people out there! Don't go!" Tucker sat up in bed, his glassy eyes wide and wild.

"I checked, Champ. The cameras are clear. I'll be back before your mom has the water heated." With one last longing look at Tucker, he turned his attention to her. "Keep an eye on the cameras. I love you both. We always come back to each other."

"We always come back to each other," both Kris and Tucker automatically replied.

Then Tucker went wild again. "But Daddy, no, don't go, please…" He pleaded until his outburst sent him into another coughing fit.

Kris soothed him, her heart breaking for her son. He had such trauma from his dad leaving as often as he did. She nodded toward Blake who quickly and quietly escaped the bunker. The clang of the steel door shutting on them once more echoed throughout the small room and brought Tucker into sobs as soon as his coughing spell ended.

"Shh, Sweetie. Daddy's going to be okay."

"People. There's people." Tucker mumbled in between racking sobs.

Kris held him, petting his head and whispering soothing words of comfort. Her heart broke with every tear, aching with need to take away her son's pain.

Once he calmed, she eased him back on the pillows.

"Please, go watch the cameras. Watch close, Mommy. We need Daddy." With glassy eyes barely able to stay open, he looked at her with such determination she couldn't deny his request.

"I will, Tuck. I will watch for Daddy."

"Now," he insisted, no longer pleading but demanding, just like he had when he said that he had heard Blake near the fire.

"Okay, Sweetie." She kissed his forehead and rose.

He only closed his eyes once she stood in front of the screens and nodded toward him.

Tucker's earnest plea unsettled her. She found her hands shaking as her eyes flickered over each screen. A silent humming sounded within her as fear pulsed through her every nerve. The only times that Tucker had acted this earnest, his premonitions had come true...just like the catastrophe.

With her heart palpitating, drumming a manic tune against her ribs, she focused on the screens.

~*~

Closing the door on his son's sobs had caused the hair on the back of Blake's neck to raise. They still stood on end as he carefully picked his way from the concealing rock outcropping. Something about what Tucker said, or how he said it, had him on edge.

He stalked to the nearest pine tree, barely registering the coolness in the damp air or the lingering burnt scent it carried. Instead he listened to every scurry of animal, pine cone dropping, and leaf crackling, processing its source immediately.

He didn't fear for himself. The prickling sensation of trepidation that rippled along his skin centered on his family. He didn't want to leave them without protection or inadvertently lead danger into their midst. The ear bud attached to the walkie-talkie remained silent, yet a nervous sweat beaded along his brow—a sure sign something was amiss. He secured the bud in his ear. Kris would follow through if danger was near. He trusted her. In fact, he didn't know where he would be without her.

Blake ripped off a bunch of pine needles from the end of the branch, hastily stuffing them into the satchel strapped across his chest. Kris would probably have chastised him for his lack of technique, but he couldn't shake the feeling that something, or someone, was coming.

Could it be the same person who had unplugged the solar converter? The last five days of stewing over the scenario, the more certain he was that it hadn't been his forgetfulness.

Movement across the forest, near the gate, caught his eye. Instinctively he threw his body behind the large trunk of the pine. Maybe it had just been a squirrel or a bird? The bark of the evergreen bit at his cheek as he cautiously peered from behind the trunk.

Shadowy figures milled about at the edge of the property. Five. Ten. A good size group of perpetrators. His heart slammed against his ribs as his gaze longingly sought out the outcropping only ten yards away from him.

"People. There's a group at the gate!" Kris's panicked voice crackled over the radio.

"Copy," he whispered as quietly as possible.

"What does that mean? Can you get back? Where are you? They're climbing the gate!" Kris's panic increased the beat of his heart. He clicked off his radio knowing he wouldn't hear the end his wife's fury, but now was not the time to communicate. He needed to focus. He needed to make his way back to his family, once again. A panicked incessant chatter in his ear would only encumber him. He would have to give Kris some combat instruction.

He watched the intruders as they piled over the gate. Two men faced out, scanning the forests and holding rifles. Another man helped the others down. Blake knew his cover was adequate. He knew they couldn't see him, but they would if he made a go for the bunker. What he needed was a distraction.

When one of them became stuck on a throng of the gate, it diverted everyone's attention. As soon as the two lookouts turned to help, Blake used the distraction to his advantage, slipping from tree to tree until he squeezed into the rock outcropping. Why had this felt more intense than any other op he had been on?

He clicked his radio back on just in case the group headed toward him. He couldn't disclose the location of the bunker to the trespassers by the creaking sound it might make upon opening.

"Blake, are you okay? Please say you're coming back."

That's why. His family needed him. He keyed in the bunker code, slipped under the hatch and closed it slowly and silently behind him. Letting out a deep breath, he eased his way down the ladder and to the steel door where he quietly tapped out his secret pattern knock.

Kris flung open the door and buried herself in his arms. Then she stood back and slapped his arm with a glare that could kill.

"You scared me to death! Why didn't you say something? Let me know you were alive?"

A small smirk played at the corner of his mouth.

"And give away my location?" He pulled her back into his arms. "I have a lot to teach you."

She pushed away. The fire in her eyes had diminished, but he could see it still smoldering under the surface. "I could say the same to you macho soldier. You aren't a one-man team anymore."

He watched his wife while her words sank in. She might just be right. Working with his family, the only people he truly cared about in this world, was definitely different. Maybe they both had a lot to learn.

~6~

Kris hunkered next to Blake in front of the screens. Their eyes hadn't left them for the last half hour. Her mouth had gone dry the moment she had heard the alarm. Seeing the people crawl over the gate had constricted her throat. It seemed an eternity before she had finally broken free of her panic enough to radio to Blake. She knew, though, it had only been a matter of a few seconds.

After giving the alert, her eyes had shot from the screens to Tucker to the radio like a merry-go-round until she had to shut them or pass out. Tucker had been right, and she had no idea if her husband would make it back to them…again.

Yet he had.

She took solace in the warmth of his powerful body next to hers, though the tenseness his rigid muscles showed he was in no place to offer comfort. His gaze poured into the screen as he watched the intruders walk onto their property with purpose. They continued their surveillance as the group strode into the screen that showed the land next to the bunker, the piece of their property that happened to host three apple trees still laden with fruit.

"It's like they knew right where to go…" Kris trailed off, stunned.

"It appears that way." Blake narrowed his eyes and peered closer to the screen. "Have you told anyone about those trees?"

"No. I do follow some of your crazy rules." She nudged him to take the edge off her retort, but he didn't budge.

"Has Tucker?"

"He worships the ground you walk on, and every order you have ever uttered he follows like one of the Ten Commandments."

"Then the only other person that knows about those trees is…"

"Marvin." The word left her mouth as heavy as the betrayal she felt, and yet, could she blame their groundskeeper? He had to do what was needed to survive, just like everyone else.

"Marvin the Maintenance Man." Blake growled. "I should have known better."

"What other option was there? There was no way I could keep up the grounds as well as hold down a full time job and raise Tucker." She stood back, planted her fists on her hips, and glared at him.

"Of course." He eyed her like the sight of her up in arms made his thoughts flee from the danger above them to more satisfying activities. "I would never expect that. There was no choice." He pulled his eyes away to stare at the screen again. "I should have known he would betray our trust though, and prepared for it."

"Is he is betraying us, or is he trying to survive?" Kris questioned him.

She couldn't read his expression. Tucker's coughing broke them from their conversation. She was by his side in a matter of seconds.

"Calm breaths, Tuck," she soothed, caressing his head.

"Daddy…" He mumbled the words between

coughs.

"He's here, Sweetie. He's back with us."

A smile curved his lips before he racked another heaving series of coughs.

"You've got to keep him quiet." Panic turned Blake's voice into an angry snarl as his gaze shot from them to the screens and back again.

"We're twenty feet or more underground. How can they hear us?" She narrowed her eyes, wishing she could knock some sense into him. How did he expect her to keep their sick son from coughing? She sat Tucker further up, propping pillows under his head as his coughing eased.

Blake pointed to the air outtake, jamming his finger in an angry gesture.

"Well, he can't just stop coughing. Besides, if he did, it would surely turn into pneumonia." She shook her head. For someone as intelligent and experienced as her husband, he sure acted ignorant sometimes.

"And if they hear us," he whispered hoarsely, "we might as well say goodbye to the comforts we have here."

Kris rolled her eyes and turned her attention back to their son. She wasn't sure if sound escaped the bunker or not, but she knew what had to be done to keep her son alive. Her gaze flicked to Blake and back again. She also knew her husband's unyielding pessimism.

With Tucker settled again, she kissed his head before rising to get the tea started. While pulling out a pot, another one crashed, the sound echoing like a dropped candlestick in a cathedral. Kris froze. She felt Blake's searing gaze.

He murmured a curse under his breath.

Slowly Kris turned to look at him. He turned to her long enough to place a finger against his silent lips. A wash of cold tingles shot down Kris's spine. Though her legs ached from holding the squatting position, she kept absolutely still.

It felt like an hour before Blake offered her a hand to rise, though she was sure only a few minutes had passed. Her shallow breathing left her light-headed as she rose. She clasped onto her husband's thick forearm until the blackness dissipated.

"They heard?" she asked in a whisper, even the thought of it left her heart racing.

"Every head turned toward us." The finality in his quiet voice left her mind reeling.

"What are we going to do?"

"I should have checked. Why didn't I ever test the sound issue?" He rubbed a hand down his face and then paced back and forth.

Kris wondered if the floor would wear out with the constant friction.

She reached out as he passed her, letting her fingers wrap around his large hand. "We can't do anything about that now. We can only work with what we have. Stop beating yourself up and make a plan."

Blake's eyes squinted and then widened before he hung his head with a nod. He squeezed her hand and went back to his vigil at the screens.

Kris eased the pans back into place before filling the smaller one with water and heating it on the stove. As grateful as she was for having all of the amenities, she couldn't help but wonder if it would have been better to be up top. At least then they had the possibility of slipping unseen into the forest.

Her chest constricted. More than ever she felt like a caged animal, and now the predators were above, ready to sniff them out. Closing her eyes, she took a few calming breaths and willed the tightness in her chest to give way. The difference was that she had her cub to protect, and her mama bear instincts raged within her.

The satchel Blake had taken lay on the table. She reached in and pulled out the long needles, three in each group, a ponderosa pine. She nodded. The only side effect with this tree concerned pregnant women, nothing they had to worry about.

Methodically, to keep her mind clear, she chopped the needles, releasing a fresh scent into the small space. It caused her to close her eyes and imagine being above ground in the forest and fresh air. A smile pulled at her lips as she continued her task until a thwapping, a sound like distant waves, alerted her to the water boiling.

She dumped the cut needles into the boiling liquid and turned off the heat. When she pulled out the lid, she did so with utter focus to ensure no extra sound would emit from her action.

While the tea steeped, she wrapped her arms around Blake and watched the activity above. She felt him tense, but held on anyway. She knew he needed comfort as much as she did, whether he knew it or not.

~*~

Blake's jaw ached from clenching his teeth, but he couldn't relax. Kris's carelessness alerted the swarm of intruders to their presence, yet no one left the group to scout the location of the sound. Instead they set up camp near their apple trees, only ten yards from the outlet valve.

When Kris wrapped her arms around him, he almost stepped away from her touch. He had only caught himself in time to still his body. He couldn't help the anger pulsing through him. It took every ounce of his willpower to remind himself it shouldn't be directed at his wife.

Not for the first time he questioned his decision of locking his family down here, cornered in a steel box. Granted, the likelihood of the intruding group having the strength of artillery it would take to breach the bunker was slim. Yet, there were other ways they could affect their livelihood and those caused his head to buzz with horrific scenarios.

"They're staying?" Kris's voice solidified the scene, making the reality hit him like a ton of bricks.

Blake could only nod. He had no words of comfort for her. No plan or advice. He had nothing but self-degradation and words she shouldn't have to hear.

"Could we stuff the outtake?"

He shook his head, having already dismissed the thought. "We need that valve. Otherwise the air pressure will increase beyond capacity."

She nodded while silently watching the group setting up tents and continuing to scan the area like criminals on the run.

"They seem scared." She hugged her arms around herself.

"They should be. They are trespassing and stealing."

"They're trying to survive, Blake. They don't have

a bunker or a prepared husband to count on. Look, there's even a few children. They have to eat." She scanned their cupboards full of food.

"Don't even think about it," he growled. "I didn't spend all this time and money preparing only to give our food away and have to watch you and Tuck go hungry."

"We have plenty."

"Kris," he grasped her by the shoulders and turned her to face him. His eyes bored into hers. "You need to understand the extent of our situation. This isn't going to just last a couple months, or even a couple years. This might be the new way of life for us…forever."

Kris's mouth dropped open. Her eyes went wide, and then they narrowed.

"No electricity. No cars. No phones. No grocery stores. Just this." He kept his voice void of emotion, void of fear, just stating facts.

He let the realization sink home, giving her time to process what that meant. Sure they had prepared, definitely more than most. They had honed skills and immersed themselves in knowledge of survival, but she had never taken it seriously. He had always known that, but it was enough for him knowing that she would have the skills when it happened…even if she never believed it would.

When he dropped his hands from her shoulders she walked dazedly to the tea and poured it into a mug, her movements calm, measured, and completely assured.

He couldn't take his eyes off her, expecting her to plummet into another panic attack or fall to the floor in sobs, but she kept on task. Calmly. Did she still not believe him?

She tasted the liquid and then added a little cold water and tested it again. With a nod she sat next to Tucker and lovingly eased him awake with caresses and soothing sounds Blake couldn't decipher.

The boy woke and smiled at her. They needed to understand the severity of what they faced and how pertinent near silence in the bunker was. He strode over to them but stilled himself when he finally made out her words.

"…so when you cough, do you think you could cough into a pillow like this?" She held a pillow to her face and coughed into it. The muffled sound was quiet enough it shouldn't be heard above ground.

Tucker nodded.

"You're such a brave boy. I made this special tea with pine needles your Daddy brought back from above ground."

"That's why he went out there? He almost got caught for me? Why didn't he listen to me?" Tears welled in his son's eyes before the boy's body started to shake. Tucker grabbed a pillow and stuffed it over his mouth. His coughs barely sounded through the barrier.

"Great work using the pillow," she soothed, caressing his head. "We would do anything for you, Tuck." Kris handed him the tea. "It tastes pretty good."

"I would drink it even if it didn't," he said seriously.

"You're amazing." Kris kissed his forehead.

Blake turned away from them and went back to the screens. He had been gone so long that now he felt like an intruder in his own family. Maybe he was wrong about them needing him. He watched the people camping on his property. A couple of them hoisted rifles and handguns. Blake ground his teeth. No, they needed him. Their innocent souls had no idea of the terror people were capable of committing.

~7~

Kris lay in bed. The darkness cloaked them like a blanket, a thick, restricting blanket. Her husband's snores drowned out Tucker's raspy breathing. Should she wake him? Surely his snores were louder than Tucker's coughing. She nudged him gently with no response. Several more attempts with the same result built up a panic in her. She elbowed him hard in the ribs.

Blake sat upright. She couldn't see him, but heard his unmistakable abrupt movement.

"What happened? Are you okay? Is Tucker okay?" The fear in his whispered voice was palpable as she heard his hand rummaging in the blankets for their son's chest.

"He's fine. You were snoring. I feared it would alert them," she whispered, doing her best to keep the fear from her own voice. A part of her felt guilty for waking him so roughly, especially when hearing his first concern was for her and their son.

"Was it really that loud?" he grumbled while situating himself, causing the mattress to move and shake.

"Yes," she said simply.

Tucker groaned. She reached out a hand to settle him. They had resorted to giving him the medication at night so they all could get some sleep. Yet, she hadn't been sleeping.

As her boys settled back into heavy breathing, her

mind began to whirl again. She couldn't show her emotions during the day. She had to be strong for her son and her husband. It was only at night that she could allow her emotions to release.

Tears wet her pillow as she stifled the sobs of fear, exhaustion, and a desperate need for mercy. She silently pleaded, prayed, and begged for her son to recover, for the people above to pass on, and for a way to survive what the world had succumbed to.

Blake's words earlier that day had hit her hard. Hearing him state her fears out loud that this could be their new norm created wave after wave of terror within her. She tried to process how to survive, and yet she continued to wonder about things beyond survival, things that enhanced the quality of life.

Like, would her son ever get to play with another child? Without that socialization, what would he grow up to be like? Her thoughts continued to wondering what would happen if something happened to her and Blake. Tucker would be alone, with no one. A shiver ran through her body. Her heart ached for her son and what this life might mean for him.

Sometime later, spent and numb with exhaustion, she finally slipped into a fitful sleep.

~*~

Blake shot out of bed, adrenaline pumping through his veins, his body ready for the fight he knew waited for him. Yet, as he blinked his eyes to focus all he saw was the dark inside of the bunker and heard his wife coddling their son.

"Shh, it was just a nightmare. You're safe." Kris soothed.

Blake hit the battery powered light near their bed, illuminating the room in a soft amber glow. Nothing else moved, only his wife who shot a cursory glance to him before returning her attention to Tucker.

Blake breathed deep to calm his racing heart. What had awoken him in a way that made his heart pump and muscles tense, ready for an attack? Had Tucker screamed in his sleep, a scream—loud enough to wake him from a dead sleep? He hurried over to the screens, ignoring the cold air prickling his bare skin.

Outside the sun lit the bustling camp. It was so difficult to tell what time it was down here. Kids ran around playing tag in the trees, picking apples, and eating as they pleased. He shifted his gaze to his son who had just fallen into a muffled coughing fit. A rock of guilt sat heavy in his gut. On the ground, the day looked beautiful. Here the air smelled stale and stiff, the bunker cold and sterile.

Blake's mind warred with options. In the end he shook his head. His family was safer here, safer than anywhere else. No one could get in and harm them. They had everything they needed to survive. If they kept their location hidden, they had nothing to fear.

Except insanity. His entire body erupted in a shiver.

Warmth surrounded him as a blanket covered his shoulders. He hadn't noticed until then that his body shook from cold. Turning, he saw Kris walking back to the kitchen area. She turned and smiled at him before filling a pot with water.

She looked haggard, like she hadn't slept in a week. Her eyes were puffy and her skin pale, much paler than usual. It made her fiery red hair stand out even more. It also made him wonder how she could offer smiles and attention to him and Tucker like she did. Kris moved carefully, like she used to when Tucker was first born and she feared waking him.

Watching her move as if terrified a single sound could take her son away from her left his gut heavy with guilt. He ripped his eyes away and back to the screen.

The scene had shifted to a less peaceful display. Marvin talked with another man, his posture stiff and tense. Blake wished he had sound to put with the actions. The men obviously were in the middle of a disagreement. The other man angrily pointed in the direction of the rocks that hid the entrance to the bunker.

Blake held his breath. Had he found the hidden entrance?

Marvin shook his head, gestured to the trees and the camp. The other man's agitation only grew. He stormed into the camp and disappeared into a tent, coming out a moment later with a rifle tucked under his arm.

Blake ground his teeth. He needed to check the locks, needed to prepare, and needed to put some clothes on. Yet he couldn't pull his gaze off of the screens. He had to know what that man planned to do with the gun.

As if reading his mind, Kris stood next to him holding a pair of jeans and a sweatshirt. He yanked them on with barely a nod toward her, his eyes never leaving the screen.

"What's going on? That man with the gun looks angry and so does Marvin," she whispered, glancing from their son once again asleep and back to the screen.

"They're arguing," he grunted, still enthralled in the show.

Marvin came up to the man with the gun, adamantly shaking his head. He reached to take the gun away, but the other man pulled it back. He shoved his face into Marvin's yelling and pushing his chest. Marvin reached for the gun again. The man decked him, sending Marvin to the ground.

Kris sucked in a breath and grasped Blake's arm.

On his hands and knees now, Marvin shook his head. The man with the gun stormed out of the camera's view. The women had brought the children against them, sheltering them as best they could from the disruption. The other men looked from Marvin to where the man left and back to Marvin.

It no longer seemed like such a beautiful day up top.

Blake's heart raced. He swiftly moved about the room, grabbing guns and knives. He laid them out on the table, taking count of the resources he had pulled together.

"Blake what are you doing? Where do you think that man is going?" Kris still watched the screens.

Blake didn't answer her. He didn't know for sure what that man's plan was or where he headed. Yet, he found himself waiting for a pounding on the outside hatch, but it never came. It had looked like the man had pointed in the direction of the rock outcropping, but other things lay in that direction as well, like…the house.

"Marvin went after him," Kris whispered, eyes glued to the screen.

Blake took two long strides to stand next to her, his breath blowing a few loose strands of her hair in a rhythmic pattern.

Sure enough, Marvin had left the camp. He searched the other screens until his eyes landed on the house. On the porch, the angry man checked the ammunition in his rifle and then scanned the area. His eyes fixated in the direction of the rock outcropping.

The man with the gun yelled toward something in the opposite direction from the house. His lips, distorted in anger, were unable to be read. The silent movie did not give anything away. A moment later, Marvin entered the camera's view in front of the house. The men argued again, arms flinging to make points as Marvin made his way up the porch steps. Marvin pushed past the man to knock on the door. He knocked again, and then seemed to call out.

"Is he trying to see if we're home? To warn us?" Kris chewed on her nail like she did during the intense parts of movies.

Blake shrugged, unable to speak with all of his attention on the performance that starred his house.

Marvin turned toward the man, tried to take him by the shoulder and turn him away from the door. The man shrugged out of his grasp and kicked at the front entrance.

"He's going to raid our home!" Kris whispered harshly.

Blake ground his teeth, clenched his fists, and fought each reaction that pushed him to arm himself and protect his home. Yet, the fiery red-head next to him and the sick boy in the bed were everything to him, not the items in a house. They had everything they needed right here. He blew out a breath, forcing his feet to stay put.

The man continued to kick the door and fight

Marvin off him. When Marvin finally pushed his way between the door and the angry man, the man stood back and raised his gun.

"He won't shoot Marvin, will he? Not over a house." She sucked in a breath as he leveled the gun at Marvin's chest. "Marvin's going to die trying to protect our home…" Kris put a hand over her mouth and gasped. Her other hand dug into his arm.

Growling and breathing through gritted teeth, Blake cemented his feet. If he left the bunker now, the whole group would know their location. It would put his family's lives at risk. This man wouldn't be the only one willing to fight, or kill, to get what he stored in there.

Blake watched the man with the rifle thumb off the safety and tense his hand ready to squeeze the trigger.

"No…" Kris cried and squeezed her eyes shut. Blake tore his gaze away for a split second to pull her into his arms.

The echo of the shot sounded only like a muffled thud in the bunker, but the reverberation made Kris flinch in his arms. Blake watched the screen, fearing to see Marvin falling to the ground and the mob ransacking their home. What he saw instead left his mouth hanging open.

Marvin stood, a smoking pistol in his hand. The other man lay head down the porch steps, legs and arms at awkward angles, and the rifle inches away from his right hand. Blood oozed out of a gaping hole in his chest.

Marvin killed to protect their home. Blake nodded his head and something greater than respect filled him. If he ever came face-to-face with Marvin again, he would treat that man like family.

"Is he..." Kris peaked up at him, unwilling to face the death that littered the screen.

"Marvin is not, but you probably don't want to look at the screen." He took his wife by the hand and led her to the pot of water boiling rapidly on the stove. "He protected our home."

"Really?" Kris open her eyes wide as she turned off the flame and filled the pot with pine needles.

Blake nodded, unable or unwilling to speak his wrong accusations aloud. He turned away from his wife, retracing his steps. He owed Marvin. Even though his gaze once again rested on the screens, he didn't really pay attention to the people dragging the body off of his front porch. He worked something out in his mind, a way to show Marvin his gratitude without giving away their location.

Marvin had shown his worth, his true character, but what other type of men camped with him? There could be others like the man with the rifle willing and ready to raid their home. He couldn't risk being found, but maybe there was still a way to reciprocate in kind.

~8~

Kris tried not to think about what Marvin had done to save their home. An uneasy flutter began in her chest the moment she heard that muffled shot. People had changed, just like Blake foresaw. Had she got humanity all wrong?

She couldn't have if Marvin had done all that to protect their home. He could have ransacked it himself, but still, to kill someone over a house, whether protecting it or to raid it…she shook her head and concentrated on the task at hand.

It had been two days…or had it been three, since Tucker had fallen sick. The days ran together. She looked at the calendar but couldn't remember if she had crossed a day off yesterday or not. An exasperated sigh blew out her mouth.

"What's wrong?" Blake asked. He squatted in front of one of the storage cupboards, slowly compiling a supply of provisions next to him.

"How did people remember what day it was before cell phones and computers?"

Blake smirked, the lopsided grin touching something deep within her. "Same way we did as kids, before people carried cell phones with them everywhere."

"Guess you're right." She reached up and crossed off the day, hoping it was correct. "Probably doesn't matter anyway. Not like there's school today…"

Blake rose and wrapped his arms around her. He

shared no words, no verbal comfort, but his warmth, the smell of his skin, and his steadfast strength gave her all she needed in that moment.

"Mommy?" Tucker croaked out.

Kris reluctantly left the safety of Blake's arms to go to their son's side. "Hey, Sweetie." She smoothed back his hair, feeling his piping hot skin. Her brain wracked through all the knowledge she had. How many days should a fever last? Three days? A week?

"I'm hungry."

Kris smiled. "That's good news."

"I just found some chicken noodle soup." Blake rummaged in the pile he had pulled out of the cupboard.

"Does that sound good?" she asked.

Tucker nodded. His eyes still held that distant, glassy look, and it scared her. High fevers had a way of changing children.

"I'll make you some right now." She kissed him on the forehead and rose to get some water on the stove. "We're boiling a lot of water. Will we have enough fuel?" she asked Blake quietly.

"We have plenty for now. Things will have to change anyway. This is only a temporary situation. We can't stay down here forever."

Kris stood, pot in hand and frozen in mid-air. Something had shifted in Blake. She watched him as if she could decipher it in his movements. When he went back to sorting items, she blinked several times before completing her own task.

"What are you doing, Daddy?" Tucker asked quietly.

"I'm checking the inventory and calculating if we have enough to spare."

"To spare for what?" Tuck sat up in bed a little, grabbing the pillow and coughing into it.

Kris's heart ached for her son. He was so responsible, remembering to stay quiet even when so sick. When he returned his gaze back to Blake, she did too. What *was* he doing? Enough to spare for whom or what? He had nipped that in the bud without her hardly even opening her mouth earlier.

"One of those people up there protected our home when he could have just raided it along with the others. I want to show him our appreciation." Blake's eyes briefly met her's before a sheepish expression filled them, and he turned back to his task.

Kris had to turn away. A smile as broad as her face overwhelmed her. She knew her husband had a giving heart tucked away in his tough exterior. She wouldn't make a big deal of the situation. His ego would balk, but she would hold this kind act close to her heart.

"How will you get it to that man?" Tucker asked.

"I'm still working on that one."

Tucker nodded and eased back against his pillows, his own eyebrows furrowed in thought.

He still held that expression when Kris brought the soup over ten minutes later.

"Let's get you sitting up higher, Sweetie." She draped a towel over his chest to catch any spills and then handed him the soup.

"Are they good guys?" Tucker asked her.

"Well, they are families trying to survive just like we are," Kris answered.

"Families? You mean there are kids up there?"

Kris nodded, watching him spoon soup into his mouth, happy that he fed himself. He hadn't wanted to eat since he first got sick. A spark of hope began to smolder inside of her. Tucker remained silent until he ate a good portion of the broth.

"Mommy, I'm done." He handed her the bowl. "Could you please bring me my cars?"

"Sure, Tuck." She smiled, pleased he ate and now wanted to play.

Yet, when she brought him his tub of cars he didn't play, instead he sorted them methodically. He gave each one his attention and either placed them to the right of him or the left.

"How many kids are there?" Tucker asked.

"I…I'm not sure." Kris shrugged. "Three maybe?"

"Four. There are four kids." Blake said as he packed items into a box.

"Four." Tucker repeated. He sifted through his cars once more. Took one more car from the box and added it to the pile on his left. He put the cars on the right back into the tub and picked up the four cars. "I want to give these to the kids up there."

Kris turned toward her son. Tears blurred her vision, and she was unable to stop them from silently streaming down her face. She sat down next to Tucker and brought him into her arms.

When she sat back up, Blake stood there, his large presence overpowering. With one look, she moved away and let him take her place.

"You're sure you want to give those cars away? There aren't any stores. We won't be able to get more." The seriousness in Blake's voice made the truth clear.

"I'm sure. They might not have any toys. I have a whole tub full of cars, and if they didn't break into our house, I have all of those still too." He handed his dad the four cars.

The lump in Kris's throat grew larger when she recognized the cars as his favorites. Love overwhelmed her. She turned away to let her tears fall silently. What did she do to deserve such a kind-hearted boy?

"Daddy?"

"Yes, Tuck."

"I have an idea on how to get the box to them."

Blake smiled. "I knew you would come up with something." He squeezed Tucker's hand and looked up at Kris, pride glowing in his eyes.

Kris felt pretty proud too, for both of her boys.

~*~

Blake stood at the door, silently looking back at his family and hoping he was doing the right thing for them. The box he held under his arm contained a bucket of freeze-dried meals, two extra blankets, a water purifier, and an extra saw, not to mention the four cars that Tucker added to the mix.

It wasn't much, but he hoped that it would show gratitude without endangering his family. Marvin had proved himself, and he hoped the others would follow his moral code. Yet, he didn't have enough trust to show himself or invite them to more. He wasn't sure if he could ever trust a group of people to have his family's best interest in mind.

"We always return to each other," he whispered.

"We always return to each other," Kris whispered back. She wet a cloth and laid it over their son's forehead before rising to meet him at the door.

He wrapped the arm that wasn't holding the box around her and hugged her to him. The sweet scent of his wife almost made him change his mind. He appreciated Marvin, but if this act brought an end to the safety he created for his family, it wouldn't worth it.

"I'm proud of you," she mumbled the words into his neck almost as if she was afraid to utter them aloud.

Her words did it. He had to follow through now and pray there wouldn't be consequences.

"I'll watch the screens. You have your communications gear?" She looked to ensure the black bud was in his ear.

"It's midnight out there. You won't be able to get a visual. Should have spent the extra on night vision cameras. At least I have my goggles. You may be able to see movement especially across the camp, but that's about it. With these," he pointed to the goggles on his head, "I'll be fine."

"I'll watch just in case." She leaned up and let her lips linger on his for a few seconds longer than usual. "I love you."

"I love you too. I'll be back to show you." He chuckled with the thought and then turned the handle before he lost his nerve.

"I'll hold you to that." Her playful tone gave him all the motivation he needed.

As the bunker door closed behind him, he closed his eyes to focus on the task at hand. Thinking about his wife would distract him and put him in danger out there. He took a moment to visualize his path.

Tucker's suggestion was to go when the entire camp slept and leave the box by the apple trees. They would be sure to find it there, he had said. It was far enough away from their camp that he wouldn't be heard, and hopefully if someone woke to use a tree, common sense would be that they used one far away from the trees' whose fruit they eat.

Blake almost wanted to include a note. A camp in this situation should always have at least one sentry, someone standing watch to ensure they weren't snuck up on. Tonight it worked to his advantage, but it wasn't safe for the group in the long run.

With his path mapped out, he silently walked up the steps to the hatch and slowly, carefully, opened it to the starlit night and fresh crisp air. Stealthily, he escaped from the hatch and closed it without sound. Readjusting the box under his arm, he spied around the rock in the direction of camp.

The night vision goggles he pulled down fit snuggly and for an instant, flashes of memory shot through him. He had to remind himself where he was, his purpose, and the need to get back to his family. The night lit in an eerie unnatural way, but he could see.

Nothing stirred. The land was silent except for the occasional hoot of a night bird and the scurry of a mouse scrambling across the pinecones near him. Using the silent walk taught to him in the Special Forces, he carefully stepped between the pine cones from tree trunk to tree trunk.

When he arrived at the apple trees, he gingerly set the box of supplies down and wrapped one of the blankets all around it. The food was in the bucket so it should be safe from critters, but better to be as safe as possible.

A crisp wind blew across his face as he stood erect. Winter was coming. Snow wouldn't be too far off. They didn't get much here, but enough so it would make it hard on those without shelters. These people should head to lower elevations.

Movement and a thud caught his attention to the right. He turned just in time to see an apple rolling down the slight hill. The fruit was near the end of its life. He pulled a few down and stuffed them into his pockets. It had been a long time since he had an apple from his own tree.

The extra time he took harvesting the apples began to creep into his subconscious. A tent rustled through the trees and he froze.

Soon the rustling quieted and the camp lay still once again. Blake took that as his cue to get moving.

In a matter of moments he was opening the hatch and easing down the stairs. He already missed the fresh air and expanse of the sky. A heaviness filled him. Then he made a vow. After winter, he would get his family out of there. By then things should have settled. They could look forward to spring and breathing in the fresh scent of Kris's favorite season.

~*~

Kris met Blake at the door. She had started to pace in front of the dark screens. She couldn't see anything and it had drove her crazy.

"That took longer than I expected." She watched him, wondering what he saw, wondering what it was like to see the stars and breathe fresh air…or walk into a camp with people who could shoot you without a chance for explanation.

"I got these." Blake pulled a few apples from his pockets.

Kris hungrily took one. It had only been slightly more than a week, but that apple represented something she couldn't get right now—freedom. The crisp bite sent sweet and sour juices down her throat. She moaned in pleasure.

"That good, huh?" Blake chuckled. "How's our boy doing?"

"Good," she said and walked toward him realizing he had been sleeping peacefully. She reached out and touched his forehead. It was wet. He was coated in sweat. She met Blake's eyes. "His fever broke!"

"With the meds?"

"No, I didn't give him any tonight. It broke naturally! He's made it past the worst." She felt the smile tease her mouth as relief filled her. She took a breath, and it felt freer than it had in several days. Tucker would make it through.

Blake sat next to her and felt Tuck too. "It's a miracle."

"Maybe it's a show of mercy for your act of mercy?"

"That could be reading into it a bit much, but if it makes you smile like that I'll agree to just about anything."

"Anything?" Kris leaned into him.

"Just please don't ask for something you know I can't give you…something that would be unsafe."

As much as she wanted to go above ground, she knew that now wasn't the time with the people camping right on top of them. She could bade her time.

"I wouldn't do that to you."

"Then how about we get back to bed now." The hint of suggestion in his voice caused her heart to race and a warmth to fill her. It was good to have her husband home, in more ways than one.

~9~

Over the next few days Tucker slowly improved. His cough still clung to him, and he carried a pillow wherever he went, but his energy grew each day. In fact, as his energy returned to normal Kris racked her brain on ways to keep him busy and quiet. By a week after the night his fever broke, she was exhausted and close to losing her mind.

"Daddy, tell me again about the night you left the box by the apple trees," he requested for the third time that day.

"Again, Tuck, really?" Blake asked, wiping a hand down his face.

If Kris was exhausted, Blake was near death. She saw the internal struggle within him day after day as he realized just how active and demanding their six year old could be.

"Yeah, act it out like this." Tucker took long steps on tiptoe and hid behind a chair.

Blake chuckled lightly.

"You got the footwork wrong. You want to move your foot like this." He followed Tucker, landing his heel silently on the ground and slowly rolling up to his toe.

"Oh!" Tucker retraced his steps and barely made a sound as he carefully walked across the bunker.

"That's great, Tuck." Kris watched him, admiring his natural skill set.

"Told you I could do it. Then you hid behind the

trees." He slipped behind a chair.

"Yep, just like that." Blake eased against the wall, a smile lingering on his lips.

"And when you woke up, the box had disappeared."

"Yep." Blake nodded.

Kris saw her husband's mind working. She wondered who had found it too. Did Marvin even know it was there? Did he know that it was from them?

The camper's actions hadn't changed since that night. No evidence of the food or the blankets surfaced. Kris watched Blake stride over to the cameras again.

Tucker followed him, using the silent walking skills he had just learned. "What do you see, Daddy? Can you see the things you shared with them? Are the kids playing with the cars I gave them?"

"Tuck."

"Maybe they hid them. Or they can only play with them in the tent. Or they could be keeping them in their pockets and never take them out because they're so special. Or…"

"Tucker." Blake finally broke through to the boy who looked at him with wide eyes. "There is a reason you have two ears and one mouth."

"Oh, yes, I know this one. We have ears on both sides of our head so we can hear all around us. Can you imagine if we only had an ear on one side of our head? We could never tell where the sound was coming from. It would be like…"

"Tucker." Blake's irritation lined his voice and the gruffness of it stopped Tucker mid-sentence.

Kris's heart went out to the boy, and yet the

constant ongoing chatter without a break wore on her nerves too.

"Hey, Sweetie." She grabbed a notepad and a pencil. "Do you know what scientists do when they study something and they have so many questions?"

"They observe."

"Right. And do you know how they record what they observe?"

Tucker eyed the things in her hands. "They write it down!" He reached for the notebook and pencil. "This can be my scientist notebook."

"That's right." Kris kissed him on his head and then met Blake's eyes. He nodded with a sideways grin and blew out a breath.

Kris hoped it worked for at least ten minutes, but she knew long-term focus was not Tucker's specialty, unless he was hyper-focused. She watched him carefully write down a few words and then turn his eyes toward the screens again.

She took the moment to rest on the bed and soak in the much needed peace.

Blake joined her minutes later.

"He's really intent," Blake said while watching their son.

"Yes, when he wants to be. He has the brain of a scientist, always observing and making conclusions."

"That type of thinking will help him survive this new life."

Kris's shoulders fell. She hated being reminded of the long-term aspect of this situation. "When does it become more than just surviving, Blake?"

Blake turned to her and searched her eyes. She knew he struggled to find words that weren't harsh. He had always been good about not talking to her like she was one of his special ops buddies, well, at least when they weren't out-running a fire or scrambling over dangerous scree slopes.

"I'm not sure, Kris. I wish I could say…"

"He can't grow up without other kids. It's not fair."

Blake's brows scrunched together. "What are you saying?"

The way he looked at her caused a strange stirring to awaken inside of her. She pushed it away though and focused on the conversation, one she had been formulating in her mind for the last couple weeks.

"Have you put any thought to what Hannah and her dad might be doing now? Or even the group above us?"

"You mean joining a mob of roving people?" Blake's features contorted in an expression of disgust. "I thought you understood that your and Tuck's safety is my number one concern. I can't keep you safe if we are surrounded by other people all the time."

"You have such the lone wolf mentality." Kris rolled her eyes. "Look at the history of humanity. People didn't evolve by living alone. They formed groups, small communities that brought different skills together in one place for the benefit of all."

"They also brought wars, death, and the corruption that led to this collapse."

"You are so pessimistic!" Her frustration raised her voice.

"And you live in a make-believe world!" Blake said as he stood up.

"Shh," Tucker narrowed his eyes at them. "I'm trying to be a scientist here."

"Oh great, now I'm getting shushed by a six year old." Blake growled low and the muscles in his jaw pulsed.

He dropped and began doing push-ups. The abrupt change almost caused Kris to burst out laughing. Almost, but her anger kept it blocked. How could he really think they could survive the rest of their lives with just the three of them?

~*~

Blake blew out his frustration with each push of his arms. How could Kris not understand he was just trying to keep them safe? People represented danger. The more people, the more danger.

He thought about Tucker's lack of socializing too. He hadn't decided on a solution yet, but many ideas ran through his mind. Maybe the solution would just drop into their laps, like an orphaned child that needed a home. Now he was thinking like his idealistic wife. He pushed faster until sweat dripped from his head, spattering on the floor, and his breath came in gasps.

When he couldn't push any more, he squatted and wiped the sweat from his brow. Kris watched him with an amused expression. Well, at least it wasn't the dagger eyes she had been shooting at him before.

"I think we need a routine." Her words crashed into his ponderings.

He mulled over the idea before nodding his head. That's what they had been missing since Tucker got sick. A routine. "You're right."

The smile that spread across his wife's face lit up the room, and instantly his frustration melted away.

They had months to figure out what to do, and looking at his wife, maybe, just maybe, he thought, the solution would find them.

He sat up on the bed next to her. "What are your thoughts?"

"That's the problem. I have too much time to think, and so do you. Tucker doesn't have enough focused outlets. Now that he's feeling better, he needs to be kept busy."

"He also needs to understand how to be silent and still," Blake interjected.

"Yes, those are good skills too, though I wish you luck teaching him them," she whispered on an airy laugh.

Blake watched her. She amazed him. Her mental strength and undying positive attitude left him in awe. It was one of the many things about her he had fallen in love with all those years ago. They could be hovering over death's doorstep on one of their adventures, and yet she always found something beautiful about the situation, whether it was a tiny flower holding onto life at the top of a barren mountain, or the stark contrast of the snow on the black scree of granite. She always found something to appreciate.

"I love you," he whispered, pushing a stray red lock behind her ear.

She blinked several times before a smile warmed her face. "I love you too."

Nothing else in the world mattered to him. He had his family. He had their love, and he would protect them with his life.

~10~

The next couple months crawled by with their days broken up by routine. The constant time-table helped them to keep their minds from going places they didn't need to.

Kris watched her family. They had five more minutes left of their morning quiet time. As much as she wanted this day to be special, she understood Blake's reasoning to keep to the routine as close as possible. It could be easy to lose it again, and when they lost routine, they tended to lose their minds. So they decided that today, rather than the normal combat training they did for an hour before lunch, they would celebrate the day they believed to be Christmas.

The break from the monotonous days felt so needed. Kris sat up and then hung her head as the world went black for a few seconds. She worried for her health. The last several weeks she had been feeling off, light-headed, and a bit nauseous. It was probably a lack of sun, fresh air, and fresh fruit and vegetables.

Once her vision cleared, she let her gaze linger on Tucker again. He read a book, a finger in his mouth and eyes roving back and forth over the words. The instated quiet time had led him to become an even more voracious reader. She sent up a silent thank you, for he hadn't even had the slightest sniffle since he recovered from the respiratory flu he had succumbed to a week after being in the bunker, and neither she or Blake had caught it either.

Blake stirred neared the screens. He spent less time over there since the group left with the first snow. Ever since they left a few weeks ago, her family had felt a little adrift, almost as if they had lost friends. A good part of their day had been spent observing that group prepare for winter.

Kris shivered. Could she actually be grateful for the bunker now? Up on top, with almost a foot of snow, and no real protection…she shook her head. Hopefully that group moved lower down the mountain where it would be warmer, for the children if nothing else.

The timer dinged and Tucker quickly put down his book, Blake stepped away from the screens, and they both turned toward her. She smiled at her boys, feeling blessed to have her family all together. Tucker blinked a few times, and she knew he was trying to come back to the world after being lost in his book.

When he did, a slow, huge grin lit up his face. "Is it Christmas now?" He bounced and jumped all the way to her. She couldn't help but imagine a grasshopper being trapped in a small box. He had become good at controlling his super high energy, at least most of the time. The routine had really helped with that, especially the exercise and training Blake instilled.

"Yes, Sweetie!" Kris brought him into her arms. "I'm sorry we don't have a Christmas tree, or music…"

"Or decorations, or presents…" Tucker added with a small pout. Then he brightened. "I did make you and Daddy something!"

He bounded away toward a little cupboard full of

his toys, art supplies, and school materials. While he dug around in there, Blake came over and slipped his arm around her.

"Merry Christmas, Wife." He kissed her tenderly and pulled her into his arms.

"Merry Christmas, Husband." She smiled and snuggled deeper into his warmth.

"Here they are!" Tucker came to them, his hands behind his back. "Merry Christmas, Mommy and Daddy!" He handed them each a drawing. They were almost identical. Each one had Blake, Kris, and Tucker standing together with stick arms around each other. In the background each picture also had a sun, trees, and a house.

"This is beautiful. Thank you, Tuck." Kris brought him into her arms and kissed his head.

"I like how you drew us all together," Blake said and ruffled his hair.

"That's how we belong." Tucker grinned.

Kris looked at hers a bit closer, her tendency to critique children's artwork taking over. Tucker had drawn him and Blake with block bodies, but hers with a round circle. She went through the child development theories in her head in attempt to decipher the reason behind the difference.

"I have some presents too." Blake stood up, interrupting Kris's thoughts.

She watched him curiously wondering how her two guys had become so thoughtful. Blake rummaged around in his gun cabinet and produced a long object wrapped in paper. He handed it to Tucker.

"Merry Christmas, Champ."

"Really?" Tucker bounced with the wrapped object that could only be a gun.

Hopefully a bb gun, Kris darted her narrowed eyes at her husband. He only shrugged with a sheepish smile.

"A real gun! It is real, isn't it, Daddy?"

"Yes, son, it's real. It was mine when I was your age. I stashed it in here when we first installed the bunker."

"Yes! Thank you! I can't wait to shoot it."

"That will be a couple months, but I'll teach you everything you need to know about it so that when you do get that chance, you'll know exactly how to shoot and care for it."

Kris watched the exchange. As much as she didn't like guns, she couldn't disagree that knowing how to use them might be a good idea. The image of that man, who now was no longer, aiming that rifle at Marvin caused shivers to run down her spine. She hoped that Blake didn't have a surprise gun for her in there. She would have to learn to wrap her mind around that thought.

"I didn't forget you," Blake said as he wrapped an arm around her.

"I don't know how you two pulled this off anyway." She smiled. She actually had thought about it sometime ago and had stored a few special treats she came across, hiding them where they would never think to look.

"It's snowing again. Pretty heavily and looks like it will be for some time." Blake smiled.

"Are you asking me for a thank you?" she teased.

"No, though living up there would be miserable right now, especially since having a fire would give our location away..."

Kris shook her head. "I do appreciate the warmth

here." She nudged him, biting back the nausea the movement caused her.

"I know it's been difficult for you down here. More difficult by the day it seems." He looked up as if he could see the land and sky above them. "With the snow coming down like it is, tracks would be covered in minutes."

Kris tried to follow his meaning, but it took her a moment before dawning hit her, causing her to grin. "Really?"

"Would you like that?" he asked, almost shyly.

"You know I would!"

"Like what?" Tucker asked, watching them curiously, finally not fully focused on his gun.

"To go above ground." Blake stood, helping Kris up. "Dress warm."

Less than fifteen minutes later, they stood at the bunker door in full winter gear. Tucker bounced up and down. Kris wished she could show the same enthusiasm. A part of her feared getting her hopes up only for them to not be able to leave.

Her family had been stuck under the ground for two months now—two long months. Creating a strict routine had been their saving grace. They learned many skills from that time as well, skills that would help them survive this next stage in their lives. Skills they would need above ground.

Blake reminded them again of the proper safety steps to take. She and Tucker both answered with unrestrained impatience. Finally Blake checked the screens one last time. Looking into each of their excited eyes, he turned the handle and allowed them to step foot into the corridor to the surface for the first time since entering the bunker.

Kris's heart raced. She couldn't wait to breathe in that fresh, crisp air. Holding Tucker's gloved hand, she felt his excitement in his quivering fingers...or was it her shaking? Blake had motioned them to stay there while he checked the area.

"I can't believe we're really going above ground!" Tucker squealed quietly.

"Me either." She hugged her son to her, hoping that something wouldn't happen now to keep this moment from happening. Half of her feared that they wouldn't actually make it up there, that Blake might find something he didn't like and send them back into the stiff, lifeless air of the bunker.

"The flakes are massive," Blake said as he lifted the hatched door and smiled down at them. "You've got to come see this."

Kris's legs shook and wobbled as she walked up the steep steps behind Tucker. The fresh air whooshed through the open hatch, filling her senses with pure delight. Each step she took she feared the dream would end.

Yet, as her boot crunched on snow at the top, she assured herself she was actually above ground, breathing in real fresh air, seeing the cloud-filled sky, and feeling actual cold wetness of snowflakes landing on her upturned face.

"Good present?" Blake's whispered words warmed her neck, a tantalizing difference from the crisp and frigid air.

"The best," she whispered, kissing him lightly before closing her eyes and focusing on the sensation of the snowflakes melting on her face.

"I caught one on my tongue!" Tucker giggled and ran around in the snow. "Let's make a snowman and a snow angel and have a snowball fight!"

"Slow down, Sweetie." *I want to soak this in.* A snowball blasted against her side in a poof of fresh powder. "Hey!"

Tucker giggled as he gathered another handful of snow and lobbed it at her again.

"Oh, you think you have skills?" Blake intervened. "I'll teach you to attack my wife," he teased as he swooped down to scoop up an armful of snow and chase Tucker.

The delightful, pure joy that bubbled forth from her son filled Kris with even more peace than the fresh air and expanse of nature around her. She clung to that thought, knowing she would need this memory to get her through the next few months.

She wasn't allowed to get lost in that thought though, for the next moment Blake swept her up and then preceded to run with her through the snow with Tucker chasing after them, squealing in delight.

~*~

They stayed above ground until their growling tummies threatened to eat them alive. Still, no one really wanted to go back. Blake had brought them both into his arms before opening the hatch.

"Thank you. This time out here will help get me through the next couple of months." Kris reached up and kissed him.

"Yeah, this is the best Christmas ever." Tucker hugged them both in a family hug.

His statement left Kris blinking back tears. Even with the world falling apart, their lives succumbed to living underground, having no one other children to play with, her son still thought this the best Christmas ever.

Now as she made lunch for them, she wondered if maybe she needed to reframe her way of thinking. Maybe during this period of time, socialization and being around other kids wasn't as important. She didn't know, but she was grateful for her optimistic, positive son. He made this trial so much easier to push through.

She grabbed the counter as she wavered and her stomach threatened to rebel. The smell of the food sent her over the edge. She must have waited too long to eat. Yet, how could she not have stayed outside until she absolutely had to crawl back underground?

She served the food to her boys who inhaled it while she picked at her plate. She did her best to make a good show of eating though the food didn't sit well in her. When they boys were almost finished, she excused herself to the bathroom. Now was the time to pull out the surprises she had stored away after she found out they would be here for months.

In the cramped bathroom, she opened the cupboard where she kept the extra toilet paper and feminine hygiene products. She stood on the toilet to get a better line of sight into the high cupboard. Immediately she found one package—a just add water cookie dough dessert. She sifted around looking for the freeze-dried ice cream she knew was there too.

While trying to balance and sift through the supplies, several boxes fell to the ground. She grunted in frustration until her hand felt the crinkling package she searched for and pulled it out. Setting the packages down, she squatted to pick up the boxes that had fallen. Several unopened boxes of tampons littered the floor. It was when she shoved the sixth box back into the cupboard that she realized it—not one of the boxes had been opened.

Her mind reeled, and she plopped onto the toilet seat. The lightheadedness, the nausea, the feeling off…how had she not realized? It hadn't been something she had worried about for a year, but still. Two months with no period, all the signs, and she had ignored them all.

Excitement warred with complete terror.

A knock startled her, and she fumbled the box, catching it right before it fell on the floor again.

"Kris, you okay?" Blake's voice was filled with worry.

Her heart raced, and she tried to swallow the lump in her throat. "Ye..yeah. I…I'll be right out."

She heard his footsteps shift back and forth a few times before walking away. Kris took in a few deep breaths, trying to come up with a way to tell Blake, or find out for sure, or… She grabbed her head. What in the world were they going to do?

Shoving the unopened box back into the cupboard, she picked up the special treats she had come in to get, looked at her pale face in the mirror, and then walked out with a deep breath.

"Mommy! There you are!" Tucker ran to her like she had been missing for a week. "Wait, what do you have in your hands?"

"Well," she started, her voice as shaky as she felt, "they aren't as wonderful as your presents, but I have some special treats for us." She handed the packages to Tucker.

"What?! Cookie dough and ice cream as survival food!" he screamed before covering his mouth and opening his eyes wide. "Sorry. Can we have some right now?"

"Yes, Sweetie." Kris got out spoons and filled the cookie dough package with a small amount of water.

Blake and Tucker sat and ate, sounds of pure-delighted moans escaping them. Once again though, the food didn't sit well with Kris. In fact her stomach tied up in knots. She watched her boys, indecision weighing her down.

"Are you okay, Kris? Do you need to rest?" Blake's concerned eyes held hers. Her mouth opened and shut before any words came out.

How did she tell him? Did she know for sure? What would they do? Would he flip? Questions challenged her every thought.

"Is this all you have for us, Mommy?"

Kris blinked and turned her attention to Tucker. "I'm sorry, Sweetie. Not much else I could do from down here."

"What about the other thing? Aren't you going to tell us your other surprise?" Tucker's eyes gleamed.

"What other surprise?" Kris's gut twisted. The poor boy didn't understand she couldn't give him all the toys she usually did at Christmas, or his yearly book or pajamas.

Tucker jumped up and ran to where she had put up the picture he had given her this morning. He sat it in front of her and Blake and pointed at the drawing of her.

"This surprise. How long will it take for my sister to be here?"

"What?!" Blake and Kris said at the same time.

Blake turned narrowed eyes toward her. She felt her eyes widen further. Her heart thrummed so loudly she couldn't speak. She couldn't think.

"Kris?" Blake growled.

"I...I..." she stuttered.

"Tucker you need to go read a book while Mommy and I have an adult talk."

"Why do you sound angry?" Tucker stood and thrust his chest out. "You're acting like you don't want my sister! She's going to save us and all you are is angry!" Tears filled his eyes before he turned away and strutted to the far end of the bunker.

Kris rose to go after him, her heart breaking for her son.

"No," Blake said as he stilled her. "You are going to tell me what's going on."

Kris narrowed her eyes. "You act like I've been unfaithful."

"Have you?" His voice choked as if he had swallowed a fish with all its bones.

"No! How could you even ask that?" Anger consumed her.

"Then what is Tucker talking about?"

"Maybe if you would have given him a chance to explain, we would understand more." Then the truth hit her like a ton of bricks and she slumped into the chair.

Blake watched her, his presence overwhelming.

She took a deep breath, but couldn't meet his eyes, so she stared at her fidgeting hands. "Just a few minutes ago while I was in the bathroom a bunch of unopened tampon boxes fell out while I grabbed the desserts. I haven't used any since we've been in the bunker. It could be stress?"

"And you haven't been feeling well." He hung his head. "When was your last one?"

"I had just finished before the night you returned…before the night of the auroras."

Blake swore under his breath. He slammed his fists down on the table startling Kris so much she sat back and sucked in a breath.

"You're not on birth control?" The condemnation in his voice sent her over the edge.

"Why would I be on birth control with my husband gone for a year?!" She stood and thrust her hands on her hips. "You act like this is my fault Mr. Casanova. It takes two to tango you know."

Blake stood just as abruptly. "And you act like this is no big deal. You don't understand the risks. There are no hospitals. No doctors. No prenatal care. No one to deliver the baby, not to mention if complications happen…"

Kris stood her ground, anger consuming her as she stared down her husband. His temper wasn't going to make her run any more. It was time that he learned to control it, and she learned to stand up against it.

Blake spun away from her, threw open the bunker door and slammed it behind him. Her body shook, but she listened with every ounce of her attention, yet the hatch to the outside never opened. He must be cooling off in the space between the bunker and above ground. Two minutes later she could finally breathe, but only to have her heart break as she heard the quiet sobs from her son, curled up in the far corner of the bed.

With a deep breath and settling of her own emotions, she made her way to Tucker and drew him up into her arms.

"I'm sorry you heard us fighting, Sweetie." She

kissed his forehead and hugged him close as he clung to her.

"Why is Daddy so angry?"

"He's scared, Sweetie." Stating the fact helped quell her own indignant anger.

"Why?" Tucker wiped his eyes and sat up to look at her.

"Well, babies are usually born in the hospital. Life has changed now. There are no doctors and nurses to help with the delivery." She realized then she talked as if it was an absolute fact she was indeed pregnant. A resounding vibration of affirmation thrummed inside of her and she swallowed audibly.

"You're scared too." Tucker watched her with knowing eyes.

"Probably." She nodded. "But tell me, Tuck. How did you even come up with this idea?"

"I saw it." He hid his face in her.

"What do you mean saw it? In a dream?"

"No, I was awake, but my mind switched to a different time, and I saw her and just knew things." He leaned back up and fervently met her gaze. "You don't have to be scared, Mommy. She will be fine. She's going to save us."

He clung to her again. Kris held her son while wrapping her mind around the possibilities: her son having premonitions, her being pregnant, and Blake having fits about it all. She closed her eyes. Right now she would just revel in the feeling of her son in her arms. Everything else would come or not, and she would deal with it then.

~*~

Blake paced the tiny room, which only fed his frustration. He finally leaned against the steep stairs and completed set after set of inclined pushups until he couldn't do another. Physical exercise was the only thing keeping him sane.

Pregnant.

He couldn't wrap his mind around it. Kris had always wanted more kids, but Blake knew the world would become a dangerous place soon. With danger so close on the horizon, he had asked her to get on birth control to keep pregnancy from happening. Having a young child would be difficult enough. An infant though? He growled.

He loved his son and would never want to change that. Having another child now, with no medical teams, no hospitals, no one but him to deliver the baby...it was too much. It put Kris's life at risk. A strangled sound emitted from him at the thought. He couldn't do this without Kris.

Fear pulsed within him, creating a sensation that made him feel feral like a wild animal, except there was no enemy to fight. There was nothing he could do but wait and watch and hope and pray.

His mind calmed enough and he remembered Tucker's words. First his warning of the people and now this. Was his a kid a psychic? Most people thought it all make believe, but he knew the government, especially the military, used people with clairvoyance skills to locate things like lost subs. It wasn't something that made it into public reports, but those skills were put into use to benefit the country. The clairvoyants were sought out with possessive force.

He swore quietly. Another thing he would have to

hide from others. If people found out his son could see the future, they would kill to get to him.

Blake resisted the urge to bang his head against the steel wall. Instead he took a few deep breaths, trying to remember what Kris had been teaching them of mindfulness. Blake had rolled his eyes when she chose that as the skill she wanted to teach in their routine, yet he couldn't deny the effects it had on all of them over the last couple months.

Twenty minutes later he could easily count the steady beat of his heart. Guilt had sunk in when he remembered his accusations and his reactions. Why did he always lose his temper and let anger control his words? It shocked him when Kris had stood her ground. It had shocked him enough he realized he needed to put distance between them before he damaged the tentative hold they had on a happy relationship.

He had repair work to do, with his wife and his son. Poor kid. It must be a heavy load to carry, the ability to see the future.

Steeling himself for the onslaught he deserved, he knocked on the bunker door, hoping that she would actually open it.

The door slowly creaked open. Hesitant eyes met his gaze. He could sense no anger or hate or any of the things his actions deserved.

"Thank you for opening the door." He could have hit himself for being so lame, yet sorry didn't roll off his tongue easily.

"I wouldn't let you freeze to death out there." She walked back into the bunker and poured three cups of hot liquid, hot chocolate by the rich scent of it.

"We're having hot chocolate, Daddy. Since it's

Christmas and all." Tucker glanced at him while swinging his leg back and forth at the table. His subdued tone told him everything he needed to know.

"Sounds good, Champ."

Tucker swung his head up. "You're not angry anymore?"

"Don't tell, Mom, but I did some of that breathing and it calmed me down," he whispered to his son, watching Kris from the corner of his eye.

Her movements had frozen as he spoke, a sure sign she heard his words just like he intended.

"It really does work," Tucker affirmed seriously.

Kris placed the mugs on the table and sat with her boys. "Seems like the perfect time for a family meeting."

"And to read the Christmas story. We always read it today. Let's do that first." Tuck jumped up and dug through his books. "We don't have it!" His bottom lip quivered as he ran to Kris.

"I bet we have it memorized anyway." She wrapped her arms around him. "It will be fun to see how much we can remember." Kris kissed the top of his head. Blake could see the pain and regret living in her eyes, but she didn't let it reach her voice.

"Okay, but first we all have to say what we're most grateful for. We always do that too." He climbed into her lap. "I'll start. I'm most grateful for Daddy being back home and Mommy always being here for me. I'm also grateful that I'm getting a sister."

Blake shot his gaze toward Tucker who met him defiantly. Then he lifted his gaze to look at Kris. Her expression held a look of trepidation.

"Mommy. Your turn."

Kris swallowed and let her eyes tear away from his

to gaze at Tucker. "I'm most grateful that we are safe, all together as a family, and for the time above ground breathing in fresh air today."

Blake hated the way his throat constricted. He cleared it trying to expel the ball that had grown there.

"Daddy?"

He cleared his throat again. "I am most grateful for being here with the two most important people in my life."

"Umm, three, Daddy. We are a family of four now." Tucker met him with an intensity.

Where did his young son acquire such an intimidating look? Then Blake looked at his wife and saw the same expression. He almost laughed, but covered it up with a cough.

"Okay, Tuck." He kept his voice calm, choosing to just enjoy the moment instead of letting fear overcome.

~11~

Kris bent down to pick up the last of the linens and once again was reminded their family was growing. Though her stomach wasn't large by many standards, at just about five months she definitely showed. There could be no denying that she was pregnant, that Tucker's premonition had been spot on—again.

Blake had slowly become used to the idea. He watched her like a hawk, but he didn't cater to her or baby her. She needed to be strong in order to survive this. He knew it and she knew it. There would be none of the coddling that she had received when carrying Tucker. They couldn't afford that.

"Oh!" she exclaimed, putting a hand on the baby as it kicked her stomach. Secretly she had been enjoying the little one's movements rolling around inside of her. It had been one of the most amazing feelings while pregnant with Tucker. With this one, she couldn't help but feel a spark of hope with every movement.

She would never be able to see the baby on an ultrasound or hear its heartbeat before it was born. How spoiled they had become as a society. Now she had to rely on the old ways to know if her baby fared well.

Kris organized everything they would take out with them, specifically clothes and linens that needed to be washed. She did the best she could with the provisions in the bunker, but they needed fresh air and a better scrub than her little hand held tub could accomplish.

Tucker practically bounced off the walls in excitement, and in truth Kris wanted to join him. She knew they still had to sleep in the bunker for now, but today marked the end of the mandatory hibernation.

"Mommy?" Tucker caught her attention, having stopped bouncing for the first time since they woke up and Blake announced for sure that this would be the day.

"Yes, Sweetie." She leaned down and kissed him on the forehead.

"May I feel her?" Tucker reached out his small hand.

"Of course," she said as she placed his hand over the last place the baby kicked, laying her palm over the top of his.

Tucker had been curious and observant with the pregnancy, asking questions and wanting to know everything about the process and what *his sister* looked like right then. Kris delighted in the conversations. Not only did she feel the bond with Tucker growing, but she felt the pull that he had toward his sister. He would be a wonderful big brother.

Blake's secret knock sounded on the bunker door. He had been scouting the property to ensure it was safe for them to go above ground.

"I can't wait!" Tucker jumped and clapped.

Kris opened the door, greeting her husband with a wide smile.

"Ready?" Blake asked, looking intimidating with guns and knives holstered all over.

Yet, her heart caught. That daunting man was her

husband, the father of her child, no…children, and the love her life. He had saved them. As horrible as it had been to be stuck underground for five months, she knew it would have been worse for them above ground. Here they had everything they needed: warmth, food, water, security, and most of all each other.

Blake's hand rested on the handle as if uncertainty warred within him. His eyes rested on hers, speaking more than words could convey. Then they shifted to their son's. A brief flash of fear danced within his gaze and then vanished as he set his face in determination.

The massive door released in a sigh, a sigh months in coming.

Blake released a loud breath and heaved the door open, motioning them to stay still and silent.

Kris's eyes closed as a gust of warm, fresh air blew across her face when he opened the hatch. Their silence was broken by the song of birds greeting the morning. A joyful tear silently rolled down her face.

"It's still clear." Blake's deep voice set little Tucker free.

Her son ran across the green ground, bounded off rocks, and climbed up low-branched trees.

Kris soaked in the moment. The sun filtered through the green leaves. Pines and oaks rocked gently in the breeze.

Life was beginning anew this spring. The world as she knew it may have ended, but their new one proved to be just as full. She rested a hand on her growing belly—even fuller.

"This is the beginning of our new life," she whispered.

Blake wrapped his arms around her. "Yes, and I will do my best to make it as fulfilling as possible."

Kris snuggled into his warmth, moved his hands to feel the delightful activity of their child in her womb. She watched her son enjoy the freedom of nature, and thanked the powers that be for the mercy of allowing the world to still surround them.

****

INSTALLMENT THREE

~1~

DATE: May 23   10:18

Not again.

Kris wiped the sweat from her brow and leaned on the barrel that held the squash plant she worked on. The pain rippled through her stomach, tightening and clenching like a wide rubber band stretching across her. Her eyes squeezed shut as she blew her breath out. She had pushed too much…again.

Her son's squeal of delight traveled to her from a hundred yards down the hill. The happy sound drew her back from the cramping. She was glad that Blake and Tucker couldn't see her. The worry in their eyes made her heart ache.

Peeking through the bushy plant, she saw Tucker skip to the target they had set up on the edge of the forest below their house. At times she could almost pretend it was an ordinary early summer day. She worked in her barrel garden up near the house. Below her and past the play structure, the boys practiced shooting their bows—not for fun, but in preparation for a hunt, a hunt for meat necessary to live.

"Bullseye!" Tucker shouted. After pulling the arrow from the target, he held it up in victory. His eyes roamed up to where she was working on their garden barrels.

She stood then, letting him see her smiling down

at him. With hands around her mouth, she yelled back, "Proud of you!"

He waved his hand before Blake walked up and patted him on the back. He leaned down to give him further instructions, and the boy's eyes turned away from her once more. Though she was happy to see the pride Blake took in their son, there were moments she missed when it was just her and Tucker. These days she took a back seat in the relationship, especially since her *condition* kept her from the more rigorous activities.

Hands on her hips, she bent back, stretching her tight lower back. The Braxton Hicks spasms had become more frequent the last couple weeks. They increased to the point she couldn't be sure if she lied to Blake when she told him they were nothing to worry about. It was too early to have early labor. She still had two months to go, and those two months were needed. She had a lot to accomplish to have enough food to last through another winter in the bunker.

Her chest tightened with the thought. She didn't want to spend another winter in the bunker, especially not with an infant. She had two more months to convince Blake he didn't either. Her husband's sanity would not last being in such close proximity to a crying infant for so long, not to mention how in the world would she wash all the diapers?

Her mind spun with too much to think about and consider. If she allowed herself time to worry about everything, she would lose her grip on her own sanity. She had to be strong for her boys. Besides, Blake worried enough for all of them.

She focused on her task. They had twenty barrels,

all full of vegetables. The self-watering system made this type of gardening so much easier. She moved on to a strawberry bed, happy to see a couple dozen red strawberries. Popping one into her mouth made her wish she could just eat them all right then.

She had found the video describing this system of gardening almost seven years ago, when she was pregnant with Tucker. Remembering the look of pride in Blake's eyes when she asked if he could help her create this self-watering garden made her knees feel weak. If only he would look at her like that now.

Yet, every time she actually caught his gaze, the expression was far from pride. Fear and resentment filled them, leaving her wanting to cower and hide. She wrapped her arms around her stomach, feeling her baby wiggle under the pressure. She couldn't change what happened, and she wouldn't want to. This baby was a part of her now, whether Blake could wrap his mind around it or not.

The baby was due in the midst of harvesting time, so she had to train Tucker on how to care for the plants, harvest them, and store them. Not that she would be able to be down for long. She prayed for an easy delivery, one that she could bounce back from quickly.

Her baby wiggled and kicked against her, causing a smile to erupt. Every time she felt the baby move, she couldn't help but feel that everything was going to be okay. She took a hesitant glance toward her husband showing Tucker how to pull the bow farther back. Would Blake change his mind about the child after it was born?

~*~

Blake glanced up at his wife as she leaned against one of the barrels. He knew her spasms came more frequently, and fear shot up his spine with every one. He gritted his teeth to keep the harshness out of his voice while coaching his son. The boy was sensitive. Blake struggled with wanting to harden him up. Life would only get more difficult and harsh, and Tucker needed to be tough. Yet, he loved the innocence in his son's eyes as he stared up at him with adoration. Blake hoped his weakness for the boy wouldn't put him in danger later on in life.

"Tilt your elbow more. Pull back all the way until your thumb can hook on your jaw. There. Now shoot."

Tucker released the arrow, and not only did it pierce the bullseye again, but it buried itself to the shaft. The boy had talent, but could he hit a moving target? Could he kill? It took more grit than most realized to kill. It took a hardened heart, and each life, animal or human, cost a piece of you.

Even with the pressure of their survival on his shoulders, Blake could not stop the smile when his boy squealed his triumph. He should quiet him in fear of others hearing, but he just couldn't crush the joy in his son's eyes. Not yet. Let him enjoy his childhood a little longer. Hopefully, there would be time before he saw that zest for life destroyed.

While Tucker reenacted his triumph over and over, Blake struggled over their position. For now, they seemed safe enough. Marauders hadn't bothered them since they left the bunker. In fact, the world seemed void of other human life. He knew that wasn't the case. There would be other survivors, and grizzly ones at that. For now, they had sanctuary and he would use it to his advantage.

The issue at hand was food. Their well still worked. The solar panels still supplied the energy needed for the pump. He knew one day that would fail and more than likely he would not have the correct part to fix it. That was a problem for another day, though. Right now, he needed to hunt, and he needed to test his son's readiness.

He hated to leave Kris for too long. The way she acted, the baby could come at any time. If he left her, what would happen? She couldn't birth the baby alone, could she?

As soon as Blake sanctioned a trip to the house, Kris had found the old, tattered birthing book she had dissected while pregnant with Tucker. Every night after Tucker had fallen asleep, he would ask her to tell him a bit more about it. He needed to know what to do. Fear propelled him forward.

"That's enough practice for today, Champ. You're a great shot on the target. Ready to see what you can do for real?"

Tucker visibly swallowed, but he pushed a smile to his lips. "I can't wait!"

Blake pushed back all the other fears and knelt on a knee in front of his son. "Killing isn't easy, Tuck. This is for our survival. Without meat, we can't live. We're doing this for your mom and for us."

"And for my baby sister."

Blake nodded. He had no doubt now that his son could see certain parts of the future. Part of him quelled the desire to ask him what to expect so he could prepare, and the other part wanted to dismiss the whole idea and pretend the *gift* didn't exist. At least here, alone, he could protect him.

As always, he scanned the area. He was acutely aware at all times of any movement, whether it be the wind, a squirrel, a bird, or whatever. Watching his son skip up the hill to his mom, he realized he needed to instill that capability in Tucker as well. Blake needed to teach him to keep constant vigilance of his surroundings, never turn his back to another, and always be ready for an attack…from anyone.

How did you teach a child to be wary of everyone, even friends?

~2~

Kris paced the living room. She knew she should be resting, but as comfortable as the recliner looked, the anxiety coursing through her wouldn't let her sit still. Blake had left with Tucker early that morning promising to return a little after noon. Though they didn't power the clocks in the house, she knew they were late because the sun had started sinking behind the trees an hour ago.

Life had been too easy with the use of cell phones. She had gotten accustomed to checking on Tucker whenever she wanted, not that he was away from her all that often. A few playdates here and there and, of course, school, but she always had been there on campus. Knowing she could run into his classroom at any time had set her heart at ease.

What she wouldn't give to have a cell phone now.

The radio she clutched like a lifeline crackled in her hand. She rushed it to her ear, trying to make out anything besides the static.

"Blake, Tucker, was that you?"

Nothing. She waited, counting her heartbeats. One. Two. Three. Four. Five.

"We're here, Mommy. Just got back on the property."

"Thank goodness," she sighed into the walkie-talkie.

"See you in a few. Miss you."

"Miss you, too, Sweetie. So glad you're okay."

Kris finally lowered herself into the chair, hung her head, and allowed the sobs to release from her. They were okay. Tucker was safe. Her arms circled her stomach as she breathed slow and deep. Their footsteps creaked up the deck, urging her to wipe away her tears and calm herself.

"Mommy!" Tucker ran to her, throwing his arms around her. "Oh, sorry, sister." He moved back and laid a hand on her stomach. "She's really active right now, isn't she?"

"She's excited to hear her brother's voice." Kris soaked in the sight of his beautiful face.

Tucker smiled and kissed her belly. "Soon you'll be able to see, my little sister."

"Not too soon," Blake said as he entered the house, his presence overwhelming as always.

"Not too soon," Kris echoed. She took her son's hand. "So, how did your first hunting trip go?"

His bottom lip trembled a moment before he pushed forth a smile. "I got a deer."

"Really?"

"Yeah, but I wounded him, so we had to chase him clear across the forest until we got to the creek."

"Oh, no," Kris said as she squeezed his hand.

"We got him in the end, though, and ended his suffering. Dad carried him all the way back…after he…gutted him." Tucker looked down, hiding his eyes.

Kris shot a glance up at Blake, whose eyes had hardened.

"It's what we have to do to survive. It's not an easy lesson, but he did well." He reached over and squeezed Tucker's shoulder. "I'm proud of you, Champ."

Tucker nodded. "Can I go play with my toys?"

"Absolutely—" Kris started to respond.

"We need to dress the deer and..." Blake cut in.

Kris stood up cumbersomely and put a hand on Blake's arm. He looked down at her, a fire blazing in his green eyes, but he nodded. "You can learn that part on the next one."

Tucker sped from the room as if he feared his dad would change his mind.

"Thank you. He has reached his limit. I'm not sure how he is still holding it together," Kris whispered, her eyes lingering to where her son had disappeared.

"He's learning to be a man."

"He shouldn't have to learn that yet. He's only six."

"You can keep saying *only* for every age, Kris. It doesn't change the fact that these are skills he has to learn in order to survive. Life is not guaranteed. If something happens to you...to us...he needs to know how to take care of himself."

Kris lowered her head as Blake spun on his heel and strode out the door. His angry words spoke loudly of his own fear As much as she wanted her young son to be able to enjoy his childhood, she knew he had to learn these skills, too.

They had to find a balance.

~*~

Blake growled as he shoved the tip of the knife into the deer. They had gutted him where they finally found him, but he needed to skin it and start smoking the meat so it would keep. Night was closing in and that would be the best time to cook the meat so the smoke couldn't be seen.

He didn't want his son to have to miss out on his childhood, either, but Kris fighting him at every turn made his job that much more difficult. The boy had to learn, plain and simple. He had cried when he shot the deer and sobbed when he realized he had only wounded the animal.

His tears had torn at Blake's heart. Yet, rather than coddle Tucker, he spoke matter-of-factly. *It's part of survival, son. You take the life of the deer to give life to yourself and your family.* His boy had nodded and sniffed back his sobs, but Tucker had been silent the whole hike back. Blake did his best to congratulate him and encourage him, yet it had probably reached deaf ears.

In truth, despite the emotional reaction, Blake was proud of his son. At six years old the kid had shot his first deer, a moving, living target. It really had been Blake's fault the deer only had been wounded. Blake should have known the boy's bow didn't have the power for a kill shot on an animal that large. He should have been prepared to take down the deer in case something like that happened.

He yanked on the deer's hide. Why hadn't he started the boy off with a rabbit or a squirrel? Something he could for sure kill?

Being a constantly present dad was harder than he had ever thought. Every decision he made affected his son and his way of thinking. Push him too far, and he would pull away. Don't push him enough, and he might not survive.

Kris coddled the boy, and he feared Tucker wouldn't have the strength to pull through and do the tough things needed to survive. He didn't know if Kris could, either. The responsibility lay heavy on him. He had to ensure they could. Taking them on all the hunts wasn't a possibility, and he had to hunt in order for them all to stay alive.

He had to push, even if it did distance them from him. They needed to know how to take care of themselves for periods of time at least. Yet fear raced through him. What if someone showed up on the property when he was hunting?

Tomorrow he would put them through a few scenarios, run some more drills, and work on some moving targets for practice.

~*~

Tucker crawled into bed with Kris later that night. After Tucker had healed from being sick months ago, Blake had insisted their son sleep in the hammock and not in their bed. Kris missed having her son with her where she could reach over in the middle of the night to assure herself that he was safe and breathing.

The compromise, though, was fair. Tucker took to the idea, happy that he didn't have to be in a room by himself. As her belly grew, she realized the separation was needed. Having a wayward foot kick her in the stomach during sleep could cause all sorts of problems.

Though tonight, she didn't resist him as he crawled under the covers with her. Blake softly snored on the other side of the bed as she wrapped her arms around their son. She didn't want to upset her husband, but her son needed extra nurturing tonight as he was being forced to mature so quickly.

Tucker hadn't talked anymore about the hunt, and she wouldn't push him. Doing something that needed to be done but didn't feel right was sometimes better left to the recesses of the mind. So, she would just hold him and whisper her love to him as he drifted into troubled sleep.

Kris, though, couldn't fall back asleep. Her mind kept going over scenarios, trying to visualize what their life would be like from here on out. If her baby was a girl like Tucker foresaw, would she grow up rough like this? Would Blake also have her hunting at six? What would happen as her children grew older and wanted to find someone to live their life with?

The questions wouldn't stop. They wouldn't let her sleep, and the baby within her rolled around and kicked as if she, too, was unsettled. Tucker finally slept soundly. She hated to disturb him, but she needed to move. Carefully, she scooched out from under him, settling him back in place as she crawled out of bed.

After a few moans and shifting, the boy continued to sleep, his snore a slight echo of his father's. At times like these, she was glad that Blake had insisted they sleep in the bunker. The bathrooms didn't work in the house anymore, so she would have had to go outside. As the baby grew, she had to take more nightly trips.

Out of habit, she tiptoed over to the surveillance cameras just to ensure all was well. She couldn't see much normally, but tonight the moon glowed brightly, casting shadows that loomed across their property.

Blake had positioned one of the cameras on the smoker. He had played with the idea of sleeping out to protect their meat, but he had ended up crawling into bed late that night. Kris understood. The bed called to her as well. She yawned and started to walk back to snuggle into that very bed when movement on one of the screens caught her attention.

She froze. The hairs on the back of her neck rose. The shadow moved, circling the smoker.

"Blake," she whispered, not wanting to wake Tucker. She couldn't peel her eyes away from the screen. The shadow didn't move like a human, but it looked big. Could it just be the angle? Maybe a raccoon whose shadow stretched along the ground from the low moon?

"Blake," she tried again.

Then the shadow rose to stand on two feet, its long nose sniffing the air. Bear.

"Blake," she yelled.

"Mommy?" Tucker called out.

"What's going on?" Blake finally bellowed.

"A bear's after the meat."

Blake shot out of bed and was by her side in an instant. It didn't take Tucker long to scramble up beside him.

"I'll be…" Blake muttered before striding to his clothes and shoving his legs into his pants. "Tuck, grab my shotgun and make sure it's loaded."

"Blake," Kris warned. No way would he take Tucker out there to face a bear.

"I just need his help to prepare. He's staying inside." Blake had read her mind.

Her lips thinned, unsure if she should be angry at him for assuming correctly or thankful that he didn't push the issue. For once, Tucker didn't argue about being left behind.

"You going to kill him, Dad?" he asked while loading shotgun shells into the gun.

"If I can," Blake stated without emotion. "Bears have good fat and a warm coat that will be needed come winter."

"We have blankets, Dad."

Blake took the gun from Tucker. "Those blankets will become threadbare eventually. A bear's coat will keep longer and work better." He roughed up his son's hair. "It's hard to transition to this way of thinking, Champ. Just try to trust me for now."

"I do, Dad. I do trust you."

"Thank you," Blake said, and bent down to kiss his son's head. He kissed Kris's cheek as he glanced at the screen again. "Just watch in case I need help for some reason."

"Maybe you should just let the bear be." Tucker pulled on his sleeve.

"I can't. He'll eat the deer you hunted. We need that meat."

"Watch your back then."

"I will."

Kris watched her husband leave, armed and ready for battle once again. Would she ever get used to him disappearing into dangerous situations? A shiver ran down her spine while she refocused on the camera screens. She didn't think she would ever get used to him putting his life at risk.

~*~

Blake couldn't help but wonder if his son saw something he didn't want to express. The thought sent a chill down his spine.

In fact, that warning kept him turning around and jumping at every slight breeze as soon as he exited the bunker. Getting to the smoker near the back of the house meant crossing the stretch of open land between the forest and there. The shadows on the camera couldn't tell him much. Having no idea of what he was stepping into sent a rush of adrenaline through him.

Blake couldn't say he looked forward to facing the bear. Hunting never had been a pleasure for him, and he had respect for the massive creatures. Yet, he couldn't have the animal taking their meat. They needed that meat to help them get through winter.

Kris always reminded him they had plenty of packaged food left, but they needed to extend that life for as long as possible just in case things became worse. No, he needed this bear. With that meat, he wouldn't have to worry about winter any longer.

Now focused, Blake silently stepped toward the smoker, where he heard the bear grunting and nosing around. Bears were scavengers. They would find the easiest food possible, and what could be more tantalizing than a smoking deer?

Once Blake was in range, he raised the gun, leveling it on the bear. The massive animal stood and sniffed the air, like it knew Blake was there waiting to steal its life. Blake stared down the beady eyes that reflected the moonlight. He had the perfect shot, and yet he couldn't pull the trigger.

It was only a youngster. The not quite full-grown bear was still large, but its mannerisms and fuller face gave it away. Had the bear just been kicked out of the cave by its mom? Blake couldn't help but think of Tucker while he watched the animal sniff the air once more and turn away.

Blake focused the gun again. He needed this bear,

young or not. He blew his breath out, his heart pounding with indecision.

That hesitation could have cost him everything. Just as Tucker's words echoed in his mind, a tingling warning shot through Blake. He shifted just in time to avoid the full attack of the mama bear lunging toward him. The move saved his life, but the bear caught him in the shoulder, searing claws biting into his flesh.

Blake rolled over just in time to fend off the large mama bear with the shotgun. Blocking another swipe with the barrel, he pulled himself back, sliding in the dirt. He needed to create enough distance to aim the gun into the bear.

Yet the bear rushed at him again, pounding him down with its front feet bouncing off Blake's chest like it was a trampoline. The air shot out of his lungs. On the second bounce, he heard the sickening crack of his ribs. Was this it? Was he really going to leave his family stranded because of a crazy bear?

Blake grit his teeth. While the bear reared up again, he scrambled away, fighting for purchase on the ground. The bear humphed and prepared for another charge as Blake fumbled with the shotgun. What he wouldn't give for his pistol right now.

Then he heard the shot. His pistol.

The bear heard it, too. She raised up on her back feet and turned toward the sound.

"Rrahhh!" Tucker yelled.

Blake shifted and saw his son running fearlessly toward the bear, releasing his arrows as he sped toward it. The sight left Blake even more breathless.

Kris ran alongside, shooting his pistol, eyes wild and belly bouncing.

She shouldn't be running. The whole thing

distracted the bear from him as she swiped at the arrows that barely nicked her hide. It distracted Blake, too. By the time he got his wits about him, the bear had turned and loped down the hill along with her large cub.

Tucker cheered, pumping his fist into the air. Kris smiled, but then her face fell as she met Blake's eyes. She made it to his side, searching his body, gasping when she saw the wounds on his shoulder.

~*~

Elation at having run off the bear only lasted a moment. Blake had been injured. Blood oozed out of angry slashes on his upper arm. With the way he held his arm across his chest and breathed shallowly, she feared his ribs had been broken, too.

She had been watching the screens with baited breath. When she saw the bear lunge toward him, she grabbed the pistol and came running. She had told Tucker to stay in the bunker. Yet, there was no stopping the boy, who quickly passed her lumbering jog, his bow in hand and arrows flying as soon as they were close enough to see the bear.

Having someone you love in trouble brought out the deepest courage a person had. She saw it in herself and her son. They weren't going to let that bear take Blake from them.

"What were you two thinking?" Blake rasped out, but he couldn't stop the smile tugging at the corner of his mouth.

"We saved you, Daddy." Tucker raced over to him. "Are you going to be okay?"

"I'll be fine." He grunted as he rolled over onto his knees and slowly stood up.

"You don't look fine." Kris took his uninjured arm. The weight of him overpowered her. Relief washed through her that he could walk on his own. Otherwise, they would all be camping out here tonight.

"Check the deer meat," Blake said through his teeth.

Kris dropped his arm, maybe a little forcefully given the growl he gave, and checked on the smoker. It looked undamaged and smelled delicious. She pushed down her irritation at her husband as best she could, but she felt resentment for the lack of appreciation for rescuing him and then being dictated. Sure, his ego had been damaged, but she and Tucker stepped up. That deserved some acknowledgement at the least.

A surge of adrenaline had shot through her as she pulled the trigger on the pistol. She hadn't aimed it toward the bear, afraid that she would miss and hit Blake instead. Just the act of discharging that bullet, feeling the kick of it in her hands, sent waves of confidence through her. It felt like power.

Holding a weapon that could stop something as massive as a bear gave her a sense of security. She could protect her loved ones, even as small as she was, if she had skill with such a firearm. Sure, she could shoot a bow, but not with the skill her son had and not with the force her husband did. With a gun though…that bear ran.

She still detested the weapons, but she understood the importance of their use now. Once Blake could, she would have him teach her how to use a gun with skill. If she could aim with confidence, she could injure rather than kill.

"Come on," she said with a new confidence. "We need to get that wound cleaned and stitched up."

Blake narrowed his eyes, but he didn't argue. His jaw clenched as he made his way to the bunker.

"If we had shot that bear, we would have had enough meat for winter." Blake's words sounded harsh.

Kris knew that he especially meant him, but she couldn't help the jab, knowing he was also upset that she hadn't actually shot toward the bear. "You can teach me how to aim, but after you heal."

Blake stopped, his eyes dark in the shadow of the rocks hiding their bunker entrance. "You liked it, didn't you?"

Kris pushed her lips into a thin line. She wouldn't give him the satisfaction of the smile that wanted to expose her. "Tonight just made me realize the importance of knowing how."

"Fair enough," he said, grunting as he lowered to open the bunker door.

"Let me do it, Dad. I know how." Tucker shot ahead, keyed in the code, and pulled the door up. Quite the feat for a boy his size.

"Thanks, Champ," Blake grumbled.

They slowly made their way into the depth of the bunker. Right now, it didn't feel so constraining, but safe from the hazards that lay in wait above ground. Kris shivered. Now safe in their hidden place, she realized just how close she was to losing her husband.

Reality sunk in. It wouldn't only mean a broken heart and a broken-hearted son, it could mean life or death for her and her children. Without Blake, where would they be?

She pushed the thought down just as she directed

Blake to sit. The lights blared to life, giving her all that she needed to see the extent of the wound. She swallowed back her nausea and her fear. The injury was gruesome.

"Tucker, grab the saline solution and the first aid kit, and then you should go put on your headphones and read a book."

"Why, Mommy? I want to help." He grabbed the items asked of him and came back to where his dad sat. Tucker gasped and backed away.

Kris came and wrapped her arms around him. "You don't need to see this, Sweetie. Go distract yourself."

"It's bad, isn't it? Really bad." Tucker's voice trembled.

"It will be fine, Champ." Blake's words didn't match his pallor. He handled the pain well, but right now it looked like the slightest breeze would push him over or he'd pass out before it had the chance.

"It's going to take some work and lots of time. Go read and try to fall asleep."

Tucker shook his head. He pulled out items from the first aid kit, laying them out like a triage nurse. "We're a team."

Kris watched him, reading the stubborn set of his jaw and the determination in his eyes. She nodded. "Yes, we are. Grab some towels." She turned toward Blake. "Do you want something for the pain? A local at least?"

He shook his head. "We need to keep those for more dire situations."

"I don't know if you have seen your arm, but this is pretty dire."

"After you wash it out with the saline solution, use

that antiseptic spray. It will kill off any remaining bacteria and numb it slightly. You need to sterilize everything in the suture kit by boiling it." He met her eyes. "Can you do this?"

"There's no choice, so yes." She wouldn't tell him her stomach wanted to rid itself of dinner, or every time she thought about having to sew his flesh together the blood would drain from her face, making her feel like she would pass out. Turning away from him so he couldn't read her eyes, she started water to boil.

"It wouldn't be the first time I've had to stitch myself up." He grunted.

"Great. Well, you can tell me about that while we wash this out then." She took the towels from Tucker and placed some under his arm and then held some against his arm, under his wound.

"Tucker, if you really want to do this, you can hold the towels here. Neither of us will think less of you if you need to go to the other side of the bunker."

"I can do this."

Kris met his eyes and nodded. Her son was turning into a little man. She didn't know whether to be proud or mourn the loss of his boyhood. Right now, she had to focus on the task at hand. The bear had done a number on Blake. Though it had been only a glancing blow, the claws had dug deep into his flesh.

As she washed away the blood with the saline solution, she was happy to not see any bone though she still wondered if the muscle would heal properly. She was sure that if he were at a real hospital, they would stitch up his muscle and then his skin.

She had no idea how to do that.

The water boiled on the stove. She placed all the suture equipment in a tray and covered them with the boiling water. As they sterilized, she blew out a breath. When everything was ready, she squared her shoulders and spaced her feet wide apart. She would need every advantage to keep herself stable.

"Okay, tell me how to do this. I'm assuming it's not as easy as stitching up a seam in cloth."

"No, there's a bit more to it." He took in a deep breath and winced, confirming her thought of probable cracked ribs.

"Well, give me your emergency suture 101, and I'll do my best not to make you look like Frankenstein."

"Who's Frankenstein?" Tucker asked.

"He's not important right now," Blake said, though he looked as if he tried to smile. "First thing is to thread the curved suture needle. Use the hemostat and don't touch the tip of the needle."

"Hemostat?"

"They look like scissors with blunt, grippy ridges instead of sharp edges."

Kris picked up the tool, which actually looked more like tweezers to her. "Got them." Her tongue slipped out of her mouth while she threaded the tiny curved needle. "Okay. Now what?"

"Start in the middle of the wound. You'll have to push through by piercing the flesh and then turning your wrist. Just one side first, pull through, and then in the opposite side."

Kris shook out her hands and blew out a breath.

"Are you sure you can do this?"

"I got it," she bit back. "You can't do it one-handed. I got it."

She glanced at Tucker who watched with wide

eyes. For once, he was silent. It actually scared her more than anything.

"Hey Tuck, why don't you talk to your daddy. Help distract him."

Tuck blinked a few times. "I didn't know bears attacked humans."

"They usually don't, son. In fact, I once heard a report saying that no one had died from a black bear attack for over a hundred years."

"Then why did that bear attack you?"

"Who knows? Things have changed. Maybe the animals feel that as well. It was a mama bear, too. Moms can get quite protective of their young."

Kris let them keep talking, but she focused on her job. Piercing her husband's flesh felt just as sickening as she feared. She swallowed down the bile rising in her throat, closed her eyes, and found the inner strength that she knew she had. This was their new life. She needed to meet it head on. She would do what had to be done to keep her husband here with them. They needed him.

She pushed the needle all the way through and then into the other side. Blake hardly even flinched. She had no idea how he did that. She would have been hysterical, crying and flinching and more.

"Do I continue like sewing or…" she interrupted their conversation about bears' natural lives.

"No. Each suture is its own separate knot. To make the knot, hold the hemostat parallel above the wound, wrap the line around it twice and then grab the end and pull through."

She did as instructed and pulled the string tight, watching it tug his flaps of skin together.

"Not too tight." He grimaced. "Just so the skin

touches. And then loop it around the hemostat just once this time and pull it through again. Do this a few times and then cut the ends."

Kris paid careful attention to ensure she didn't pull the suture too tight as she knotted the string. Tears threatened to spill in fear of doing something wrong and costing him his life or the use of his arm because of her negligence. She sucked the emotion back as she tied off the last knot on the first suture and snipped the ends of the string.

She felt like she had just run a marathon as exhaustion hit her. She looked at his arm and the one suture she had completed—one of probably a few dozen.

"It's going to take you until noon if you keep going at this pace. Start the next one. Do it halfway between the first suture and the end of the gash. Then the same on the other side and keep doing it halfway between until there's enough to keep the skin closed all along the wound."

Kris focused. She rolled her shoulders and prepared for the next suture. It went quicker than the first. And the third went even faster. By the time she had finished the second wound, Tucker snored from his hammock and Blake's head nodded. How he could sleep through such a painful procedure was beyond her.

Two more gashes to go. She stretched her neck, her hands, and rotated her shoulders. Just as she was about to start the first suture in the next wound, she felt Blake's eyes on her. She froze and met them.

"You're doing great, Kris. Thank you." His words, though muddled with exhaustion, held all the encouragement she needed to hear.

His words lent her strength and purpose. Her husband needed her, and she was able to do what was necessary. She slipped the needle in, and in no time at all she was tying the last stitch. Finally, she gobbed antibiotic cream over her handiwork.

Blake stretched his neck to look at the wound. "You'll make a medic yet, Krista. Nice work."

She didn't hide her smile this time while she bandaged his arm, feeling proud of what she had been able to do and praying that it healed well, that it didn't become infected, and that he would have full use of his arm.

As she cleaned up, she found an Ace bandage. "Stand up," she directed her husband. A smile tugged at the corner of her lips when he raised his eyebrows at her. She knew he wasn't used to be directed, but he didn't argue as he stood.

She lifted his shirt up.

"You know, if you wanted to undress me, all you had to do was ask."

"You're in no shape to do that," she said as she wrapped the bandage around his ribs. There wasn't much else besides time that she could do for them. "Do you think they are broken?"

"Just cracked, I bet. Maybe even only bruised. We'll see in a few days." He lowered his arms and tentatively took a deep breath. "Better. Thank you."

"You're welcome."

She packed up the rest of the things and put them away, avoiding his eyes. Emotions were starting to overwhelm her, and she was too exhausted to stuff them anymore.

"Hey," Blake said as he caught her arm. "You did good tonight. You both did." He pushed a strand of hair behind her ear.

"We could have lost you." The words tore from her.

Though it probably hurt him, he pulled her into his arms and held her. "It's going to take a lot more than a bear to take me away from you."

Kris let him hold her for several more minutes before helping him gingerly into bed. She kissed her son on his forehead before carefully climbing in beside her husband. He already had started snoring before she had settled. Though her mind swirled, once she closed her eyes, exhaustion took over. She settled a hand gently on her husband, feeling his chest rising and sinking. He was here by her side. Her family was safe, at least for now.

~3~

Blake growled low in his throat, sounding like the bear that had attacked him. He squeezed his eyes shut and blew out an explosive breath. Controlling his language took a strain on him. His wife and son were so sensitive it left him having to calculate each and every word, a fact that drained him further. If they were his men, they would have the full wrath of his frustration.

"Why don't we take a break, Tuck?" Kris wrapped an arm around their son while glancing back at Blake. Anger didn't flash in her eyes, but empathy. Somehow, that felt worse.

What he wouldn't give to be able to run a mile or do a few sets of push-ups to dispel the pent-up frustration and self-condemnation. Yet, just kicking at the rocks on the dusty ground sent his ribs into spasms.

"You need a break? Want to go for a walk or want me to try?" She nodded toward the deer meat they had been trying to strip and salt.

The chore took strength, one that his wife or his son didn't possess. It just tacked on another thing to the list that he had failed at. He should have been hunting and procuring meat for the winter. Now, he sat around barking orders at his family and getting frustrated when they didn't have what it took to complete them.

"I should be hunting. We need to be stockpiling

meat."

"We have enough to supplement the freeze-dried rations. Plus my crops are coming in nicely. If I am able to can enough before…" Her hands possessively wrapped around her belly, and her eyes wouldn't meet his.

He knew why. Try as he might, he couldn't be excited about another baby. It could take Kris away from him and leave Tucker motherless. Every time he thought about it, he broke out in a cold sweat.

"Anyway, I can teach Tuck, too. He's a fast learner."

"Yes, he is." He looked at his wife, her red hair wild around her glowing face. She always had made pregnancy look beautiful. "I don't enjoy being hard on him."

"There are different ways to do it. Between us, maybe he'll be balanced." She smiled weakly before her eyebrows scrunched together and she turned away.

"How often are they happening?"

"Huh?" she asked, pretending to be busy with the meat.

"Kris, don't pretend like I don't know what's going on. How often is the cramping happening?" His fists clenched. It was too soon. The baby wouldn't survive. He feared what that would do to Kris.

"More frequently, but I'm fine." She turned back around, her forehead smooth once more. "Just Braxton-Hicks. Nothing to be alarmed about."

Blake knew different. He knew that it concerned Kris and that they were happening more often than they should. What should he do, though? As much as she should rest more, if she did, no one would be preparing for winter and they would be in dire straits.

Without a word, Blake stormed out into the forest. Kris would be flaming mad, but it would be better than his mouth spouting off in ways it shouldn't to his wife. He needed to calm down and think. Panic only complicated and clouded the situation. He could figure out a way to help them survive. He had to.

~*~

Kris grit her teeth as she tugged the knife through the meat. Since Blake had stormed off, she had sliced into thin strips nearly three-quarters of the meat he had quartered and smoked. She stood to wipe the sweat beading on her forehead with her arm.

"Great work, Tuck," she encouraged her son as he salted the meat before adding it to the rest of the pile.

"I'm hungry, Mommy."

"Me, too. Let's munch on this venison that some fine hunter got for us." She cut off two fresh strips and handed one to Tucker.

"Thanks," he said, before taking a tentative bite. "I don't think I'm a fine hunter."

Kris held her breath. She had been waiting for him to open up about the hunt. "Why would you say that?"

"I cried when I shot the deer." He lowered the piece of meat and stared at it absently.

"Why would that mean you aren't a good hunter?" she asked, hoping he would keep talking.

"Hunters don't cry." He hung his head.

"I'm sure most hunters do after their first kill. I know I would."

"You would?"

"Absolutely," she said as she wrapped an arm around him and sat with him on the log. "If you enjoyed the killing part, I would be worried."

"Really?"

"Yes. It's hard to kill another living being in order to keep your family alive."

"Maybe we should just become vegetarians." He shuffled his feet in the dirt, still holding his slice of meat.

"Well, that can be an option I guess, but the meat gives us vital nutrients that we can't get from the plants we grow here, and it's something we can eat year round. We have to see it as survival food."

"Like that disgusting freeze-dried stew."

Kris laughed. The stew had been quite horrid, but they made Tucker eat every last bite. It's survival. Nothing can go to waste.

"Yes, Sweetie. Something like that."

He nodded, inspected his meat, and then tugged off a bite with his teeth.

"I'm proud of you, Tucker. It takes a strong person to do what has to be done to help their family survive, even if it's really hard."

She kissed her son on the temple before attacking the piece of meat in her hand. Luckily, the nausea had worn off last month. Now, she felt ravished all the time, and this baby craved meat.

Learning how to navigate killing their food was a lesson Kris had never wanted to learn. She watched her son with empathy. If hunting was left up to her, they just might have to become vegetarians. The baby rolled around in her stomach, kicking and pushing. Kris rubbed her belly, letting a smile crease her lips. Baby didn't like that idea.

The deer had been cut and salted and the sun sat low on the horizon by the time Blake decided to grace them with his presence again. Kris pushed the annoyance down as her eyes fell on his arm in a sling. The man didn't know what to do with himself. He had been injured almost beyond capacity, and she was sure he worried about all that he couldn't do right now.

"Time for practice," he said as a greeting.

Kris swallowed the groan that stuck in her throat. For Tucker's sake, she would keep it to herself. She hoisted herself off her seat, wishing her courteous husband who had spoiled her during her first pregnancy would return. Now, all she had was this stern, watchful man who scrutinized her every move.

The irritability grew as the day had grown longer, as did the cramping in her belly. She needed rest, whether he thought so or not. He had disappeared around the corner of the house, as she figured out how to state the words. Should she come up with an excuse to go into the house or just come straight out and tell him she was going to go inside and rest?

When he came around the corner with the shotgun in hand, though, she knew she wasn't going to get out of this practice.

~*~

"Grab your bow, Tucker." Blake nodded to the boy as he held Kris with his gaze.

She was exhausted. He could read it in her expression, but this was something that needed to be accomplished and now. Tomorrow might be too late.

"Come on. You can sleep in tomorrow." He did his best to grin, though it felt more like a grimace.

Kris rolled her eyes, but she followed with Tucker running at her heels.

"Mommy, wait until you see what I can do now."

She smiled and let her hand touch his slim shoulder before he ran ahead to put up the targets he had made by wrapping wild grasses together. The kid's ingenuity always surprised Blake. If things had been different, he bet his son could have had a lucrative career at just about anything he wanted. Instead, he had to use those skills to stay alive.

He pushed away the negative thoughts. Staying on task meant staying alive. Left alone in your head too long, you would lose your grasp on sanity. Another thing he needed to reinforce in his son. He added that to the growing mental list. How would he ever teach him enough?

"Watch!" Tucker called as he loaded an arrow into his bow.

Concentration settled into the boy's eyes. He held the bow in his left hand, pointed his feet perpendicular to the target, grasped the string below his nocked arrow with the two top pads of his fingers, took a breath in as he pulled back, and held it while he aimed. His breath rushed out and his fingers released the arrow as if he blew it to the middle of the target.

"Bullseye." He grinned proudly up at his mom.

Blake breathed a sigh of relief. He had feared that Tucker's hunting experience would cloud his desire for archery. It seemed it hadn't, as Tucker slung his bow over his back and skipped toward the arrow wedged into the bundle of grass.

"He's really improved," Kris said, her gaze still on their son.

"As you said, he's a fast learner. As his strength grows, so will his skills." He handed her the shotgun. "Now let's see if Tucker got his speed of learning from you."

Kris hesitated before she took the shotgun from his hands. He thought long and hard about which gun he wanted to train her on. The pistol would be easier for her to carry but harder to aim, and had a short range. The rifle was meant for long distances, and he couldn't see her sniping someone or something like that. The shotgun, though, could kill small game and whether close or far, would be deadly to an attacker.

Tucker returned and watched raptly while Blake awkwardly helped with his one good arm to get Kris holding the gun in the correct position.

"Now, the safety is on. We won't release it until it's time to shoot, but we still…"

"Never point the gun at anything we don't want to kill," both Tucker and Kris stated.

"Well, I guess you two do listen to me. At times at least." He chuckled, enjoying the feeling of the laugh even though his ribs caught with the action.

"When it's a topic I know you are more knowledgeable in, at least." Kris's smile made the jab worth it, and besides, she had a point. He surely didn't know everything. Trying to cook the other night proved that to him…and everyone else.

"Okay. Okay. Now let's get to business. The shotgun is a powerful weapon. It's most effective within thirty yards and uses a scattered shot, so it's harder to miss your target."

"Should I learn how to use it, too?" Tucker asked while peering around to see everything Blake talked about.

"No, not yet. It has quite the punch. Nestle it more in the crook, here." He touched the place between her shoulder and collarbone. "We don't want you to dislocate a shoulder."

He continued his instruction, and thankfully Kris listened with only one or two small eye rolls.

"Are you going to have me shoot it or what? I'm getting hungry."

"Me, too," Tucker added.

"I hear ya. Okay, let's shoot. Aim for that middle bundle. Good. Hold your breath and squeeze the trigger slowly."

The echo of the gun exploded throughout the land around them. Blake immediately stood and looked around. Why hadn't he thought about the sound of the gun alerting people?

"I hit it!" Kris's enthusiasm pulled his attention back to her.

"So you did." He smiled and squeezed his good arm around her. "Looks like you're going to have to rebuild that target tomorrow, Champ."

"Whoa, Mommy shot it to smithereens!"

"Yes, she did."

"Should I try another shot?" Kris asked, a shine of excitement in her eyes.

"I think we better not. You've proved you've got the skill and can handle it. Best to save the ammunition." He spoke the truth, but as he looked around once more, listening to the birds still protesting the loud explosion, he worried.

What if someone had heard that shot?

~4~

The weeks slowly crawled by. Kris became slower and slower as her stomach grew. She enlisted help from Tucker so much that he practically ran the harvesting and canning by himself, though she wouldn't let him do the boiling water part yet. Every time he got near the massive pot of scalding liquid, it scared her. A shiver ran down her spine with the thought of those consequences.

Blake strode toward them, walking better every day. He grasped a rake in his healing arm. The sign reassured her. She felt blessed that it had healed as nicely as it had with no signs of infection and that he had the ability to fully use his arm, as least as much as she could tell.

Blake had never complained, though she could see the lines etched in his brow when it pained him.

"How's the body?" she asked as he sat in the shade near where she and Tucker stood.

"Almost as good as new. In fact…" he paused and looked up at her.

She took the moment to sit as well. Her swollen feet surely needed a rest. Besides, with the news he was springing on her, she might wish to be sitting rather than standing.

"I'm thinking I'm ready for a hunt."

"Really?" she asked and shook her head. "I really don't think you should stress that arm or your ribs with trying to stretch that massive bow."

"Not bow hunting, rifle." He watched her like she should know the importance behind his words.

"And that means?"

"I will need to travel farther from the house so my shots aren't trackable back here."

"You're not taking Tucker." The words flew from her mouth before she could stop them. The thought of Tucker out there in the wilderness overnight without her...she shook her head adamantly.

Tucker stopped, a handful of green beans in his hands. He didn't say anything, but he watched them with rapt attention.

Blake cleared his throat, looked at their son, and back to her. "I would actually feel better if he was with you."

Kris blew out the breath she had been ready to barrage him with. Thank goodness the man had some sense.

"I need to travel light so I can carry the deer back, and," he looked at Tucker, "I need you to keep your mom safe for me."

Tucker nodded. Kris saw the mixture of emotions on his face: relief, hurt pride, and the protectiveness she had seen rise in him with her pregnancy.

"I will keep Mommy and my sister safe."

"Good boy. I'll set out before dawn tomorrow. With any luck, I could be back late that night."

"That would be preferred." All of a sudden she realized the implication of all of this. Her husband wouldn't be with them at night and possibly longer.

"We need the meat, Kris. I don't like this idea, either, but we're out of options."

"I...I can shoot another with my bow, Dad." Tucker stood tall, puffing out his chest and sucking in his lower lip.

"I'm happy to hear you say that, Champ. Can I tell you something?"

Tucker nodded.

"I should have said something before. I'm sorry. That bow of yours just isn't strong enough for a deer. The last hunt proved that. It had nothing to do with your skill, just the strength of your bow."

"I can use Mommy's," Tucker offered.

"Eventually, yes. Right now, though, your arms just aren't long enough. Maybe by next year."

Tucker looked at his arms. "Maybe when I'm seven."

"Maybe then."

"You're going to be seven in a couple months, Sweetie."

"Really? My birthday is coming?"

Kris nodded before the pain of another cramp rippled through her. She squeezed her eyes shut. When the pain passed, she opened them to find both her boys staring at her.

"Maybe my sister will be my birthday present!"

"That would be a wonderful gift," she said, thinking that if she waited that long it would be a gift.

"Tuck, why don't you go and see what kind of food we have that will travel well."

"I can do that," he said as he ran off to the task.

"Kris," her husband said in a voice that she knew she couldn't ignore. "You have to be honest with me."

She looked him square in the eye, though she still did her best to hide her own fear.

"Will the baby come soon? Do I need to stay?"

"I don't want you to go, but no, I don't think birth

will happen in the next week." She shrugged. In truth she had no idea when true labor would start.

"They're progressing."

"As they have for the past month. If I rest, they dissipate." She bit her lip. She wanted to tell him that he needed to stay, but she knew he would be like a wild animal if he did, especially if nothing happened. Which she did believe wouldn't…she hoped.

"This meat is important. We need to keep as many of those rations as we can in case…in case things get worse."

"Worse?"

Blake shrugged.

Kris knew she wasn't the only one hiding fears.

~*~

Blake turned for one last look at his family standing on the deck of their house. An unnerving feeling filled him, causing his hands to shake and gut to gurgle. Every part of him was torn, battling with the need to go and fear of leaving them alone.

He hadn't been away from them in close to a year. At times, he almost went insane with the constant presence and chatter, but being with them meant he knew they were safe. It meant he could protect them.

"Promise me you'll go to the bunker if anything feels off," he had asked them. "And in the evening before dark."

They had promised, and from the look in his wife's eyes, he didn't doubt she would. He half wanted them to just stay in the bunker the entire time. Yet, food had to be collected and the gardens watered. Work still had to go on.

For probably the thousandth time, he chastised himself for getting injured.

"We always come back to each other!" he shouted.

Their response echoed to him, a sweet harmony that would carry him through. He lifted his arm in farewell and then headed into the forest. Luckily, the fire hadn't made it past his property so the forest and meadows beyond were still green and full of life.

The creek meandering through the meadow had still been running when he and Tucker had hunted a few weeks ago. He hoped it still did. It was far enough away from his property to not attract attention to them in case there were people near enough to hear.

It had been strange when Marvin's group had left at the beginning of winter. They hadn't seen another person since. A strange pull tugged at his heart, but he shook his head. People only brought danger. Yet he wondered where that little group went and, once again, wondered if Hannah's dad, Arland, had taken his advice and if they had made it through the winter.

If he was lucky, no one would find their little oasis and they could live out the rest of their lives secluded on their property. Unless order was restored.

Twenty-year rations. That's what they had filled the officials' bunkers with. Twenty years. Would they really stay that long?

A deep curiosity filled him as he wondered what state the country was in. That solar storm must have been huge for the aurora to appear this far south. Had it cut power for the whole country? The whole world?

The thoughts drove him mad as he stomped through the pine needles and fallen cones. He kicked one of the pine cones, startling a squirrel who scampered away to scold him from the safety of a tree. It reminded him that he hadn't been paying attention to his surroundings. He growled while readjusting his pack and continued on.

Yet, once again he lost himself to ponderings. This time, he found himself corralled by a thicket of brush. Angry at his lack of attention, he just pushed through the bushes. The action caused a stirring to his right.

Blake froze as three deer sprang from the brush. Without thought, he raised his rifle and let out a shot at the largest buck, a two-prong. The shot echoed, reminding him too late he wasn't far enough from his house.

He swore and then swore again when he realized he had missed the deer. Great. Now they would know he was here, and it would be more difficult to find deer near the meadow. Blake crashed through the bushes, his frustration violent as he left behind destruction.

~*~

Kris had hardly slept. The bunker had been eerily silent and empty without Blake. Tucker acted nervous and silent. It played on her own nerves, which were frazzled already. The baby even moved more actively. Every time she awoke, sensing Blake's absence, she would hope and pray that she would hear the echo of his steps down the ladder and the pounding of their secret knock on the door.

It remained silent, and finally she couldn't stand just lying in bed any longer. She pulled her arm from where Tucker pinned it beneath him. Blake might be upset that she allowed him to sleep with her, but it had brought them both comfort. She missed sleeping next to him, being able to reach over and feel his chest rise and fall, reassuring herself that even if the world had collapsed, she still had her son.

Blake will be back today, she told herself as she started a pot of water for coffee…coffee she didn't drink. Well, she'd make herself some tea. She searched through the cupboards, the feat becoming quite challenging as of late.

"What are you looking for, Mommy?" Tucker sat up and rubbed his eyes.

"Some tea," she said, pushing herself back up to stand.

"I'll find it for you." He jumped out of bed and padded over to her. "What kind do you want?"

"I was thinking chamomile." She watched her son, amazed at how he and his dad could just wake up running.

"Are you stressed?" he asked.

"You've learned a lot from that herb book, haven't you?" She loved the fact that he wanted to read books that would serve his survival.

He shrugged and scourged around the cupboard for less than a minute before he produced the tin of chamomile.

"Thanks, Sweetie."

"Of course." He stopped and looked at her, then rested his hands on her belly. "How's my sister?"

"Super active."

"Maybe she misses Dad, too."

"Maybe, Sweetie." She kissed the top of his head and let him go. He tugged out the herbal book and snuggled back on the bed.

They took their time getting through the morning

routine and leaving the bunker. Part of her wanted to just stay within the security of its walls. The other part feared that she had even had that thought. As always, leaving the bunker and breathing in the fresh air settled her nerves, yet something still felt amiss.

"What's the matter, Mommy?" Tucker came up behind her.

"I'm not sure. Just have a weird feeling." She shrugged and smiled at her son. He didn't need anything extra to worry about.

"Probably because Daddy isn't here. He's been with us this entire time."

"It's been nice, huh, Sweetie?"

"Yeah. Though I do miss it being just you and me sometimes."

She squatted in front of him, no easy task with her large belly. "We will always have that special bond."

He wrapped his arms around her, clinging as if his whole world had crumbled as it had. She wasn't sure if she would be able to get over it, either.

She strapped the surveillance remote back to her belt and pushed herself up again. "Well, shall we do some more canning?"

"Canning, canning, canning." Tucker stuck his tongue out.

Kris knew that this new way of life took a lot out of her six-year-old. It broke her heart. "I have an idea."

Tucker stopped to listen.

"How about we just play in your room for a bit?"

"Like old times?"

"Exactly."

"Okay!" He gripped her hand and pulled her toward the house.

She laughed, enjoying the feel of it bubbling up from her chest. Something stirred on the wind. She stopped to smell the light breeze. Fire. Like the smoke from a campfire. Was Blake camped downwind?

"Come on, Mommy!" Tucker tugged on her.

She shook her head. Her sense of smell had increased like crazy with this pregnancy. Maybe it had become a bit overzealous and imaginative, too.

~*~

Blake hadn't expected to sleep out overnight. If he hadn't allowed himself to be distracted, he wouldn't have had to. He couldn't go back without a deer. He piled up a bed of pine needles in a grove of trees. The warm night air enveloped him like a blanket.

As much as he wished he were with his family, sleeping under the stars with a canopy of trees surrounding him brought a sense of peace over him. It had been a long time since he had been able to sleep in the forest.

His family was safe in the bunker probably hours before now. Knowing they had that safety allowed him to settle into the deep bed of needles. His body relaxed as the day's disappointment slipped away and he fell into a restful sleep.

~*~

"No, Mr. Dinosaur! Don't eat me," Kris said, contorting her voice while she moved a tiny plastic bug on the carpet.

"I'm hungry! I need to survive. Yum, yum, yum."

Tucker pretended the dinosaur he had tried to eat the bug but kept missing. "Hey, get back here, little bug."

They laughed while Tucker and the dinosaur chased Kris and the bug around.

Beep. Beep. The surveillance remote interrupted their playing.

Kris and Tucker froze, eyes wide. Kris's heart hammered.

"Maybe it's just Daddy coming back over the property line?" Tucker asked.

"Let's see." She looked at the remote and saw that sector five had been breached.

"That's the front gate. Why would Daddy be coming back that way?" Tucker said after he peeked at the remote.

The frantic beat of Kris's heart made it difficult to breathe. She picked up the walkie-talkie.

"Blake. We have a breach in sector five. Do you read?"

Only silence answered her.

She ran to Tucker's window where she could see their long driveway.

"Mommy?" Tucker's voice quivered as he pulled on her arm.

Nothing moved outside the window. She glanced down at her son, who had his bow in his trembling hands.

"It'll be okay, Sweetie. Let's go ahead and get into the bunker. Just to be safe." She grasped the cold metal of the shotgun and led Tucker to the door. "I'll take one more peek. Then we will practice our ninja moves to get to the bunker. Okay?"

"Okay," Tucker whispered.

Kris pushed a smile forth for his sake and then

cracked the door open. She saw nothing, so she opened it wider and looked back to give Tucker the signal. Before she did, she caught movement out of the corner of her eye.

She quickly refocused on the long driveway. A man stood there, rifle in hand, seemingly staring straight at her. With the distance between them, she wasn't sure whether or not he could see her in the crack of the doorway.

She quickly and quietly closed the door and locked it.

Flattening her body against the door, she squeezed her eyes tightly shut as if just her will would push the scene she saw out of her head. Her mind swirled with all the scenarios Blake had run them through. First, if at all possible, make it to the bunker.

The back door.

She grabbed Tucker's arm and raced to the door leading to their deck and the back of their property. At the door, she glanced down at her wide-eyed son and placed her finger on her lips.

He nodded, grasping her hand tighter.

She set the gun down long enough to ease the door open and then immediately grabbed the cold steel again. They ninja-walked down the deck toward the back entrance of the bunker. Before they rounded the last corner of the house, she motioned Tucker to stay as she peeked toward the driveway.

With a gasp, she threw herself against the rough wall of the house, her heart hammering so fast she thought she might faint.

Instead of the one man, a group of more than a dozen armed men slowly moved toward her and her son.

~5~

Blake watched the meadow, looking for any movement. Sweat rolled down his back from the heat of the summer sun. Another wave of nervous energy showered him. He kept vigil on all sides, trying to decipher where the feeling came from.

Something was about to happen, the instinct fired within him.

The area was clear. Just birds and squirrels doing their happy chattering and singing. Nothing seemed amiss, but the hair on the back of his neck prickled.

He wiped the sweat beading on his brow. He had run out of luck. Maybe he should just get home. If he left soon, he would be able to make it before Tucker's bedtime. A tingle of fear pricked his skin again. Yes, he should go home. He should never have left his family there without him.

Just as he stretched his leg out to rise from his brush cover, a movement to his left caught his attention. It was only a small flicker of an ear, but he saw it. The deer watched warily, turning its ears this way and that before taking a tentative step from the bush he hid behind.

Blake held his breath. Only a few more steps and he would have a clear shot. Carefully, soundlessly, he raised the rifle and set the sights on the deer. A fly landed on his finger, but he ignored it, concentrating only on his sights lining up for the kill.

Adrenaline surged through him as it always did

while hunting. It wasn't that he enjoyed killing the animal but the challenge of hitting his target. Besides, his family needed this food and the other supplies the kill would offer.

The hide would have to be used for baby clothes. The few items Kris had saved from Tucker for memories wouldn't be enough.

One more step. Blake blew the air out from his lungs in a slow controlled manner and then sucked some more in to hold it. His finger tightened, squeezing the trigger. The resounding boom of his rifle echoed across the valley. Flocks of birds flew from the tops of the pines and firs.

The deer fell.

A sigh of relief came out with Blake's exhale—a clean shot.

With a furtive look around, he rose, keeping aware of all his surroundings. He would drag the deer back behind the brush to gut it. The more concealed location would allow him to focus on his task instead of worrying about being a sitting duck in the open meadow.

He rotated his shoulder as he warily made his way to the fallen deer. Would it be up to the task of cleaning the deer? He clenched his teeth. It would have to be.

~*~

Kris squeezed her eyes shut and calmed her breathing. *Panic causes your mind to shut down. You need a clear head to stay alive…to keep your son alive.*

She inched her way back around the house to where Tucker stood, drawing in the dirt with an arrow.

"Is it cl—"

Kris slipped a hand gently over his mouth. Once his wide eyes met hers, she placed a finger on her lips and slowly took her hand off of him. Using the signs that Blake had taught them during the months in the bunker, she signaled that a group of armed men approached. Then she motioned to the back door and made the signal for a silent approach.

Every sound their steps created sounded like explosions to her. She kept her mind focused on her task and off running scenarios. *You must stay calm. Keep breathing.*

Tucker squeezed into the house, and her heart began to ease slightly. After silently shutting and locking the door, she slipped low under the windows to Tucker's bedroom, where she peeked through a crack in the curtain.

The group almost had made it to their house. There were more than a dozen. Mostly men, and a few women. Their clothes were tattered and dirty. They turned their heads constantly as if they feared being attacked. Maybe feared wasn't the word—prepared.

She couldn't see their faces yet, but it didn't look like the group with Martin. This was a new group, better armed and more prepared.

Tucker stood by her, readying his bow. "I'll protect you, Mommy."

She lowered to her knees and put her hands on the sides of his cheeks. "I love you, Sweetie. More than anything in this world. You want to know the best way to protect me? Hide in the closet hole."

"But Mommy!" he whispered frantically.

"We can't make it to the bunker. There's only

enough space for you in the hole. If I don't have to worry about you getting hurt, I can keep myself safe."

"Mommy..." Tucker's lower lip trembled as he threw his arms around her.

"I need you to be brave, Sweetie. I need you to crawl into that hole, stay silent, and don't come out until I come get you." A small flash of fear shot through her. What if she didn't make it?

As she opened the closet door, peeled up the carpet, and opened the hatch, she reassured herself that he would be okay. Blake would make it back before Tucker would die in there. It already had a survival pack with food and water, and Blake had fashioned air vents of sorts. He would be okay.

"I'm sorry I didn't see this happening. Maybe I wasn't paying attention. Maybe I..."

"Tucker." Kris took his face in her hands again. "It's not your responsibility to see things. You are given a gift when you are meant to see it. You understand. It's not your responsibility."

Tucker nodded, tears in his eyes.

Boots scuffled outside.

"We always come back to each other," she whispered and kissed his forehead.

"We always come back to each other." He nodded, bit his trembling lip and crawled into the dark hiding space under the house.

Closing the hatch on his wide, scared eyes was one of the hardest things Kris had ever had to do. She quickly replaced the carpet and scrutinized it to ensure it didn't show the hidden door it concealed. Then she silently shut the closet door, grabbed her shotgun, and let a few pent-up tears escape.

The porch squeaked as someone approached the

door. The bang of the knock echoed throughout the house, causing Kris to jolt and the baby to kick at the sudden noise. The pounding resumed before more boots approached and muffled voices spoke.

"We know you're there. We saw you. Why don't you come on out? We don't mean any harm." The voice boomed, loudly reverberating into Kris's head.

They had seen her.

So much for stealth training.

She hung her head, said a quick prayer for strength, and then stood to her full height. Intimidation. Act like the big dog, become the big dog. Blake had taught her many things, but the fake-it-til-you-make-it was hers. She knew how to play a part.

No way would she give them the satisfaction of mousing out the front door. She worked her way to the back and listened for movement on the deck. After feeling confident they hadn't rounded the corner yet, she silently edged her way out the door and ninja-walked on the deck toward the front of the house.

Just before rounding the corner, she stopped. Squeezing her eyes shut once more, she took three deep breaths. She positioned the shotgun in the nook of her shoulder, flicked the safety off, and faced the armed group.

"What do you want?" she asked, not recognizing the strength and tone of her own voice.

"Well, hello to you, too. Why don't you put that big old gun down and just talk to us?" the man in the front said as the rest of the group raised their guns of various sizes and types toward her.

"I think not." She kept her voice firm, strong, even

though inwardly she trembled. Something about the man's voice tugged at her memory, but she pushed the distraction away.

"If we meant you harm, you do realize that you are vastly outnumbered." The man cocked his head to the side.

Kris, stretched her trigger finger, replaced it with a slight squeeze, and said, "Sure, but I'll get at least two. You first."

"Spoken well." The man chuckled.

Kris blinked and focused on the man. That chuckle placed his voice.

"Arland?"

The man actually stepped back before cocking his head to the side again. He had changed, Kris noticed. His posture spoke of confidence and hard work. His voice commanded. She almost lowered the gun, but you never knew about people. The collapse had changed him and maybe not for the better.

He shaded his eyes from the glare of the sun behind her. "You wouldn't be Kris Chantry, would you?"

"What in the world are you doing, Arland? You've resorted to raiding houses? I guess my husband chose wrong." Kris widened her posture, now feeling more confident. Blake never misread people.

He folded his arms across his chest. "Put the gun down, Kris. I owe you. You have nothing to fear from us."

Kris hesitated. She didn't know if she could trust the group behind him to follow his lead. "You've changed," she said, relaxing her aim but not her grip.

"Survival can do that to you. Your husband told me that." He took a tentative step toward her. "How much longer do you have, Kris?" He nodded at her belly.

"A month at most."

Arland nodded and turned toward the group standing silently behind him. "This lady and her husband, The Survivalist, saved my daughter's life."

The others lowered their guns and looked around with more curiosity than fear.

"Where are Blake and little Tucker?" He glanced around and at the house.

Kris watched him. She knew she was supposed to keep intel to herself, but Arland was a friend, right? Don't trust anyone, Blake's words echoed in her mind.

"He'll be back shortly."

"Hunting?" Arland asked, leaning against the side of her house like an old friend just stopping by to have a conversation. "And Tucker?"

"Learning how to hunt." She kept her tone even. It hadn't been a real lie, which was good. She could never lie undetected.

"You can put that gun down, Kris. You're amongst friends."

She looked over the group. Men and a few women of various ages watched her, curious and eager. They didn't look like hardened warriors or people who have killed. Their eyes still seemed bright. Though many looked thin, too thin.

"Where did you end up, Arland?"

"We've set up a nice camp yonder." He nodded absently toward the forest beyond their back property. "We heard shots, a couple times now."

"Hunting. Preparing for winter."

"Have you had any trouble here? No marauders?"

Kris shook her head. Where was Blake? She feared she might be too trusting, yet a part of her craved for the conversation with another human besides her family.

"What is it like out there?" she asked him, wanting to believe she could see him as a friend.

"Chaos. Much of it has died down…and I do mean die." Arland watched his boot for a moment. "Hannah is well. She'll be excited I found you."

"I'm glad to hear she is well." She lowered her gun further. "How did you guys survive the winter?"

"It wasn't easy. Some lost fingers and toes, but we didn't lose a single person."

"Thanks to Laurie," a woman added in.

"Yes. We can all agree Laurie's knowledge kept us alive." He let his gaze drop to her belly again. "Speaking of Laurie, you might be needing her help soon."

"She a doctor?"

"No, better. She's a midwife and skilled in foraging and healing herbs."

A midwife. Kris grit her teeth to keep the smile turning up her lips. She did close her eyes and give thanks for the mercy she had been shown. What was the chance of having a midwife just showing up at her door with less than a month to go? Then reality clutched her heart. Would Blake allow the woman to assist her?

~*~

The fluttering of anxiety urged Blake to tug on the hide of the deer a bit quicker than normal while he field-dressed the animal. The hide tore, leaving a chunk large enough for the baby's shoe ruined. He pulled away the knife and eased back on his haunches. Squeezing his eyes shut, he blew a few breaths out.

Each piece of this deer would be needed for their survival. He needed to focus. Finish the task and then hoof it out of there and back to his family.

Willing his hands to still their trembling, he kept his mind focused. Expertly field-dressing a deer would make a better hide for clothes for the new little one. Tucker would need more soon, as well. Luckily, Kris had stockpiled several bags of hand-me-downs from friends in the basement. They probably had at least another year or two until they would have to make him some.

Flashes of horrible war images popped in his mind as he pulled the deer's entrails out. Images he wished he could erase. And people wondered why he didn't enjoy hunting. It was something that had to be done. Something he had to do before to keep his skills sharp. Now it was for his family's survival, and he would do anything to make sure that happened.

The sun sank low and would soon drop below the peaks in the distance. Blake stood and stretched his back, keeping his eyes constantly scanning. His shoulder throbbed and ribs ached, but he had completed his task.

Warily, he stepped out into the open meadow. He needed to wash the blood off his hands. The land had erupted in the cheerful song of birds greeting the cooler air. The mosquitoes, which had hid during the intense heat of the day, buzzed around Blake's head. He swatted at them as he crouched at the edge of the creek.

The cool water felt glorious, and he entertained the

thought of jumping in, but only for a moment. Need drove his movements. Something was wrong. He felt it in his bones, like a constant high pitch thrumming, making him jittery and shaky.

Next time, he would bring his family with him on a hunt. Kris would like it here. Picturing her, though, brought another wave of fear rolling through him. She was heavy with child. Even a short journey like this could send her into labor—a labor he had no idea how to navigate.

He pushed away from the creek and made his way back to the deer. Flies already had swarmed the entrails. He swatted at the few on the meat before digging out some paracord from his pack. It wouldn't be easy. The buck was a good size. He tied the deer's legs together in a way he could loop them over his back.

Carrying it like this from where they had finally caught Tucker's deer had taken a lot out of him. Now he was injured and a good five or more miles further out from the house. He thought of the trek back, the landscapes, the hills and climbs. He normally would make camp with a big enough fire to ward off predators and start the journey fresh in the morning.

His feet, though, itched in need for movement, and that thrumming urged him to get home. He didn't have Tucker's gift, but he knew something was wrong. Had Kris gone into labor?

Without hesitation, he flung on his pack and then squatted low to shoulder the deer onto his back. Removing the entrails had lightened the animal, but not by much. The weight slammed down on his bones and joints, causing his ribs to grind in pain. They had healed enough not to be damaged but not enough to be without pain.

For a split second, doubt at his ability had him falter.

A crow cawed in the distance, as if calling him to act.

Blake ground his teeth, took that first step, then the next, and eased into a rhythm he would be able to keep up. Memories filtered in, and soon he was too exhausted to fight them away any longer. He would go from knowing he carried a deer home to being back at war carrying his buddy who he knew wouldn't make it. Leaving a man behind was not an option, regardless the extent of his injury.

The urgency pushed him forth as he traveled from the present to the past and back again.

~*~

Kris bit her lip, indecision playing a wicked game within her mind. She watched the group who were now assembled in her backyard, lounging around, laughing, talking, and enjoying the reprieve. While she had given them each water, she saw just how gaunt they were. Some looked like just skin and bones.

Yet, they sat amidst her barrels of home-grown vegetables and next to the smoker that had just smoked a whole deer. Blake would be furious. His wrath would be like none she had seen thus far, of that she was certain.

She scanned the forest line, half-hoping and half-fearing he would show up right now.

The lower the sun sank, the more she knew she couldn't send them off. She had snuck inside once to whisper to Tucker that she was okay but the people hadn't left. Should she pull him out? It would show her as a liar, and she still didn't quite trust the group.

The thought of Tucker in the dark hole, scared by himself…She bit her lip so hard she tasted the metallic blood.

"You okay?" Arland walked up next to her.

"Yeah," she said, pushing a smile on her face. "It's been a long time since I've been around other people."

"Your family should join us. Having comradery is important. We're building a new community, one where we rely on each other and build upon one another's skills." He eyed her before looking back at the group. "The only skill we're missing is The Survivalist."

"The Survivalist, huh?" Kris's smile felt less pushed. "Is that what they're calling Blake?"

"Yes. He has made quite the name for himself without even knowing it. His advice saved lives, not just mine and Hannah's but over three dozen people. These families have become my own. A tribe of sorts."

Kris nodded. How she longed for the companionship of another woman. She glanced at the few mixed in the group. Two of them looked young, but the older one, the one who had spoken of Laurie, she looked to be about forty—wise, watchful, and she stared right back at Kris.

"That's Rachel. She has proved herself this past winter. She showed up, alone, starved, and grieving."

"She lost her family?"

"Yes. When society crashes, it doesn't care who it takes with it. We have given her a home and made her one of our own." He turned to look at Kris again.

"Would you come with us?"

Emotion filled Kris. It could have been her pregnancy or seeing people still surviving, still pulling together. The need to be honest pulled forth from her.

"Arland, I have to tell you...Tucker...he's here."

"I know." He nodded and smiled.

"What? But how?"

"I know the look of a panicked parent." He took her hand in his. Hands that had once been smooth and weak, used to pounding keys instead of using axes. Now they were rough, scarred, strong. "He is safe with us, Kris. We want you to join us."

Kris's heart hammered. She longed to be with people, have a community, and have children for Tucker to play with. She dropped her head, knowing the truth. Blake would never agree.

"What if we decide not to? What would you do then?" she asked in a half-whisper.

Arland narrowed his eyes, dropped her hand, and looked toward the group.

"You know I only met your husband briefly. He's not a difficult man to read. I know he prefers solitude, thinking that is what is best for his family. I get it."

Kris wrapped her arms around her stomach wishing it could be different.

"It's not, though. It's not what's best. Eventually, he will realize this, and when he does," Arland met her eyes again, "the invitation will still be open. Now, go get Tucker. Two of my men caught turkeys on the way here. We'll feast on meat tonight!"

Arland's confident steps set the beat of her heart. Could it really be that easy? She glanced back at the house, wanting Tucker in her arms. Then she watched the group again. All of their guns had been leaned against rocks or barrels. They smiled and relaxed. Surely nothing could go wrong, right?

~*~

Blake swore as he tripped over yet another downed tree. He hefted the deer off of him with a grunt. So close. Less than a mile to go and he would be home with his family. The blood from the deer mixed with his sweat, and the night's breeze passed through his soaked shirt, cooling him down.

He lifted his face to the wind that now came down canyon from toward his home. Thinking of home made his mouth water. He swore he could smell cooking meat and roasted vegetables. Breathing in deeper only intensified the scent.

He held his breath, and a rush surged through him. That smell of food did float in on the wind. He looked up into the night sky. The moon was almost full again. A quick thought of the bear shot through him but didn't stay for long as reality crashed down on him.

Kris wouldn't be cooking this late at night. She would be in the bunker, cool and safe, probably snuggled in bed with Tucker.

The hair on the back of his neck stood on end. His body protested as he donned the deer once more and took long, purposeful strides toward home. His property began just a few hundred yards away. Once he was there, he could use the walkie-talkie. He could hear his wife's sweet voice telling him they were okay.

Blake pushed through the pain, ignoring it and every other instinct except getting back to his family.

Once he crossed the property line, he pulled out the walkie-talkie from his cargo pocket without hardly slowing down.

"Kris. Back on property. Do you read?"

He held the device to his ear while he pushed forward, sweat dripping down his face. Nothing. Only static greeted him, not the sweet voice he longed to hear.

He tried again. Then again a few moments later.

She's a sound sleeper, he placated himself. She must be in the middle of a dream cycle. He would go directly to the bunker, leaving the deer in the entrance. It should keep for the rest of the night.

His self-talk kept his feet pumping closer and closer to his family.

He remained blissfully optimistic until he heard the voices. At first, he thought it had been his imagination. When he heard it again, he paused, held his breath and listened.

Sure enough, voices and laughter flowed down from where his house stood. A forest between him and his family and whoever held them captive.

He dropped the deer where he stood and ran. Heart pumping and mind imagining a million scenarios a minute, he released his pistol from its holster, crashing through the brush until he was within a hundred yards of the house.

There he slowed and moved more stealthily. The scent of food cooking caused him to drool even with danger so close, danger to his family. The cheerful voices put him off.

Maybe Kris and Tucker had made it to the bunker. Maybe those people camped on his property had no idea they were there. He held onto that hope as he eased closer and closer to the opening of the forest where he saw the firelight flickering right in his backyard.

He evened his breath, calmed his racing heart. He had to act smart. It could mean his whole existence ending with one wrong move. Surveillance first. Tactile action after intel.

~*~

Kris pulled Tucker closer. He sat stiffly beside her since she brought him out after she had spent twenty minutes convincing him it would be okay. Did he react this way out of fear of repercussions from Blake or fear for their lives?

Right now, though, she wished she would have left him in the safety of the house or somehow had gotten him to the safety of the bunker. That would have been a chancy move, though. It wasn't that she feared Arland, but she might have pushed Tucker further than she should have. Maybe she should have let him stay in the house.

She scanned the perimeter again hoping for a sign of Blake. Arland had guys roaming the edges of the forest *for their protection* Surely they would have called out if they had seen him.

Kris attempted to enjoy the banter between the people. She had longed for something like this for some time now, some interaction with other humans, other good humans. And they were good, weren't they?

Tucker's uneasiness made her uncomfortable. His wide eyes watched the people and then looked out toward the forest the way his dad had disappeared.

Back and forth. Back and forth.

"Tuck, it's okay. These people won't hurt us. It's Hannah's dad, remember?" She leaned down to whisper in his ear and kiss his temple.

"They're so loud. Others will hear. Dad…he's angry. I feel it." Tucker tucked his head into her.

"I wish your daddy was back, too, Sweetie. He may have handled this situation differently, but having contact with other people is important, for trade if nothing else."

"Like tonight? We shared some vegetables with them and they shared some turkey with us?"

"Yes, Tuck, just like that." She looked back at the crowd. "If things don't go back to normal, having people to trade with will be important. Some will have skills we don't have."

Tucker screwed his face up as he looked at her. "We're survivalists. We have all the skills we need."

Kris smiled and kissed his forehead. "I'm sure we do. Isn't it nice, though, to see other people?"

Tucker shrugged and watched the forest's edge once again. He gasped slightly and turned toward her, but right then Arland approached them.

"It's a lot to get used to, isn't it?" Arland sat on the bench next to them, looking over his group lounging around the yard.

"It's definitely different," Kris said, trying to push forth a smile, her mind still wrapped around what Tucker could have seen. He scooted closer to her when Arland spoke and wouldn't look at the forest again.

"I have to admit, there are times I would love to trade it for some peace and quiet. They're a good bunch of people, though. We're doing our best to survive and regain some humanity."

"I always wondered if people would pull together after events like this." Kris soothed her son with her hand. "Or if everyone would be at each other's throats."

Arland nodded. "I never really thought about it before all this happened. It was a struggle at first. We haven't been without our contradictions. We've had to protect our group a few times."

"Is it well-known where you are?"

He shook his head. "We're pretty protective. The Survivalist, I mean Blake, gave me the advice I needed to find an ideal location. Though there has been word about roving groups. Hence the security measures."

Tucker couldn't sit still. He squirmed and wiggled his way until he sat in her lap.

"What's gotten into you?" she whispered.

"Dad…" Tucker choked out.

"I'm sure he'll be back soon, Sweetie."

Movement at the forest edge to her right caught her attention then. Out of the darkness came two men, one with a knife on the other's throat.

As they slowly made their way up to the group, Kris could only watch in horror. The others scrambled to their feet, raising guns and shouting threats. She immediately recognized her husband as the man wielding the knife.

"Blake," she said in a soft warning.

"You can all drop your weapons now." His steely voice held barely controlled rage. "Kris, Tucker, inside now."

"Daddy," Tucker shouted and started running toward him.

"Inside now!" he growled, stopping Tucker in his

tracks.

"Blake, it's Arland. You know, Hannah's dad?"

Arland lifted a hand in greeting with a wide smile. "I told you to be extra cautious, didn't I, David? I told you the Survivalist would be returning."

"I never heard him, sir," the man with the knife to his throat whispered hoarsely.

Blake shifted his gaze from Arland to his wife to the group with the guns.

"Drop your weapons," Arland ordered his crew, who immediately followed his command.

Blake shifted his weight, but he hadn't let the man go.

"Blake," Kris tried again.

"I won't tell you again, Kris. Take Tucker inside now." His tone of voice left no room for discussion.

Kris seethed, her fists clenching and unclenching as she thought about repercussions of not following her husband's directions.

"Come on, Tuck," she finally said through gritted teeth. Once she had her son's hand, she turned toward Arland. "I apologize about the rudeness of our departure. Thank you for the turkey and company. May we see you again." She nodded her head and stiffly walked Tucker away from the group and into their house.

At the door, she looked back once more. Blake still held the knife to the man, David's, throat. A tingle of apprehension swept down her spine. What was he going to do?

~6~

Blake could smell the man's fear, a sour stench that made him want to let go. Yet, the man was his only bargaining chip, and he needed all he could get. His mind swam from the emotion of seeing his wife and son in the midst of an armed group.

Hearing that it was Arland made no difference to him. People changed when the world collapsed, and Arland certainly had. He could tell by the hardness in his eyes and the confident set of his shoulders. Who knew what his intentions were?

"What are you doing on my property, holding my family hostage?" Blake's words sounded as edgy as he felt.

"Whoa there, Blake. No hostages. We were just visiting friends, and we're happy that you returned before we left." Arland smiled, holding up his hands.

Blake didn't move. There was a hardness in Arland's eyes that hadn't been there before. The man had been working, and he had done things he wasn't proud of. His eyes told Blake that.

"Do you see how he's holding his feet?" Arland turned and asked the people in his group. "One foot in front of the other so he has time to react in any direction."

The quick turn of conversation floored Blake. He held one of Arland's guys by knifepoint, and yet, the man gave a lesson on his tactics.

"We've been working on learning defensive and

offensive positioning. Hope you don't mind being an example." Arland watched him carefully, keeping his smile spread widely.

"I see you acquired followers," Blake said evenly.

"I didn't ask to lead. I just wanted people to survive." Arland cocked his head. "Do you feel ready to let David go yet? I don't want him having a heart-attack. His wife and young children would be devastated."

Blake almost smiled, but he kept the grin in. He had chosen well. Arland had turned into the leader that Blake thought he had seen in him.

"You have nothing to fear from us, obviously." Arland motioned to the group.

"Why are you here?" Blake asked.

"We heard shots. Wanted to see what we were up against. I can't tell you the joy at finding your lovely wife, even if she was quite intimidating holding that shotgun aimed at my heart." Arland laughed.

This time, Blake did allow a small smile to tug at the corner of his mouth. The image of his wife eight months pregnant and holding a shotgun at an armed group made him want to go up there and hug her. His grip on David loosened, but he didn't release him.

"Tell your people to leave all their weapons on that table over there." Blake nodded toward the picnic table he had planned on setting the deer on before finding this mess.

"You do as he says," Arland motioned to them.

The group watched Blake with something between fear and appreciation.

"Why are they looking at me like that?" he asked.

"You're the Survivalist," Arland said as if it were common knowledge.

Blake grit his teeth, like that answered anything.

Once all the weapons were on the table and the group had moved away, he dropped the knife from David's neck. The man still stood there until Blake gave him a little shove.

"Go on," Blake said, still not sheathing his knife. He closed the gap between him and Arland and was impressed the man didn't move back. "They need more training."

"Yes, I know. You want the job?"

Blake watched him, trying to read any hidden agenda behind the question. Why would Blake want to make a group stronger than it already was? He could see that turning against him as time unfolded.

"You don't have to answer now." Arland looked back over his group, nodding for them to return to their conversations. "They're a good bunch. None of us are soldiers, but we do what has to be done to save our families."

"How's Hannah?" Blake asked, biding his time while assessing everything going on around him.

The group still watched him. David glared, rubbing his neck and getting jostled by his comrades. Blake watched him closely, trying to judge what kind of man he was. He might not have the skills, but that didn't mean his retribution might not be dangerous.

"Well, she's taking on the art of herbalism taught by our midwife…" Arland trailed off looking at him pointedly.

Blake grit his teeth. He didn't look forward to being the only one to help Kris birth their baby, but the implication that he needed help grated on his last nerve.

"At times like these, Blake, survivalist or not, you

need a community of people in order to thrive."

Blake looked at him closer, took in the gauntness of Arland's cheeks, the tough but slim arms. Then he scrutinized the group. The whole lot of them looked malnourished.

"Thrive?" Blake asked, an eyebrow raised.

"Winter was tough. We were caught unprepared. This one won't be as bad," Arland said with a shrug.

"What of news?" Blake had to admit he had wondered what others were doing to survive. How bad had the chaos become after he secured his family in the bunker?

"Not much. Societal collapse as you foretold. Marauding groups. We've kept to ourselves as much as possible. Picked up some people adrift here and there. Fought off a few attackers. No one knows the extent of the damage, but the rumor is that it's large. Too large to fix for quite some time."

Blake nodded. He knew how long the scientists expected the need for bunker security was. Twenty years. He glanced back up at the house in time to see Kris step away from the window. Even though he was proud of her for facing off an armed group, the fear of what could have happened, and her letting them all stay, and, by the looks of it, eat their food, caused a flame of anger to consume him.

Sure, he could send Arland and his gang off in a fit of rage and threats, but then he would have enemies out there, enemies that knew where he lived, where his wife and kid lived. Kris had better have a good reason to have met them, armed or not, instead of hiding away like he had told her to.

~*~

Kris finally gave up on Blake coming back up to the house. Her eyes were heavy. She couldn't keep them open any longer. Bed called to her...her real bed where Tucker curled up in his old spot. Easing in beside him, she wrapped a protective arm around her son. It was awkward with her huge belly, but she needed to feel him against her.

His heart beat rhythmically against her palm, soothing her. She had locked the doors, and Blake was out there. Besides, Arland had proved himself a friend, hadn't he?

Another yawn sent her pulling the lightweight covers over her. The feeling of her old bed beneath her ruined any last chances she may have had to stay awake.

She had slept hard, so hard that waking to the light of dawn sat her straight up in bed. Her heart pounded as she frantically searched the room and reminded herself of where she was. As she calmed, the quiet, happy chirping from the birds outside sent her back under the covers with Tucker, a smile now spreading across her content face.

How she missed waking to natural light and the songs of nature.

Before long, Tucker stirred as well, snuggling into her. She missed this, too.

"Morning, Mommy." Tuck's sleepy voice made her kiss him on the forehead.

"Morning, Sweetie."

He stretched and then threw an arm around her. "Is it exercise time already?"

"No, you can sleep a little more." Though she did wonder what had transpired overnight.

"Then why do I hear Daddy leading drills?"

Kris held her breath for a moment. If she listened past the beauty of the song birds, she could hear Blake's voice calling out commands.

As much as she didn't want to, she kissed Tucker on the forehead again and crawled out from under the covers to investigate. Her feet hit the carpeted floor, and she sighed. It was so much more welcoming than the floor of the bunker.

She tiptoed to a window that looked into the back property. Sure enough, Blake stood there calling out commands to Arland's group. Her brows squeezed together at her husband's sudden change of thought.

"Tuck, I'll be right back."

"Mmmhmmm," he murmured, snuggling deeper into the covers.

She locked the door behind her and made her way purposefully toward her husband. Several of the members from Arland's group nodded at her, but Blake kept his back toward her the whole time.

"Now, pair up and use those same techniques to disarm your partner. Use the sticks as weapons. No one wants to get shot today." Blake watched intensely at the group before him.

"So, now you're training them?" Kris whispered once the group was busy with their practice.

Blake didn't turn toward her, didn't acknowledge her more than a slight nod she would have missed if she hadn't been staring at him.

Kris's eyes narrowed as she felt the rage building up inside her. She tasted it in the bile that rose to her throat, feeling it burn.

"You dismissed me in front of everyone last night without even asking what had happened, never coming in to see if we were all right, or anything. Now, you have turned your back on us to train them?"

"You didn't leave me much choice. Now stop. We don't really want to be having this conversation now, do we?" His words came through gritted teeth, foretelling the animosity he felt, or was it exhaustion?

She could read the lines in his brow and the paleness of his eyes. How he still stood was beyond her because everything in his body spoke of pure fatigue.

"Fine, but I'm not keeping Tucker holed up in the house."

"Suit yourself." Blake turned back toward the group. He stepped away from her, kneeling down next to a pair of Arland's people. "Grab him like this." Blake took the man's hand and twisted it up behind his back.

The man let out a groan.

"See, now he's immobile. You try it."

Kris shook her head and walked away. She didn't understand her husband. She could read him, though, and she knew he hadn't slept a wink last night. The guy probably watched everyone like a hawk, thinking that at some point they would try to overpower him.

Poor guy. It must be difficult to always think everyone was the enemy.

Arland came running up to her just as she neared the steps to the back deck.

"Morning, Kris."

"Good morning, Arland. Did you all get any sleep?"

"Oh yeah. I think most of us slept well, though that man of yours kept watch all night, I think."

"He's paranoid." She shrugged.

"It's kept him, and you and Tuck, alive, though. Hasn't it?"

"True." She looked back over at her husband, trying to quell the anger that stewed inside of her. "How did you get him to train them?"

"Power of persuasion." He smiled. "In truth, I think he misses being in charge of a group of soldiers."

Kris watched Blake. He didn't look like a man doing what he wanted to do. He looked like he needed rest. No one else probably could tell he favored his left shoulder and hunched slightly from his ribs paining him. His shirt was caked in dried blood, something she hadn't noticed when staring daggers at him. He must have gotten a deer because she couldn't see any fresh blood or other evidence of new injuries.

"Miracles do exist," she finally stated.

Pain rippled through her, and she bent over, gritting through it. Another cramp. She wouldn't call them contractions—too inconsistent and way too early. After it passed, she panted for several seconds before she opened her eyes and saw Arland's offered hand.

"You should be resting, Kris. You're going to put yourself into labor."

"I'll be fine." She straightened, easing her breathing and pushing forth a strained smile. She felt Blake's watchful gaze and didn't want to elicit any further anger from him.

"I think I should bring Laurie over. She could help you."

The thought of a midwife coming to her filled Kris

with a lightness she couldn't quite grasp. The intenseness of Blake's glare, though, brought her crashing back to reality.

"I'm not sure he would be happy about that."

"I'm sure he would want the best for you and his child."

Kris shrugged, biting her cheeks in order not to let the tears escape. So close to having just what she needed, and yet the barrier of her husband's distrust in others would stand in the way. She knew it.

Arland laid a hand on her shoulder. "I'll convince him. You go rest."

Kris nodded, unwilling to trust her voice at the moment. As she took the steps slowly up to her house, she allowed a few tears to escape. It had to be a miracle that they arrived when they did and with a midwife in their community. How could Blake not see that as a gift?

~*~

Blake watched the men and women packing up their bags, laughing and joking while getting ready to head back to their camp. He hadn't taught them much, but maybe it would be enough to save a life or two should an altercation erupt.

"Thank you, Blake. If nothing else, you gave them a sense of confidence." Arland stood next to him, watching his group like a proud father.

Blake nodded. "Keep them practicing. When it comes down to it, protecting their families will give them the urgency they need."

"You sure I can't convince you to come with us? It's a great community of people with a wide range of skills."

"We have everything we need right here."

"I see that you do." Arland scanned his property again until he stopped, and Blake saw his gaze had fallen on Kris.

Blake grit his teeth. He never would have thought he would be jealous of a man like Arland, but he sure didn't like the way he kept watching his wife.

"Maybe we could arrange a trade?"

"A trade?" Blake growled, giving his full attention to the man.

"Yes," Arland said with a slight hesitancy. Then he stood tall and faced him squarely, a fact that Blake had to respect.

"What exactly did you have in mind?"

"You seem to have a great many crops. It's a lot for just three of you." Arland put his attention on the barrels.

Blake nodded, hiding the relief that rushed through him. Why he thought the man spoke of something other than food had him thinking he really needed that sleep now.

"And just what do you think you have to trade for some of our crops? As you can see, we have everything we need."

"Everything except what you will be needing shortly." He nodded at Kris. "I mentioned before that one of the women," he cleared his throat, "with me is a midwife."

Blake did his best not to react. The thought had been playing on his mind since last night. A midwife. Someone who knew how to birth babies, someone besides him. Then he locked the hope away. He had no idea who that woman was or if she could be trusted.

"I appreciate the offer, but we will be fine."

The shock of his refusal was evident in Arland's expression. "Then I assume birthing babies is on the list of your skills?"

Blake just held his gaze.

"You do realize she is having contractions, don't you? She said she has a month to go. These contractions are coming too soon." Arland rubbed his face with his hands, but Blake stayed impassive.

He didn't need anyone. He could protect his family. How could he trust his whole world to a woman he had never met?

"Do you have a flare gun?" Arland asked.

The absurd change of subject caught Blake off guard, and he nodded before he thought better.

"When it comes time, you shoot it off. We'll return with a flare so you know we saw the signal. It might take several hours to get here, though, so don't wait too long."

"Arland," Blake warned.

Arland held up a hand. "I'm not saying any more." He scanned his group. "Looks like we're all ready. Once again, Blake, thank you for your hospitality and your time to train them on a few things."

Blake nodded and shook his offered hand.

"You know where we are at in case you change your mind."

"I do," Blake said as Kris and Tucker joined them.

"You guys taking off?" Kris asked, and Blake hated the longing in her voice. He knew she wished they could go with them. They were safer here. She would realize that soon enough.

"Yes, but we hope to see you all soon. We plan to

have a harvest celebration in two more full moons. You are welcome to join us."

"A harvest celebration?" Tucker asked. "Like the Pilgrims?"

"Something like that, Tucker." Arland knelt in front of the boy. "You know, my daughter still talks about you all the time. You made quite the impression on her. She's going to be happy when I tell her I saw you."

"Tell Hannah hi for me, too." He looked up at Kris. "Mommy, can we go visit Hannah sometime?"

Kris looked at Blake, or should he say glared at him.

"There are other children as well. A couple even closer to Tucker's age," Arland said as he stood.

"Please, Daddy?" Tucker now looked up at him with those green eyes full of hope.

"We'll talk about it, Champ." The thought of taking them into a group of people made Blake's palms sweat. How could he protect them with that many others?

Kris gave Arland an awkward hug, the belly getting in the way. "May we see you again," she said to him seemingly reverently.

Blake knew her desire to be among people, but it wasn't safe. Here, he could protect them. Here, they would be safe…and yet, if it had been a different band of marauders and not Arland? Blake squeezed his fists tighter. He wouldn't be leaving them alone again.

He opened his fingers long enough to shake Arland's hand one more time and then wave farewell to the rest of the band. As soon as they crossed the property line, he would be able to breathe a little easier. He would be able to figure out why Kris had let them on the property in the first place.

Before all of that, as much as he wanted to just sleep, he needed to grab the deer, if it still lay in the forest where he had dropped it. He hadn't heard animals out and about last night, but some of them were sneakier than others.

He dropped a hand to Tucker's head. "I need your help, Champ. You up to helping to me prepare a deer carcass?"

"You got one?" he asked.

"Yeah, if it's still where I dropped it last night." Remembering the rush of fear that coursed through him at that particular moment had him glaring at Kris again.

"You act like this is my fault." Kris wrapped her arms around herself. "You have no idea what happened or how I handled the situation. So go on believing whatever you want. Just know I disagree with you on needing a community. You know where I stand."

She turned on her heels and waddled away from them. Yes, she waddled. Arland was right. The baby would be coming soon, much too soon.

~7~

Kris glared at Blake's back as he and Tucker disappeared into the forest. She had enough of his controlling, unappreciative ways. Not that she had a choice. She needed Blake. She sighed as she set the squash into the basket with the others. And she wanted him.

Her heart squeezed as she finally let out a few tears and the pent-up emotions of the last twenty-four hours. She had held onto her anger last night in order to stave off the fear. Today, though, she just wanted that feeling of belonging with Blake and with others.

Having Arland's band here reminded her just how much she missed out on with only her boys. She wrapped her arms around her belly, wondering if Tucker was right about her baby being a girl. The idea resonated with her. She would love to have a girl, even in the craziness the world had become.

"What should we name you?" Kris spoke to her belly. "Megan is a nice name or even Elise."

Thinking of her baby, she went back to work picking and canning her produce. The crops were producing well this year, of that she was grateful.

By the time the boys had made it back with the carcass and begun the butchering process, Kris's anger had subsided. In fact, she was still so wrapped up in thinking about baby names that she even smiled at Blake. When he saw her smile, he stopped, his face a mixture of confusion and indecision. It pained her that he didn't return the gesture, but she shrugged it off and went back to work.

During their fresh venison dinner that night, she couldn't help but bring up her baby name ideas. "What do you guys think of the name Megan?"

Tucker froze, his hand halfway to his mouth. He shook his head.

"No? Well, what about Elise or Alissa?"

Tuck shook his head again.

"What if it isn't a girl?" Blake asked, before putting another bite into his mouth.

Kris watched Tucker. The thing was, she believed him. He had been right so many times before. Tucker's fist clenched around his fork. He blew out a breath and then narrowed his eyes at his dad.

"She is a girl, but you won't name her Megan, Elise, or Alissa."

"What do you think we should name her?" Kris asked Tucker quickly before Blake spat out the words he looked like he wanted to.

"It's for you to find out." Tucker pushed back from the table. "I'm full. Thank you for dinner." He glared at his dad one more time before grabbing a book and climbing into his hammock.

Kris watched Blake. His brows scrunched together, and the muscle in his jaw twitched. He had a lot to say, and somehow Kris knew she would be hearing all of it before she fell asleep that night.

Sure enough, almost the second she walked away from the sleeping Tucker, Blake stood to meet her.

"Tell me," he commanded.

In fact, it was such a blatant command that Kris wanted to spit it back into his face. Instead, she went about making herself a cup of tea, silently calculating what words she would use. By the time she sat down at the table where Blake paced in front of, her anger was manageable.

"Sit, please." She watched as Blake followed her request. "We are in this together, so we are going to have to learn how to trust each other and be kind for Tucker's sake if not for our own sanity."

"I trust you," Blake said between his teeth.

"If you did, you wouldn't have treated me like a disobedient child."

"That's not what I—"

Kris held up her hand. Already, the conversation had escalated. "It's how I perceived it."

"I told you to go to the bunker at first sign of any thing. Did you not have the remote on you?" The look in his eyes filled her with dread, like he thought she was the stupidest woman on the planet.

"I had it, but by the time it went off, it was too late. We even attempted to go around the back of the house."

"So you just walked right out there?"

"No." She said the word in a hard-lined way. How dumb did he think she was? "There was no alternative. So, I snuck Tucker back into the house and hid him in the hole beneath the closet. I couldn't fit in there." She pointed at her huge belly.

"I didn't realize you had hidden Tucker."

"Well, that was option two in your plan, wasn't it?" Her voice bit more than she intended, her frustration tempering her words.

"Yes," he said with a nod. "Arland told me you met him with the shotgun."

Kris wondered at the slightly amused expression on his face but only nodded.

"Did you immediately lower your weapon when you saw it was Arland? People change. You had no idea what his intentions were." His fists squeezed together on the table.

"I didn't lower it right away. It took some convincing."

Blake narrowed his eyes as if he tried to detect if she was lying.

"I followed all your protocols, Blake. You have no reason to be angry with me."

Blake's hands fumbled on the tabletop. The grinding of his teeth made Kris want to cover her ears. It was like nails on a chalkboard.

"You know how I feel about groups of people. You just invited them to stay for dinner! Do you know the panic I felt when I heard them and then saw you and Tuck in the middle of a group of armed people?"

"I didn't invite them. They stayed. What was I supposed to say? My husband doesn't want company and I have no idea when he will be home so could you please kindly leave our property. Really? Sure, I had a gun...they had over a dozen."

"And you brought Tucker out of hiding!" he hissed at her.

"That was a judgment call. I felt awful leaving him in that dark hole when I felt like it was safe for him."

"It was a poor call."

Kris glared at him as she pushed off of her chair. "If you can't trust my judgment, then I suggest you don't just abandon us like that." She turned before leveling her gaze on him. "And don't you ever speak to me like that in front of others again. I don't care who they are."

Kris locked herself in the bathroom and turned on the hot water. She fumed until she didn't know if it was the steam or her anger fogging up the tiny room. The warm water felt heavenly pouring down her body. The tension eased from her muscles as she slowly relaxed.

A pang of guilt squeezed in her chest. Here she was enjoying a nice hot shower when Arland and his community hadn't had one in almost a year now. They only had a cold creek to bathe in. She shut off the water. Her anger had turned into guilt and sadness. She wished she could help those people. She wished she had other mothers to talk with and prepare with.

Her stomach clenched as another spasm caught her. She felt a wetness between her legs, and her heart dropped. Her water hadn't broken completely yet, but this meant the baby was coming and soon.

~*~

Blake sat on the edge of the bed doing his best to stay awake. He hadn't slept more than a few hours for the last three days, and it had caught up with him. He wiped his face and blinked his eyes. Kris had shut the water off ten minutes ago. Why hadn't she come out yet?

He didn't want to go to bed so angry. Not that he didn't feel justified in his right to be upset about her decision, but it never sat well with him to go to bed without repairing a perceived hurt at least slightly.

When the door finally opened, he looked up, his mouth already starting to form words. Those words faded when he saw the stark whiteness of Kris's face.

"What happened?" he asked, rising quickly from the bed.

"We have to prepare." She wrapped her arms around her pregnant belly.

Blake looked down at the large protruding belly, watching another ripple squeeze its way around it.

"It's time?" He swallowed, his throat all of a sudden feeling parched.

"Soon," she said after the contraction ended. "I lost my plug. It's a matter of days or maybe just hours."

Blake paced as Kris got down low on her hands and knees to search the cupboards. He knew he should search for her, but his mind swirled, pushing out rational thoughts. She rose with a few towels and placed them under the sheets on her side of the bed.

"What are you doing?" Fear tightened his voice. She had said days. Why would she be getting things like that ready now?

"In case my water breaks. I don't want to ruin the mattress." She lay down on them and pulled up the covers around her.

How in the world was she acting so calm? She would be in labor soon. Their whole lives would change with so many uncertainties. What if he couldn't deliver the baby? What if there were complications?

Yet, she snuggled onto her side and calmly closed her eyes. "Good night," she said.

Blake watched her in horror before the yawn overtook him. Maybe she was right. He better get some sleep, too. If the baby came later tonight, he would need to have a fresh mind. He tugged off his filthy clothes and took a quick shower to wash off the grime and carcass stink before he crawled into bed beside her.

He wanted to pull her into the crook of his arms, hold her and feel that connection that they used to have. What had happened to take that away? What if he lost her before he found out a way to restore it?

He reached out a tentative hand before pulling it back, turning over on his side and pushing himself into sleep.

Blake woke with a start, finding himself sitting upright in bed and surveying his situation. Kris moaned in her sleep beside him, writhing in her blankets. Tucker watched her wide-eyed from the hammock.

"Kris," he said quietly, laying a hand on her.

She calmed for a moment and then curled in on herself, wrapping her arms around her belly and moaning more.

"How long has she been like this?" Blake asked Tucker.

The boy blinked and then met his gaze. "She woke me up. Is Mommy okay?"

"How long, Tuck?"

"A half-hour maybe? I don't know. She starts moaning and then stops for awhile before doing it again. Is my sister coming?" he asked, dropping his eyes back to his mom.

Blake watched Kris again. She had calmed, her forehead smoothing. Maybe it had just been a bad dream. He should wake her, but if it was the start of labor, she would need all the rest she could get. He scooted to the edge of the bed and tried to clear his head enough to remember what all the books said.

They didn't have a bed with stirrups, but babies

used to be born in beds all the time. Plastic sheets, towels, water, his head swam. Where was that book?

He pushed off the bed and pulled on his clothes. As he slipped his shirt over his head, he watched the cameras for any signs of intruders or anything amiss. After several minutes, he glanced back over at Kris. She still slept peacefully. Maybe it was just a false alarm.

He tried to laugh at himself for getting in a tizzy over nothing as he started to heat the water for his coffee. Just a dream probably. Relief swept over him. He had more time, and he would dedicate it to memorizing that book from cover to cover.

Tucker rustled in the hammock as he climbed out of it and crawled into the bed by Kris. The boy pet her head and sang her a song. Blake realized, then, Kris had started moaning again.

Not a false alarm. He had to get that book.

~*~

Kris was pulled from the dream by excruciating pain that wrapped around her entire middle and settled in her lower back. She heard a strange moaning sound, finally realizing it came from her while she curled in around her belly.

"Shhh, Mommy. It's going to be okay. Shhh." Tucker's little voice filtered through.

A moment later, the wrenching pain eased off. She panted and focused on the feeling of her son's hand brushing her hair back.

"There you go. Just relax, Mommy."

She blinked open her eyes until his little face came into view.

"Hi, Mommy. Are you okay? Is my sister coming?"

Kris took his hand and brought it to her lips. "You are so sweet, my son. How long have you been here?" She sat up, realizing how weak she felt.

"Long enough that you have had four rounds of pain."

"Four rounds…" Her mind jumbled as she sat and swung her legs off the bed. A quick look showed that Blake wasn't in the bunker. "Where's Dad?"

"He said something about a book before he ran out the door a few minutes ago."

Kris nodded, doing her best to push the sleep out of her muddled mind.

"Mommy?"

"Yes, Sweetie."

"Why won't anyone answer my question? Is my sister coming?"

"I'm sorry I didn't answer. I'm not sure what's going on. I'll have to see how consistent the contractions are and how far apart. It won't be very long though." She smiled at her son.

"I can't wait for her to be here!" He jumped on the bed.

"Me, too, Sweetie. Me, too." She couldn't. Once she had her baby in her arms, she would be past this huge thing hanging over her and her husband. Once they were all safe, she knew Blake would relax.

"I'm hungry, Mommy."

"Okay, Tuck. I'll get some breakfast going." She pushed off the bed, holding onto the counter to steady her swimming head.

"It's going to be so fun having a little sister. I'll teach her how to shoot bows and walk like a ninja. I'll even teach her how to read."

"It'll be a while until she's ready to do all of that."

Kris smiled, trying to push away the fear of labor and focus on the beauty of having another baby. "At first, she'll mostly just sleep and eat."

"And poop. That's what Daddy said."

Kris laughed. "Yes, and that, too." For a moment, she allowed herself to worry about not having everything in place, like diapers.

"She'll need lots of care and love and..." Kris doubled over, grasping her belly, the pain ripping through her, stealing her breath, and leaving her panting by the time it finished.

"Another round?" Tuck asked.

Kris nodded, trying to catch her breath. "I need to track them, Tuck. Please go check the time on the cameras and write it down in your notebook."

"Got it." Tuck hopped off the bed and ran to his notebook, flipping it open to a blank page where he wrote down the time. "Daddy's coming back. I see him leaving the house."

"Thanks, Sweetie." She wanted to ask him what his mood was like so she could prepare. Instead, she took another deep breath, stood upright, and made the decision to keep her own peace no matter her husband's mood.

~*~

At first, Blake believed that maybe Kris wasn't in labor. When he had returned, she was up, making breakfast, and smiling like any ordinary day. Yet every few minutes, if he paid attention, she would stop her movements and quietly breathe. Like now.

When she turned back around, she acted like nothing was amiss. Her eyes, though, held a determination that Blake recognized. He had to admire her strength of composure, for every time she looked at their son, she would spread a smile across her lips.

The boy bounced around as if it were Christmas Day. Blake wished he could feel excitement, but Tucker didn't experience what Kris went through to bring him in the world. He had no idea what it would take out of her or how precious life balanced in the midst of it.

"Tuck, you're wiggling around a lot. Do you need to take care of something?" Kris asked him.

"I'm trying to wait until we go up top. I'd much rather use a tree." Tucker danced.

"I don't think your body wants to wait that long. Go on," she said, nodding her head toward the bathroom.

Tucker mumbled and groaned, but he went into the bathroom, sliding the door mostly closed behind him.

"I don't think he'll ever get used to that composting toilet," Kris said as she took his empty plate.

By his calculations, she should have another two minutes before another contraction.

"Why are you pretending like you aren't in labor?" Blake asked, trying to keep his tone even.

Her movements froze momentarily before she continued to wash the dishes. "Things have to be done. Might as well do them while I can."

Blake blew out his breath. "We need to prepare."

"I need to ensure Tucker can take over the canning for a day or two."

"Canning can wait. It won't go bad in a couple

days." He swiped his hands through his lengthening hair. What he wouldn't give for a haircut today. He stood up to pace the floor. His hair was the least of his worries.

"Have you decided where you want to do it?"

Her question stopped him. His eyebrows scrunched together while he contemplated her meaning. Oh…the labor. She would be more comfortable in the house, he knew that. Yet, if marauders chose that time to arrive, and given his track record that's when they would, he wouldn't be able to protect her.

"It has to be the bunker. You'll be safer here."

Kris's shoulders fell as she looked around the tiny quarters. "We'll have to put a waterproof sheet on the mattress. Otherwise, it will be ruined."

Blake nodded, mentally adding that to his list of supplies. "What else?"

"You've read the book, haven't you?" She had thrust her hands on her hips, her eyes glaring.

"Yes, I…fine. I'll just double-check with the book then." He plopped down into the chair and opened the book.

Moments later, he still felt the glare of her eyes on him. He glanced up, and her look of determination told him he was in for it.

"I need a woman, Blake. Can you add that to your list?"

"Sorry. I'm all you got."

"There is a midwife an hour's walk from here. A MIDWIFE! From a trusted group of people. Why won't you give me that?"

Blake swallowed the angry words that filled him. In her condition, he shouldn't anger her further. Yet, her lack of respect or understanding for his views made it almost impossible.

"They aren't to be trusted, Kris. Yes, it's Arland. Yes, we rescued his daughter. People change. Even if he still is someone to rely on, how do we know we can trust the others with him…or this midwife woman who we have never met?"

He stared hard ar Kris. He had started with his tone calm, soothing, but it had escalated. The fear in him turned into indignant anger, building and growing to the point he didn't know if he could contain it any longer.

Kris's glare burned through him. Her nostrils flared with each breath she blew through them. As her mouth opened, she doubled over and started a different type of breathing.

He wanted to go to her, should go to her, but the anger rooted his feet.

Tucker chose that moment to finish in the bathroom and enter the room. He immediately ran over to his mom and talked soothingly, wrapping his arm around her in support.

That should be him, not his six-year-old son. Blake worked on his breath, too. He tried to push the anger away, tried to focus on what needed to be done.

When the contraction ended, Blake stood and walked over to Kris. "You should be resting." He took her arm gently and led her to the bed.

"There's a million things to do before this baby comes, Blake. Are you going to do them?" She spat at him, but that contraction took more energy from her and the words were weak.

"I will do what needs to be done."

"On top of what we need for labor, I need diapers,

wipes, towels, baby clothes, blankets, my nursing bra, the baby wrap—"

"Kris." Blake swiped down his face. "One thing at a time. We still have a few hours, right?"

"Hopefully," she said, biting her lower lip.

Right then, Blake knew she was as scared as he was, and it diffused all the anger within him. He had to be her rock right now. She needed him to be the one who stayed calm, who kept his wits when the stress got high. There was only him.

~*~

Labor progressed much faster than Kris had anticipated. She hardly had time to catch her breath between the contractions. Tucker hadn't left her side. She didn't want to have him see her like this, but what other choice was there? They couldn't tell him to go in the other room. There wasn't one.

Blake thankfully had stepped up. With Tucker, he had been her constant support, doting on her and filling her with encouragement. Her mom had planned to fly out, but Tucker had decided to come early. She had missed her mom being there, but it had bonded her and Blake in a way nothing else could. She felt that now, as his hand lay on her head and he spoke gentle words in her ear.

She didn't remember active labor lasting this long. It felt like an eternity had gone by. Without the lighting to help decipher time, she really had no idea how long it had been, but it felt like a lifetime. As the contractions came and went and her strength waned, she picked up on the panic in Blake's voice and his hands shaking as he wiped her brow with a cool cloth.

She should have had pushing pains by now.

Kris closed her eyes, remembering the comforting sound of the heart monitor they had for Tucker. She knew he was okay by listening to the steady rhythm of his heartbeat. She didn't have that now. There was no way to know if her baby was distressed.

"You need to check me. Am I not dilating?" She pushed out with her ragged breathing in between contractions.

"Check..." Blake thumbed through the childbirth book.

He was reading when she went into the next contraction.

Tucker took over with the cloth. "You got this, Mommy. I know you can do it."

His voice gave her the thread to cling onto while the pain threatened to steal her away. She didn't remember labor hurting this much. Yet, isn't that what her doctor had told her. It was the woman's gift that pain could not be remembered. She sure could feel it now.

Kris went back to focusing on her breath and trying to feel her body and what was going on.

"Okay, I think I got this." Blake touched her face, and she blinked open her eyes. "I'm all washed up and going to position you so I can check. Okay?"

She nodded, feeling too fatigued to even talk.

She felt the tentative pressure from Blake as he did his best to perform something he probably never had wanted to, at least not in this way. His fingers pulled out.

"My best guess is that you are fully dilated, but the baby's head isn't entering the canal."

The news brought Kris to an almost sitting

position. "What?"

"It's still farther than your cervix, but maybe I'm wrong..." For the first time, Kris heard the unsureness in her husband. "Maybe you should try pushing?"

Kris nodded. It couldn't hurt, right?

Blake helped her up into a similar position she was in when Tucker was born, without the stirrups of course. Then she instructed Tucker to sit up by her head. He didn't need to see what happened down there.

When the next contraction came, she bore down, doing her best to will the baby into this world. Her body felt like it couldn't go any farther, like she had reached its full limit. Yet, when the next contraction came, she pushed again.

Her life became the pushing, the brief rest and panting in between, and back to the pushing.

~*~

Blake reached his fingers in again to feel for the baby's head.

It hadn't budged.

He didn't understand. His heart raced as panic flooded his veins in a fiery river of fear. He sat back on his haunches, watching his wife fade away before his eyes. His son watched with a look of pure horror. Had he just committed his wife to death because of his lack of trust?

He stood with a roar, controlling the urge to propel things across the room.

"Blake..." Kris's weak voice reached him.

He squeezed his fists and took the two quick steps

to reach her side. "It's going to be okay, Kris. You just rest now. No more pushing."

"The baby?" she asked, her words barely louder than her breath.

"Everything is going to be okay." He lied. He knew if the baby didn't come out soon it would go into distress, and he probably would lose Kris. Clenching his teeth, he bent over and kissed her on the forehead. "I'm going to get help."

"You're leaving us?" Tucker squeaked.

"You keep Mom as calm as possible. If she feels like she has to push, you will have to try to guide your sister into this world."

Tucker gulped, but pushed his shoulders back.

"I knew I could count on you." He cupped his son's chin. "I shouldn't be long. I'm only going to shoot the flare gun and wait to see a return. I'll have the walkie-talkie, so alert me if anything changes."

"I will." He took the walkie-talkie and clutched it to his chest.

Kris went into another contraction. Blake soothed her through it. As she relaxed back into the bed for her brief respite, he rummaged in the cupboard and withdrew a flare gun and his pistol.

Before leaving, he walked back over to his wife and son to kiss them both on the forehead. "We always return to each other."

"We always return to each other," Tucker repeated.

"…always…return…" Kris breathed out.

"Let me know if anything changes, Tuck."

Blake took one last longing look at his family, hating how many times he had had to do that recently, and quickly pushed out of the bunker and into the world above.

The night was quiet, as if it knew something was happening. He ran to the clearing, hoping the flare would burn out before it hit the dry ground. Summer was not a smart time to use a gun like this, but he had no choice.

He hung his head for a brief moment before raising the gun over his head. "Grant us mercy," he whispered as he pulled the trigger.

The flare burst into the air like a sad firework. As it trailed back down, a smoke trail following, he realized the slight chance that it actually had been seen at Arland's camp. Should he have welcomed Arland's help before? Yet, they still hadn't expected it to happen this soon.

Blake stared up into the starlit sky in the direction of Arland's camp. So much had changed. Had it been different and Kris been in a hospital now, would he be more excited rather than fearful? She scared the pants off him then, too. If it hadn't have been for the doctors, he would have lost all of his nerves.

Blake let his head hang forward as he stretched the kink out of his neck. No return signal. Nothing.

"Tucker, what's the update," he asked over the radio.

"Still going, Dad. She's getting weaker, though."

"Keep doing what you're doing, Champ. We're going to get her through this." *Somehow.*

Blake tried to keep the panic under control. He did his best to focus on the night sky as he prayed for mercy. He couldn't go through this life without Kris. Tucker needed her. He needed her. Blake fell to his knees, letting the tears stream down his face unabashedly as he begged for her life.

He became so lost in his pleading that the movement he saw at the forest's edge caught him completely off guard. Still on his knees, he raised his pistol, aiming at the two figures standing in the shadows.

"Hello, the camp!" a voice rang out as one of the shadowy figures raised a hand.

Blake immediately lowered his gun and allowed his face to fall to the ground. His prayer had been answered.

~*~

Kris panted. She didn't even have the strength to moan through the last contraction. She lost herself in the waves of pain, feeling as if she teetered on the edge of something otherworldly in between the moments of agony.

Through the haze between worlds, she recognized the sound of the bunker door opening and closing. Voices filtered to her through the thick thrumming air, voices she didn't recognize. A female voice.

A scent of herbal freshness wafted toward her as she felt a cool, soft hand reach out and touch her forehead.

"Kris, my name is Laurie. I'm a midwife. How about we get this baby to your arms?"

Kris mustered enough strength to nod.

"I'm going to check you now."

Her cool hands felt all around her stomach and then checked her dilation. She heard murmured questions and Blake's deep responses. Another contraction ripped through her, leaving her to the point she thought she had lost all sanity.

"Kris," Laurie said. "We need to reposition you. I need you to get up on your hands and knees. Do you think you can do that?"

Kris shook her head. "I...can't...I'm done...save the baby..."

"You can, Mommy. You can do this."

"Come on, Krista. I know you're exhausted. You've got more mountain to climb," Blake whispered into her ear.

Kris shook her head, her body refusing to move. Her grip on this world quickly faded.

"You name her Mercy," Tucker said so closely she could feel the warmth of his breath on her ear. "I saw you. You held her. She has red hair like you and green eyes like me and Daddy. So you see, I know you make it. I know you can do this."

Kris clung to her son's words. Her beautiful, gifted son. Tears leaked through her tightly closed lids. Mercy. She would give Tucker his sister. God was granting her Mercy, in a way she never thought.

She drew in a deep breath, grit her teeth and rolled over to her hands and knees. Hands helped her into position, right as another contraction hit.

"Now push, Kris. Give it everything." The midwife encouraged while she pushed, prodded, and manipulated Kris.

As Kris rested, the midwife checked her. "We have movement!"

The bunker erupted in cheers, and it gave Kris strength. The feeling flooded her as a gift granted, not one she pulled from within, but one given, infused with the love from everyone surrounding her.

With the next contraction, she pushed even harder, knowing that she could do this, knowing that soon she would be holding that baby in her arms—Mercy.

~*~

Blake hadn't believed his eyes when Arland and the midwife had stepped from out the forest. After rising from his gratitude, he had ran to them, the question leaving his mouth before any sort of greeting.

"How?"

"As soon as I told Laurie of Kris's condition, she packed up and said we needed to come right away," Arland had told him.

"You're just in time. She's been in labor for almost twenty-four hours." He turned, expecting them to follow him. "Something isn't right. The baby hasn't dropped into the birth canal."

He hadn't thought about revealing the bunker to them. His attention had been so focused on getting Kris the help she needed and grateful it had been so close. It wasn't until they stood at the rock outcropping and both Arland and Laurie stopped talking abruptly.

"I should have known you had a bunker." Arland patted his back.

The rush of fear that had overtaken Blake must have caused a change in his expression, because Arland immediately reassured him.

"Your secret is safe. No one will know about it. It won't go beyond Laurie and myself." Arland looked to Laurie, who nodded.

"Let's just worry about your wife and bring that baby into the world," Laurie said, touching his arm.

With the mention of Kris, Blake had pushed his misgivings behind him.

The memory played in him while he watched the midwife, Laurie, work with Kris. Watching her assured movements and hearing her calm yet authoritative tone took the pressure off him. He knew he had done the right thing by bringing her here. Labor already progressed, the baby's head even showed down below.

"We're almost there, Kris. A few more pushes and you'll be holding your baby," Laurie soothed his wife.

He repositioned himself to take more of Kris's weight. He leaned down to whisper in her ear.

"You have more grit than anyone I have ever known. You can do this." He kissed her head, overcome with emotion. "I love you, Krista."

She nodded, her panting unable to produce words.

"Let's get her into a more upright position. Blake, you will need to take most of her weight."

Blake positioned himself in front of Kris.

"Have her put her hands on your shoulders so she is kneeling but pressing on you with her upper body."

Blake helped Kris into position. Feeling her weight on him was reassuring.

"Good. Okay, Kris. These last couple pushes will be the ones," Laurie encouraged.

As another contraction came, Kris bored down on him. She turned so red that he feared she would pass out. Instead, she let out a cry of pure strain and effort. One that seemed to say, *I will do this*!

With that push, Blake craned his neck so he could see the baby's head. He dropped his forehead to Kris's. "I'm so proud of you. You're doing this. Our baby is almost here."

The next push did it. The baby dropped into Laurie's hands. Kris panted and cried in his arms. He let the tears stream down his face, too. She made it. She did it. Kris brought their baby into this world…this post-apocalyptic, no hospitals, no doctor world.

Yet, the baby didn't cry.

The realization hit him like a bullet to his chest. He hugged Kris tighter to him while frantically looking toward the limp baby in the midwife's arms.

Laurie quickly unwrapped the cord wound around the infant's neck. The baby's skin, blue instead of pink, made Blake's blood run cold. He didn't want to say anything. Didn't want Kris to know.

Laurie cleared the baby's mouth and pressed gently down on the tiny chest.

Come on. Come on, Blake inwardly chanted.

Tucker stepped up to the still infant.

"That's my sister," he said in awe.

"Honey…" the midwife started.

Kris writhed in his arms. "Why isn't she crying?" When she laid eyes on the tiny infant, blue and still, she broke down in wracking sobs.

"Wake up, Sister. Mommy needs you now. Wake up." Tucker bent down and kissed her forehead.

At the moment he pulled away, the baby's eyes blinked open wide and then squinted. Her little fists began twitching until they beat the air. Then the bunker echoed in her squall of protest.

Kris stopped crying, rubbed her eyes, and then reached for their daughter. He had a daughter! A beautiful little girl.

Kris nestled their baby into her arms, holding her close and whispering soothing sounds.

"Oh, thank goodness," Arland whispered, drawing Blake's attention to him. He had forgotten the man was there in the dark recess of the bunker, his face pale but eyes steely.

"Here comes the afterbirth," the midwife said, but Kris hardly even scrunched her brow with the pain of the last push.

Laurie kept busy taking care of things and ensuring Kris didn't need stitches or anything else. Blake hardly paid attention. His wife and his daughter enamored him. When Tuck came up to be a part of the first family meeting, Blake wrapped an arm around him.

"You were right, Champ. Look at your miraculous little sister."

"I told you. Next time, you'll believe me."

"Yes, Tuck." He kissed the boy's head. "Next time I will believe you."

Blake saw Laurie watching them. He knew that she now would not only know where their bunker was, but also that his son had a gift. A tingle ran down his spine, but he pushed it away and instead lost himself in his daughter's open, curious eyes.

~*~

Kris couldn't believe she held her daughter in her arms. Thankfully, she had attached right away and nursed like a champ, eager and relentless. Just like her brother. She kissed her daughter's head, breathing in her scent and memorizing it.

Tucker lay next to her, curled up with his hand wrapped around his sister's little foot. Even when she kicked and punched the air, she kept that one foot still, as if she needed the contact with her brother as much as he did.

A tear slipped from Kris's eye. The bond between them already had grown. A bond they would need to survive this new world...together.

She looked up into Blake's eyes while he watched her. He had hardly moved since their daughter arrived. He had fallen in love with her already. A smile curled Kris's lips. What a daddy's little girl she would be. She would find the weakness in this big tough guy she had promised to spend the rest of her life with.

He bent down and kissed her. A kiss that spoke to Kris in ways words could never touch. All anger and resentment disappeared. They would start fresh today. Build this new life together. Now a family of four.

The midwife washed at the counter, meticulously cleaning all the items used in the process. She had taken the soiled sheet and replaced it with layers of towels. The water boiled on the stove, and she dropped in some herbs before replacing the cover.

Arland walked over to her then, letting his hands rest and massage her shoulders. Laurie leaned back into him. In that moment, Kris realized Arland had found love once again. The thought warmed her heart as she refocused on her little miracle.

When Arland came over, he slapped Blake on the shoulder and then touched their daughter's little fist. "Have you decided what to name her?"

Kris gazed down into her daughter's wide eyes, eyes that seemed to hold all the knowledge of the world and beyond. Wise, old-soul eyes. Kris leveled her gaze with Blake's. Then she looked back down at her daughter.

"Her name is Mercy. Mercy Grace Chantry." She

had asked to be granted mercy, and now, she had. She held Mercy in her arms. Life would be changed forever. It wouldn't be easy surviving with an infant, and yet the little girl in her arms filled her with peace. A peace stronger than fear. A peace that would give them strength to thrive in this new world. A peace that granted them Mercy.

****

INSTALLMENT FOUR

~1~

DATE: September 21   11:06

Mercy was the miracle that they had needed. As much as Blake would never admit that out loud, he felt it, especially during moments like right now as he held her and her little hand reached up to touch his face. These last few months had been a challenge to say the least. Having an infant in the middle of a post-apocalyptic world was probably the hardest assignment he had ever faced.

Mercy cooed and gurgled, happily kicking her feet and telling him everything she thought.

"Oh, really?" he asked, letting her chubby hand clasp around his finger.

"Is my sister talking again?" Tucker ran up to them.

Mercy let go of Blake's finger and started kicking her legs and waving her arms in excitement. That little girl loved her big brother, and he was infatuated with her.

"Hi, little sis. Are you ready for your first journey?" Tucker asked.

The reminder made Blake tense, his body going rigid with the idea of bringing his family into a group setting. He questioned his sanity when he agreed to take them to Arland's community for their harvest celebration.

Mercy's face scrunched as she became still and made a different sound, something low and grumbly.

"Oh, that's a new one," Blake said. "I'm not sure she's happy about this trip."

"It's okay, sister. I will protect you." Tucker leaned over and kissed her cheek.

"We'll be fine," Kris said with a happy lilt to her voice.

Blake looked up from his children to see his radiant wife. She looked like she had never been pregnant. Yet, that fateful day she gave birth had shifted something in him. Understanding of what his life would be like without her dawned upon him, and he didn't like it. He wouldn't want to live this life without her. Once again, Kris's amazing strength of mind and willpower left him in awe as she pulled through. If he had been in that situation, could he have pushed on like she had?

Then, with Mercy being born not moving and the kiss of her big brother causing her to take that first breath…Blake shook his head. It was nothing short of a miracle—a true granting of Mercy.

It had reinstated his faith, and he would do what he needed to pass that on to his children.

~*~

Kris watched the mixture of emotions cross Blake's features. She knew he had misgivings about today, but a promise was a promise. It was the least they could do to show their gratitude to Arland and Laurie, for without them, she and her sweet girl might not be here.

"Come to Mommy," she said as she lifted Mercy

from Blake's arms.

The look on Blake's face showed his disappointment of no longer holding his treasured daughter. He laid a hand on Tucker's shoulder instead, and smiled down at the boy.

"Do you have everything, big brother?" Blake asked their son while she situated Mercy.

"Yep, got my sling. I'm getting really good at it!" He held it up before stuffing it into the pouch he had started wearing anytime he went outside. "My bow and quiver are over there with my pack, just in case we see some things to hunt on the way. And," he patted his thigh, "my knife that you gave me for my birthday, as always, is right here."

Her son looked like a mini-version of her husband. He had spent more time with Blake since she had Mercy. The changes in Tucker showed in his confident strut as he did his best to emulate his dad. Part of her heart ached knowing she was losing her sweet little boy. The other part of her knew the change would benefit his survival. It was just so hard to let go.

"I'm proud of you, son. You have been providing your family with meat." Blake ruffled his hair.

"I try, Dad." However, a shadow filled his eyes.

Kris knew that Tucker still did not enjoy taking the life of animals, but he did his best to embrace his new role in the family. He had brought home several squirrels and rabbits now. Not only did he provide meat but moccasins for his sister, and Kris worked on a pair for Tucker as well. His poor toes were jammed in his boots, and the soles wouldn't hold up much longer. As it was, they were held together by twine.

She fit Mercy into the wrap, holding her close to

her body. When Blake had found the baby wrap and cloth diapers stuffed in the attic right after Mercy was born, Kris had been overcome with gratitude. She thought they had gotten rid of them after Tucker had no longer needed the baby items. That one find changed their situation from surviving to thriving.

Wearing her daughter like this, she could do everything she used to. In fact, Kris was more productive than she had been the months before her delivery. She shouldered her bag and adjusted it. With Mercy growing, the weight she carried increased, but her strength did as well.

The trip to Arland's camp was about five miles of up-and-down hiking through forests and meadows. It would take them most of the morning to get there. Tucker's endurance had increased with their little forays out into the forests to hunt, so she hoped it wouldn't be too exhausting for him. She wanted him to have energy to play with the other kids.

They now hunted as a family. According to Blake, that wouldn't change if it could be helped. His last solo hunt, when he returned to find her and Tucker in the situation he perceived as a threat, left him scarred. He had clung tightly to them ever since. Rather than it being overbearing, they had settled into a comfortable, cohesive family. That brought peace to Kris.

She knew enough about life and marriage to know that this honeymoon period wouldn't last, but she sure would enjoy it while it did.

Blake checked his pack for the second time. Part of her wondered if today would push him past his threshold, and she might see her grace period fade away. The set of his jaw definitely warned her it might be so.

Yet, when he looked up and caught her stare, he smiled.

The worry in her melted away. Mercy cooed and snuggled in. Tucker reached up and took her hand. He wore his backpack and had his bow slung over his shoulder. Everything would be fine.

"Ready, Mom?"

When did he stop calling her Mommy? It tore at her heart a little, but she still smiled down at him.

"Ready, Sweetie."

Blake scanned their property one last time.

"We're not leaving forever, Blake. Just for one night." Kris wrapped her free hand around his arm and leaned into him.

He reached around and pulled her and Tucker into a family hug that encompassed Mercy.

"I don't like this. You know that. Everything we have is here." Blake squeezed them before letting go and donning his own, very heavy-looking backpack.

"It will be here when we get back, Dad." Tucker took his hand.

Kris shook off the feeling Tucker had more to say about that. Sometimes she wished he had never realized his gift. It was a heavy burden for her now seven-year-old to carry. When he looked up at her, that sad, faraway expression had faded away, and he smiled. Hopefully seeing other children would remind him of how to be a kid.

Excitement bubbled up in Kris. She couldn't wait to see Tucker playing carefree with other kids and to show off Mercy to Laurie. The midwife had come for a visit six weeks ago with gifts of herbs to help milk production and some ideas for natural absorption for diapers. Her timing had been impeccable, just like with the delivery. She wondered if Laurie had a gift as well.

It was during this visit that Arland convinced Blake to come to their festival. Kris had overheard the conversation and choked on her food when she heard Blake say they would go. Laurie then had told her about her son, soon to turn four, and the other children at the camp. Would Tucker remember how to just be a kid? It had been a year since he had that chance.

~*~

The closer to Arland's camp they came, the tenser Blake felt. He was walking his family into an unknown situation. What had he been thinking? Just because Arland and Laurie had proven themselves didn't mean this camp would be safe for them.

He glanced back at Tucker. The boy had pushed through. With less than a mile to go, his face held a determined expression, but Blake could see the exhaustion in his movements. He needed Tucker at his best when they arrived.

"Let's take one last break before we get there." Blake stopped at a rock pile and released his pack from his aching shoulders. Kris had insisted they bring the last of their fall squash to add to the celebration. Right now, he wished her sweet smile hadn't convinced him to pack them into his bag.

He took Tucker's pack off as well and set it against the rocks. Kris leaned against a rock and loosened her straps to lower hers off her shoulders. His wife continually impressed him with all she bore. He couldn't take his eyes off her, enthralled with the graceful way she moved.

Mercy, fussing at the stop in movement, pulled him out of his day-dreaming. "Shh, girl. Let's get you out of there for a few minutes." Blake approached Kris to help get their daughter out of the wrap.

At a little more than three months, Mercy had begun to really interact. He enjoyed her smiles and excited cooing when she saw him. He bounced her as he walked her around and pointed things out to her like he always did.

"Tree. See the rough bark that looks like a puzzle?" Blake talked to his daughter.

"That means it's a pine tree." Tucker answered. "See the long, pointy needles? Those are its leaves."

Mercy reached out for the pine needles that Tucker held. She grasped a few and immediately put them in her mouth.

Blake laughed. "Not yet, girl. Those pine needles are edible, but they aren't for you just yet."

"Yeah, and they can make a tea. Have I told you about how Dad saved me by escaping the bunker to get me some needles for tea when I was really sick?" Tucker asked his sister.

He continued his story while Mercy looked as if she actually listened to every word Tucker uttered, cooing in response and reaching for the tree again. When Tucker finished his story and took off after a squirrel that ran past them, Mercy whimpered.

"Okay, it's feeding time. Best to have a full belly when we meet everyone." Kris reached for their daughter.

Blake grudgingly let her go. As Kris nursed Mercy, he couldn't help but be grateful that Laurie had brought the herbs to help Kris produce enough milk. Once again, Laurie had proved herself. Kris's milk hadn't started producing as much as it had with Tucker. They didn't have any formula. Blake had worried about how they would keep their miraculous daughter alive if Kris's milk dried up completely. He had even played with the idea of journeying to the grocery store ten miles away on the off-chance there would still be formula on the ransacked shelves.

As much as he didn't want to be going into such an unnerving and unknown situation, Blake knew they needed to pay their respects to the two people who had allowed his family to be all together. He just didn't like it. He blew out a breath, knowing he wouldn't breathe easy until they were back in their bunker.

"Tucker," he called over to the boy. They needed to go over protocol before they stepped into the camp.

"Ugh, I almost had him." Tucker kicked at the pine needles on the ground as he stuffed his sling back into his pouch and joined them.

Blake handed him a piece of deer jerky and some water. Kris chewed on hers while sitting against the rock and nursing their daughter.

"Okay, let's go over protocol again." Blake looked pointedly at both Tucker and Kris.

He knew it annoyed his wife, but she smiled in a way that showed him she would go through the motions. Tucker sat forward, eager to show how much he had learned. Blake was relieved the kid liked running scenarios as much as he did. It solidified the knowledge that he needed to impart to his son.

"Always keep your eyes open. Never turn your

back on anyone, even if they say they're a friend." Tucker looked off into the distance, a sign that he struggled to remember what else to say. "If something goes down, first try to find Mom or Dad. If I can't, escape to the rendezvous point. Where is the rendezvous point?"

Blake looked around. "How about here? What would your point of references be?"

Tucker stood up, stuffing the last of his jerky in his mouth. He scanned the entire area for a minute and then turned back to his dad.

"The rock pile," he said.

"Great, but from a great distance you won't be able to see that marker." Blake folded his arms. They had played this game many times in the last several months, and by the glint in his son's eyes, he knew he had more to say.

"That's why those two dead pines on each side of that large cedar will be my other reference point." Tucker stuck his little chest out.

"That's right, Champ." Pride filled Blake.

"Which direction is the camp?" Kris asked.

Blake cocked his head and decided to challenge her. "Northwest."

Kris smirked, craned her neck to look around, and then met his gaze. "So, we will be crossing that little creek and then heading up that rise."

"I'm impressed," Blake said with a small chuckle.

The pride that shone in Kris's eyes almost made this whole trip worth it.

"We forgot one thing," Tucker said.

"What's that?" Blake asked.

"We don't give up our assets."

"Very true. Do you know what that means?" Blake

asked, watching Kris tuck Mercy back into her wrap. He rose, as did Tucker, and they all walked to their packs. Blake appreciated the seamless way they worked together.

"Yes. We don't tell people what we have, where we live, how we live, or anything that could be used against us." Tucker tightened his straps and slung his bow over his shoulder.

"I'm very proud of you, Tuck. You know one more thing you should focus on?" Kris asked him, as she bent down to kiss his forehead. "Having fun."

"Thanks, Mom." He smiled, but Blake could see the hesitation in his eyes, a look that mirrored his own misgivings.

"We'll probably run into the guards in a quarter-mile. I'm thinking I should scout ahead and let them know we're coming. I don't want someone to make a poor decision." Blake looked pointedly at Kris.

"I'm sure they are expecting us, but you do what you need to." Kris blew him a kiss.

"I won't be that far ahead of you." Blake nodded in the direction they were headed.

"I have my whistle, Dad."

"That makes me feel better. Thanks, Champ." He ruffled his hair. "Take care of Mom and your sister."

"Always. And we always return to each other."

"We always return to each other," Blake said along with Kris.

He waved farewell before he started at a jog up through the forest. Blake didn't worry about them so close behind. He just didn't want one of the guards to get carried away and take a shot before they knew who they were.

Even with his heavy pack, he made good time.

From where he stood, he could smell the campfire smoke and hear a murmur of voices. A shuffling to his right made him sneak behind the large fir. He watched the guard walk toward him, scanning the area.

When the guard was close enough, Blake recognized the man named David. Seeing that the guard was the one who he had held a knife to his throat back on his property made Blake grateful that he had the forethought to come ahead. Who knew what kind of angry feelings the man may have for him?

Blake had planned on just stepping out and making himself known. Knowing the guard was the same man he had overtaken just three months before, he couldn't help but see if David had learned anything. Besides, Blake didn't feel safe just stepping out into the open with the guy. David's reaction was unpredictable given their history. Blake slipped off his pack, soundlessly set it down, and then snuck out from behind the tree.

Blake stood right behind the guy, a smirk covering his lips. David hadn't learned a thing.

Then David turned abruptly, catching Blake a little off-guard. Blake ducked just as a long knife sliced at where his head had been.

Blake smiled, reached down, and grabbed for David's leg. David twisted at the last second, leaving Blake rolling and landing on his haunches. He looked up to see David posed for attack as well.

David smiled and nodded. "We meet again, Survivalist."

Blake stood with a chuckle. He had missed training with a true competitor. "You've learned a lot, David."

David stood and reached a hand out to Blake. "I was given quite the motivation." He looked around, scanning the forest. "Where's the family?"

"Coming up behind. I wanted to make sure you knew it was us approaching."

"We've been expecting you. The whole camp is excited to meet The Survivalist and his family." David slapped him on the back and looked in the direction of the camp. He motioned for Blake to follow him. "I know how you are. Right up here is a good vantage point to see the layout of the camp."

Blake watched him. It felt odd to feel a comradery with someone again. He didn't quite trust David, but he smiled to keep up appearances, if nothing else.

At the viewpoint, Blake stopped abruptly. The camp was much larger and more organized than he had anticipated. He had expected some worn-out tents haphazardly thrown together and several fires spread out in a big open area. Instead, he saw a few tents, but mostly bark shelters spaced around a large central fire. Around the dwellings were small piles that looked like the beginnings of barriers.

Blake nodded, scratching at his chin.

"Impressive, huh? We have really come together." David turned to watch Blake. "Of course, there is always more to learn."

People milled about the encampment. Children ran and laughed. Some people were at the fire cooking something that smelled delicious. A group of women sat, busy with something that looked like basket making. A few men stood at the edge of camp practicing archery.

From out here, it looked like a peaceful situation. Blake couldn't believe it, though. There had to be underlying contention, something that made living like this unsafe. He couldn't see it from here, but if his training taught him anything, it was there, and he would do what it took to find it.

~2~

Tucker shook under Kris's hand. She squatted, not an easy feat with her pack and her daughter. Tucker didn't take his gaze off the camp, so she touched his face gently to bring his attention to her.

"Tuck, it's going to be okay. I won't lie. After all this time with only us, it's going to seem really loud and busy. Remember how we talked about our bubble?"

The boy nodded, his eyes wide and roaming from her to the camp beyond.

"You have everything you need right here." She flattened her palm on his chest, feeling the pounding of his heart.

"What if I don't want to play?" he asked, his gaze following the children running around.

One of them shouted and pointed up at them. They cheered, jumped up and down, and started running back to the main fire. It seemed then that the entire camp stood and looked toward them. Kris could feel the heat traveling up her neck. She had forgotten that she would have to deal with the unaccustomed noise and attention as well.

She focused on Tucker again, a new understanding finding her. "Of course, you don't have to. You do what you feel comfortable with, and if you need a break, we'll go into our tent for a while."

Tucker's expression softened into relief. Had he thought she would make him play with the children if he didn't want to? She pushed back up to standing, and Blake held out a hand to help.

"Thank you," she said, squeezing his hand, needing his reassurance more than she thought. "We'll be okay," she said, more to herself than her family.

Mercy whimpered against her and hid her face in her chest. Kris pulled up the wrap to cover her head and then rested her hand on her back, murmuring soothing sounds.

"Well, of course you'll be okay. It's like a huge family waiting to greet a long-lost brother and sister." David winked at her and slapped Blake on the back. "Come on. They can't wait to greet the prodigal son."

As they entered the camp, Kris couldn't help but reach out and touch the bark dwellings. She had taken her class on field trips to learn about these homes the natives in the area had built. A smile tugged at the corner of her mouth, wondering if the idea had been Laurie's.

In front of each home lay a grass mat. Some had shoes by them, others had baskets. Kris resisted the urge to peek into each one. At one of the homes, Laurie had pushed aside the heavy curtain that looked like animal skin long enough that Kris could see herbs hanging from the rafters inside.

"You made it!" Laurie came with open arms and pulled her in close. She looked at Mercy's covered form. "May I?"

"Of course," Kris said as she pulled the wrap off her daughter's face.

Mercy scrunched her eyes and grimaced until she focused on Laurie. Then she cooed and reached for the midwife's curls.

"She recognizes you," Tucker said from beside her.

"I'm happy to hear that," Laurie said and kissed Mercy's head before covering it back up. She squatted in front of Tucker. "You have grown, Tuck."

Tucker threw his shoulders back. "I'm seven now."

"Oh, wow! Growing so fast," Laurie said. "Do you want to meet my son? He's not big like you, but he will love following you around."

Tucker bit his lip, but he nodded.

Gratitude for Laurie filled Kris. She had a way about her that instantly soothed.

"Ethan," she called into the group that watched them.

A small boy of about four peeked from behind legs, a finger in his mouth. He slowly came toward his beckoning mom, his eyes staring at Tucker and then his mom.

"Ethan, this is Tucker. I've told you about him. Would you come with us and help show him around?"

Ethan's eyes widened, and he reached for Tucker's hand.

After a glance up at his mom, Tucker took the smaller boy's hand and bent down to him. "You have a big camp."

Ethan nodded and then looked at Kris and Blake.

"That's my mom and dad. I have a sister, too. Her name is Mercy." Tucker pointed at her. "Do you have a sister?"

"Hannah." Ethan shrugged. "She like my sister."

"I know Hannah," Tucker said in awe.

The boys kept up the hushed conversation as

Laurie led them through the throng of people toward the main fire. The center of the camp opened as groups stopped what they were doing to watch them approach. The rectangular fire-pit ran about ten feet in length with various poles and cooking apparatuses stretched along it.

Many people tended meat skewered over the fire or pots heating on large rocks or over the coals. The fragrant air tantalized her senses, making Kris's mouth water and tummy rumble. It had been a long time since having a feast or a variety of food to choose from.

Arland walked toward them with his arms outstretched and a warm smile.

"Friends!" he called and gave them each a hug. "We welcome you to our camp." He spread his arms wide and then looked towards the people of his community. "These are the Chantrys, the people I told you all about. At some point today, take the time to introduce yourself and your family to our friends. For now, though, let's allow them to settle in. Please go about your business. We have a feast to prepare!"

The camp cheered and, with longing looks, faded back into the daily activities that had kept them busy before they arrived.

"We don't get many visitors." Arland laughed. "Come, sit. Relieve yourself of your packs and rest your legs before I take you on a tour."

Kris gratefully dropped her pack before easing onto a log bench in front of a large fire. She patted the wood next to her to entice Tucker, who still talked with Ethan, to do the same. As her hand touched the wood, the smooth feel made her look closer. Someone had taken care when making this bench. She glanced at the many others around the fire. Each one held the same rounded smoothness.

Blake didn't seem to notice while he held onto his pack as if his life depended on it. Just because he didn't look like he took notice didn't mean he hadn't. The man seemed to observe every nuance that happened around him even when looking completely preoccupied with something else. His hands clutched the pack, and Kris knew he would carry it everywhere with him, but the weight had bored down on him. She could tell as he rolled his shoulders.

"I brought some squash to add to the feast." Kris nodded at Blake, hoping lightening his pack would take some stress off him.

He opened the pack and handed an armful of squash to Laurie and another woman.

"These will be a delicious addition to our vegetable harvest. Would you like to come see?" Laurie asked, starting to walk away. "When you're rested, of course."

"Yes, thank you," Kris said. As much as she wanted to inspect everything they did in this community, her feet and shoulders could use a break.

~*~

Blake pulled his pack close. He didn't trust all the eyes on him. Without the squash, it would be like carrying nothing now. He glanced at Kris's pack, haphazardly dropped without a care. She had their food rations and water, plus their stove. He wanted to take them discreetly from her pack and put them in his now that there was room.

He scanned the camp in between conversations

with Arland. Already he had found the ideal location to place their tent, at the edge of camp butting up against a rock outcropping. From there, they could escape easily if needed, and no one could sneak up from behind them.

"What do you say, Blake? Want to check it out?" Arland stood.

Blake nodded and stood, donning his pack at the same time. He saw that Arland noted it, but the man respectfully said nothing. Blake didn't expect Kris to put her pack back on, but he still swallowed his displeasure as she walked away from it like it was nothing.

His expression must have given him away, for she went back and set her pack neatly against the log bench alongside Tucker's.

"Arland, are our packs safe here?" she asked.

"Why, of course. No one will bother them. Though, if you feel more comfortable, you can leave them in my home."

"I would, actually," Blake said. He reached over and picked up the packs before Kris could. "You've done well, but I got it now." He smiled at her, hoping to not dispel the peace they had since Mercy arrived.

"Thank you." She looked over to where Laurie waved for her and then back to him.

"Go on," he said and bent to kiss her temple and whisper, "We always return to each other."

She leaned up and whispered the same to him, and then she bent down to Tucker.

"Ethan wants to show me his house. He says he lives with Arland, so I will be with Dad."

"Okay, Sweetie. You know what to do." She leaned in close to Tucker, and Blake knew she whispered their saying and their son did back to her.

Kris stood there, indecision playing on her features. Blake understood. He didn't want to be away from any of them during their time here, but he also knew that would be unrealistic. Besides, they could gain more intel if they split. He nodded encouragingly to his wife.

"I've got him, Krista."

She smiled, took a step back, turned and made her way to the group of women where Laurie stood.

Blake watched her, feeling his heart torn. She needed other women. He had seen her brighten with Laurie's visits. He didn't understand the social nature of females, but Kris sure seemed to blossom as she approached the group. She let them peek at Mercy. He heard their exclamations even from where he stood.

"She'll be safe." Arland shouldered up next to him. "We have a great group of people. We had to do some weeding here and there, but we have come to be one big, happy family."

A hundred feet away, a woman yelled, and a man returned the banter. Blake shot an eyebrow up at Arland.

Arland laughed. "The irony of the moment." He shrugged. "Marital disputes happen no matter the circumstance. Surely you understand that."

Blake narrowed his eyes, but he did. The argument had already dispelled, with the woman huffing off, toting a large basket of something toward the fire. She eyed him but kept her focus forward.

"Come, Tucker. I show you my house!" Ethan pulled on Tucker, who looked up at Blake.

Blake nodded to his son, took one last lingering

glance at Kris, and then followed Arland and the boys into the area where close to a dozen bark dwellings stood. He had to trust. They wouldn't have made it this far just to lose everything here, right? He held tight to his faith and opened his eyes to what he could learn.

~*~

Kris enjoyed the women's excitement over Mercy. It filled a craving she had for the last year, but the constant chatter now overwhelmed her and Mercy. She bounced her daughter as she started to fuss and felt her smile being forced rather than easy.

"Would you like a quiet place to nurse Mercy?" Laurie touched Kris's arm, a softness in her hazel eyes.

"Thank you," Kris breathed the words out with relief. She stood and waved to the women. "It was a pleasure meeting all of you. I'm sure we'll visit more."

"We have so many questions for you," a woman with short blonde hair said.

"Yeah, like what's it like being married to The Survivalist," a young woman said as she winked and laughed.

A few of the others joined in, but several blushed along with Kris.

Laurie took her arm and led her away from the group. "Don't mind Bailey. She's young and her baby-maker has just started ticking. She'll be married before the end of winter if you want my guess."

"Married?"

"Oh, yes. One of our community is a pastor, not that we have all the paperwork, but hey," Laurie shrugged. "There's no government to file it with right now, so what are we supposed to do?"

"I think that's wonderful that even in a survival situation like this, people are still getting married and moving on with their lives."

"Me, too." Laurie ducked her head, but not before Kris saw the pink fill her cheeks. "Here we are."

She stopped in front of the bark dwelling Kris had seen her exit when they first arrived. Laurie lifted the rough deer skin and gestured her in. It took Kris's eyes a few moments to adjust to the dimness. Light streamed in from the opening in the center of the room. A small fire-pit had a few embers smoldering inside of it, giving the circular room a smell of camping mixed with the herbal aroma that always lingered on Laurie.

Mercy squealed happily as she fought her way out of the wrap.

"You like it in here, huh?" Kris asked her as she took her from her wrap.

"Here, you can sit on the bed Ethan and I share to nurse." Laurie smoothed some blankets on a raised platform.

Kris marveled at the construction. As her sight fully adjusted, she saw two other beds lining the circular walls around the room. Against one of the other beds, she saw her and Tucker's packs. It didn't surprise her that Laurie and Arland shared a dwelling.

She positioned to nurse Mercy, who ate greedily. Kris lost herself in her daughter's eyes like she always did when feeding her.

"Would you like some privacy?" Laurie asked after stirring the fire and adding a small piece of wood.

"I understand if you have other things to do, but I

enjoy your company." Kris smiled, hoping the woman would stay.

A flash of light brightened the room as someone walked in.

"Oh, hi, Laurie. I just need my basket. The kids and I found a great patch of gooseberries. I thought it would be a great addition to the feast." She glanced at Kris. "Sorry. I didn't realize you had company."

"Hi, Hannah," Kris said, happy to see the girl she had rescued on the side of the road a year ago.

Hannah blinked a couple times and stepped closer. "Kris? Oh my goodness! You guys made it." Hannah bent down to give her a hug. "This must be Mercy." She smiled down at the baby. "Oh, sorry, didn't realize you were feeding her."

"It's okay," Kris said. "It's so good to see you."

Hannah had grown and, although thin, she seemed healthy and full of life. "Is Tucker here? I've missed that little guy."

"Hannah has become our community nanny. She takes the kids out on hikes and teaches them about the plants."

"That's wonderful, Hannah."

Hannah shrugged before digging out her basket near her own bed. "The kids are great. Do you think Tucker would join us?"

"He's with Ethan somewhere, probably with your dad and Blake," Kris said, hoping that Blake wouldn't let him go out of his sight.

"I'll try to find them before we head back out. It was good seeing you, Kris. We'll catch up more at the feast."

"I would like that."

"Anything else you need, Laurie?" Hannah asked.

"I'm good, Hannah. Thank you." Laurie smiled, and Kris could see the love for the girl in her eyes.

Kris watched Hannah duck out of the dwelling. "It's so nice to see her doing well."

"It is. She's quite the young lady," Laurie said and looked down. "Arland suggested we share a dwelling."

"I'm not judging, Laurie."

"Oh, I know. Many of us have decided to share dwellings. I just didn't want you to get the wrong idea." She sat down on the bed opposite. "This is his bed."

"I'm sure it helps to share resources, and I can imagine it feels safer with him here."

"Yeah." Laurie looked up at her. "We both lost our spouses years ago. It's hard to let go, you know."

"I can imagine." The idea sat close to home. During the year before life had changed, Kris had thought of what she would do if Blake never returned. It sent a shiver through her, causing Mercy to whimper.

Kris sat Mercy up and patted her back. As she thought of a life without Blake, her whole heart shuddered. Not only would it leave them at a detriment for their survival, how could she ever look at another man? No one could compare with her husband.

She put Mercy back into her wrap and decided she needed to feel Blake's arms around her right then. Hopefully, he wouldn't be too hard to find in the large encampment.

~3~

Blake marveled at the bow he held in his hand. He had learned how to craft a bow out of PVC pipe and other scavenged materials while in the service, but the craftsmanship of the bow he held now went beyond scavenged materials. The smooth wood bent seamlessly, and the string made from deer sinew made a nice thrumming sound as he loosed his arrow, hitting the target exactly where he had aimed.

"This bow is unbelievable," Blake said softly, not meaning to say it aloud.

"Our resident carpenter, Frank. A retirement hobby that has now become a necessity for our survival." Arland nodded at the bow. "I bet he would trade you for one."

"Think he would trade to teach me how to make one?" Blake rubbed his hand up and down the bow. With this skill, he could make one the perfect size for Tucker, one he could pull back and have enough strength for a kill shot on a large animal.

"You teach our group of hunters how to shoot like that, and I'll teach you all I know." A man with greying hair and a lined face reached out his hand toward Blake. "Frank Anderson."

"Blake Chantry." Blake took his wrinkled but strong hand in his own.

"I know who you are," the man said with a wink. "What do you say? Trade?"

"A skill for a skill." Blake nodded. "I like it."

"I can see it now, Blake. You'll learn to love us." Arland slapped him on the back.

Movement in his peripheral vision caught his attention. He had hoped it would be Tucker. He didn't like the idea of him traipsing off into the forest without him or his mother, but he was with Hannah and the other kids. He should be fine.

Yet, a nagging fear ate away at him. He would give the group a few more minutes to return before he excused himself to go find his son.

The person coming toward them wasn't Tucker as he had hoped, but his wife. The closer she came, the more he worried. Her eyes shined as if she were about to cry, and her steps quickened until she was in his arms.

"What's the matter, Krista?" he asked, holding her with their infant daughter between them.

"It just feels weird being away from you and Tucker." She blinked and looked around. "Where is Tucker?" The quiver in her voice didn't hide the anxiety that he knew coursed through her.

"He went with Hannah. She said she told you," Blake said, looking off in the direction they had disappeared into the trees.

"Hannah takes the kids out there all the time to learn about edible plants, how to snare, and just to get them used to being out in the forest." Arland stepped up to them. "They stay within our guards so there is no reason to worry."

"We are never apart, Arland. It's hard on a mom's psyche." Kris's voice remained calm, but her hands squeezed Blake's shirt.

"Well, I'll come with you to find him and soothe your worries." Arland took a few steps toward the woods, and they followed him.

"Thank you," Kris said.

Blake thought the words, too. Kris provided the perfect excuse to ensure their son was safe.

As they walked through the wooded area, Blake noticed there was a path carved out by all the footsteps. Better for the kids and foragers, but easier for people to follow the trails to the camp. Sure, Arland had guards roaming the outskirts, but how well did they patrol such a large area?

His question was answered as they came around a bend to find an older child running toward them.

"Arland!" The kid who looked about twelve panted and bent over to catch his breath.

"Scott, what is it?" Arland bent down to his level.

"Someone's here," he said, before gulping in air. "I think it's Jake, but he's all beat up. Hannah told me to come get you."

"You did well, son. Now, continue on to camp and tell Mitchel to grab a couple guys and bring them back. Which trail is he on?"

"Stay to the right the whole way."

Blake didn't stay to hear the rest. With one look at Kris's wide eyes and a nod of her head, he took off in the direction the kid had described. He took note of the well-worn trails and the surroundings, but he focused on getting to his son.

When he rounded the bend to see a group of kids huddled around a man on the ground, he saw Tucker looking right at him. His boy stood back from the group, a hand on his knife, and eyes constantly scanning. Tucker ran to him and wrapped his arms around him.

"You okay?" Blake asked, checking him over.

"Yeah, Dad, but this guy doesn't look too good. We found him like this." Tucker pointed to the man in the middle of the trail where Hannah was offering him sips of water from her canteen.

"You're doing great, son." He stood and walked over to squat next to Hannah.

Hannah looked up, briefly assessing him before turning her attention back to the man. His face was a mass of contusions and blood. His eyes were nearly swollen shut, but they widened slightly when he saw Blake.

"It's good to see you, Blake. Can you help him?" Hannah asked, hope lining her voice.

"I've got my kit, Dad." Tucker had pulled out his first aid kit and handed it to him.

"I think he's a bit beyond your kit, Tuck, but thank you. We need to get him home to camp and washed up to assess the damage."

"Jake doesn't live here. He brings news now and again, but he's not a part of our camp," Hannah said.

Blake felt for the pulse on the man's throat. A strong beat let him know the man would more than likely make it through. Something pulled in his memory. He had met a Jake the day he brought Hannah home. Could this be the same one?

Jake's hand shot out and weakly grasped Blake's wrist. "They have my family…" The words were rasped and weak, but his eyes were full of urgency.

"Who?" asked Blake, the hairs on his neck bristling.

"Men from the city," he rasped before trying to push up.

"He has two young children," Hannah whispered, horror in her eyes.

"Arland!" The kids cheered as he and Kris, holding Mercy, came around the bend.

Blake stood. "I don't think your perimeters are secure. If he was followed…"

"No one's following…" Jake muttered.

"Let's get him back to camp and figure this out," Arland said with authority.

This was his camp, so Blake would not overstep. He wrapped his arms around his family, wishing they were back home where he knew how to protect them. If it were his camp, he would be sending men to check each perimeter, double the guard, and be interrogating the man on the ground before bandaging him up.

Blake felt Arland's stare then. The man nodded up the trail. Blake kissed his family on their heads and followed the community leader up the trail a short way.

"I see the look in your eyes. Care to share?" Arland stood, arms crossed, gaze intense and earnest.

"I would be securing the perimeter and finding out what's going on before taking him back to camp." Blake squeezed his fists, trying to keep himself from ordering Arland around. This wasn't his fight, but his family was in the midst of it.

Arland nodded.

Footsteps running around the bend drew their attention. Four men approached with the boy they had run into on the trail.

"Mitchel," Arland said, walking back toward the group, "take two of these men and secure the south perimeter. Look for any other signs of movement. We'll be doubling the guard tonight."

"Will do," Mitchel said and looked at the two men

closer in age to Blake, and they jogged up the trail.

The young man left hadn't taken his eyes off Hannah.

"Tyler," Arland called to him.

The young man tore his eyes off Hannah and looked toward Arland. "Yes, sir."

"Escort Hannah and the children back to camp and sound the bell. We need to be on alert just in case trouble is coming this way."

"Yes, sir." He nodded and then turned toward the kids. "Let's go, guys. How about we practice our ninja moves on the way back to camp?"

Blake saw the small smile on Hannah's lips as she rose, her gaze on Tyler. The look lasted only a moment but long enough so that Kris would be talking about the love interest. Yet, Hannah's eyebrows scrunched as she looked down at Jake one last time. She came up to her father, who draped a long arm around her.

"You all right?" Arland asked his daughter.

"Yeah, Dad. Jake says men from the city have his family. We will help them, won't we?" Hannah's eyes teared up.

"You know we will do what we can." Arland nodded. "Now, take your charges back to camp and stay safe. We'll know more soon."

She nodded, kissed his cheek, and followed the group of ninja-walking kids.

Tucker, though, stood by Blake's side, his hand still on his knife.

"Do you want to go with the kids, Tucker?" Blake lowered down to ask his son.

"No, I want to stay with my sister." A stern expression of protectiveness filled his eyes.

"Sounds good to me," he said and rose, meeting Kris's eyes. He read them as he did and knew that she wouldn't allow him to whisk them off to safety. He prepared for a battle he wished he had never heard of as he squatted next to Jake. "Tell me everything."

~*~

As much as Kris wanted to pull Tucker out of hearing distance of Blake's interrogation, she couldn't stop listening. Blake had talked about what things would be like after an apocalyptic event, but hearing it from the bruised lips of a man in desperate need to save his family sent chills coursing through her.

He described the men as sick skeletons with no morals. They wanted food, food that Jake didn't have. The threat they had given if Jake didn't return by sundown sent her covering Tucker's ears and finally pulling back down the trail.

"They wouldn't really do that, would they, Mommy? They wouldn't really hurt a baby." Tucker's eyes were wide as his gaze dropped down to Mercy, sleeping in her wrap.

"I would like to say no, Tuck, but starvation does strange things to people." Kris squeezed her eyes shut, wanting to rip out the image from her mind and that of her son's.

Tucker's face had gone pale, and he wrapped his cold fingers around her hand while his other hand drew his knife from its sheath.

"I will protect my sister. No one will ever even look at her that way!" The grim line of his lips and his steely words made her wish she would have taken Tucker down the trail when the other kids had left.

"No one will hurt your sister, Sweetie. We're safe here." She pulled him into her arms and repeated her words. "We're safe here."

"I wish we were home." Tucker's whispered words hit her hard.

She looked back up the trail as Blake walked toward them, his own lips a mirror image of her son's. He was going to save that family, just like she had known he would. Blake brought them into the protection of his arms.

"I have to," he whispered.

"I know," she whispered back. She wouldn't expect any less of him.

Would Arland's men have a chance without Blake? She didn't know, but with Blake, she had every confidence that the family not only would be saved, but that the men accompanying him would be as well.

Arland came into view, helping a limping Jake along the trail. Blake let go of them to help support the man as they traveled back to camp.

"Dad won't let those men near us. He'll send them on to the Maker." Tucker's determined words shocked Kris. They had never talked about killing before, and the words he used were nothing like she would expect from him. Where had he heard this?

As much as she wanted to admonish those thoughts, she couldn't help but wonder if that wouldn't be the best thing to do. Men that stoop that low could never be trusted, and there were no jails to house them to keep them from hurting others. Her stomach lurched, and she sent up an apology for her line of thinking...pushing the thought from her mind. She didn't want to know. That decision lay on Blake's shoulders, and as much as she wished it didn't have to, she was grateful the burden wasn't hers.

~*~

Blake clenched his teeth as he sat in the meeting on the outskirts of camp. Men and women shouted opinions. Some were angry at Jake for making this their problem, some saying it had nothing to do with them. Others said they should just move camp and avoid the altercation altogether.

When consulting a mass of people like this, it never ended well. That was why the services had ranking officers to tell others what to do, no opinions needed. Without the intel or experience, those opinions didn't matter in the first place.

Arland patiently listened to everyone, a look of calm on his features.

Blake growled low and pushed up to walk away from the group. He couldn't stand the non-action a moment longer.

"Blake, you have something to add?" Arland asked, a look in his eyes saying he wanted him to share with the group.

"This is your group, Arland. It's your choice to make." Blake turned away.

"We would be honored to have your opinion." Arland's words stopped him.

Blake rubbed a hand down his face and turned back toward the man who had grown into a leader, although lacking in any tactical experience.

"If men from the city have made it this far, they won't be the last. People will go beyond what a person would assume sane when they're starving. Can you save everyone?" He looked at the faces turned toward him. "No, you can't." Some of those expressions now turned dark. "Do you do everything you can to save your own?"

The whole group roared in agreement.

"But Jake isn't one of us!" someone shouted.

"He might not live here, but he was our neighbor. He has been providing us with valuable information," another countered.

Arland held up his hand calmly and turned back toward Blake. "Let's say we decide to try to save Jake's family. How would you suggest we go about it?"

Blake held Arland's gaze for a long moment and then looked at the others watching him, trust brimming in their eyes. He had done nothing to earn that trust. These were men and women surviving the best they could with the resources they had, pulling together as a group, a group he had no wish to be a part of.

Yet, he couldn't stand by while a family was being tortured. Those men wouldn't stop there. They would keep assaulting more families, families that used to be his neighbors.

Blake looked Arland right in the eye and said, "You put me in charge."

~*~

Kris watched as the men prepared. The sun glinted off their guns, and she looked up, seeing that it hung just over the mountains. Dusk would come sooner than later. The family only had a short time left.

After being under Laurie's care for the last couple hours, Jake was now recognizable. He stood unsupported, his eyes hard and knuckles white, grasping a weapon in his hand. A touch of insanity lived behind his eyes. She understood. If it were her family, she would be a bit insane as well.

Blake issued a few last instructions before swiping his face with mud. The others followed suit as he stepped away from them to bring his family into his arms.

He kissed Mercy's head as she reached out to grasp his mud-covered nose. He bent down and looked Tucker in the eye. "You keep your mom and sister safe. Do not leave their sides."

"I won't, Dad. You bring those kids back."

"I will do my best, Champ." He ruffled his hair and stood.

He bent down and kissed Kris, long and hard. "I'm sorry I'm leaving you again," he whispered, his forehead resting on hers. She didn't mind the fact he made her muddy.

"You'll be back. You always come back."

"Nothing would stop me from protecting you."

"I know," she said, kissing him one more time. She had every confidence that he would be back. He had been on far more dangerous assignments. "We always return to each other."

Blake and Tucker repeated the saying, and even Mercy cooed a response.

"Look at you, joining in already." Blake kissed the top of Mercy's head.

"Ready?" Arland asked, drawing Blake away.

"You're staying here, Arland."

Arland squared his shoulders.

"I told you, if I did this, I would be solely in charge. I need to know my family are in hands I trust."

Arland's features relaxed, and his arms dropped. "I will keep them safe with my life."

Blake nodded. With one last look at Kris and their children, he turned to the half-dozen men ready to follow him. "Let's go."

As Kris watched her husband lead the men from camp, something settled deep within her. She was used to him leaving, going off on dangerous missions, but not like this, not when she knew the situation he walked into. This was the first time she saw him in action, saw the mask of command control his features, and saw him lead men as if he had been born to. She always thought of her husband as special, but seeing him this way and the awe in the faces around her cemented the knowledge. Her husband was The Survivalist.

~4~

Blake had taken three of the four men who had military experience. The fourth was old enough to have fought in the Korean War. The other two men who joined them were David and another guy he remembered from training at his home. Counting himself and Jake, there were seven of them. More than enough to take on the four starving men Jake had said were at his house.

Blake had watched Jake closely for any signs of dishonesty or scheming. What he found was a man determined to get his family back. The idea burned in Blake's gut. He would do anything to save his own family.

Jake held the carcass of a rabbit taken from the feast's stores. He had been told to bring back food. Bringing more than a dead rodent would cause suspicions to rise. He needed to have the surprise on the men holding Jake's family hostage. The best way would to have Jake return with something they demanded.

Blake had gone through the scenario several times in his mind and made the difficult decision. He knew how to weigh the cost of taking a life.

At the edge of the neighborhood, he gathered the men together and looked each one in the eye. "We don't leave survivors."

Men like this couldn't be left loose to kill others, or worse. According to Jake, there were several other families still trying to live in their homes. If they rescued Jake's family and left the men alive, they would just move on to the next home. There were no cops, no judges, no jury, and no jail. There was only survival.

The men all nodded. He didn't worry about the ones with experience. They had killed before. They knew the stakes. David and the other guy, though, swallowed as if they didn't like the taste of the command. They needed motivation.

"You heard what Jake said the men would do if he didn't arrive in time?" He glanced at the sun, only inches away from the peaks, and then looked at David and Neil. "Think of your own children."

Their eyes hardened, and they nodded.

"We don't have time for surveillance. I will scout the house upon approach, but as of now the plan is to surround the house. Jake and I at the front. You two," he nodded to the two younger military men, "at the back. The rest of you take a window. Shoot to kill at first shot."

After everyone nodded, they dispersed to surround Jake's house. Blake followed a discreet distance behind Jake in case they had someone watching. Jake had stuffed the pistol Arland had given him into the back of his pants. His hands gripped the rabbit tightly.

Yelling from the house hastened Jake's footsteps. He barged through the door, leaving it open, giving Blake a view of the chaos behind it.

"About time, boy. We just heated up the coals." A dirty, emaciated man with stringy hair yanked the rabbit from Jake's hands.

"We almost gave up on you," another just-as-unruly man said, pretending like he was going to take the young child from Jake's wife's arms. The older boy clung to her legs and sobbed.

"Don't touch them," Jake said, reaching back for his gun.

Blake ran, closing in on the house as Jake aimed the pistol right at the man's head. Jake didn't hesitate, he pulled the trigger. His wife screamed, and the man dropped.

The one holding the rabbit dropped the animal as he reached for his own gun, but Blake dropped him before the rabbit hit the ground. Two more single shots at the back of the house signaled the end. Could it have been that easy?

Blake stepped into the house, checking right and left and moving carefully down the hall. Each room was empty. He swung open the back door only to be greeted by two guns cocked and aimed at his head. He pushed a breath out as he recognized his men…yes, his men.

"Stand down," Blake said, eyeing the two dirty scoundrels lying in the dirt. "All clear."

He holstered his gun and walked back into the house.

Jake was on his knees, holding his family and weeping. Blake didn't avert his eyes. Instead, he pushed that image into him, grounding it in deep until it became a part of him. He wanted to always remember what he fought for. It was this, people willing to put their lives on the line for their families. Family…the one thing that even an apocalypse couldn't destroy.

~*~

Kris paced in front of the fire. Tucker sat in the dirt with Ethan, playing with the cars he had brought. Every once in a while, Tucker would look up, scan the tree line where his father had disappeared, and then focus back on the toy in his hand.

Laurie walked up to her with a steaming metal mug of tea. "To help calm your nerves."

Kris took the cup gratefully. Mercy had fallen asleep an hour ago and would soon wake up, but she couldn't stop her nervous pacing. She had all the confidence in the world when Blake had left, but now as full darkness took over the camp, a tingle of worry began to nag at her. What if he didn't return?

"It's hard being married to a man who constantly puts his life on the line." Laurie sipped on her own tea, watching her with compassionate eyes.

"You speak as if you know." Kris stopped her pacing to watch the woman she felt like she could now call a friend.

"My husband was a firefighter." Her gaze lifted to the heavens where stars began to peek out, showing them they weren't alone.

"And one day he didn't return?" Kris asked, dread filing her.

Laurie nodded. "I was pregnant with Ethan."

Kris put a hand over her mouth, and her eyes brimmed. "I'm so sorry." Empathy rushed through Kris in waves like a tsunami. She brought Laurie into a hug because words didn't seem enough.

"They're back!" Tucker shouted and took off into the dark.

Relief filled Kris in a guilty rush. She pulled back, seeing the firelight dance in Laurie's eyes.

"Go. You need to welcome your husband back." Laurie smiled and walked in the other direction.

Kris sucked in a breath as she walked to where she could see the shadows of all seven men and a woman. As she neared, she saw the woman and Jake each carrying a child. Blake had done it. He brought them all back.

As soon as his strong arms wrapped around her, Kris's body shuddered with the pent-up emotions. Tucker had already been in Blake's arms, and Mercy cooed in her sleep. She had her family. She let that gratitude fill her until she overflowed with it. The strength and urgency of the embrace showed her that Blake, as well, had some extra emotions.

When the world slowly filtered back in, she heard Jake and his wife tearfully thanking everyone. Kris disengaged herself from the tangle of arms to see the community welcoming them with open arms, offering them places to sleep, food to eat, and warm blankets. She glanced up at Blake to see if he noticed the generosity of the group. Had the events today helped him to see the benefit of living within a community?

She wouldn't push the subject. That wasn't how Blake worked. He had to take things at his own pace and come to the conclusion on his own. Otherwise, it wouldn't work.

Arland stood on a large stump near the fire and called everyone's attention.

"Our community has pulled together to save a family that we now will call our own. Join us in welcoming them. Before we begin the feast, let's hear a prayer of thanksgiving from Pastor Rob."

A man in his fifties took Arland's place on the stump. He looked around at the people gathered.

"We are truly blessed today! Not only have we added to our family, welcomed friends with open arms, and have each other to rely upon, but thanks to our entire community down to our children, we have a feast that is beyond any I have ever participated in."

The crowd cheered in agreement.

"Now, let's take a moment of silence to express our gratitude for all we have." Pastor Rob bowed his head.

Most everyone else did as well. Kris watched Blake reverently close his eyes, his lips moving in a quiet prayer. Tucker took her hand, his eyes wide as the whole community embraced this moment of thanksgiving.

A moment later, Pastor Rob lifted his head and said, "Amen."

Several others repeated the word, and Arland exchanged places with him.

"Let's enjoy our feast!" Arland's words rang out and the people cheered.

Women passed out plates as everyone formed a line starting at the fire. Kris said thank you as she was handed a beat-up camp plate. Tucker and Blake received wooden plates. As they neared the fire where all the food was laid out on a series of flat rocks, the scent of the now uncovered pots blasted them in delicious aromas that made Kris's mouth water.

She scooped fresh green salad onto her and Tucker's plates, adding what looked like roasted root vegetables, and then some meat, whether it was venison or rabbit or something else, she didn't know. She had seen the woman in front of her drizzling a sauce over her meat, and after one whiff of the tangy aroma, Kris did as well.

"Look at all this food, Mom. Where did they get it all?" Tucker asked as they found a seat on an empty bench.

"From the land, Sweetie," Kris said as she sat, situating Mercy to a position where she could eat easier.

"May I sit with you?" Laurie asked, standing in front of them with her own steaming plate.

"It would be our honor," Blake said as he scooted down, inviting Tucker and Kris to follow so there was enough room for Laurie at the end.

"Tucker was just commenting on all the different types of food you have," Kris said.

"Yes, this year has been bountiful."

"Did you really get all of this wild?" Tucker asked as he shoved another bite of meat into his mouth. "And what is this stuff on the meat. It's so yummy," he said around his full mouth.

"Tucker, don't talk with food in your mouth." Blake eyed him.

"Yes, all of this food comes from the land around us. You saw some of the plants when you were out with Hannah, right?"

"I did. I memorized them so I can tell you, Mom."

"I'm sure you did," said Kris with a laugh.

"The sauce is made from holly leaf and madrone berries. Wait until you have the gooseberry jam with the acorn bread for dessert. That is a special treat!"

"You guys are resourceful," Blake said.

Kris knew Blake didn't give compliments freely. She saw the way he scanned the crowd, the careful way he ate, and she knew his mind was processing. She gave him the space to do so and continued a conversation with Laurie on the different ways to prepare foraged greens.

There would be a lot of changes coming, whether they wanted them or not. Eventually, their prepped food would run out and their tools would break. They had to learn to adapt and use the natural materials the environment provided. Arland's camp was a great resource to learn how that could be accomplished. The question was could they do it on their own? She didn't want to, but it would take something huge to sway her husband into that way of thinking.

~*~

Blake watched how the people of Arland's camp worked together. Each person had a job and seemed to complete it without grudging behavior. The food was delicious, and he had to wonder what daily rations would be like. Certainly, they couldn't eat like this every night.

The people he had seen before at his house now looked healthier, less lean, and more alert. They must have had a difficult winter. With that thought, he had a difficult time swallowing his food. This group of people survived a winter with absolutely no preparation, no stored food, no bunker, no more than tents and what they could put together in a rush and carry on their backs. He and his family had been warm and had plenty of food and even hot showers.

"Do you not like the acorn cakes?" Arland asked as he approached him. "They aren't the cake we're used to, but you can acquire a taste for them."

"No, they're good." Blake watched him, thinking of the lanky self-conscious man he had spoken to only a year ago.

Arland's shoulders were now set back, his hands were rough and work-hardened, his eyes held determination and confidence. This man had accomplished something huge. He had saved the lives of a dozen or more families, not just one.

"Your feast is impressive, Arland." Blake cleared his throat, reaching for his canteen.

"They have done an amazing job harvesting under Laurie's directions. We didn't have the time to do this last fall before the snows came." Arland sighed as he sat down next to him. "This winter will be better."

"Do you have enough to last all of you through?" Blake asked, aware that Kris now watched him in earnest.

"With some supplementation from meat and some winter foraging, yes."

"Even with the new additions?" Blake nodded toward Jake and his family scarfing down their food.

"It will be a bit tighter, but not much. We could squeeze in a few more?" Arland raised an eyebrow, the effect a bit comical in the dancing flames.

Blake laughed. "I haven't changed my mind, but I'm seeing the benefits you have created with such a smooth-running community."

"I'll take that," Arland said with a nod.

"Can I go play with the kids? It looks like they are playing some sort of game." Tucker stood expectantly in front of Kris.

Blake glanced at a group of kids sitting in a circle near the fire. There were some sticks of wood and rocks that they flicked around. A few erupted in cheers while taking the acorns from the others.

"They are playing a game that the natives in our area used to play. One of our community used to volunteer at the museum. She taught us the game." Arland stood and offered his hand to Tucker. "If you don't mind, I would take him over with the other kids to explain the rules."

"Of course. Thank you, Arland." Kris smiled. "Enjoy yourself, Sweetie."

"I will!" Tucker skipped over to Arland and took his hand.

Blake watched the delight on his son's face. Was he being selfish for keeping them isolated?

Mercy squealed happily, bringing his attention to his daughter. She bounced on Laurie's lap, chewing on a finger, and being a delight as always. He wanted to swoop the girl up in his arms, and the disappointment in knowing that it would be rude to steal her away from someone else tugged at his heart.

Instead, he stood and decided to go for a little walk. Surely there had to be something amiss going on, something besides the poor border patrol.

Once Blake made his way past the first row of dwellings, he stood still and closed his eyes. Without the light from the fire, he needed his eyes to adjust. When he opened them, the starlit sky came into view. Something about the pockets of stars pulled at him. It always had, ever since he was a boy.

Living here, there were so many trees that he could rarely see the sky in its entirety, but the pockets gave glimpses at the heavens, glimpses like he saw in his children.

The moon peeked out from behind the mountains beyond the trees. Soon, it would be overhead, and the entire camp would be bathed in moonlight. Now, though, he could walk around without being seen. He convinced himself he wasn't spying, but yet he needed intel to make a decision and know if he should allow himself to sleep tonight.

Each dwelling glowed dimly, and he wondered about the safety of keeping hot coals in a structure made out of wood when no one was around. Yet, those coals would keep them from having to restart a fire every time they needed it, not to mention keep the dwelling warmer.

As he reached the edge of camp, a soft murmur of harsh voices made him freeze. He evened his breath and strained to make out the words.

"You could have led them straight here, Jake," a voice he didn't recognize accused.

"But I didn't man, just let it go. My family was in jeopardy." Exhaustion lined Jake's voice.

"It could have put ours in jeopardy."

"Give me a break, okay. I'm trying to make things right."

"By giving us more mouths to feed?" the man asked in disgust.

"I'll do my part. I heard those city guys talking about bunkers. If we could find…"

Blake's blood went cold. He should have known.

"We don't raid houses here. That's not what we do." He could hear the firmness in the man's tone.

"But—"

"No, buts. Now, come on. Arland wants to talk with you and your wife. We need to know what we're up against."

Blake's nerves were on edge. If one of them wanted to raid bunkers, what would it take for all of them to decide it was a good idea?

Blake followed the two men to a dwelling more toward the center of the camp. When they entered, the hide swayed, allowing a brief glimpse inside. Arland, Jake's wife, and a few other people sat within the dwelling. Blake balanced on his feet, walking silently toward the side of the dwelling where he crouched down. He swallowed the disgust at eavesdropping. There was no helping it. He needed to know where people stood when they didn't think he was around.

"Thank you for coming, Jake," Arland greeted. "Sara was just telling me about the men that held her captive."

"Yeah, did she tell you they were there searching for bunkers?" Jake asked

"She did. She also said they claimed to have come ahead of the main party in order to get first dibs on the bunkers in this area." Arland kept his voice calm, but to Blake's trained ear, he could hear the tightness within it.

Someone sighed heavily, and another let out a soft sob.

"Do we have to do this now, Arland? Sara has been through the wringer." Jake sounded as exhausted as Sara was emotional.

"I do apologize, but it's best to find out all the information when it's fresh. Then she can move past it and embrace the safe environment of our community," Arland said, and Blake couldn't help but think the scientist should have been a diplomat.

Jake snorted. "No one's going to be safe once the city arrives here."

"Why do you say that?" Arland asked.

"The group those guys kept spouting about is large and organized. I've told you the bits and pieces I've heard in the past, but this new information goes way beyond what we thought."

"Tell me," Arland encouraged.

"Those guys said that this CME thing was a global event. More than half of the population has already died of starvation. Even more in the cities closest to us."

"The experts predicted about ninety percent of our population would die. People don't know how to live like our ancestors," Arland interrupted.

"Anyway, the cities closest to us formed something like a coalition. These guys said they had to do unthinkable things to survive, and only those willing to go that far lived. The rest were...well, they perished."

Sara erupted into more sobs.

"If we don't find those bunkers first, we will be next," Jake said, panic filling his voice.

"We have everything we need right here," someone else said.

"That sure worked well for you last winter, didn't it?" Jake scoffed.

"I know this is hard on you," Arland said soothingly. "Why don't I give you a minute to calm down? I want someone else in on this meeting. I'm going to fetch him and return."

Blake stood, and as quickly as possible while staying silent, he disappeared into the darkness to the edge of the camp. While walking back toward the fire, he pondered what he had heard. Jake just might be right about one thing. With the city coming, no one was safe.

He approached the fire from a completely different direction, happy to see his wife still comfortably conversing with Laurie and another woman and his son playing with the children.

His body was tense, rigid with the probability of people like Jake searching out his bunker, raiding it, and taking what he had prepared for over a decade. Blake needed those supplies for his family's survival. He clenched his teeth as he made his way toward his wife. Why did people who had no thought to prepare think it right to take from others who did?

"There you are," Kris said as he arrived. "Arland is looking for you."

The statement relaxed Blake's jaw. He was the other person Arland had wanted in on the conversation. Part of him now felt guilty for sneaking around and listening.

"Where is he?" Blake asked.

"He's in the counsel dwelling. It's where Jake and his family will be staying until they have theirs built. I'll take you," Laurie said as she stood.

"You're okay?" Blake asked Kris.

"Yes. Janene and I are talking about baby stuff."

Blake looked at the other woman who held her expanding belly, another addition to the community. He nodded and glanced at Tucker.

"I won't let him stray. Go see what Arland needs." Kris took his hand and gave it a squeeze.

Blake bent down and kissed her and his sleeping Mercy. As much as he wanted to, he would quell the urge to do the same to Tucker. The boy looked engrossed in a game.

Laurie smiled and beckoned to him. He followed her back to the dwelling he had stood behind just a few minutes before.

"Arland is questioning Jake and Sara right now. He wanted you to hear the information for yourself,"

Laurie whispered before she pulled the flap back and entered ahead of him.

"Oh, good, they found you." Arland said, and patted the seat next to him. "Of course, you know Blake Chantry?"

"We are grateful for his help in getting my family back," Jake nodded. He sat next to his wife with his children sleeping behind them.

"The team did well," Blake said as he sat.

"Blake, Jake and Sara were just telling us the news they heard from the men holding them captive. They claimed to have gone ahead of a large group organized by a coalition from the city in search of bunkers." Arland stared straight at Blake.

Blake could tell Arland did his best to keep his face blank, but in his eyes he saw his intention. He had to wonder if the man really cared enough to warn Blake, or if he used it as more incentive to join them. Blake shifted in his seat. He didn't understand why Arland was so adamant about Blake and his family being a part of his community.

"I think we should go ahead of them and search for the bunkers before they get here." Jake sat forward, looking straight at Blake.

Blake never was good at poker, but he knew how to keep from showing emotion when needed. He took a moment before responding. "And how do you suggest finding these bunkers?"

"The men said that the main guys had a map. Some guy who worked for one of the companies that installed bunkers created one from memory."

Blake forced his body to stay calm. "Do you have that map?"

"No, they didn't have it. They only remembered a

couple roads that were on it. One was ours, Mountain View Drive. The other was Ridgecrest."

When Blake heard the name of his road, the hairs on the back of his neck rose. They had signed legal documents stating that no records of his location would exist and all the employees signed nondisclosure agreements. Not that paperwork, or laws for that matter, made a difference now.

"Why, Jake, would you want to take the chance of robbing bunkers that are probably still being inhabited when we have everything we need right here?" Laurie asked in that kind way of hers.

"I saw what you all went through last winter. It was hard on us, too, but not near as much. The pickings in the houses close by are becoming thin, but there are many more neighborhoods around. Those bunkers would have surpluses. That's what those preppers did. They stockpiled food and tools and ammunition."

Arland sighed. "You are new here, Jake, so please let us educate you. This community strives to live off the land, with the land, without raiding others. The people that have prepared for an event like this have the right to keep what they worked so hard for. We have everything we need."

"Last winter caught us unprepared," Laurie added gently. "This year we have plenty. Enough for you and your family, too."

"It's safer," Sara pleaded, touching Jake's arm.

Jake fell silent, but he nodded.

Blake didn't trust that he had let go of the notion of raiding houses or bunkers. This guy would be one to watch.

~5~

Kris waited until Tucker's breathing eased into deep sleep before she reached out to touch Blake. He had been lying stiffly on top of his sleeping bag from the moment they had all crawled into their tent. Ever since he returned from the meeting, he had seemed preoccupied, but she knew better than to put him on the spot in front of others. The way he acted, it was information that Tucker didn't need to hear unfiltered.

"Blake?" She sat up on an elbow and looked down at her husband. "What's troubling you?"

"I need to get back and check on the bunker." Blake's tight words made her feel on the defensive, but she breathed through it.

"Did something happen when you went with Arland to make you worry more?"

Blake sighed and rolled over to face her. The moonlight lit their tent enough that she could see his eyes searching hers.

"You can tell me. We are in this together. I will trust whatever it is you advise." She leaned over and kissed him before drawing back so she could read his face as much as she could in the dim light.

Today, besides the excursion to save Jake's family, had reminded her of how nice it was to have people around. It also made her grateful for a little solitude. There were pros and cons to everything. When Blake left to bring Jake's family home, she realized that all that really mattered to her was her family being together. Yes, Blake had trust issues and didn't like being around big groups, and maybe that part of him was right. In any light, she would follow him wherever he led. She trusted he would make the right choice for them.

"The people that survived in the city," Blake started and then cleared his throat. "They aren't the most moral. They are the fighters, the people willing to do whatever it takes to survive."

"We do whatever it takes, too."

"Not like this. We won't harm others or take what is not ours." He wiped a hand down his face as if he wanted to wipe out memories.

Kris nodded, understanding dawning in a rush of fear.

"These people have started forming gangs," Blake said.

"I'm so glad we don't live in the city."

"Well, that's it. Those guys that took Jake's family hostage are from one of those gangs."

"Oh," Kris said, sitting up.

Blake sat up with her. "Kris, they have a map of the bunkers in the area."

Her hands covered her mouth so her gasp wouldn't wake her children. "What are we going to do?"

Blake shook his head and looked down at his hands. "From what they said, it sounds like we might have a couple months and maybe until after winter before they make it all the way up here. I don't know."

"Can we fight them off? How can they even open the bunker without our code? I thought it was armored." Scenarios coursed through her.

"It is, but I'm sure they have their ways. Otherwise, they wouldn't be going to so much trouble to come find them."

Kris's heart raced. If their bunker wasn't safe, what would be?

She lay back down, feeling her whole body shiver, and it wasn't with the cold. Blake pulled her sleeping bag over her and brought her into his arms.

"I'll figure something out, Krista." He kissed her head and pulled her in closer.

"You always do," she said, and let his comfort push out the dread filling her.

Blake would take care of them. He always did, just like he always returned.

~*~

Blake reveled in the warmth of his wife in his arms. The kids slept peacefully. Tucker snored in his sleeping bag next to him, and Mercy slept in her little Moses basket that one of the women had gifted Kris. Kris had fallen asleep what felt like hours ago, but he didn't want to let her go despite his arm going to sleep and his shoulder cramping.

The moonlight had traveled all the way across the tent, and the moon now seemed to be setting. Dawn would come soon. Nothing had stirred in the camp as far as he could hear. The whole land seemed peaceful, but he knew that peace could just be the calm before the storm.

He knew Kris wouldn't be too happy with him, but his plan was to leave right after morning meal with Arland's people. He needed to get home and figure out what he was going to do. So many ideas ran rampant within him that he couldn't think straight. Being home at the bunker, taking account of all he had there, figuring out escape routes and contingency plans...he needed to be home.

A month or more seemed like a long time, but it would go fast, too fast. It could be that the group never arrived, and it could be they decided to beeline for this area and work their way back down into the valley instead. It was difficult to put yourself in the enemy's mind when they weren't in their right ones. This lot were starved, half-crazy, ruthless, and only there for one thing...survival. That made them the most hostile enemy he would ever encounter.

They got lucky with the lot at Jake's house. They weren't the brightest bunch, obvious just by their leaving the mass group without all the information. Maybe they had thought they would only encounter hillbilly bumpkins. They were wrong about that. Mountain folk were tough and, with a group like Arland's, worthy adversaries.

A stirring near the fire roused him from his daydreaming. He silently pulled one arm free and unzipped the tent a few inches to peek out. He would recognize that lanky, now-confident stature anywhere. Even without seeing Arland's face, he knew the leader was up and contemplating.

Blake watched his wife for a moment longer before easing his other arm out from under her. Once free, he shook it to bring the circulation to his hand and arm, pins and needles infusing it. Tucker rolled over in his sleep, moving more into Blake's place. He most likely sought out the heat. A smile tugged on Blake's lips, knowing that when he returned to the tent he would find Tucker cuddled up with Kris. Let him have those small moments of boyhood.

He slipped on his coat and pulled a beanie over his head. His once-again short hair didn't provide much warmth on these cold fall mornings. He eased out of the tent as quietly as possible, his breath visible in short puffs. Once he turned back toward the fire, Arland lifted a hand in greeting.

Blake met him with a handshake and stood next to him, enjoying the fire he stirred up from the embers.

"Morning, friend. You enjoy meeting the sun, too?" Arland asked, his gaze lost to the flames.

"Always been a morning person," he said.

Arland looked up at him and then back to the fire. "Even when you don't sleep."

Blake shrugged.

"You know, you are safe in my camp." Arland sounded a bit saddened.

"I didn't sleep in fear of our safety."

"It's the trouble coming, isn't it?"

Blake nodded. He could feel the stress coming off Arland as well. He tried to hide it with a smile and calm movements, but Blake could read it sitting under his skin, readying him to pounce when needed.

"What are your thoughts?" Arland asked, meeting his eyes in the firelight.

Blake watched him for a moment and then simply said, "We're not safe."

"By we, do you mean your family because of your bunker?"

"That, and the collective we. Once people like that make it here, it's not just the bunkers that will be at risk, but every house, shed, outbuilding, and person."

Arland nodded and returned his gaze to the fire. A

pot boiled, and he took it off the flame, pouring the steaming liquid into two mugs sitting in wait. Blake almost chuckled at that. Arland had expected him.

He handed him a steaming mug. "It's not as good as coffee, but a close replacement."

Blake cooled the liquid with his breath before taking a tentative sip. It wasn't like coffee at all, more like a bitter tea, but it was warm and strong, something he needed right now.

"What will you do?" Arland asked.

"Prepare. What will you do?"

Arland shrugged. "We'll have council meetings about it. Probably for weeks." He laughed, a laugh built out of desperation.

"I saw the trail blazer marks on the way back from Jake's."

Arland nodded. "In hindsight, not the best move on my part."

Blake read the defeat in him. His shoulders had slumped, his hands fidgeted with the mug, his head hung. Arland had a heavy burden, one he hadn't prepared to shoulder.

"You've done well," Blake said and clasped his shoulder.

Arland looked up at him, his eyes glassy in the firelight. "You mean that?"

"Yes, I do. Your camp runs smoothly. People listen to you. You have utilized all the skills and knowledge of every person in your community."

"But? I know there's a but. If there wasn't, you would be joining us."

Blake blew out a breath. "Do not take it personally. I like my solitude. I like knowing that I can protect my family."

"And heaven forbid, what if something happens to you? Where would your family go then?"

"To you, hopefully." Blake smiled, a brief humorless smile.

Arland chuckled and turned his eyes heavenward as dawn began its glow on the distant peaks. "You know, I always daydreamed about being a hermit one day. Just taking off into the mountains, finding a cave, and living my days out in peace. In that dream, I never thought I would have more than three dozen people joining me."

Blake understood that. He hadn't realized the weight he had put on Arland's shoulders that day he dumped Survival 101 on him in a matter of minutes, but what the man had done with that taste of information impressed Blake. The guy was a survivalist and a leader, one that had his respect.

"We're going to have to move camp," Arland stated, depression and regret lining his words.

Blake nodded. It was the best chance of survival. "Have a plan to where?"

"Into the wilderness…somewhere." He nodded toward the forest east of them and shrugged. "Care to offer advice on that one?"

"When are you planning on the move?"

"I'm hoping to make it through winter. We have stores of food here, a semi-defensible position, and friends," he said with a smile.

"Talk it over with your council if you want. Give me a couple weeks to focus on our preparations. Then come for a visit. We'll go over the maps and see what we can find as a suitable location."

"Thank you," Arland said as his hand dropped on Blake's shoulder. "You are the reason for all of this."

He spread his other arm wide. "You do realize that, don't you?"

Blake rose and looked down at Arland. "No, I'm not. This grand creation is yours, my friend, and one you should be proud of."

Blake left Arland's side in search of some peace in the forest. He needed to think. He needed time to himself, to build a plan of his own, and to figure out, once again, how he would keep his family safe. For a moment, he wondered if they had an inside man locating all the bunkers, was there someone doing the same to the government bunkers he had helped to hide?

~*~

Kris woke from a nightmare only to find Blake gone and Tucker in his place, but Tucker wasn't sleeping. He sat wide-eyed, staring at nothing. The image sent her heart racing into overdrive. Was Tucker having a vision? What would happen if she disturbed him?

A moment later, Tucker blinked several times and found her watching him. Tears brimmed in his eyes so much like Blake's.

"What is it, Sweetie? Are you okay?" She pulled him into her arms.

"We're going to leave Forest Glen. We all are." Tucker's voice was soft, remorseful, and reverent.

"What did you see, Tuck?"

"I saw everyone here walking through the woods, carrying everything they could. Fear lived in everyone's eyes. Fear and sadness." Tucker sat back. "I don't want to leave our home, Mommy. I want

Mercy to grow up in our house like I did. She won't know how to swing or go down a slide."

As if Mercy heard him, she started whimpering and fussing in the basket next to them. Kris kissed Tucker on the head and then reached to pick up his sister.

"It's okay, sweet girl. No matter where we are, you will have all of our love and the best big brother you could ever wish for." Kris soothed her baby, wishing that she could have a normal life full of playtime at the park, playdates with friends, and a warm bed and house to return to.

"I will teach you everything I know, little sister, and I will find a way for you to learn how to swing." Tucker kissed the top of her head.

She kicked her legs and beat her fists, babbling away as if everything she said made sense.

"I know, sister. You will." Tucker moved away then to start rolling up his sleeping bag.

"What do you know, Sweetie?" Kris asked when he didn't elaborate.

Tucker stopped, looked at her, and then went back to rolling up his bag. "That's between my sister and me."

Kris bit her tongue. She didn't like secrets, and her curiosity screamed at her to make him share what he meant. A brother and sister should have their bond, though, even if it didn't make any sense to her. It would come out eventually, and until then she would do her best to respect her son's wishes for privacy. Yet, she wondered at what it could be that he heard in his sister's babbles, and what exactly he thought she would be doing.

~6~

Blake knew it would be hard to get Kris to leave, but he hadn't expected the entire camp to be upset. Yet, person after person came up to ask if they could stay. They offered up their own homes, half their rations, goods, tools, and more. Blake didn't get it. Why were they so important?

He graciously thanked each one for their offers, and despite the pleading in Kris's and Tucker's eyes, he stood firm on leaving. Promising to come for another visit soon did seem to appease most of them, including his wife and son. Even he felt a little comfort with the idea of visiting again.

He hadn't realized how much he had missed male companionship. Not that he needed it on a daily basis, but having it available when he did eased some of his stress. This visit proved to him that he could fully trust Arland, something that came hard for him to believe.

He would help Arland find a suitable location for his camp. If nothing else, then he would know where they were, and his family would know, too. He was serious when he said he would want Kris to go to the camp if something ever happened to him. She would be safer there than on her own. So, why then did he not want to join them?

He could no longer say it was the safety of the bunker because ironically the bunker might just be what led people straight to them. He shook his head and wiped down his face.

"You okay?" Kris asked from beside him. "You've been quiet ever since we left camp."

Blake blinked a few times, realizing that he had lost himself in all his planning and ponderings. What had he missed? What if someone had ambushed them? He admonished himself with a growl.

"It's okay, I didn't mean to interrupt your thinking." Kris slowed her pace to ease behind him where Tucker hoofed it.

He had been going at a breakneck pace, and no one complained. Tucker's face had turned red, and he grunted with each big step up the hill. Kris labored as well with her pack full of herbs and food people sent them off with and, of course, their Mercy, whom she soothed quietly.

"She needs to eat?" Blake asked looking back at his family, hating the fact he had pushed them so hard without realizing it and without the need to do so.

"It's okay. I can readjust her and nurse while we hike." Kris started rearranging the wrap.

"No, a break would do everyone good."

Blake took her pack off her and set it against a tree. He then turned to Tucker who had already removed his pack and walked off to sit in a beam of light on a rock. Blake continued to watch him while he took off his own pack. It seemed that they all had things on their minds today.

"Any idea what has our boy being so contemplative?" Blake asked Kris as she got herself in a comfortable position to nurse a fussing Mercy.

She blew out a breath, waited until he met her eyes, and then said, "He had another vision."

"It's burden I wish he didn't carry."

"Me, too."

"Did he tell you this one?" Blake squatted next to her, enjoying the feel of his muscles stretching.

Kris nodded. "He said we're all leaving, Arland's camp and us." Her voice caught, and Blake reached out to touch her face.

"Whatever happens, we will face this together." He repeated her words.

Her eyes moistened as she nodded, attempting a small smile. "Will you talk with him?"

Blake rose. "On my way." He looked down at his beautiful wife nursing their miraculous daughter. Life sure wasn't turning out as he had thought it would, but he had to admit he wouldn't change it. "As long as we're together, we're going to be okay."

Kris smiled before he turned to talk with Tucker. The boy sat with his eyes closed and face upturned toward the sunlight. He didn't want to intrude upon his serene moment, so he stopped and soaked up the silence as well.

In a life where you didn't know what would happen next, taking the time to appreciate where you were was vital for your peace of mind. Blake had learned that years ago, but seeing his boy already using that wisdom settled him. Tucker would be okay. He would be able to carry this burden, as much as Blake wished he could take it off his shoulders.

"It's peaceful here, isn't it?" Tucker's words broke into Blake's contemplation. "It is. I'm glad to see you enjoying it." Blake climbed onto the rock next to him.

"We're moving," Tucker said straight forwardly, as if it were happening in the moment.

Blake nodded. "Your mom told me you had another vision. Why don't we break it down?"

Tucker turned to him. "You believe me?"

"Of course I do, Champ. So we were with Arland's camp?"

"Yes, sort of. I still felt apart, and we were ahead of them."

Blake nodded. "Do you know when this will happen?"

Tucker shook his head. "I don't want to leave, Dad."

"I know, son. Me neither, but if you saw it, we should prepare. I'm sure there's a good reason. Now let's look closer to determine how much time we have. Could you tell what time of year it was? If it was cold or hot? What did the trees look like? How old did your sister look?"

Tucker closed his eyes and stuck the tip of his tongue out of the corner of his mouth. "The oaks have no leaves. We are bundled up. I can see our breaths, and there is snow in the shade. Mom is carrying Mercy in her wrap. She smiles at me…she has a tooth!" Tucker's eyes open. "Little sister is going to get a tooth."

"I'm sure she will get plenty." Blake smiled encouragingly at his son even though his mind went a million miles a minute. It sounded like this winter. They didn't have much time. A heaviness settled on him. He didn't want to leave their home either. "You did well, Champ."

Blake patted his son on his back and handed him a chunk of jerky and his canteen. "Eat up and rest up. We're more than halfway home."

Home. What would they call home after they left? He pondered what it meant as he settled himself beside Kris.

"When will Mercy get her first tooth?" Blake asked.

"Tucker got his around six months. Why?" she asked while handing him their daughter.

He took her in his arms and sat her up. Her goofy toothless grin and milky drool made him smile. "Do you think visions can be changed?"

Kris didn't respond. She watched him, biting her lip. Mercy did respond, a babble of response, her eyes intense and purposeful. Too bad he didn't speak baby. He felt for sure she had the answer.

~*~

Kris still played Blake's question in her mind, even three weeks later. Could a vision be changed? She laid Tucker's baby picture reverently on top of her wedding dress with a few other special mementos. There were some things she wanted to ensure would survive. If they really did leave, one day maybe Tucker or Mercy would return and find these treasured keepsakes.

"Say it again, Sweetie," she told Tucker as he dangled a toy in front of Mercy.

She liked having the house to be in during cold days like today, days that reminded her how lucky they were to have all they did, and how much she would miss it.

"Little robin, listen to me, start at the twisted tree and count to three. One. Two. Three. See the apples high in the boughs, follow them down two rows."

"Good, Tuck. Keep practicing. It's important that you can remember these rhymes." Kris knew he understood, but she hoped repeating the words would cement them into him to the point he couldn't forget.

The rhymes just might save his life one day.

Blake came through the door, dirt smudged across his face and no coat despite the cold. He stopped to say hi to the kids before he came over to her.

"This just about ready? It's time to close up the hole."

Blake had decided they should stash their extra supplies in underground caches. In that case, if the bunker did get raided, they would still have a good supply to draw from.

"Do you remember this day?" she asked, holding a picture of her and him standing near a waterfall along granite slabs.

"Like I could ever forget." He smiled at her in a way that made her remember why she said *yes* all those years ago. "That's the day you agreed to deal with me for the rest of my life."

"For the rest of mine," she said.

"Oh, no you don't. You aren't leaving me here alone." He pulled her into his arms.

Kris wanted to melt into him and disappear from the ordeal they faced. Reality crashed into her serene moment with Mercy's fussing.

"She's not happy today, Mom." Tucker earnestly tried to interest his little sister with the giraffe toy they had found in his room.

"No, she's not." Kris gave Blake a quick peck before pushing away to pick up her sweet, fussy girl. "Yes, I think I am done with that for now. We have two more caches right?" she asked Blake while bouncing Mercy.

"Yes, at least two more."

"Can I come help, Dad?" Tucker said as he rose

off the ground and puffed out his chest. "I'm strong and can carry a lot."

"I know you can, Champ. You can use those strong muscles to carry the bag your mom just packed." Blake nodded to the bag and grabbed a couple others.

"How long are these going to remain underground?" Tucker asked as he met his dad by the door.

"As long as needed," Blake said, his voice giving away his despondence. He glanced at Kris with a sad smile before taking the bags and her son out.

Kris focused on Mercy, pushing away thoughts about why they had to bury their treasures and extra food underground. She wished they had their Jeep or at least a wagon or something so they could take it all with them. She sighed. They didn't have any idea of where they would go yet or even what would cause them to leave all they had prepared to sustain them during an event like this.

Mercy whimpered, chewing on her finger.

"What is it, sweet girl?" Kris looked at her finger to make sure it was okay and noticed an increase in drool. Her breath caught, and she examined Mercy's gums. They were red and swollen on the bottom in the middle…right where her first tooth would erupt.

They should have two more months at least! Kris ran her finger along the gums, and sure enough, she felt the sharp edge of her first tooth pushing under the surface.

Mercy cried and tore her head away to put her finger back into her mouth.

"I'm sorry, Honey. I know that hurts." They didn't have any teething gel or the ability to freeze a teether.

How would she help her daughter through this for the next year? She wished Laurie were here. She would have some remedies from the forest.

As if her prayers had been immediately answered, she heard the monitor beep. The area on the northeast perimeter lit up. Probably Arland and hopefully Laurie coming for their promised visit. Yet, her heart raced, knowing the threat coming toward them. They had to be careful.

She held the radio up, breathed out to calm herself, and contacted Blake. "You there?"

"We're here," Tucker responded.

"There's a breach on the northeast perimeter."

"Probably Arland, but I'm sending Tucker back and will investigate," Blake said.

"Be careful."

"You, too. In fact, meet Tucker at the bunker and lock yourself in, just in case."

"You really think that's necessary?" Kris asked.

"For my peace of mind? Yes. Please, Krista."

"I'm going," she grunted into the radio as she packed all of Mercy's things into a bag and headed out the door.

"Thank you," Blake's voice crackled over the walkie-talkie.

"Just radio as soon as you see it's Arland, okay?" Kris requested, knowing she would be worrying until she heard the visitors were their friends.

"10-4, over and out."

"Love you. We always return to each other. Over and out." Kris needed to hear him say it.

"We always return to each other. Out."

Tucker was waiting for her with the bunker door open. "Do you think Arland brought Ethan with him?"

"It's a long trip for a little guy," she said as she ushered him in ahead of her. She handed the bag down and secured Mercy before climbing down the steps while closing the door behind them. The finalizing whoosh of the door closing would never be her favorite sound. Yet, with the thought of having to leave the safety the bunker offered, she realized that she had come to depend on it as much as Blake.

What would they do for safety out in the forest or wherever they went?

~7~

As Blake closed in on the northeast perimeter, he moved stealthily from tree to tree. He hoped that the intruders were just their friends. Friends. He liked the sound of that. Yet, there was a tingle of warning that made him cautious. Life had taken a turn in the last month again.

He had accustomed himself to their new survival way of living and become almost comfortable on their land. He had become complacent, though. The idea that people traveled toward him and his family with the intention of taking all that he had prepared for themselves left him in the constant need to be on the watch and take nothing for granted.

The sound of leaves crunching made him suck in a breath and freeze behind the tree he had been approaching. Every muscle tensed, his breathing stilled, and all he could hear was the pulsing of his own racing heart. Then he heard another step and another.

The sound of labored breathing reached him. The person had to have just climbed the bank at the edge of his property. It would leave even the fittest person breathing hard. The leaves and pine cones that littered the ground made walking silently difficult. Blake did his best to peer around the tree to see if the person was friend or foe.

He slowly pulled out his pistol and flicked the safety off. Being prepared could be the difference between life and death. It wasn't as if he wanted to scare Arland if it was he, but if it wasn't, not being ready might mean his family being left in jeopardy without him. The idea left him leveling the pistol as he stepped silently toward the person who seemed to be waiting at the top of the hill.

Blake kept his eye on the incline as well, for he could hear one or two others trudging up with smaller steps.

"You're almost there, Ethan. Think about how excited your friend, Tucker, will be when he sees you."

Blake breathed out a sigh and holstered his gun as he heard Laurie encouraging her son. Then he stepped out from behind cover.

"That he will be. Welcome," he said from beside Arland.

Arland stepped back, a hand on his chest. "You're going to give me a heart attack one of these days."

"Not my intention, my friend." Blake reached out a hand to him.

Arland clasped it and pulled him into a hug. "Good to see you, Blake."

"Hello, Blake," Laurie called up from about three-quarters up the incline.

Blake bounced down to them, gave Laurie a quick hug, and hoisted Ethan to his shoulders. "Tucker is going to be so impressed that you walked all the way here."

Ethan giggled. "I walk long way to play."

"Yes, you did. I'm proud of you." Laurie smiled and nodded her thanks to Blake.

"I am, too, Ethan. You have a strength of mind that will serve you well," Arland told the boy as he and Blake came alongside him.

"I am survivalist!" the boy said while making big muscles.

"That you are," Blake said, bouncing him on his shoulders. "We're almost there. Kris and Tucker will be—" He stopped so abruptly Ethan crashed into his head and wrapped his little arms around Blake's face. "Sorry there, buddy. Just got to make a call."

"A call?" Arland asked.

Blake held up his walkie-talkie. "You there?"

"We're here," Tucker returned.

"Tucker!" Ethan cheered.

"We have visitors, with one very special one." Blake squeezed Ethan's foot and started walking again.

"Did Arland and Laurie bring Ethan?!" Tucker's voice crackled through, excitement making static.

"Why don't you all come out and see?"

"We're on our way! Oh, over and out."

"Over and out, Champ." Blake stored the walkie-talkie back on his belt loop. "I think you just made Tucker the happiest boy in the forest."

"No. I the happiest boy!" Ethan clapped his hands and squealed before grabbing back onto Blake's head.

Blake couldn't help but appreciate the cheer the visitors brought to his day. Maybe he wasn't quite the lone wolf he thought he was.

"How long you guys staying? I'm sure the camp needs you." Blake asked.

"We're hoping for at least a night, maybe two depending on how much we can accomplish. David has really proved himself quite the leader after his run-in with you. Between him, Mitchel, and a few other council members, they'll be fine. We have runners ready in case they need us."

"It's nice to get away from the hustle and bustle for awhile," Laurie said with a sweet smile.

Blake understood, but he hadn't expected Laurie to feel that way. She was always calm, patient, and sweet. Yet, she was in high demand at the camp. That would get exhausting.

"I will pull the maps out as soon as you are rested. Kris had put on some stew earlier. I'm sure she can add more to it. It won't be a feast like yours, but we do have fresh veggies from the garden and a rabbit that Tucker got this morning."

As they neared the cleared-off acreage of his property, he saw his family coming toward them. Tucker took off at a run to meet them.

"There's my little hunter now," Blake said, hearing the pride in his voice. Tucker had proved himself since the birth of his sister. He was a dedicated student and followed directions to a T.

Tucker stopped short as he reached them. His head cocked sideways to look up at Ethan on his dad's shoulders. Blake reached up, lifted the younger boy off, and put him on the ground in front of Tucker.

"I came to play with you." Ethan held up the car Tucker had let him keep when they left camp before.

"Wait until you see all the other toys I have in my room!" He took Ethan's hand and started pulling.

"Tucker," Kris said as she arrived. "Your manners?"

"Oh," Tucker ducked his head and then turned toward the adults. "Hello, Arland and Laurie. Thank you for bringing Ethan. May I take him to my room?"

"Hello to you, too. Of course. You boys have

fun," Laurie said.

"Yay!" Tucker cheered, and the boys ran off toward the house.

"Well, you just made his week," Kris said as she hugged Laurie and Arland. "Happy to see you."

Mercy whimpered from her wrap.

"She's having a rough day." Kris unwrapped her and held her out to Laurie.

"Oh," she said as a bit of drool dripped down as she brought her into her arms. "Are you teething, little one? Aunty Laurie brought you some yummies to help with that."

"She's teething?" Blake almost choked on the words. He trapped Kris's eyes in a hard gaze, not angry, just intense. Could this really be happening already?

"After you took Tucker outside, I noticed her gums were inflamed." Kris gently pulled down Mercy's lip to show him. "You can feel the tip of a tooth right here."

"I thought we would have more time," Blake whispered to himself, but the others heard it.

"Oh, it's just teething. Nothing to be so glum about. I knew it would be coming soon, so I brought some things for her."

"You are so thoughtful, Laurie." Kris tore her eyes off Blake, pushing a smile to her face as she faced Laurie.

They didn't need to share Tucker's vision, not yet at least. Arland already planned to move camp. He didn't need to know that Blake's son foresaw them joining. That might just change. A vision could be only a warning, right? He would heed the warning and prepare, but he wouldn't not pray that events would shift, allowing them to stay in the comfort of their home.

~*~

Kris and Laurie sat in the living room of the house with Mercy while the boys played in Tucker's room. The happy noises of boys filled her house, leaving Kris with a nostalgic melancholy.

"It's so nice to hear the boys playing. It brings back memories of before." Laurie sounded like she missed those days, too.

Kris nodded and stared down at her beautiful little girl in her arms. Mercy would never get to know what it was like to play in a room full of toys.

"She'll be okay." Laurie reached out and touched her knee. "She won't know the difference. Our boys, on the other hand…they will, but kids are resilient. With the right nurturing, they'll make it through."

"Yeah," Kris said. She usually could see the positive in everything, but she struggled right now.

A melancholy had settled in her ever since Tucker shared his last vision, and she couldn't shake it. She wished she could openly share it with Laurie, but the look in Blake's eyes let her know that was currently off limits. It wasn't in her nature to keep things from a friend, but her loyalty to her family made more of an impact.

Laurie pulled out two small jars and a pouch with what looked like sticks in it. "These are for Mercy." She held up the jar with herbs in it. "Chamomile and chickweed for tea. You make the tea and soak a small cloth and let her chew on it." She held up the second jar. "Lemon balm mixed with animal fat to rub on her gums." She held up the pouch. "Here are two roots. One is licorice root and the other arrowroot. I have been growing them from my supply, and they have done quite well. She can gnaw on these for relief."

Kris took the items. "Thank you so much, Laurie. Your foresight and gifts always amaze me. I appreciate you so much."

"And us you and your family. Arland's stress has lessened dramatically since he has found your husband."

"Blake has seemed to actually enjoy his company, which is really saying something for him. He has always been one to keep to himself."

"Well, I think our men have found their counterparts." Laurie laughed. "Our boys get along well, too, and who knows, maybe Ethan and Mercy will pair up one day."

The men entered as she finished her own prophecy.

"Are you playing matchmaker again?" Arland asked as he and Blake shrugged out of their coats.

Having the woodstove in the house was one nice thing about the winter. Blake had to do some modifications to make the smoke dissipate, but he allowed them to have a fire for now, something Kris knew would probably be revoked soon with the threat of the city encroaching upon them.

Laurie laughed. "I can't help it. We have the survival of children to think about. So much of the population has died off, we need to think about repopulation. At least keeping our own community alive and prospering."

"I don't want to think about our little Mercy getting married off." Blake groaned as he gave their sleeping daughter a kiss.

"Tell me about it," Arland humphed. "Miss Matchmaker has decreed my Hannah being married off in under a year."

"I haven't decreed that." Laurie knocked into Arland playfully. "That is an observation. She and Tyler have been virtually inseparable."

"Well, there aren't many other kids her age." Arland crossed his arms.

"She's not a kid anymore," Laurie said gently.

"So you keep telling me," Arland said glumly.

Kris smiled in understanding. It was difficult to think about your children growing up and moving away, but they wouldn't move away anymore, would they? In a community like Arland's, when Hannah decided to marry Tyler, she would only be a dwelling away. The thought brought some comfort to Kris. She liked the idea of her children always being close.

"Well, talking about the future," Blake said, clearing his throat, "we thought we should get your opinion, Laurie, on a location with all the resources you need to continue your foraging and gardening."

"Thank you for thinking of that, Blake."

"Well, I can't take the credit. That was Arland's thought, but I do agree it's a necessary component of finding a location where your community can survive."

"Oh, we plan on thriving," Laurie said.

Kris watched the confident woman and realized she had every intention of following through with her statement. The way she said it made Kris wonder if she had over thought the whole move. Maybe Laurie was right. Maybe living off the land in a hidden, secret community wouldn't be nearly as uncomfortable as she feared.

~*~

Blake spread the cracked, smudged, and torn map carefully on the table.

"Wow, this is one well-used map," Arland said, touching a torn edge.

"It's decades old and extremely precious." Blake eyed him, not liking other fingers on the delicate paper.

"Oh, a keepsake?" Laurie asked.

"No. A resource that can no longer be found."

"There still might be some if we looted the forest service station. I even have some at my house," Arland stated.

"Not one like this." Blake pointed to a road. "Does yours have this road? Or this one? I can promise you, it doesn't."

"It's for the same location." Arland watched him closer.

"Those roads have been blocked off for a decade now. According to the new maps and most people, they no longer exist."

Laurie gasped and then met his eyes. "You mean this can lead us to places no one else will know about?"

"Exactly." Blake stood back and snuck a prideful glance at Kris. She had always complained about the old map.

"Great. Now his head is going to grow so large he won't be able to carry it around anymore," Kris said wryly from where she sat letting Mercy chew on a stick.

"Are you really letting our daughter chew on a stick?" Blake said.

"It's licorice root." Kris nodded toward Laurie.

"It helps the inflammation and pain in her gums," Laurie said.

"Oh." Blake didn't like the reminder that time was closing in on them. What was going to push him far enough to leave his place of safety? Sure, people might be searching for his bunker, but how would they find it? How would they get into it? Fear clutched his heart with an icy grip. Did he want to find out?

Tucker ran into the room. "You have the map out! Can I see? Where are we going?" Then he took a step back. "I don't want to leave…"

"Tuck, we are looking for a new location for Arland's camp. You can look at the map later. Enjoy your company."

Blake avoided the curious stares from Arland and Laurie. He glanced at Kris, who also focused anywhere but at them.

Tucker walked back to his room, but with much less joy than before. Blake watched him retreat. He didn't want to leave either.

Blake cleared his throat and looked at the map. "We're looking for a place to house about three dozen people, right?"

Arland stared at him for a moment and then glanced at Laurie. "We have grown by two families, another nine people, and have word that at least one if not two more families want to join us as well."

"The news of the city marauders is scaring the few people left who have been surviving in their neighborhoods," Laurie said.

"More people who like to raid houses and bunkers." Blake crossed his arms. He didn't like the idea of more people like Jake joining the community, but then again, it wasn't his camp or his decision to make.

"They are only accepted after they take an oath to follow the community's rules," Arland said, his gaze unwavering.

"New Forest Glen won't stand for stealing, even if it is survival," Laurie said.

"You've named your camp. I like the name," Kris said.

It was good. Having a name for the community would instill a sense of belonging that would help everyone want to come together to make it successful.

"Okay, so we're talking close to fifty," Blake started.

"Could be fifty-four," Arland said.

"And don't forget the babies that will come," Laurie added.

Blake swiped a hand down his face, noticing the stubble that had begun to grow. If they left, he wouldn't have the option of using his electric razor anymore. He scratched at the growing beard. He would have to get used to facial hair, as Arland had. Though he obviously had a pair of scissors or something because Arland's beard wasn't nearly as unruly as many of the other men's at his camp. He shrugged, a beard was the least of his worries.

"Let's find a location suitable for one hundred then. We won't make it that big at the start, but there will be room for expansion." Blake looked closer at the map, reassessing his ideas.

"We? Does that mean you're joining us?" Arland

just wouldn't let it go.

"No decisions are being made today, Arland. Let's just say I want a suitable location that will keep everyone safe and fed."

"Good enough. I'll stop pestering." Arland sat back in his chair, a smug smile on his face.

The fact that Arland pushed for Blake to join them didn't make him angry. It made him feel good that he wanted him around. He didn't understand it, but just the same, it was nice to be wanted. Leaving his home was something he never foresaw in his preparations. Leaving might be something he's preparing for, but that didn't mean he wanted to think about it.

"I have three locations I think might work." He pointed to all three on the map.

"What are the elevations?" Laurie asked.

"They are all valleys that sit from three to four thousand feet with peaks close by that range from five to six."

Laurie nodded.

"So, it will be a lot like here. We'll get some snow, but not much." Arland scratched at his beard.

"Yes, but there will be snow between here and there. That will deter people from searching out there in winter, at least." Blake pointed to the peaks and ridges encircling the valleys.

"Wouldn't being down in a valley be a disadvantage for defense?" Arland asked.

"Being as we are more dependent on survival right now than a massive defense, I think it would be okay. Each of these valleys is nestled in between ridges and peaks. The only way to see them would be to climb the peaks themselves, something not many who are struggling to survive will want to do. Of course, we will have outposts on each one that will give us the advantage of knowing of any approach."

"So, which of the three are you leaning toward?" Arland asked.

Blake turned to Laurie. "That's going to depend on the foliage."

Laurie smiled, and her eyes focused on the map. "I've never been good at reading these things. It would help if I could see the landscape."

"Do you have a few weeks?" Blake asked and sat back. "Because it will take several days for us to walk there, and each location is at least a day's walk apart or more."

"If it was just the two of us, we could cover that much quicker." Arland watched Blake, reading him.

Blake hardened his eyes. "Absolutely not. Every time I leave my family, something awful happens."

"They could stay with…" Arland started, but when Blake hardened his gaze further, he stopped. "Okay, then let's do our best from here and see what we can figure out."

"Each location has a creek or small river running either through it or close by. This one here has a spring. I have actually drunk from that one before. Good water."

Laurie and Arland followed his fingers on the map and then sat back and looked at each other.

"Water is a definite must for foraging and for growing crops. The spring is a plus. Do you remember the type of brush, trees, or other plants there?"

Blake shut his eyes. It had been ten years ago that he had gone hunting out there. Part of him hadn't wanted to share that location for it had been his original bug-out plan before he started working with bunkers. Yet, if they did end up having to leave, there might be advantages to having Arland's camp, New Forest Glen, close by.

He remembered how ecstatic he had been to find the spring. Springs were always good finds. They were water that damming upstream wouldn't affect. Survival situations needed consistent water, water that couldn't be affected by things outside of their immediate surroundings.

"It was well shaded. Not only did it have the normal evergreens, but I remember being shocked to find a grove of oak trees and, of course, the normal alder trees. There were dogwoods down by the creek. I almost didn't find the place because of a wall of manzanita on the ridge around the valley. That would actually be a good defense."

The more he pictured the location, the more he recognized that it would be the perfect spot for a community...and even a small family who wanted to live close but not within the hubbub.

"I don't know much about plant life, so I can't help more," Blake said. The decision had to be theirs. He wanted a place he knew he could reach and a place he and his family could retreat to if needed, but he still hoped that visions could change. That something he did or didn't do would change the outcome, and they could stay in the place he had spent years preparing.

"And you can lead us there?" Arland asked. "You'd be willing to take your family on that long trip?"

"I want them to know how to get there, and you can't leave markers. It would be unsafe."

"I realize that now. Before, I left a trail for people to escape the fire. I had no idea what that would turn into."

"None of us did," Laurie said, laying a hand on top of Arland's.

Blake nodded in agreement. He had an idea. Being surrounded by scientists and politicians, you gleaned information that the general public didn't want to know. This scenario was one of them. He had heard the statistics. He knew about the percentage of population decrease, the gangs, and the looters. Those were all things he had expected. The one thing he didn't expect, and should have, was the person who memorized the locations of all the bunkers he had helped install.

Blake's jaw muscles twitched. There was no going back. All he could do was prepare to be found and hope they weren't.

~8~

By the time Mercy's two bottom teeth were in, Kris had grown weary of expecting something crazy to happen. Her teeth were in, and nothing had transpired to make them want to leave. Maybe something had shifted and the vision wouldn't happen.

It had been four weeks since Arland and Laurie had visited. Kris started to feel lonely. She missed having her new friend to talk with. Tucker moped around, too.

"Can we go to New Forest Glen Camp again?" Tucker asked as if he read her mind.

"This storm coming feels icy, Tuck. It probably means snow," Kris told him, wrapping her jacket around her and Mercy tighter. They didn't come out of the bunker much when it was cold like this, but she wanted Tucker to run some energy out before the storm hit.

She readjusted the weight of the shotgun she always carried when outside now. The cold metal against her made her think about Laurie and the others living outside during the snow. How did their camp run then? Did they still have communal meals and work outdoors?

The thought of a warm shower soothed her, but guilt came with it. No one at that camp had had a hot shower for over a year now. The idea made her feel woozy. No hot water. No shower. Yet, that's what they would face living out in the forest like Tucker foresaw.

Maybe it had passed. Tucker hadn't said anything more about it. He hadn't seemed nervous or upset when he saw Mercy's teeth pop out. This line of thinking would drive her mad. Instead, she just focused on the moment, enjoying watching Tucker speeding through the trees.

Blake walked back to them from a perimeter check. He had taken off his coat, his arms bare to the cold. She wrapped her arms tighter around herself and Mercy, thinking of how cold that must feel. Blake, though, didn't have a trace of goosebumps.

"All clear. How are things here?" Blake asked, picking up Tuck as he ran into his arms. "You still have energy to burn off?"

"Tons!" Tucker squealed as Blake hung him upside down over his shoulder.

"How about you show Mom how you can find all three cache pits?"

"Okay!"

"All three?" Kris asked, watching her boys while love filled her. She wouldn't change how close they had become for the world. It warmed her heart, making the chill a little easier to bear.

"Yep. Number one: Little robin listen to me, start at the twisted tree and count to three. One. Two. Three. See the apples high in the boughs, follow them down two rows."

Kris followed him as he completed the riddle to find the location. Of course, as he stood over the prized spot, there was no marker indicating he was correct. Well, except the look of pride on his father's face.

"Nice work, Sweetie. You are really getting good at memorizing."

"You haven't seen anything yet!" Tucker said and scrunched his brows while he concentrated. "Number Two: Little squirrel on the rock, what do you do? Run past big pine trees numbering two. Collect acorns as you go, and look to see where they grow."

Tucker made his way through the trees around rocks until he stood with his little chest puffed out on the second spot Blake had hidden their supplies.

"This one could get tough later depending on how big this oak tree gets." Tuck touched the leaves of the tree no taller than he was.

"Well done, Tuck," Blake said. "Yes, as the oak tree grows, this one will be tougher to get at. All the better to hide it, right? Now, we haven't practiced three for very long. Do you think you can do it?"

Kris enjoyed watching the pride that filled the boy at meeting a challenge his dad threw at him. He had always pushed himself to meet the expectations of others and of himself. He had turned it from academics to survival scenarios very quickly.

"Little stellar jay picking up sticks, count the madrone trees numbering six." Tuck stopped, stuck his tongue out while he concentrated, and then finished the riddle and his steps. "Build your nest in me, says the tall fir tree."

"Yes!" Blake high-fived him. "You remember those in the years to come, and one day it just may save you and your sister."

"What about you and Mom?" Tucker's euphoria dimmed as he looked between them.

"It could save us, too, Sweetie. I think what Dad means is that you may be the one to come get them, right?"

"Yeah. We don't know what lies ahead of us in this life, Champ. All we can do is be prepared and learn skills that will help in every situation."

"Including how to stay calm in intense situations." Kris gave him a hug. "I'm very proud of you."

"I'm proud of you, too, Mom." Tucker kissed her on the cheek.

Kris stood, shock and love overwhelming her. "Why?"

"Maybe he means because of your strength of mind." Blake took her hand as they walked back to the bunker. The riddles took them a good half-mile away.

"What does strength of mind mean?" Tucker asked as he ran up to catch them.

Blake stopped and looked at Tucker. "It means when it seems all odds are up against you, your body feels like it can't go on, your fear tells you that you won't make it, you keep pushing on."

"Oh, like Mom did when little sister was born."

"Exactly like that." Blake dropped Kris's hand to muss their son's hair and then wrapped his arm around her.

Kris warmed inside, knowing that her boys thought so much of her. Strength of mind really was a trait that led to success and thriving, especially in the situation they found themselves in right now.

They ambled back to their warm bunker arm-in-arm, feeling that even in a post-apocalyptic world, life wasn't all that bad.

That was until a beep from their remote froze them all in their tracks. Within a moment, their life had taken a drastic change. Kris could feel the cold travel from her toes all throughout her until her heart almost stopped. Her eyes found Blake's in a frozen moment of fear.

He yanked the remote off his pants. "It's at the gate."

Kris pulled Tucker to her, his eyes round, and for once he was silent. The bunker was still about two hundred yards away and in the direction of the gate. Could they make it in time?

Blake grabbed her by both shoulders, the jar waking Mercy, who whimpered. She had been fussy the last couple days. Her cries, and Blake's earnestness, woke Kris out of shock.

"You have to run. Take the kids to the bunker." Blake's gaze was intense, full of urgency.

"What about you?" Fear shrilled her voice. Blake would do something stupid to keep them safe.

"I'm going to do my best to keep them away from you." He pressed his lips against hers. "I love you, Krista." He kissed Mercy with a sheen in his eyes and kissed the top of Tucker's head quickly.

"We should stay together, Dad."

"You take care of your mom and sister. Now run!" He gave Tucker a little shove and took off in the opposite direction.

"We always return to each other!" Tucker called out after him.

Kris whispered it, too, but Blake hardly paused in his urgent quest. Her heart lurched as she grabbed Tucker's hand, readjusted the shotgun so she could run, and tugged him toward the bunker. In a few steps, he pulled his hand out and stopped.

"We have to go, Sweetie."

"He didn't say it…" Tuck's lip trembled, but then

he pulled off the bow he constantly wore anytime he was outside and nocked an arrow. "Let's go."

"That's my boy," Kris said and kissed him.

She squeezed an arm around Mercy in the wrap, and they took off in a run toward the bunker. Shots echoed across their property. She and Tuck stopped.

"Dad," he whispered.

Tears stung at Kris's eyes, but as more shots rang out, she urged her son to keep going. They were almost there, but she pulled Tucker to a stop at the edge of the apple trees. Three men stood at the rock pile that hid their bunker door.

The men looked up at them, their frozen movements showing their shock.

Her heart racing, she pulled up the shotgun, aiming at the men. Her hands shook as she reached for the safety. Mercy cried. The sound stopped her in horror. What would the blast do to her baby? She didn't want to cause Mercy to go deaf.

Before she could stop him, Tucker had released his arrow, hitting one man in the shoulder. The man's yowl sent the hairs on the back of her neck raising.

"Get them," another yelled.

Her hands shook so much she couldn't get the safety off or load the chamber. Ice ran through her veins. "Run, Tucker! Run!"

Tucker stood his ground only a moment before he took off through the forest. Kris followed as closely as she could with Mercy held close into her, screaming her displeasure. Doom closed in on her as she heard heavy steps behind her. A moment later, her neck burned with the grasp of a rough hand.

Kris twisted, swung at the man with the shotgun, and kicked out. The man grunted as the barrel of her gun glanced off his shoulder before ripping out of her hands and flying across the ground. Despite the blow, he tightened his hold on her. She continued to fight with every ounce of her strength while protecting the baby wrapped against her. When she felt the cold metal against her cheek, though, she froze. The reality of being captured settled like a rock in the pit of her stomach.

Blake would come for her if he survived, Tucker, too, and she just might be the death of them both. She hung her head, praying for an act of mercy. She had to keep her children safe.

~*~

Blake ran toward the group of armed men climbing over his gate. There were close to a dozen men on this side of the gate. A few of them started toward the house, which sent Blake out of his training and into protecting mode. He had to keep them away from his family.

A roar erupted from his throat as he opened fire on the group. The men that could ran for cover, but Blake continued in a suicidal run toward the others until they had found shelter and started returning fire.

A bullet grazed his shoulder, burning across his skin. He fell to the ground and rolled until he could stand behind a tree. When he was safe, he glanced at his arm, seeing that that the bullet only scratched him. He flattened himself against the tree as bullets flew past him. His heart raced as he did his best to get into controlled fighting mode, but all he could think about was his family. Had they made it to the bunker? Would they be safe there?

The firing stopped. Blake peered out. The surviving men, about a half dozen, were checking those that had fallen. From what he could see, he had taken out at least four or more. The three that had taken off toward his family were not among them.

He banged the back of his head on the tree, murmuring an oath beneath his breath. Pulling out another magazine from his cargo pocket, he reloaded his pistol. It was his last magazine. He had to make each shot count. He took a steadying breath. Getting to his family would be key.

He readied himself for another run, but this time covertly. He peered around the trunk of the pine that had saved his life, cocked and aimed his gun. Two shots. Run. He blew out his breath, aimed at the man holding a rifle pointed toward the tree he hid behind. Blake fired two shots as he ran for the cover of the next tree, getting him that much closer to his family.

Shots fired after him, but stopped as he hid behind the next tree. They must be short on ammo, too. In this survival situation, you couldn't afford to waste bullets. He checked his clip. Thirteen more. Two shots. Run. He followed the same protocol until he made it to where he could see the rock outcropping where the bunker hid.

What he saw made his heart stop and his mouth go dry.

A man had his wife and baby daughter, a handgun shoved into her cheek. Blake's blood boiled as his hands squeezed his gun until his knuckles refused any more pressure. He evened his breathing and looked again. No sign of Tucker. Movement on the other side of the forest caught his attention.

Tucker.

The boy had his bow raised, peeking out from behind a tree. Blake now could see the several arrows he had stuck in the ground before him. He planned on rescuing his mom. Blake started to step out to stop him. What if Tucker missed and hit his mom or sister?

A single shot sent him cowering behind the tree again, leaving him only able to watch as his son tried to be the hero that he had pushed him to be. Tucker was right, they shouldn't have split up. They would have had a better chance going together with Blake covering them while they made it into the bunker. Now, he had to figure out a way to rescue them.

He checked his clip just in case he had miscounted, but it was empty. There was nothing he could do.

Every inch of his body tensed as he watched Tucker on the other side of where Kris was held hostage. He held his breath while he saw his son cock his head like he did every time right before he released the arrow.

The arrow flew straight at the unsuspecting man holding a gun against Kris. The man screamed, dropped the gun he held on Kris, and grabbed his face, blood pouring through his fingers. With bated breath, Blake watched Kris use the distraction to her advantage. She kicked out, dropped the guy to the ground, and grabbed for the gun.

Blake quietly praised her while she pointed the unfamiliar weapon back at him.

The man rose to his knees, holding his face, and spouting words that Kris shouldn't have to hear. The man glared at her. The look in his eyes must have been terrifying for Kris's hands started to shake.

"Don't you move," Kris said with more conviction than Blake thought she would have.

"Your family is crazy, lady." He spat and wiped at his oozing cheek. "But you're not going to win in the end. I have more men coming."

"That doesn't do you any good right now, does it?"

"Oh, you're going to shoot me?" He laughed, a cruel, menacing sound, and stood.

"If you come toward me, I will."

Blake watched, immobilized by the inability to do anything to help his wife who so bravely stood her ground.

"Do it," the man said with a smile as he reached for her.

Blake held his breath. He started to move toward her, but a shot chipped the bark the second he moved.

Kris hit the trigger over and over, but only clicks resounded.

"You've got spunk. Too bad there aren't any bullets left." He went to reach for the gun, but another arrow whipped in and pierced his hand clean through. The man screamed again, holding his hand. "Someone get that crazy junior Robin Hood!"

Two more men took off toward Tucker. That was the last straw for Blake. He might get a few bullets in him, but he wasn't going to let them get his boy. His muscles bunched in, ready to jump out from behind the tree when a sound crunched behind him.

Blake spun and ducked at the same time. A rifle butt barely missed his head, cracking into the trunk instead. He kicked out and knocked the man to the ground, but in his distraction, Blake missed the second man whose fist pummeled him to the ground.

The hit sent sparks behind his eyes, but he came up yelling, going full body into the man. They fell to the ground in a heap of writhing fists and knees and elbows. Finally, they ended up with Blake on top, grabbing for his knife.

He heard the air whistling too late, and a blinding white pain lanced his head before the world turned dark.

~*~

When the arrow pierced the man's hand, Kris had taken advantage of the distraction and run toward her son, fear propelling her feet. Mercy screamed as Kris tightened her arm around her baby's jostling body, but she needed to get to Tucker.

Only a few more yards and she would be there. The boy released three more arrows at the men running toward them, and with each release, she heard a grunt or cry of pain. All out of arrows, he now held his bow like a sword and waved it at the men still coming at them.

Before she could pull Tucker into an embrace, she was grabbed from behind by strong arms that pulled her hands behind her in a grip that brought tears to her eyes. Luckily, the wrap kept Mercy safe against her, but she could only watch while two others grabbed her wildly fighting boy. He kicked, punched, and bit, but eventually they had him, face down in the duff and hands pinned at his back.

"This one is half-wild," one man said.

"Half? He's like a crazy wild Indian. He ruined my jacket, and I'll probably have to stitch up my arm."

"Let go of me! Leave my mom and sister alone!" Tucker yelled and squirmed, though Kris knew every move hurt his arms, for hers screamed almost as loudly as her daughter.

A circle of birds flew overhead, unnaturally cawing and squawking, seeming to yell at the men below.

"What in the world is going on?" The man with the oozing wound on his cheek and an arrow still in his hand looked up at the birds and then to her. "We could have done this peacefully."

"You come onto our property armed and ready to take what is not yours and you expect a peaceful welcome? You are the crazy one."

"We have mouths to feed, too, my dear." He smiled in a way that made her think he really was crazy.

"Then go and hunt like everyone else who is trying to survive." She leveled him with a hard glare.

"Oh, we are hunting."

A chill ran down her spine, the shivering making her arms sear in pain.

The man grabbed his head with his good hand. "This racket is too much. Quiet that baby and your son, and someone make those birds leave!"

"Let me go so I can!" Kris said as she tried to free her arms.

The man with the arrow in his hand nodded. It was good to know who was in charge. The fact that he hadn't outright killed Tucker for what he had done to him was a good sign and one Kris would use while she tried to find a way to keep them alive…until Blake rescued them. If Blake was still alive.

All that shooting…. Her blood ran cold. What if they had killed him?

Her hands now free, she rubbed Mercy's back and murmured soothing sounds while she took small steps toward the still struggling Tucker. With Mercy now only whimpering, she kneeled next to her son.

"Save your energy, Sweetie. You did well."

Seeing his face smooshed in the dirt and the wild fear dancing in his eyes made her heart ache. With her hands she motioned calm, surveillance, and then the *I love you* sign. That one Blake didn't teach them, but it was just as important as the others.

Tucker settled, and the men relaxed their hold slightly.

"You better tie that one up. He's a dangerous little brute. Get me Hank so he can patch me up."

The man squatted in front of Tucker, whose arms were now tied behind his back. "You still might be trainable, boy. I would have a use for a guy like you."

Tucker glared at him. Kris had never seen such a hard look in her young son's eyes, and it tore at her heart.

"You just wait until my dad gets his hands on you. He is going to be so mad that you have us."

The man smiled, one of those smiles that make you wish you could wash after seeing it. "Oh, you don't know yet. We already have your dad, Rambo man and all. He's still mortal, just like you."

Kris's heart sank. Yet, he didn't say that Blake was dead. If he was still alive, there was a chance. If anyone could get them out of this, Blake could, even captured.

"Bring the kid's dad," the man yelled.

"Hank's here, Chuck." The man with the ruined jacket came with a guy toting a black backpack.

"Stick around. Looks like the kid got you, too." He

turned toward Hank. "Get this arrow out of me and stitch me up. We have a bunker to raid."

He looked up at the sky where the birds had dissipated, reminding Kris of the impending storm. A snowstorm was the least of her worries at this moment. If she could get a big enough distraction to free Tucker and have him run to Arland's, at least he would be safe.

Chuck, who seemed to be the leader, sucked in a breath as Hank broke the arrow and pulled it out.

"I can't believe you guys let that kid get the best of you," Hank said as he jammed a cloth onto both sides of Chuck's wound.

"You didn't see him. He's like some sort of ten-year-old Robin Hood," Chuck said, almost good-naturedly.

"Ha! By the time I'm actually ten, I could use a bow that would have killed you," Tucker said.

"See? I'm telling you, we need this kid with us. I can see the whole ploy now. Poor starved boy begging for food, and then, Wham, he turns Tasmanian devil and wipes them out, and we get all of their supplies." Chuck laughed, and Hank shook his head.

"You and your ploys, boss." Hank said. "Need a stick? Both the hand and the cheek will need stitches."

"Nah, just do it."

A heavy slump with a grunt took Kris's attention from the men. She gasped when she saw what the newcomers had dropped—Blake.

"Dad!" Tucker struggled against his ropes.

"Quiet down, boy. He's alive," Chuck said before bracing himself for Hank's ministrations.

Kris watched Blake. His chest rose, but the back of his head and his arm oozed. She couldn't see his face. It was a shock to see the husband she once thought invincible in a bloody, banged-up heap. As much as she wanted to hang her head and cry, she had to stay strong for her children. Blake was alive. There was hope.

As much as she didn't want to be vulnerable with the men around, she knew she could keep Mercy from fussing by feeding her. In the privacy of the wrap, she fed her daughter while sitting next to her son and doing her best just to breathe and find calm in the situation.

At least an hour had passed since the arrival of the men on her property, maybe more. She could feel the cold seep into her even with the adrenaline that raced through her. Tucker shook, whether from shock, fear, or the cold, she didn't know.

Mercy settled, and Kris scooched closer to her son, wrapping an arm around him.

"No funny business." Chuck eyed them as Hank finished the last knot in his stitches.

"He's cold," she said simply.

Blake stirred, and she held her breath.

"Perfect timing. Thanks, Doc." Chuck nodded at Hank and stood up, making his way toward Blake. He nudged him with his foot. "Wakey, wakey, Rambo."

Blake tried to kick at the man, but his hands and feet were tied. After a few moments of struggling, he stopped.

"Where's my family?" His voice was a hardened growl.

"We're here," Kris called out.

In a movement she hadn't thought possible, Blake

shimmied onto his knees and turned toward them. His face was a mass of bruises, his left eye swollen shut, his lips bleeding.

"Are you okay?" he asked her.

She nodded, biting her lip to keep herself from crying.

"I've been worse, Krista. It'll be fine." As swollen as his face was, it was hard to tell, but it looked like he tried to smile.

"Dad," Tucker said, his voice trembling. The boy's hero lay bleeding before him, and Kris wished she could hide the image from her son.

"You did exceptional, Champ."

"I'd say you trained him well," Chuck said. "Okay, enough with the reuniting Hallmark scene. Let's get down to business."

"Let them go," Blake said between clenched teeth.

"I don't think you're in a position to negotiate." The guy stood and held open his arms. "You may have killed a half-dozen of my men or more, and your spitfire son may have injured most the rest of us, but I have more coming. We have the guns and your family. So let's try this again."

Chuck squatted in front of him, though far enough away that Blake couldn't touch him.

"What exactly do you want?" Blake asked.

"The code to your bunker."

"Surely you have other ways of getting inside. Otherwise, you wouldn't have traveled so far to find them."

"We do, but it's winter, and I would like a warm place to ride it out." Chuck smiled, and Kris had an uneasy feeling that this man wasn't well in the head.

"Maybe you should find a different one. Ours isn't

suitable for an outfit of your size."

Chuck laughed. "They can stay in the house or in a tent for all I care."

"Let my family go. Then I will give you the code."

"Yeah, I can't do that, Rambo. You see, I don't trust you, and besides, I've grown quite fond of your family. Your boy I think is still young enough to convert, and your wife, well, there are not too many women left, especially of her caliber."

"They aren't yours for the taking." Blake growled out the words.

"Give me the code."

"No."

Chuck closed the gap between them in less than a second, his good fist hammering down on Blake's cheek.

"Don't touch my dad!" Tucker yelled.

Blake's head whipped back up to glare at Chuck.

"I usually let the inhabitants go," Chuck said, shaking out his hand. "Your family just has really surprised me. With so many losses, I need compensation." He squatted down and cocked his head. "Let's try this again. Give me the code."

"No," Blake said, squaring his shoulders the best he could.

Chuck nodded at one of the other guys. He came up, gut-punched Blake in the stomach with his rifle, and then knocked him on the side of his face.

"Stop it!" Tucker yelled.

Kris averted her eyes and tried to cover Tucker's, but he shrugged out of her hand, doing his best to crawl with his hands behind him to get to his dad. She wanted to comfort him, but what could she say?

Blake slowly shifted until he was on his knees

again.

"You have endurance. I'll give you that." Chuck shook his head.

Something cold landed on Kris's cheek, and she saw a snowflake land on Mercy's head. The storm was starting.

Chuck noticed as well. "I've run out of patience. Thanks to your son, my head and hand are killing me, and I just want to get into that bunker and ride out this storm. So, one last time." Chuck took a pistol from one of the other men and held it to Blake's head. "What is the code?"

"Just give him the code, Dad. It's just the bunker," Tucker pleaded.

"It's not worth it," Kris added.

"Your family is smart. So what do you say? You going to end this nightmare and tell me the code?"

Blake shook his head. He peered at them and hung his head. Then he looked straight at Chuck.

"Maybe I'm going about this the wrong way." Chuck closed the gap between him and Kris and her kids. He held the gun pointed at them. "What about now?"

Kris held her breath. Tucker tensed beside her. Even Mercy struggled in the wrap, reaching out toward her dad. Her whole body tensed as if she pulled from her innermost depths.

"Dada!" Mercy called out, clear as day.

Blake's head swiveled toward his daughter.

Mercy's impeccable timing to say her first word may have just saved their lives. While watching her husband, Kris prayed for it to be so.

~*~

Blake couldn't believe his ears. His daughter just said her first word, and it was his name! He had missed that first word with Tuck, but he hadn't with Mercy, and he didn't want to miss anything else. He took a deep breath and nodded.

"You'll let them live?" Blake asked. All he cared about right now was his family's safety. He wanted to hear Mercy's words, each one of them. He wanted to see the elation in Tucker's eyes when he accomplished a task. He wanted to see the love in Kris's eyes when their gazes met.

"If you all behave," Chuck said, a smile of victory already spreading across his lips.

Blake glanced back at his family as they all watched him. Giving away this information might be his death warrant, but it might also be the only way to keep his family alive.

Blake nodded. "Alright. There is plenty enough in there to compensate. So you can let them go."

Chuck stood. "This might have been the hardest bunker to acquire yet, boys, but we got it, and if I am right, we just hit bank!"

He turned triumphantly, but as he did, a shot rang out, and then another and another. Chuck fell to the ground, his open eyes staring blankly at Blake.

Blake rolled over to his family, doing his best to cover them, but ended up with Kris covering them all.

The shots came from the northeast of their property. Somehow, he didn't think it was from the same group, especially with three of Chuck's men on the ground, unmoving.

"In my boot," Blake whispered urgently.

Kris slid her hand down his leg and loosened the tiny knife he kept hidden there. In a matter of moments, his hands were free. He took the knife from her, sliced the binding around his ankles and then made quick work of the ropes around Tucker's hands.

Immediately, Tucker threw his arms around him. Blake pulled him and Kris and Mercy into his arms. While shots fired around them, all he could do was hold his family and pray. The image of Jake holding his family that day ripped through Blake as he held his.

A moment later, Arland was by their side. "Are you guys alright?"

Blake stared at his friend with tears burning his eyes. "You came?"

"We came as soon as we heard the first shots. We don't leave a friend behind. You aren't alone."

With that one statement, a torrent of emotion flooded Blake. He grasped his family to him. Nothing in this world mattered besides their safety. That meant everything. And as he looked up at the men and women now surrounding them, he realized his family had just grown.

~9~

Blake sat atop his favorite rock outcropping on his property. He looked over his land, his house, Tucker's play structure, their archery practice area, and everything he had worked so hard to create for his family.

This was where he spent part of nearly every day. Not that he would tell anyone that. Others didn't know he took quiet moments to appreciate the beauty of the world that they lived in or account for all that he was blessed with.

Blake pushed himself to an upright position on the jumbled rock formation. He liked looking over his property, remembering it and life as it once was, a simple safety that felt so far behind him, a life blind and ignorant to its fragility.

He shook his head. No. He needed to remember it as it was. For this just might be the last time he could. In only minutes, he would be leaving it behind: the memories, the safety, and the past.

He threw his pack over his shoulder, and with one long glance, he joined the rest of the group headed back toward Arland's camp. They had cleaned out the bunker, taking whatever food, tools, and other supplies they hadn't stashed already. Everyone was loaded down and some even pulled travois full of supplies. Cleaning out the bunker had been an easy choice for him. It was either take what was left to share it with the people who treated them as their own or leave it for the next group of marauders.

Besides, he had all that mattered with him. He searched until he found his wife holding their daughter and their son, bow over his shoulder. The land, the house, the bunker, none of that mattered. His family was the only thing that did.

Arland came up beside him and slapped his back. "Well, brother. Let's go home."

Home, Blake realized, went everywhere with him. It wasn't a location. It wasn't just one place. If he was beside his family, no matter where that might be, he was home. He would follow home anywhere and through any trial. They were his everything.

****

INSTALLMENT FIVE

~1~

DATE: December 2   09:12
What in the world?
An arrow landed two feet in front of Blake. He heard its whistling warning in time to duck behind a tree. Where had that come from? The hair on the back of his neck stood on end. His morning patrol to check on the guards at the perimeter had never been this eventful.

He didn't think the arrow had come from one of the city marauders since they used guns. Besides, it came from the direction of camp. After ensuring no more arrows were careening toward him, Blake stepped out and plucked the arrow that had pierced deep into the ground. Near the feathers were two red stripes with a black dot in the middle.

Tucker.

He peered in the direction the arrow had flown from. The brush moved a hundred yards down the hill before two boys came pushing their way through it.

"I told you I could shoot far," Tucker's voice traveled to him.

"No way your arrow made it this far. We must have passed it already." An older boy about ten stomped past Tucker, a scowl on his face.

"No, it came this way."

The other boy stopped in front of Tucker and shoved his hands on his hips. "You think just because you're the son of The Survivalist you're better than us."

"No, I don't. I just shoot better than you because I've practiced more." Tucker didn't back down from the boy who towered over him.

Blake watched, tamping down his desire to end the altercation at once by putting the older boy in his place. He didn't want Tucker to be bullied, but he also knew boys, and if he stepped in, it would be difficult for Tucker to live down his dad rescuing him.

So, Blake planted his feet and watched, wondering when he would be seen. He thought he saw Tucker glance in his direction, but the boy acted as if he didn't see him.

"Whatever, pipsqueak. You aren't better than me. You're just a baby with a tiny bow."

"Then why did we find your arrow way back there, and we still haven't found mine?" Tucker stuck his chest out. "Come on. I saw it go this way."

Tucker stayed to the side of the other boy, just like Blake had taught him to do. Never turn your back on someone was a rule he had the boy repeat many times. When Blake saw the other boy throw a punch, he sucked in a breath, ready to shout, but Tucker ducked as if he expected the attack and rolled, kicking out the other boy's feet.

The boy landed roughly. Tucker stood over him, but not close enough to be touched. Once he saw the boy wasn't coming at him anymore, he looked up and connected eyes with Blake. His son's lower lip trembled, but his eyes held determination as he looked back down at the other boy.

"I don't want to fight with you, Darius. Let's just go get my arrow." Tucker reached out a hand to help the boy up, but Blake saw that Tucker's stance was ready if Darius decided to do something tricky.

Darius rolled and pushed up on his own. He wiped at his eyes and glared at Tucker. "Wait until I tell my dad what you did. You are going to be in trouble. No one will believe you shot past me anyway. You can't even find your arrow."

Blake couldn't hold his tongue any longer. "You mean this one?" He held up Tucker's arrow. "It almost hit me. We will have to discuss safety precautions when having contests, boys."

Darius's mouth hung open before he openly glared at him and ran down the hill.

Tucker hung his head and walked slowly up to his dad. "I'm sorry I almost hit you, Dad. I shouldn't have done the distance contest."

"No one got hurt. We can figure out a safe way to have a shooting contest." He handed the arrow to the boy and ruffled his hair.

"Well, I shouldn't have done it for two reasons. One, because I almost hurt you. Two, because now Darius really won't want to be my friend. You always told me not to showcase my skills. I'm sorry."

"It's a rite of passage for boys. It's hard to be humble when they goad you into things." He wrapped an arm around Tucker and continued to walk his route. "You'll learn."

"I will, Dad. I promise."

Blake stopped and looked seriously at his son. "I am proud of you, Tucker. You handled yourself well, with restraint and courage."

Tucker's glum expression dissolved as a small smile broke free.

"Come on. You can help me finish up the

perimeter check."

Blake felt at ease with his son by his side. He didn't like the fact that Darius tried to bully him around, but Tucker had handled it with maturity far beyond his years. The boy would be fine. It may be hard on him at times, but he would hold his own.

The last month had been a challenge for Blake and his family. Being in a group situation after surviving on their own for so long, and under such imminent stress, had taken its toll. More than once, Blake had threatened to take them and disappear in the night. Each time, Kris talked him down.

Right now, this was the safest option for them, and Arland needed his help. Every day, he trained with the men and women and even some of the children, teaching them how to shoot bows and use knives as well as defense strategies should things go wrong.

They learned things, too. Kris gleaned all the information she could on how to forage and use plants from Laurie. Tucker learned the art of getting along with other children, as well as the tips Hannah shared on her daily hikes she took with the children. And him, well, he learned how to get along in a group setting with people who have vastly different outlooks.

The storm that had dumped snow on them as they left their home for good had been the start of a series of cold storms. Finally, the snow had begun to melt away. Only patches here and there were left in shady areas. Blake knew it would only be a matter of time until the next cold storm hit. He wanted to have their shelter more insulated by then. Those first few days had been rough, especially on Kris and the kids.

This was definitely a different way of doing things, but he would find a way to help them thrive, even if it took him years to do it.

~*~

Kris bit her cheek to keep the words from pouring out her mouth. She kept glancing up to where the boy, Darius, said Tucker had attacked him. Attacked him? The boy had to be at least three years older, almost twice his weight, and a foot taller. Tucker was not one to attack, either.

She controlled the urge to call the boy a liar and demand he take her to Tucker right now. It worried her that he still had not returned.

"Whatever, Darius," Scott said. Kris recognized the older boy from their first visit when he met them on the forest path to warn them about Jake. "Why don't you tell your parents the truth?"

"What is the truth?" His dad stared down at him.

Darius glared at Scott and crossed his arms.

When he didn't say anything further and the parents didn't push it, Kris walked over to Scott. "Can you please tell me what really happened? I'm worried about Tuck."

"Well, I didn't see what happened up the hill, but I know Darius was mad because the survival kid beat his best shot."

"They were having a contest?" Kris asked, sensing the parents paying closer attention than they let on.

"Yeah, I told Darius he should know better than to think he could beat The Survivalist's kid, even if he is younger. But that guy never listens." Scott shook his head.

"He didn't beat me." Darius pouted. "His dad rigged it. He held up a different arrow at the top."

"Blake was there?" Kris asked.

"Yeah, after he watched his son beat me up, he taunted me with that fake arrow." Darius glared.

"Hmm…that doesn't sound like Blake." Kris wanted to say more, but she swallowed her words. Knowing that Tucker was with Blake eased her anxiety, giving her the energy to mind her manners.

"Nor does it sound like something an adult would do, especially The Survivalist," Darius's mom said.

"We'll get to the bottom of this when they return. Younger or not, that boy has grown up knowing how to fight. I won't have him picking on my son." As Darius's dad spoke, Kris's mouth hung open. Guess she knew where the kid got his combative attitude.

"Did you really just say that?" Kris couldn't stop her mouth. This guy really thought that her little, barely seven-year-old had beat up his oversized bully of a kid.

"What's going on here?" Arland stepped in right as Kris thought she might lose her cool and Darius's dad looked ready to get physical.

No one said anything.

"Kris?" Arland asked.

"This kid and his dad are accusing Tucker of beating him up." Kris spat the words out. She did not like confrontation, but her mama bear instincts were on high alert. She patted Mercy's back as she stirred in her wrap.

"Was anyone else there to witness this?" Arland asked Darius.

"The Survivalist was there at the end," Darius pouted.

"And you're saying that he just stood there and watched Tucker beat you up?" Arland looked him over.

Kris did as well. The kid had some pine needles on his back but nothing else. No bumps, bruises, scrapes, nothing to show he had been hurt.

"You don't look like you were beat up." Arland stood staring intently at the boy.

"He knocked me down." Darius's lip quivered.

"Oh, I wonder why he would have done that." Aland scratched at his cropped beard.

"I wasn't really going to punch him…" Darius started and then covered his mouth.

"Ahh, I see. Tucker was defending himself. Why would you even pretend to punch him?" Arland kept his voice calm and unassuming.

"He said he could shoot his arrow farther than me," Darius pouted.

"He can," Scott said simply.

Arland squatted down in front of the boy. "You know, Darius, we all have our own skills that we bring to this community. Scott here is a great leader. Tucker is a wonderful archer. I hear you are really skilled with the snare."

"Yeah, I've caught more animals than any of the other kids." Darius stood taller.

"You see. You have your own special skill to contribute. No need to compare yourself to anyone else." Arland stood, looked at all the adults and then at Darius. "So, are we all good here now?"

Everyone nodded.

Kris felt aptly put in her place. She was a teacher. She should have been able to negotiate that as well as Arland. If it had been two other kids, she would have.

With her own son being mistreated, something unruly loosened in her.

"Kris, could you come with me? I was looking for you before I came upon this non-situation." Arland nodded toward the fire.

"Of course," she said as she followed him. The warmth of the fire eased the chill creeping up her. "I'm sorry about that."

"No need. Boys will be boys. Tucker is trying to find his place, and Darius, well, he is known for pushing boundaries and being physical. He'll adapt, as will we all." Arland smiled knowingly.

"Well said. So what can I help you with?"

"Well," he said and chuckled. "I need the advice of a woman."

"Why don't you ask Laurie? I know she…. Oh, it's about her." Kris's heart warmed. "Ask away."

"Do you know she and I both lost our spouses?"

"I do. I'm sorry."

Arland nodded. "It's hard to let go."

"That's exactly what she said." Kris's eyes went wide. She wanted to stick her foot in her mouth. She always talked too much, which is why she tried not to talk at all.

"She did?" Arland asked and then nodded. "I had been fine with the idea of spending the rest of my life without another wife, but now…."

"It's different," Kris said.

"It is."

"Have you two talked about it?" Kris asked.

Arland shrugged. "Not directly."

"It might be time." Kris heard a commotion, but tried to keep her attention on Arland.

"What would I say?" he asked. A shimmer of his

old insecurity she remembered from that night so long ago now surfaced.

"Listen to your heart. Tell her exactly how you feel without tippy-toeing around the tough stuff."

"That's the hard part, huh?" Arland said as the commotion grew louder and closer.

Kris looked up just as Blake and Tucker ran around the end dwelling. They looked out of breath, and Tucker's eyes were wide as he ran to her. She stood at the same time Arland did and moved toward them. Tucker ran into her arms, hugging both her and his sister.

"They're here," Blake breathed out.

Kris took a step back, keeping her arm around her son and wrapping the other around Mercy. How could they leave now? It was full-on winter. Traveling with an infant in the dead of winter with the old and sick of the community would be foolhardy at best, life-taking at worst. Did they even have a chance of outrunning an organized, driven group of armed men?

~2~

Blake's skin prickled with urgency and the need to act. They had almost fifty people that needed to be moved. Every part of him wanted to grab his family and leave the rest to their own devices. The guilt of even that thought burned him as he sought out his wife's eyes.

So much trust lived there. She depended on him, and he needed to be the leader she thought he was. He blew out a breath. Kissing her temple, he told her to go pack up.

With one last, long look, she took Tucker by the hand to pack their belongings hastily for the second time. Blake watched his family walking urgently to their shelter. He hoped this would be their last move and the last of marauders they had to deal with. He prayed it would be, but something told him he better keep them primed.

"We aren't prepared," Arland whispered in disbelief.

"That doesn't matter." Blake looked up at the sky. Dark, billowing clouds piled low on top of them. The air crystallized their breath.

"How much time do we have?" Arland asked, his eyes scanning the camp he had worked so hard to create.

"Scouts said they were at the edge of town, discussing the trail marks they just found."

"Maybe they won't follow? They won't want to

come out into the forest," Arland almost pleaded.

"They will come, my friend. It could be a week or it could be an hour." Blake knew Arland would have a hard time leaving all he had built. It brought back the feeling of leaving his own home a month ago.

"We should have the scouts go check again and report back," Arland said.

"I called all but three of the guards to return to camp and help with packing up. The last three are to watch that perimeter, though Declan said he was going to scout a little." He dropped a hand on Arland's shoulder. "We don't have time to discuss this, Arland. You tell them or I will. Now."

Blake took a few steps over and rang the bell hanging next to the fire. People ran toward them. The nervous energy pouring off them fueled his own.

"The time we had hoped would wait until after winter has arrived. We need to pack everything that can be carried and leave now," Arland said calmly.

His calm grated on Blake's nerves. He would rather create mayhem if it meant action. People just stood there and stared.

"Tonight? Snow is coming. How are we going to keep our children warm?" a woman cried out.

"I know it doesn't seem like it, but that is a blessing." Blake did his best to keep his voice calm even though he wanted to scream at them to pack up this instant.

"Freezing to death is a blessing?" a guy spat out.

"We will take precautions so we won't freeze to death, but having our tracks covered will save our lives." Blake squeezed his hands until his knuckles were white and screaming. "Look. I know this is not ideal, but we don't have time to discuss this. You need to move. Pack everything you can carry, blankets and food before anything else."

Still no one moved.

"Go! Now! The lives of your family depend upon it!" he yelled, unable to control his urgency a moment longer. Then he turned his back on them, walking away to help Kris pack, not waiting to see if they would finally act.

By the time he made it to his shelter, the scurry and frantic voices behind him showed they had finally decided to act. He blew out a held breath. He didn't want to leave them, but if they procrastinated too long, he would have no choice but to lead his family to safety without them.

Tucker ran out of the tent with a handful of freeze-dried food and placed it in one of the wheeled carts they had made after seeing them in Arland's camp. They had made three out of Tucker's old off-road stroller. The three big, heavy-duty tires created a wheelbarrow-type cart that could be pulled fairly easily through the rough terrain.

After Arland and his men had come to their rescue, Blake had filled each of them with all the food left in the bunker. Much of that food he added to the community cache, but he had kept quite a bit for them, just in case.

They had given one of the carts to Arland in appreciation for coming to their rescue. The two they had kept sat outside their shelter, already close to full.

"Dad," Tucker said as he neared and threw his arms around him, "are we going to make it?"

"I hope so, Tuck. We are certainly going to do our best."

Kris ducked out then, Mercy, as most of the time,

wrapped against her. Kris unloaded her armfuls of supplies into the cart.

"You could work faster if you put her down," Blake stated as he did a quick check through the carts.

"And if we have to leave in a hurry?" Kris put her hands on her hips, her long, red hair flowing in the wind.

Blake caught his breath. Even with danger riding down on them, he couldn't take his gaze off the beauty of his wife all fired up.

"She's staying with me. I'd rather have to leave some of this behind because I'm slower than the alternative."

Blake smiled briefly and took a moment to kiss her. "Good thinking," he said as he ducked into the shelter to make sure they had packed all the things they needed.

Kris's shotgun leaned against the door next to Tucker's bow and quiver stuffed full of every arrow he owned. His rifle was there, as well. The dwelling otherwise looked close to bare, empty, sad. He touched the rough wood, wishing he could bring it with them rather than have to cut more trees once they arrived.

He stopped, an idea processing rapid-fire-fast through him

He rushed back out into the cold. "You guys are doing great, keep it up. I'll be back," he called over his shoulder as he ran into the encampment. Some people had travois and a few had carts, but many only had baskets and packs.

He ran up to David, who frantically stuffed as much as he could into his and his family's packs. A pile of clothes, food, and blankets sat in the middle of their shelter with no place to put them.

"Blake, are they coming now?" David asked, his eyes wild as he looked over his family, letting his eyes rest longer on his young boy.

"They aren't here yet. Help me," Blake commanded.

David followed him out of the dwelling and watched in horror as Blake pulled off the bark of his shelter.

"What are you doing?" David's wife shrilled, her eyes wet with tears.

"You need a way to carry more belongings, right? You'll need to build a shelter once you're there, right?"

David nodded and started helping him tear apart his shelter. Soon they made it down to the main structure poles. They laid them on the ground, found twine, and quickly, not beautifully, webbed them together.

"A travois," David's wife said. She pulled herself away and quickly began piling the last of their belongings on a large blanket and wrapping them up.

Blake ran to the next family, got them started on their own travois, and went on to the next.

The air was thick with panic, but a purpose filled him. He would bring these people to safety.

~*~

Kris constantly reminded herself to breathe. She laid her hand on Mercy, who gratefully slept in her wrap against her chest, and she felt her little, soothing breaths. She touched her son as he raced past her, arms laden with supplies and eyes full of determination. She had her children. No matter what, they would be together.

"Mom," Tucker stopped as she reached out to brush a hand on him as they passed, "we're going to be alright. New Forest Glen is beautiful. Wait until you see it." He smiled and raced back into the shelter.

She laid the items in her arms into the overflowing cart. Why did it seem backwards? Her son comforted her. She shook her head.

Taking a moment to straighten her back, she watched the frantic movements of the camp. People yelled, screamed, cried, ran, and yanked their shelters apart. For just a moment, it all felt like a dream. She stood apart from the chaos. Her eyes then roamed the outskirts of camp in the direction of where the trail to Mountain View Drive was. Would the marauders come careening into their camp, guns blazing?

She shook her head and refocused. Ducking back into their shelter, she found most everything was already packed. Funny how they could now pack all they owned into three backpacks and two carts. Moving trucks were no longer needed.

Tucker dug down into the cache in their dwelling. He stopped to stand and take a few deep breaths.

"I'll take over, Sweetie." She reached for the little camp shovel.

"No, I've got this." He stuck his tongue out of the corner of his mouth as he focused on digging.

When he hit something solid, he squatted down and dug with his hands. Kris knelt to help. They pulled out extra ammunition, food rations, and some cash that Kris wondered why they bothered to keep. They put those last few items into their carts.

She took two blankets she had saved for last and

wrapped them around the items in the overflowing carts. Tucker came around with twine to tie it all down.

"You are amazing," Kris said and kissed his temple.

Tucker smiled and kept working.

Their packs and carts were packed when the first flakes of snow started falling. Funny how it seemed to snow every time they fled. There was a peace to it. Soon the world would be covered in white, fresh, clean, like the new start they were headed toward.

"Let's go help the others, Tuck." She wrapped her arm around her son, feeling blessed to have such a determined, special child.

Tuck nodded and took off. She did her best to keep up. No way would she let her son out of her sight with danger coming down upon them at any moment. When she caught up with him, he had an arm wrapped around Ethan, who cried hysterically.

"It's okay, little buddy. We are going to a place with a spring, a cool little creek, and fields to play in. We will have so much fun building shelters and play areas, and I'm going to make a swing for my sister. Would you like to help me?"

Ethan rubbed his eyes and nodded.

"Good. We are going to have to make rope using long grass that will grow in spring. We can catch grasshoppers…" Tucker continued telling Ethan about their new home.

Kris found herself lost in his story and looked up only when Laurie reached out a hand to her.

"He has an amazing gift," Laurie said.

"Yes, he has always loved younger children," Kris said, taking the things in Laurie's arms.

"That's not what I meant," she said quietly.

Kris's eyes went wide, and she looked around to see who else might have heard or guessed that Tucker actually spoke from a vision and not just comfort for a smaller child.

"He's safe. Don't worry." Laurie rested her hand on Kris's arm.

"What can I help with?" Kris laid the things down in their cart, and with a glance to make sure Tuck wasn't going anywhere, she ducked into the shelter. "Do you have a bag for all these herbs?"

Laurie handed her a tall basket, and they started ripping down the herbs and stuffing them haphazardly into the basket. Laurie cringed. Kris knew she handled the herbs roughly, but they had to hurry. The men could be here any minute.

"I find it amazing that you do so much with Mercy wrapped against you." Laurie smiled at the baby now peeking out of the wrap.

"It's the easiest way to get things done. I wore Tucker, too." Kris kissed her daughter's head and returned her joyful smile, noticing that her first top tooth had broken through. A chill traveled through her as she remembered Tucker's vision.

"I wore Ethan but wasn't nearly as versatile as you," Laurie said, bringing Kris out of her thoughts.

"Times change," Kris said, stopping for a moment and looking around. "It's not going to be easy."

Laurie shrugged. "I think the hardest has come and gone. We know how to live off the land. Once we are surrounded by forest for miles, who will bother us then?"

"It will be safer from others, true, but...." Kris shook her head and continued with her work.

"We will prevail, Kris. So will our children. Because of them, the future of humanity has a chance. They will be raised in peace, with grace and love. They will be independent and kind and will change this world for the better. This move is needed in more ways than just saving us from the city marauders coming toward us now."

The conviction in Laurie hit Kris like a pummel. Her friend believed this with her whole being. Could Laurie be right? Is this their chance to change humanity? Did they have what it took to build a community of children like she prophesied?

Kris didn't know, but she knew they would find out…if they made it out of camp before the marauders found them.

~3~

Blake sucked in a breath as the scout he had sent out to double-check the marauders' current location came trudging back, dragging a bound man with him. What was the guy thinking bringing one of the city people here? He could escape and show the city people how to get here even quicker.

Blake stood out from behind the tree, his arms crossed and his displeasure burning within him. "What are you doing, Declan?"

"I caught one!" Declan held up his hand with the rope in it.

The other guards cheered until Blake quieted them with a raised hand. As soon as he had spoken, the bound man snapped his eyes up to him. Something about him seemed familiar. Flashes of what now seemed like a past life blinded him for a moment.

"Sergeant Chantry. I had an inkling this was you." The man stood erect and did his best to salute.

"Butler." Blake stepped toward him.

"Yes, sir." He nodded.

"How did he capture you?" Blake narrowed his eyes. The Butler he knew wouldn't have been caught by his newly trained scout, especially not Declan.

"I gave myself up."

Blake watched him for any signs of betrayal. "Why would you do that?"

Butler's jaw clenched. "I couldn't stay under that command any longer. They do…unspeakable things."

Blake nodded. "How did you get with them in the first place?"

"The coalitions are the only way to survive in the city, sir. I have a family. They give them rations if I fight."

"And if you desert?" Blake asked.

"They will stop...or worse." He hung his head. "You should kill me. If I die, they continue to get rations." Butler lifted his head and squared his shoulders.

Blake whipped out his bow and fired an arrow.

Everyone froze, and Butler's lip quivered before he sucked it in. He looked at himself, surprised that he hadn't been hit.

"Take off his hat and any ID markers," Blake said as he stormed past Declan and Butler.

He strode directly to the bush where he had shot his arrow and returned holding a dead rabbit by its ears. "Toss his hat and ID tags here. Lay down next to them, Butler."

Butler did as he was told, watching Blake carefully.

"How long until they march on us?" Blake asked.

"An hour. Without my return, maybe two."

"Why are they waiting?" Declan asked.

"Gathering intel from people that live in that neighborhood." Butler squeezed his eyes shut.

"There are still families there. We have to get them!" one of the guards demanded.

Butler shook his head. "Going in now is certain death. Besides, there isn't much left to save."

Blake clenched his jaw. They had had their chance to join them. They chose wrong, yet his chest felt tight knowing what they faced.

"Declan, drag Butler to the edge of that ravine."

Blake nodded toward to rock ledge.

Butler nodded. "I always appreciated the time serving under you, Sergeant. Thank you. You are saving my family."

Blake watched him. "You'll have plenty of time to show me your gratitude." He turned to Declan. "When you drag him to the edge, have him strip off his outer clothes and then stuff them with whatever foliage you can find."

Declan stared at him.

"Now! We have an hour to get our families far out of camp. You two help. Go!"

The guards did as they were told. Blake pulled his knife from his thigh holster. He cut the rabbit and drizzled the blood on Butler's hat and tags. He dropped the bleeding rabbit and dragged it through the depression left by Butler's body.

Luckily, Butler had been wearing his old military coveralls, so the stuffing was simple and the guys were close to finished when he arrived. He smeared more blood on the suit and stuffed the rabbit inside of it.

"Now, throw the dummy into the ravine making sure his backside is facing up," Blake directed.

The dummy was tossed over, landing more than thirty feet below. From this angle and distance, it looked like a real body.

"Congratulations, Butler. You are now dead." Blake turned on his heel and walked back toward the outpost. "Let's go."

"But Blake…" Declan started.

"No buts, Declan. We are not killing more than we have to. Butler will be a good source of information, if nothing else. We now have less than an hour to get back and get our families to safety. This choice is mine, and I will take responsibility for it. Now, go!"

Declan pulled the newly-bound Butler down the trail toward camp. Blake turned to the other two guards.

"Which of you can run the fastest?" Blake asked them.

"That'd be me, sir, and I don't have children to worry about yet, so my wife doesn't need extra help packing up." The younger of the two stepped up.

"Dillon, right?" Blake sized up the lean, younger man.

"Yes, sir."

"Stay hidden at the top outpost. From there, you can see a vantage point where they will have to cross a few miles out. As soon as you see movement there, you discreetly hightail it back to camp. If we have already left, you should still see our footprints. Catch up and report as fast as possible."

"Yes, sir." He nodded but then looked down toward the camp. "My wife…"

"I'll make sure she is packed and safe. You have my word." Blake met his determined stare.

He nodded. "May we meet again."

"May we meet again," Blake repeated, and the young man ran off to his post.

He and the last guard easily caught up to Declan pulling Butler.

"Don't harass the man," Blake said as he reached for his knife and sliced the bindings on Butler's wrists. "You aren't allowed to touch a weapon until I say so. If you attempt to leave, you will be shot."

"Yes, sir." Butler saluted and rubbed his wrists as he followed the other guards down into camp.

People scurried everywhere, crying and loudly protesting. Blake scanned the milling crowd for his wife and children. He found them tying off the last straps on Laurie and Arland's cart. When Kris's eyes met his, they filled with relief and love.

He ran to her, pulling her and Mercy into his arms and watching his son talk with Ethan.

"We're all set?" Blake asked.

"Everything is ready to go at our shelter."

"Good work, Krista." Blake shifted, and her eyes widened.

"Who's that?" she asked in a whisper.

"Long story. Butler this is my wife, Kris; our daughter, Mercy; and the big guy is our son, Tucker. Butler is coming with us. He served under me and will be a vital source of information."

"Not if he goes out in this storm wearing only that," Arland said as he came out of his shelter with an extra coat.

"Butler, meet Arland, the leader of this camp."

Butler's eyes went wide. Blake knew he had thought he had been the one in charge. In truth, Blake didn't know the roles anymore and didn't care. They needed to leave, and he would make sure they did.

"Thank you, Arland." Butler nodded.

Aland gave Blake a sideways glance. "I'm assuming you'll fill me in on this?"

"Later." Blake nodded. "We need to move now. It's time to ring the bell and assemble the camp, ready or not."

Aland nodded and turned toward Laurie and Hannah. "You all set?"

They both nodded.

When Arland began walking toward the bell, Blake turned to Kris. "Have you seen Dillon's wife?"

"Yes, Carly is with her parents. See, there she is now." Kris pointed to the young woman who kept looking toward the outpost.

"I'll meet you at the dwelling." Blake walked toward Carly, who turned to stare at him as he met her.

"Dillon?" she asked, fear dancing in her eyes.

"He volunteered to be the last one at the post to give us the best chance. He will catch up with us."

Carly bit her lip and her eyes brimmed. "You'll make sure of it?"

"I will," Blake said earnestly. "Be safe. Stay in the middle of the group."

She nodded, biting at her trembling lip again.

Blake squeezed her shoulder before walking toward his family.

"Let's go," he said before reaching down to take Tucker's hand and then Kris's. Butler followed silently behind them.

He second-guessed himself about bringing Butler along, but he told the guards the truth. He would be a vital source of information, someone who was trained to observe and report. He would give them all the intel needed about the circumstances in the city and the men that would be funneling into their camp in a matter of minutes.

His family, now loaded down with packs and standing next to their carts, was ready. Was he? Was he ready to take fifty people into the wilderness and survive off the land?

~*~

Kris watched in horror as people screamed and cried in the meeting area. Everyone wore packs or carried baskets. Mothers and fathers held the shaking hands of their panicked children. Terror filed everyone's voice.

"Where are we going?"

"Will they catch us?"

"We will freeze to death!"

Arland did his best to calm everyone's fears, but they were too afraid to listen to his calm rationale.

Blake shifted his weight next to Kris, urgency pouring off him. She lifted a hand and rested it on one of his folded arms.

"Blake, you have to go talk to them."

"Arland's their leader," he said between clenched teeth.

"You hold the power to break through their fear. They don't need a calming leader right now. They need a commander."

"I agree with your wife, sir. You could lead an army into hell itself." Butler met his gaze and then looked out into the chaotic group. "Either that or leave them to get slaughtered."

Kris gasped, appalled that the man could think such a thing. When she met him with her hard glare, though, he nodded toward Blake. Her husband's jaw muscles worked, and his hands clenched and unclenched. Then he strode toward the stump where Arland was doing his best to calm the crowd.

Kris saw relief fill Arland's eyes when they met Blake's. He mouthed the words, *thank you*, as he stepped down for Blake to take his place.

Whispers traveled through the crowd. She heard

the name Survivalist repeated over and over. Soon every eye was on her husband. She sent him strength and said a small prayer, asking for the others to listen to him. He had commanded soldiers; certainly he could command this community who prepared to fight for their survival—a battle for their life.

"Fear is not a bad thing. It is a tool," he called out in his most commanding voice. "A tool that needs to be managed and aimed, just like a hammer or an arrow. Right now, you need to aim that fear in a direction that will serve you best. You aim it toward survival."

A few people yelled out agreement.

"Use that fear to push your body to walk as fast and as far as possible. Use that fear to ensure you have your family's wellbeing in mind. Use it to carry you away from the danger that is advancing toward us. Use it to survive!"

The cheer this time held more strength. Kris watched the crowd and turned back to her husband. He didn't have them all yet. She watched him meet the eyes of each group and then linger on Pastor Rob.

"Right now is a time for faith. We all have been shown mercy before. We were all delivered from disaster over a year ago, and we survived. No, we thrived!"

Blake paused, waiting for the crowd to quiet. Kris's heart thundered. He almost had everyone.

"We will thrive again. Have faith we will be delivered from this darkness and kept warm by its embrace. We are leading you to a land of beauty and abundance. A place for new Forest Glen to thrive again!"

Everyone, even the children, cheered loudly. They

would follow him now, but as she saw his eyes rest once more on Pastor Rob, she knew he had an even greater plan. A way to cement that faith in them by stealing a few more minutes they really didn't have. Yet, united, they stood a much better chance than not. Yes, her husband was a commander.

He held up his hand one last time, and the crowd quieted. "Before we begin our new journey, let us have Pastor Rob send us off with a blessing and a prayer for mercy."

Pastor Rob quickly made his way up to the stump. He took Blake's hand in his and met his eyes with a deep inner faith she wished he could see in them all.

"You saved us all today," he said before stepping onto the stump.

"As Moses led the Israelites into the Promised Land, so will we be led into safety. Bow your heads with me."

As Pastor Rob led them in prayer, Kris felt a shift in the community. An inner peace filled her as if each person shared their peace with everyone else. It was an understanding, a belief that they would thrive, that they would keep their faith and make it to their own version of the Promised Land. It felt like the granting of mercy.

~4~

Blake stood at the front of the line with his family, and now Butler, by his side. Snow fell softly at first, but it rapidly increased its pace. Mercy had awakened and was cooing and gurgling happily at Tucker.

"Look at that! Mercy has her top tooth, just like in my…" Tucker's eyes grew wide as he looked toward Butler and back.

"She sure does, doesn't she?" Blake acted like Tucker hadn't almost spilled his greatest intel in front of a man he really had no idea if he could trust. Sure, he had trusted Butler with his life while they served together, but times had changed, people had changed, and every man really only fought for himself and his own family.

"My son had just gotten his first few teeth before I left, too." Butler pushed forth a sad smile. "I bet he's walking by now."

"Mercy can't walk yet, but she can say Dada. Can't you, baby sister? Say Dada." Tucker talked with her.

"Dada, Dada," she said reaching toward Blake.

Blake started toward her and her smiling mom, who held her in her wrap, when he heard the commotion. On the other side of the hill, Dillon scrambled down the slope as fast as he could.

"It's time." Blake's heart felt like it would stop, and then it began to race. "Kris, do you remember how I told you to go?"

"Yes, but…"

Blake ended her rebuttal with a kiss. He bent down to his son. "Tuck, you remember as well. I know you do. Help your mom and sister. Do your best to move the cart. If it becomes too much, push it aside and I will bring it when I catch back up. I'm counting on you, son."

"I won't let you down, Dad."

"You never do." He kissed the top of his son's head and then his daughter's. "We always return to each other."

"We always return to each other," they said together, and Kris tugged Tucker to move along with her.

"Sir?" Butler shifted his weight.

"Come with me," Blake said as he turned and started off at a jog.

"Yes, sir."

"Use that fear and faith to push you forward. Move your families along as quickly as possible," he called as he moved through the line of people.

On his way, he grabbed Arland, David, Mitchel, the military men, Kevin and John, and a couple other men with guns.

"We take up the rear. When Dillon catches up, we'll decide how to proceed," Blake told the men assembled with him.

The line felt like it lasted forever. He remembered Pastor Rob's statement. How did Moses lead that many people out of Egypt? Blake shook his head. The fifty or so he had felt overwhelming. Several of the children already complained, and they hadn't even made a hundred yards.

They would have to dump some loads in the carts and travois in order to make room for children. They would never make it otherwise, and the trek would only get more difficult as the snow piled up. He stopped his pace as he came alongside Tyler, the young man who had eyes for Hannah.

"Tyler, I need you to run ahead. Tucker will have a shovel in his cart. Take it and have him lead you ahead the trail a good mile and start digging a deep hole."

Tyler's expression showed his confusion and almost horror.

"It will be for a cache. We will need to start carrying children soon. I'd rather gear get stored for later retrieval than have some not make it."

"Agreed. Will do, sir."

He turned to Hannah. "Would you go with him and take over the cart Tucker is pulling? I'm sure Kris will appreciate your company."

"Of course, Blake." She smiled as if they weren't being chased down by marauders. The innocence of young love. He shook his head.

People were on their way to attack them, take what they had worked so hard to attain, and kill any who got in their way. Blake needed to focus on the task at hand. His family and their community were not safe yet.

It would be a taxing, arduous journey, one that he prayed everyone would survive, but first he had to keep the bad guys from following them. Otherwise, those prayers would be worthless.

Blake and his nine comrades hid themselves in the trees at the edge of camp. Several of their hands shook, with cold or fear he couldn't be certain.

"Remember those hand-warmers you could buy when you went skiing?" David asked.

"Yeah, you shook them to activate them," another guy responded.

"What I wouldn't give for some of those right now." David smiled.

"I'd be fine with a real pair of gloves," another said, blowing into his hands.

"Butler, how many are in this coalition and what is the normal protocol?" Blake asked while the men bantered about cold hands.

"This unit has about a hundred men. There are more, but we split at the Jackson junction. Meyers leads this division and sends the most expendable force in first with orders to kill anyone they feel will be trouble. This first battalion is ruthless, lawless, and downright evil, if you ask me. They don't get fed much, and that does something to a man's brain."

"I've seen that before." Blake nodded, pushing the memories into the recesses of his mind.

"Meyers' men aren't far behind, to make sure the first battalion doesn't get too out of hand. Bullets are a scarcity, though, so this first group only gets a handful. After that, they resort to their swords, axes, or whatever they can get their hands on."

"Straight out of Vikings," one of the men said.

Blake turned and watched them. Only Butler, Kevin, and John, besides himself, had any military experience. How would he hold out on an organized force of a hundred men?

Dillon had almost made it to them. Maybe he wouldn't have to face that army.

"Will they follow?" Blake asked, blinking back the snowflakes catching on his eyelashes.

Butler shrugged. "Depends on what they got from the neighborhood and what you all have left in the shelters. I'll tell you what, though, it would be the first time they ever strayed into the forest. They hit houses and bunkers. They would have no idea how to survive in the wilderness."

"Then we'll use that to our advantage." Blake grit his teeth and watched the horizon on the other side of the camp for any movement.

~*~

Kris's hands already felt tender, and she knew blisters were forming. She led the line, ignoring the discomfort. Showing weakness was not an option. Yet, every step she took weighed her down. Between the heavy pack, Mercy in the front, and the cart, she would have to pull from her deepest reserves to make it the five to eight miles Blake wanted to accomplish before sundown.

"Tucker," Tyler said as he ran up to them with Hannah just behind. "Your dad gave us a job. We need your shovel, and you need to run ahead with me about a mile up the trail."

"What's going on?" Kris asked, pulling up to a stop.

"Blake asked Tyler to have Tucker show him the trail and start digging a cache. I swear he thinks of everything. He said the kids will need to be carried soon, so caching the gear is our best bet." Hannah said.

Kris nodded. She had to agree. Blake did think of almost everything, but sending their son ahead without them? "I'll go."

Tyler stopped from helping Tucker search for the shovel and looked at her. "No offense, Mrs. Chantry, but with your baby and the pack, you won't be able to run very fast."

"Mom, I got this. I'll only be a mile ahead, and the bad guys are behind us, not in front. Animals will be holed up in this storm."

"What if you get lost?" She worried about not being able to find her son in the storm. Horror rocked through her.

"I have the landmarks, Mom. As long as you remember them, too, we'll find each other again." He looked down at the snow starting to build up on the ground. "Besides, you can follow our footprints."

As much as she didn't want to let him go, she kissed him on the forehead and whispered, "We always return to each other."

"We always return to each other." He kissed his sister and then took off at a jog. "Come on, Tyler. This way." He waved the young man to him.

"I'll see you soon." Tyler held gazes with Hannah, who nodded before he took off to follow Tucker.

"I like how you guys always say that same thing when you part. It's very sweet and meaningful." Hannah picked up the handles to the cart Tucker left behind.

"Blake started it when he had to go on his missions, and he has always made it back."

"Just like on the day it all happened." Hannah's gaze followed Tyler as he disappeared behind the trees and sheet of falling snow.

"Like that," Kris said, feeling her heart sink when she could no longer see Tucker.

"Tyler is good in the woods. He'll keep Tucker safe."

Kris nodded. Tucker was resourceful. As long as

they found each other on this nontrail, he would be okay. At least, that's what she told herself.

Mercy fussed and started rooting. Kris looked back at the long line of people following her. She didn't want to delay them further. Increasing her pace, she lengthened the distance between her and the group behind her.

"I'm not sure the others can keep up this pace, Kris," Hannah panted after a short while.

Kris glanced behind her. The distance should give her enough time. "I don't expect them to," she said as she dropped the handles of the cart and adjusted her wrap so Mercy could nurse, and then she tucked the wrap over her head. Kris quickly touched her daughter's tiny hands and feet through the wrap to make sure they were covered and warm. Once reassured with Mercy happily gulping her lunch, she pulled out her gloves from her pockets. The warmth helped soothe her hands, but not for long. Picking up the handles of the cart, her palms still screamed even through the extra layer.

"That wrap is pretty handy, isn't it?" Hannah said as she picked up the other cart and followed her.

"It is a lifesaver." It truly was. Kris didn't want to remember all the times having Mercy tied to her had saved her daughter. Too many to count. Hopefully, this new location would provide the haven that Laurie thought it would. She could use a break from constant threats and fighting for her life and the life of her family.

"You helped Janene make one, didn't you?"

"Yes, I helped her set it up before we left." Kris looked back as best she could. "I hope she's doing well back there."

"We'll be okay, right? I mean, Blake wouldn't lead us into harm?"

"We're choosing the lesser of two evils, Hannah. This journey won't be easy."

"We've been through worse." Hannah smiled at her.

"Yes, I guess we have." Kris did her best to return the girl's smile, but it felt more like a grimace.

From what she could gather with her limited skills, she guessed that they might be a mile to a mile and a half in. Her hands had already blistered even through her gloves, her feet already felt frozen, and her back screamed at having so much weight on it.

Hannah was right, though. They had been through worse. She had pushed through more physical pain than this. She could do it again.

"Wait! Stop!" a woman yelled from somewhere down the line.

Kris eyed Hannah, looked up ahead where her son's footprints filled in with snow, and then set the cart down.

"We don't have time for this," Kris could hear Blake urging.

It all hit her then. She was leading the camp. Blake and the others were at the end of the long line, probably waiting at the trailhead to make sure they weren't followed. As Hannah watched her, she realized so did everyone else.

Laurie wove her way up through the line until she, Ethan, and their cart were right alongside them.

"What's going on back there?" Kris asked.

"Marie is having a difficult time getting her three-year-old son to keep moving. She can't carry him and their pack, much less pull their cart."

"Tyler and Tucker are working on a solution right now, but we need to make it there. Can someone else pull the cart and carry the boy for another half-mile or so?" Kris asked.

People started to complain and whine. Where was Blake and his inspiring talk now? She wasn't a leader, and Laurie wasn't stepping up. In fact, the other woman looked to her, as did everyone else.

"I know herbs, plants, and things like that. I don't know how to get them moving." Laurie shrugged.

With a sigh, Kris shouldered out of her pack. "How far back is she?"

"Only a hundred feet or so."

Kris nodded and hoofed her way through the churned-up snow until she saw Marie crouching next to her crying son. David, her husband, must be with Blake. Their other two children stood by, adjusting the packs they wore.

Marie looked up at her. "I can't get him to walk any farther." The tears in her eyes spoke of her desperation.

Kris looked around at the state of the others near them. Everyone looked miserable. Kids wiped at their noses, and their lips trembled. Adults blew into their frozen hands and stomped their feet to stay warm. Two men stood by, watching. Neither had a cart or a travois or a child in their arms.

Everyone watched her. They waited for her to lead them. Where was her husband or Arland? Even Laurie would be better at this than she. Her heart raced as her body warmed with anxiety. She drew in a deep breath and blew it out. Then she met the eyes around her.

"In less than a mile, we have a cache being dug to

store some items that have become too heavy or to make room for our children in the carts or on the travois. We will be able to come back for these, but right now we have to get there."

Many around her nodded and murmured positive sounds, but still no one came forward to help Marie.

"If we want to survive, we have to work like a team. That is one thing that really impressed me when I first came to your camp. You worked as a unit. A team pulls together when times are tough. They help shoulder the load of their teammates when they're struggling. Right now, your teammate Marie needs help. What do you say? Are we going to pull together like the community I know New Forest Glen is? Because that's the only way we will all make it." Kris watched the group, finally letting her eyes fall on the men near her.

The two men looked around and then at each other. They shook out their hands, and one took Marie's cart and the other offered to take her young son. Then, the entire line started moving and talking. Several people took on more loads to relieve those who had been struggling.

"Now, this is the Forest Glen I know! Let's get home!" Kris walked back to her spot in the lead with cheers following her. Her pack felt lighter when she shouldered it back on. Her hands didn't feel nearly as sore when she lifted the cart once again.

Hannah smiled at her. "Nice work. Looks like Blake isn't the only one with a silver tongue."

"Well, I don't know about that, but it worked. I don't know for how long, and we have a long way to trek, so let's take advantage of it." Kris started in the direction they had chosen, noticing at once that barely an indent was left of Tucker's footprints. A chill ran through her once again.

There were many ways to get to their meeting point. What if their paths didn't cross? Fear made her chest prickle. Mercy must have felt it, too, for she started whimpering. The farther they traveled, the more unhappy she became.

Kris did her best to soothe Mercy, singing soft lullabies, whispering comforting words, anything she could think of to calm her. Stopping was not an option. The group had stayed right with her, and she knew slowing their momentum would mean the chance of it never returning.

Yet, Tucker's prints had fully disappeared now. Kris pushed on slowly, looking for other signs of his passing such as broken twigs or snowless branches. Her fear mounted into full-blown panic as Mercy's scream filled the air. Birds burst from trees, something that didn't happen in a snowstorm. Their cacophony mixed in the Mercy's wailing.

Kris almost stopped, putting her cart down so she could see what had Mercy up in arms. She never had been a screamer before. Then, as Mercy sucked in a breath for another round, she heard a faint sound whipping toward her on the wind. Mercy must have heard it too, for she sucked in her trembling lip and cocked her head. The bird ruckus died down just as the sound began again.

A whistle.

Three times and pause and three times more. Tucker!

Kris bent her head to brush her lips on her daughter, who now smiled and babbled as if she had never been upset. The whistle came from the right, so

Kris pushed on through the brush, clearing a path through the snow for those behind her.

The whistling became louder and louder until, at last, the sweet sound of her child called her.

"Mom! We're over here!" Tucker ran toward her, a grin brightening the situation. "I heard little sister scream. She missed me. So I whistled so she knew I was here."

Kris wrapped her son and daughter in her arms and bit her lip so she didn't cry. Once again, her children had saved them. "What would I do without you two?" She kissed them both and stood back up.

"You don't have to worry about that, Mommy. We'll always be here."

Kris's heart warmed. Then she lifted the cart once more. "So, show me this cache that you two dug."

She didn't expect much because it was only Tyler and Tucker armed with a small camping shovel battling frozen ground.

Tyler stood near a rock pile, his face lighting into a wide smile when he saw Hannah behind Kris. Then, he looked at her.

"We found something to help." He pointed at the rock formation. "Now, this won't work for food that little critters would munch, but it will for other things. We have closed off all entrances so only a field mouse could work its way in." He motioned for her to follow, and he pointed to a large hole. "Plus a smaller cache for food."

"Tyler and I make a good team," Tucker said proudly.

"Yeah we do, Buddy."

"I'm impressed." Kris watched behind her as the line of people started to gather. "Anyone else want a go at this?" she asked those closest to her.

"It's all you, Kris," Hannah said with a smile. "You're great."

Kris rolled her eyes and stepped on a rock near her so she could see everyone.

"This is the cache. The food goes in the pit in the ground and the other items in the large one in the rock pile. It will only be for a few days until we reach our destination and can send others back for it."

The thought of finding this again made her search for landmarks.

"Don't worry, Mom. Tyler and I already found the landmarks."

"Good work, Sweetie."

She turned back to the group. "Don't take too long in deciding what to keep and what to leave. The important thing to remember here is that you are making room for your younger children to have help on this long journey."

Right then a shot echoed through the woods. It was distant and devastating. She watched the expressions of all the women who had men with her husband. She imagined that her face held the same mask of horror and hope combined.

~5~

Conversation around Blake ceased as Dillon came into close proximity. He had just reached camp. Blake pushed off the tree he had been leaning on and swung his guns over his shoulder.

"What's the plan?" Arland asked. "Are we headed to join the group when Dillon arrives or...?"

"We have to make sure they don't follow us," David said. "Right?"

Blake had been toying with that idea the whole time. On the one hand, he wanted to disappear so their footprints would be covered by the snow that continued to fall. On the other hand, if the marauders found the trail before their tracks were covered, and they decided to follow...there would be casualties. He thought of the people likely bringing up the rear of the group, the older population and the ones with younger kids like David's family.

"If we go now, our tracks will be covered," Mitchel said, readying himself to leave.

"That will all depend on how close behind Dillon they are." Blake shielded his eyes from the dropping flakes as he watched the man coming toward them.

Dillon was close enough now that he could see them and slowed his pace. Through the curtain of snow, Blake could see the smile on his face.

"I made it," Dillon said right before a blast from the ridge flashed.

"Get down!' Blake yelled.

Dillon fell to the ground, but the snow around him slowly turned red. He lifted his head to look at Blake, his eyes wide and fearful. Blake motioned to stay down and still.

"Watch the ridge. Look for any movement, glint, flash, or something dark that stands out against the snow," Blake told the others where they hid behind the trees.

He scanned the ridge from where he thought the gunshot had come. Nothing moved. Nothing glinted.

"What do we do?" David whispered. "Dillon is bleeding out."

From where the blood pooled, it looked like Dillon had been hit in the leg. Hopefully, the bullet had missed the main artery. If not, they wouldn't have time to save him. It didn't make a difference to Blake how risky it would be. He would get Dillon out of there, one way or the other.

"Keep your surveillance." Blake kept his voice even.

"We need to get Dillon," another said and started moving in that direction.

"No! Get behind cover!"

It was too late. Another blast sounded as the guy stepped out of the edge of the forest. The bullet hit the tree next to Blake, sending bits of bark burning his cheek.

"Agh." The guy dropped and scrambled back to the tree.

"You were told to stay put," David spat out. "Blake, you were hit!"

Blake didn't take his eyes from where he saw the flash. As foolhardy as the guy's move was, it gave Blake the ability to locate the sniper. He reached up where his cheek burned and held his hand in front of him without taking his eyes off the sniper's location. His fingers were sticky with blood, but not a large amount.

"Just shrapnel from the tree. It's fine."

"How are we going to get Dillon? Every time we move, that guy goes at it again," Arland asked.

Blake narrowed his eyes. He knew the rifle he had wouldn't cover the distance to the sniper, even if he had his military-grade scope on it. The sniper must have a high-powered rifle. The only chance would be getting closer or shooting rapid fire toward him, hoping to distract him long enough to get Dillon out of there. Blake mentally marked the spot where the sniper hid.

"How many snipers does Meyers have?" Blake asked Butler.

"Just the one now." Butler smiled a humorless smile.

"You didn't have your rifle earlier?" Blake asked, wishing they had firepower to match.

"Nah, he only gives it to us when he has devised a plan."

Blake realized if Meyers were a distrusting fellow, and it seemed as he was, he probably wouldn't pass out artillery until he absolutely had to.

"And what do you think this devised plan of his would look like here?" he asked Butler.

"You really going to believe what this turncoat says?" one of the men said.

Butler stared hard at the man. "I see how this could look to you. When faced with life and death situations, you have to make choices you otherwise would never consider. There is something deeper, though, bred into a soldier who has served. One of which is the fact that I would never give bad intel to a superior officer."

"We aren't serving right now, Butler," Blake said, biting the inside of his cheeks while he tried to make a decision.

"Aren't we? We are trying to save the last of humanity." Butler's intense gaze was leveled at him.

"Point taken. Now, we are running out of time. Dillon needs medical care, and an army of marauders is heading our way." Blake urged him on.

"Yes, sorry. They will have all the entry points scouted. Their first unit will break off in groups and fill in from each one. The sniper will pick off deserters or aggressives."

Arland seeming to be calculating each word. "So, that sniper won't be moving until our camp is full of marauders."

Butler nodded.

"We have to leave…Dillon would understand." One of the guys looked frantically down the trail and back to the ridge.

"They'll torture him for information on our destination," Butler knew from experience.

"He doesn't know where we are going. No one really does besides Blake," the guy countered.

Arland looked at Blake. "We aren't leaving Dillon."

"No, we're not," Blake said through clenched teeth. "We don't have time for me to scout around until I am close enough to get a good shot at the sniper."

"I'll provide the distraction." Butler stood tall, a grim determination in his eyes.

"Yes, you will," Blake said. "You all will."

With a warning expression, he handed Butler his rifle.

"Sir?"

"Don't make me regret this," Blake said and then took off his pack and all his other bulky items. "Do you all see that dwarfed tree hanging off the bank on the southwest side of the ridge?"

"The one next to the dead pine?" Butler asked.

"That's the one. The sniper is hunkered down in there. On my signal, you all fire steadily at that location."

"What are you going to do, Blake?" Arland asked, his face going white.

"I'm going to bring Dillon home."

"Shouldn't someone else do it? What if you're hit? We won't be able to find the location without you," Arland countered.

"Does anyone else know how to heft a full-size man to your shoulder? Kris has the map. She and Tucker have studied it and will be able to get you there, but I don't plan on leaving them…or any of you." Blake put a hand on Arland's shoulder. "Just fire like crazy, and I'll be back before you know it."

Blake leveled his gaze on each member until they all took shelter at a tree and aimed toward the dwarfed tree. He blew out his breath a few times, calculated the distance to Dillon, and readied himself.

"Now!" he yelled as he ran toward the Dillon. No shots hit him or even the ground where he ran, and before he knew it, he was next to Dillon and hefting him onto his shoulder.

He heard the crack of the sniper's rifle just as he neared the tree line. A moment later, he felt the burn in his calf. It didn't stop him, though, and he made it to safety before landing on his knees and unceremoniously dropping Dillon into the snow.

His calf burned as if fire consumed him, but he had been shot before. This only felt like a graze. He searched Dillon, finding blood oozing out of a wound on his upper outside thigh. Not an artery.

"Thank you," Dillon groaned as he tried to sit up.

"Sit back. I need to fix this." Blake pushed him back into the snow even though the man shivered.

He tore the pants around the wound to get a better view and then turned the leg to find the exit wound.

"No exit wound," Butler whispered while leaning over him.

Blake shook his head. "We need to get that bullet out."

"Uh, I hope not now because they're here." David backed up from the tree he had stood behind.

Blake turned to see the people filing down into the camp. His body tensed as he turned back toward his man lying in the snow. He undid the belt around Dillon's waist and cinched it above his wound.

Dillon gasped but did not scream out.

"We're going to get this out, but we need to get you out of here first. Can you do that?" Blake asked the pale young man who nodded. "Good. David. Mitchel. You each take an arm and get him to Laurie. Tell Kris to keep going until the first stopping point. We'll catch up."

Blake worked his leg, making sure what he said wouldn't be a lie. His calf protested, but it still functioned. That was all he needed.

"What about the rest of us?" the guy who had jumped out of cover said.

"They'll follow the line of blood if they find it." Blake watched as the men pushed into the camp and began searching the dwellings. "We have to give them time."

"We'll go as fast as we can," David said as he pulled Dillon up to his feet and shoved a shoulder under one arm and Mitchel supported the other.

Dillon groaned but worked hard to keep up with the fast pace David set.

Blake saw that the community's tracks were almost filled in, but a group that size would leave a mark a lot longer than a single person or two. He squinted up at the sky, seeing only the snow that fell down around them. Fall faster, he prayed.

~*~

Only one shot could mean anything, but more than likely it wouldn't mean the death of her husband. By the time the second shot reached them, it woke Kris from her spell. Everyone stood frozen, fear filling their faces. She had to improvise and act fast.

"That's our signal. It's time to pick up our pace. Even if it means dumping stuff, do so. Get those children too young to run into the carts and on the travois. We need to move!"

She watched the people scurry about their duties, getting kids into carts and on travois and urging older ones to move faster. She needed to lead, but who would take up the rear to make sure everyone kept up?

Laurie laid a hand on her shoulder. "Lead. I'll take the rear."

"You know, sometimes I think you can read my

mind," Kris said to her friend as she squeezed her hand.

"You and I just think a lot alike, my friend. Now go."

"Work as a team. Help those you can!" Kris called as she looked out for the markers that Blake had taught her. "This way."

"That's my thought, too, Mom." Tucker nodded, full of serious intensity. He lifted the cart handles that Hannah had brought there for them and started off to break the snow.

"Tucker, I can—" Hannah started.

Kris touched her shoulder and shook her head. "Let him for the time he can. It won't be long until breaking the trail becomes too much, and he needs to be relieved."

Hannah nodded, but she chewed on her lower lip. Tyler moved in and around the people, helping them offload supplies and load up children. With one last look, they filed in behind Tucker.

They had only made it a couple hundred yards when the forest echoed with a volley of rapid fire.

Panic could be heard in the community's voices and some soft sobs. Some kids called their daddies, and some women screamed. The terror of the marauders at her home ripped through Kris. Tucker had stopped, eyes wide but unseeing. He closed them, and when he opened them again, he looked directly at her.

"He makes it." Tucker's voice held an assurance that gave her strength.

"Do not let fear consume you!" she called to the people. "We don't know what that fire means. What we do know is that our men are out there giving us the chance to survive. Let's honor them by doing so and hold hope in our hearts that they all return to us."

"Faith. Honor. Hope!" Tyler raised his fist in the air. He stared straight at her before starting a second time. "Faith. Honor. Hope!"

"Faith. Honor. Hope!" The crowd began to chant with them as they pushed forward.

Kris joined in as she set a quick pace through the woods. Soon they would make it to the dirt road where the brush would clear, making for much faster travel. They could get there. They would get there.

With each step, she pushed out the fear and filled in the void with the words they chanted. After a hundred yards, many people had stopped chanting, but enough continued quietly to keep the rhythm in their steps. Tucker had begun to slow his pace. She could hear his rapid breathing and see him straining with the cart.

"Time for me to break trail." Kris walked up beside him.

"I got this, Mom," he said with determination, reminding her so much of his father.

"Just like the geese, Tuck. We take turns." She kept her words soft, hoping his little ego wouldn't take offense.

He nodded and let her pull ahead.

"And Tyler needs your help. So I will take over your cart." Hannah took the handles from him before he even had the chance to protest. "Go on. He's encouraging those with young ones to keep moving."

"But stay close," Kris called out, trying to keep the fear from her voice. She wanted him by her side, but she knew Hannah's ploy. "Thank you," she told the girl.

"That is one special boy right there. I didn't want him passing out from pushing so hard. I don't think he would willingly stop until it came to that."

"You read him well, Hannah. He's always had that drive, but this last year has made him even more determined and unwilling to ask for help." Kris sighed. "I'm hoping that living in a community where we rely on each other allows him to see that it's okay to ask for help now and then."

"That is something I could try to incorporate in our hikes." Hannah paused. "You know, when we get settled in New Forest Glen, you should think about starting a school."

Kris turned to meet Hannah's eyes before concentrating on keeping on the right track.

"You don't like the idea? I don't mean like necessarily teaching algebra and chemistry. I mean, there is so much for these kids to learn about surviving, but we don't want to forget to teach them how to read and write or our history. Our culture would be lost without that."

"Hannah, I love the idea of a school for the children. You are an incredible young woman for thinking of things beyond just surviving today." Kris's mind worked, formulating tentative plans for a school already, but she also watched Hannah as much as she could. "Your father is going to be okay."

"I know." Hannah said, a determined look entering her gaze. "Blake is with him."

Kris let them be in their own thoughts for a while. She needed to concentrate on the trail. Somewhere close, they should come upon the first of the old dirt roads. Having an open area and trail would not only make travel easier, but also ease the stress of constantly losing the right path or getting stuck in thickets of brush.

Every time her worry went back to the volley of fire that echoed through the trees, she thought of Tucker's words. *He makes it.* She let the words settle over her like a warm embrace. She had to believe that. She had to believe they all would make it back.

She pushed under a branch heavy with snow. After making sure the snow hadn't dropped down to cover Mercy, who slept soundly again, she looked up and caught her breath.

The road.

"You okay?" Hannah asked from behind her.

"Yes. We made it to the road." Kris smiled, but as she stepped out from under the tree branches and onto the clearing of the road, the snow dumped in heavy sheets around her. Her footsteps left over six-inch-deep prints in the pristine white road.

Kris drew up the wrap to ensure the snow wouldn't land on Mercy and tugged her hood farther over her face. She turned to watch Hannah drag the cart out onto the road.

"Wow. It's deep." She put a hand over her eyes and looked down the road.

"Looks like the trees shelter the road a bit further ahead. Let's stop there briefly to check on everyone," Kris said. She wanted to lay eyes on her son again.

"I like it. My hands could use a rest." Hannah stretched her hands before pulling the cart the last few hundred feet before the promised break.

Kris understood. Her hands stung as she clenched them around the cart handles. Blake hadn't sheltered her completely from physically demanding work, but he had shouldered a lot of it. Her hands were proof of that.

The relief in people's voices as they saw a break so close tugged at Kris's heart. She knew they should only stop long enough to account for everyone and then continue on. When would Blake catch up? She tried to blink back the snow long enough to judge where the sun was and how much longer they had daylight. They would have to find shelter before then and make fires so everyone stayed alive.

As the last people crossed into the road, a scream shattered Kris's thoughts. She immediately searched the crowd until she saw Tucker safe, a hand wrapped around little Ethan's.

She searched for the source of the scream and saw Carly, Dillon's wife, running toward a man leaning heavily on David and Mitchel. Laurie took charge of the situation with her calm, firm tone. Kris started toward them as they headed toward the most sheltered location under a tall cedar. She saw the trail of blood following the trio of men and stopped short.

Three men were back, but no sign of Blake or Arland or several others, including Blake's new charge, Butler. Pushing through the crowd that had gathered, she made it to the area Laurie had set up as an emergency healing station.

David stood up after easing Dillon down and met her eyes. "He's alive," he said.

"He saved my life," Dillon breathed out as his wife held him and planted kisses all over his face.

"And the others?" Laurie asked, her hand holding the moss for his wound frozen in mid-air.

"Everyone else is, too." Mitchel grasped her arm. "Arland is fine."

Laurie nodded, but Kris saw the moisture in her

eyes as she set about her work.

"Blake says the bullet has to come out," Dillon said through clenched teeth.

"Do we have time?" Laurie asked.

"They are holding the edge to see if the men try to follow." Mitchel crossed his arms.

"Why didn't they just come back with you?" one of the other wives asked.

"The marauders could have followed our trail, and without being laden with gear and children, they would be able to easily catch up," David said as he held his wife and kids, who had come running as soon as they saw that he was there.

"Did Blake have any further instruction?" Kris asked, hoping for something to hold onto to know she led the group down the right path.

"Just to keep going to the stopping point," Mitchel said and then took off to meet his wife, who slogged through the snow toward them.

People were sitting where they could. Some had their feet out of their shoes and were rubbing their toes. Kris had quality waterproof boots, but still her toes hurt with the cold. She wondered how people with only tennis shoes were doing. As she maneuvered through the groups toward Tucker, she heard them.

"My feet are frozen."

"Am I going to get frostbite, Mama?"

She needed to get these people to shelter and start fires to thaw out their frozen bodies.

Tucker looked up as she approached. "Hey, Mom."

"Hi, Sweetie. How are you holding up?" She eased down on the folded blanket the two boys sat on.

"Okay." He looked at Ethan and then back toward her.

His nose and cheeks were red with cold, and he had his hands stuffed into his armpits. Thank goodness he had his gloves, but she still worried about him since he wouldn't tell her how bad off he really was.

"Do you think we'll make it to the rock overhang Dad had told us would be our first night?" Tucker asked looking down the road.

Relief flooded Kris. She had been so stressed to get to the road she had forgotten the rest. The overhang would be exactly what they needed, a protected shelter where they could make fires and dry out their socks and shoes.

What had Blake said? A mile or two and the overhang would be on their left about a hundred yards off the road. At this pace, they could make it within the hour. One more hour to warmth!

A guttural yell silenced the crowd. All eyes turned to its source. Laurie had removed the bullet embedded in Dillon's leg.

Kris blew out her breath and forced a smile as she looked down at the boys. "He'll be better now. Dillon had a bullet in his leg, but Laurie took it out. Now he can heal. Rest up. We have one last push to accomplish for the day."

She traveled through the groups of people, sharing the good news of one last push, sharing hope and faith that the rest of their men would make it to spend the night with them. As she did, she convinced herself so much that she could almost feel Blake's warmth wrapped around her.

~6~

Blake watched the people piling into camp. He didn't want to take the time to bandage up his calf, but if he didn't, he would leave a trail as well. Rolling his pants up, he saw the bullet entrance and exit. It had taken a good-sized chunk out of his calf, but still was only a graze. He counted his blessings and quickly patched it up while the others watched.

"How often do you get shot, Blake?" Arland asked, watching intently.

"Too often as of late it seems," he said wryly.

"That's nothing compared to that time we were holed up in—" Butler stopped as soon as he met Blake's cold stare.

"This is not the place for war stories. How many have entered the camp so far?" Blake asked.

"Twenty-seven, and the line is still coming." Kevin looked through a pair of binoculars.

Blake stuffed the first aid kit back into his pack and surveyed the situation. There was no chance that they could take them on, and that wasn't his intent. He merely wanted to watch, assess, and, only if needed, delay them following the community that fled into the forest—his community.

"What's the strategy?" Arland asked.

"Wait. Watch," Blake said, never taking his eyes off the people running into the camp he had called home for more than a month now.

"I don't like watching," Arland said, his voice low

enough only Blake could hear.

"That I understand." Blake nodded, thinking of when the marauders had shown up to take his bunker. He often wondered if the others that Chuck had promised were coming had ever come. Maybe he had been talking about Meyers' crew.

Arland's men had buried the bodies so the others might never know what happened to Chuck and the rest of his unit. The dark of that day constricted Blake's throat. There had been nothing else to do. It was the survival of his family or their deaths.

He forced those thoughts back into the recesses of his mind and concentrated on the current problem. Pulling his rifle out, he peered through the scope and scanned the line coming down what used to be a barely discernible path. The men looked rough, clothes in tatters, grime covering their faces, and shoes in a variety of bad-to-shredded condition.

Blake could tell instantly when Meyers and his personal guards came over the rise for their clothes weren't in tatters and their boots were good. Meyers himself stood almost regal in his commanding attire.

"That Meyers?" Blake nodded toward the line coming into the camp and then met Butler's eyes.

Butler squinted.

Blake ensured the safety was on and then handed the rifle to Butler, who immediately leveled the scope.

"Yep, that's him," he said, handing the rifle back to Blake. "You have a kill shot…"

"No more killing unless needed. Who knows what chaos would ensue if Meyers were out of the picture," Blake said, leaning the rifle against the tree. "We're only waiting and watching right now."

"The sniper, he will come check on his shot," said

Butler, staring in the direction of the bloody patch of snow slowly becoming covered by the falling flakes.

Faster. Heavier, Blake prayed.

Several cheers went through the men ransacking the camp. They came out of the dwelling that had been used to store the food, holding baskets and racks of drying meat.

"They found what we couldn't carry." Arland sighed. "May it keep them from following us. Though I bet they don't know how to cook all the greens, berries, and other foliage the women worked so hard on gathering."

"We took all that could be carried." Blake let his hand drop on his friend's shoulder. "Surely we still have more than you had last winter."

"True," Arland said, nodding.

"I think that's our sniper," Butler said as one man veered off toward them. With questioning eyes, he reached for Blake's rifle.

Blake nodded. He would have to trust him until he proved himself untrustworthy. He couldn't afford to think twice about everything. Besides, he had his pistol and knife in easy reach if needed.

Butler looked through the scope. "That's him."

"Ensure you are hidden, but move slowly." Though his calf screamed at him, Blake squatted behind a thicket so he could still see without peering around the cedar he had been standing behind.

His men followed his moves as each found his own concealed location. Blake's senses were on high alert. Adrenaline spiked through him as it did on every covert mission. His breathing eased, and his vision tunneled.

The sniper warily scanned the tree line as he

walked toward them, his rifle at the ready. He stopped at the site where Dillon had fallen and squatted, keeping his eyes focused on where they were hidden. Then he briefly looked down and swiped the freshly fallen snow away to reveal the frozen blood. He looked up again, and the hairs on Blake's neck rose for it looked as if he stared directly at him.

"Perkins!" someone from the camp yelled.

The sniper stood, keeping his eyes on the tree line and backed away. Meyers and a few other men met him partway, their voices carrying across the open space.

"What are you doing out here?" Meyers asked the sniper.

"I got one of them. His body is gone."

Meyers looked out into the forest. "Will they attack?"

"It would be foolhardy of them. I say they escaped into the forest."

"Well, we have plenty of supplies here. What a score they left behind. Come." Meyers gestured back toward camp.

Perkins' feet stayed planted. "They killed Butler, sir." Perkins held up Butler's tags.

Meyers took them, clutched them in his hands, and glared into the forest. "You sure?"

"They shot him and threw him into a thirty-foot-deep ravine."

Meyers stuffed the tags into his jacket pocket. "We will give these back to his family when we arrive back home. His sacrifice will be remembered."

"We just going to let them get away with this?" Perkins snarled.

Meyers glared into the forest, scanning the edge.

Blake watched him through the scope as he clenched his fists and tensed his jaw.

"They could pick our guards off tonight." Perkins squared his shoulders.

Meyers let loose a growl of frustration before turning toward one of his guards. "Keep twenty men and guard the loot." He turned to another. "Assemble the men. We have a score to settle."

Blake tensed. They were coming after them because of a decision he had made. There was no time for self-blame. He signaled across the line to his men to retreat. They slowly backed farther into the forest until they were several hundred yards away from the edge.

"This is crazy," one of the guys said. "We didn't kill no one."

"Not for real at least," Butler said. "I can't have the blood of your community on my hands, Blake. I will return to Meyers."

"No." Blake clenched his fist around his rifle. He would not leave a man behind, even in this situation. "This was my choice. The rest of you do not need to suffer the consequences. Go back to your families."

"So, you are going to sacrifice yourself, and thus the safety of the whole community, for one man." Arland watched him seemingly without judgment, but more of a curiosity.

"Yes. I've been at worse odds. Don't give up on me yet." He pushed forth a smile.

"I'm staying," Arland said.

"Now, that would be selfish. New Forest Glen needs its leader, and we had a deal, remember?" Blake stared earnestly at the scientist turned leader turned friend.

Arland hung his head. "You are always keeping me out of altercations, Blake."

"A leader is the head of a community. Without you, there would be no one to keep them going. Now go. All of you. That army will be descending upon us in minutes."

"I'm staying, but I would like a gun." Butler stood firm.

Blake nodded. Arland handed him his rifle, and another handed him a pistol.

"We're staying, too," Kevin and John said.

Blake gave each man a curt, appreciative nod. He looked at Arland, clasping his hand. "May we meet again."

"May we meet again," Arland returned and looked back at the three men returning with him. "Let's go."

Blake watched the four men jog through the forest, following the almost full footprints and covered blood trail that Dillon and the others had left. Their trail could be followed. Blake cut off a cedar branch and followed their tracks for a ways and then returned, brushing the snow so freshly fallen flakes could conceal them in less time.

"Walk around a lot in this area while we plan. We hunker ourselves in here. See those rocks?" Blake pointed out three different rock outcroppings set out in a line, all facing the trail the army would follow. "We have a good vantage. Use bullets sparingly. Pick them off all across the line. We need to discourage them."

"They'll send in the expendables first. Each will only have a few shots," Butler added.

"How can men be seen as expendable, especially when the human race is dying off like flies?" John sneered.

Blake wondered the same thing, but he couldn't get lost on that thought right now. He didn't like taking lives, but he didn't want to lose any from their community either.

"Change of tactic. We'll try to persuade them first. If they push on, then shoot. Aim for the weapons first or rocks and trees near them. We don't want to have to kill unless necessary."

"Are you sure?" Butler asked.

"I may regret it, but I am tired of death. We'll try to hold them back. If it looks like it isn't working, I will take the first kill shot. You all follow suit."

"Yes, sir," the three of them responded.

"Just in case we get separated or something happens to me, to find the others, keep the ridges to your left until you meet a road, then follow it east. They will find you." Blake looked each one in the eye. "Thank you for staying."

"Pleasure serving with you sir," Kevin said, and he and John saluted before they jogged off to their places.

"Butler, you stay close," Blake said as he covered his tracks until he reached the brush.

"You can trust me, sir." Butler held his gaze.

Blake nodded. He sure hoped so. Otherwise, he may have not told the truth about his making it out of this and might have brought two innocent men into the mix.

~*~

Kris could feel the temperature drop once the sun fell behind the trees. She couldn't see it behind all the clouds and snow, but she could feel it. The last of the people finally caught up to the side trail that led to the overhang.

Her stomach twisted, thinking how close she had been to passing it. If it hadn't been for Mercy squalling and needing a diaper change, she wouldn't have seen the overhang through the snow.

Blake's memory amazed her. Not only did he remember this overhang, it was the perfect size for their large group. People collapsed onto the dry dirt that still existed underneath the huge rock ledge. Exhaustion filled everyone. You could see it in their eyes and their limp body movements. Kids no longer cried, but whimpered.

She had counted every person that had come into their camp for the night. All were accounted for except eight. Looking out into the snow, she hoped Blake would make it back in time to keep her and the kids warm tonight. A shiver shook her, causing Mercy to gripe.

"You did it," Laurie said as she walked up.

"Now to keep everyone from freezing to death." Kris kept her voice quiet. "I'll ask David and others to start fires. Five or six should really help, especially with the reflective rock."

"I agree, though this wind is brutal." Laurie tugged her jacket closer to her. "How is Mercy?"

"Grumpy, but she's warm tucked in against me." She looked over at Tuck, who cuddled close to Ethan where she had left him against the deepest part of the overhang. She had immediately pulled out their blankets and tucked them around him. As soon as Ethan had arrived, she sent him to warm up underneath the blankets with Tucker.

Kris took in the scene. Everyone huddled beneath blankets or furs, shivering, eyes drooping. Some had jerky hanging limply from their hands, too tired to eat. They had made it. She blew out a breath. The worst part wasn't over yet, though.

A gust of wind whipped in from the northwest. Something had to be done or that wind would steal a good portion of their heat. She caught David's eye, and he walked over.

"You did good, Kris. Blake would be proud." David squeezed her arm gently.

"Thank you," she said, losing her focus in the snow again. "Hey, could you organize some people to start six fires evenly spaced?" Another gust blew across her frozen cheeks. "And find some guys with good gloves to build a windbreak for us. A snow-wall along the Northwestern side would do wonders to keep in some warmth."

"My thought, too." David reached out to touch her. "You need to rest."

"We all do," she said, pushing a tired smile to her face.

"People are coming!" one of the guards she posted as soon as they arrived shouted.

"Maybe it's Blake and the rest of the men!" She started toward the commotion on the road.

"I hope so," David said. "I'll get to those fires."

"Thank you, David." She glanced over her shoulder before urging her reluctant feet to push forward.

Thankfully it was still light, so when she arrived at the road, she easily recognized Arland and the three others, but no sign of Blake. She couldn't help looking down the road, hoping to see him coming.

Arland came toward her as soon as he saw her.

"He'll be coming. Don't worry. He and three others have stayed to ensure we weren't followed."

Kris nodded. "Come, get out of the snow." Her words sounded choked as her throat tightened.

"Hey," Arland said and pulled her into a hug. "He'll make it."

Kris let herself relax into the hug briefly, the stress of the day overwhelming her before she pushed off and led him and the others back to their temporary camp.

"David is leading a team in building a windbreak." She pointed to where a few men began piling snow up around the edge of the overhang. "Others are starting fires."

"You've done well, Kris. Thank you." Arland rested a hand on her shoulder. "I'm so glad you and your family decided to join us."

Kris's eyes filled, but she blinked back the wetness, turning her attention to Laurie rushing toward them.

"You made it," she breathed out and wrapped her arms around Arland.

Kris smiled and discreetly left them to their homecoming to check on the boys. They had leaned back against the rock, their heads resting on each other's and eyes closed. This would be a moment she would have normally rushed to get a picture, but all she could do now was ingrain it into her memory.

Soft sobbing broke into her memory-making moment. She turned to see Janene huddled over her baby, rocking back and forth. Kris's heart froze for a moment, and she pushed herself to approach the woman.

"Janene, are you okay?" Kris eased down into a

crouch, ignoring her screaming muscles. "Is your baby doing okay?"

"Where is my husband? He didn't return with Arland."

"Your husband is with my husband. He'll bring him back." Kris reached out, hand shaking to pull the blanket back from the baby's face. Warm breath burned her fingers. Kris let out the breath she had been holding.

"How do I keep him warm enough tonight?" Janene sniffed.

"Oh, honey, that's easy. You keep him right up against you." Kris helped her get her baby situated against her chest under her jacket, but with room to breathe. She repositioned the beanie on the little one's head and stood. "You're going to be just fine. And I'm hoping we wake to our husbands' warmth surrounding us."

"Me, too. Thank you for your help and your kind words."

"I'll be right over there if you need anything." Kris nodded toward the sleeping boys.

She longed to join them, but she had to check on the rest of the community. It would be a long night, made longer without Blake's return.

On her way to check on the windbreak progress, she spoke to each family she passed, giving out encouragement like it was candy and wishing she had extra blankets instead. She reminded each family to take off their shoes and socks and dry them by the fire. It would be another long hike through the snow tomorrow, and having soggy shoes would only lead to frostbite and dangerous conditions.

The windbreak did wonders. She could already feel

the difference. The men had built up the snow, packing it down and adding more until it was taller than they were. It almost reached the top of the overhang, and it had stopped the majority of the wind.

"Thank you, guys. This works great." She did her best to show them a gracious smile.

"If we had more time, we could extend it across most of the opening, and it would really keep the heat in," one of them said.

"I agree, but we just need to survive the night. We have a ways to travel until we reach New Forest Glen." Kris looked across the distance in the direction their new location lay. Would they reach it?

"I was thinking," David said. "What about staying here until the storm ends? If we aren't being followed, then why push through a potentially dangerous situation?"

"Luckily for me, David, I don't have to make that decision. Arland is back."

"Good, then you go rest. Blake will have my hide if you pass out from exhaustion."

"You don't have to push it. I'm headed there now." Kris turned, but looked over her shoulder and said, "Thank you."

"You're welcome. Tell my wife I'll be by her side in just a few moments," David called after her.

Wives. She decided to stop to talk with Janene and John's wife. Their men were still out there with Blake. As military wives, they knew this situation all too well, but that never made it easier. The two women huddled together near the fire closest to her. With a quick glance, she saw her boy and Ethan still snuggled and sleeping.

Gingerly, she laid a hand to rest on Mercy's back and worked her way into the wrap to touch her fingers, toes, ears, and nose to ensure her baby wasn't cold. Kris couldn't help wishing that her extremities were as toasty warm as her daughter's, but there was a peace in knowing her children were safe.

"I can't wait until we get to New Forest Glen," Janene said. "I want Kevin by my side."

"We got through all those years before. We'll get through tonight," the other woman said, clutching her two children to her side.

"We will," Kris affirmed as she squatted near them. "Blake will bring them home." She hoped she spoke the truth, but she knew Blake, and he never left a man behind.

"Yeah, but will he be shot up like Dillon?" Janene said.

Kris sighed. "You know how it is. We know the risks our husbands take and the prices that may have to be paid. Dillon will heal. He still has the chance to start a family with his new wife. We need to have faith."

"Faith. Honor. Hope." The oldest child, a boy of about ten, whispered.

"That's right. Together, we will prevail." Kris stood and touched each woman's shoulder. "Let's have hope our husbands will return to keep us warm tonight."

Kris felt chilled to the bone as she took the few steps to Tucker. She didn't want to disturb him but laid a hand on his cheek to see if he was warm. The firelight flickered across his smooth skin, and his cheeks were warm to the touch. Not a fever, but a healthy warmth. His boots needed drying. She watched him sleeping peacefully for several more seconds before she pulled the blanket off his feet and began unlacing his boots.

He moaned in his sleep but didn't wake up. Poor boy was exhausted. She yawned. She was too.

While taking his boots off him, she realized just how tight they were. His toes were scrunched and cold. She put his boots by the fire and draped his soggy socks over them. Then she dug through the carts near them until she found two pairs of his socks, which she warmed over the fire before slipping them onto his feet and wrapping the blanket around them once more.

She hesitated for a moment before reaching for Ethan's feet.

"I'll take over. Thank you for thinking of him," Laurie said as she squatted beside her.

Kris rose to pull out a few more blankets and the deer hides that Blake had cured. She laid out the hides on the ground, one over the other, and then layered the blankets at the bottom to make for easy pulling over. She watched Tucker sleeping. She needed to get him lying down so they could keep each other warm, but once again the desire to not disturb his much-needed slumber had her just watching him.

"It's sweet, isn't it?" Laurie said from where she squatted at her son's feet.

"It is," Kris said.

Laurie sighed and started tugging off Ethan's soggy shoes. "It's time to make some waterproof moccasins."

"I have a pair started for Tucker but haven't finished them yet. How do you waterproof them?"

"Animal fat or pine sap. Both work, though you

have to reapply many times. Our boys' feet are growing so fast, it will be hard to keep up." Laurie measured her son's foot against her hand. "How fast they grow."

Kris took the boots and socks from her and set them next to Tucker's and then became aware of her own. She had quality boots, but her toes still hurt from the cold. She sat on the bed she had made and tugged off her own boots. Her socks were hardly damp, but her toes were freezing. She warmed them in her hands for several minutes as she watched Laurie do the same to Ethan.

Ethan stirred. "Mama?"

"I'm here, Honey. Just warming up your toes."

"I'm hungry." Ethan sat up and stretched, waking Tucker.

"I'm hungry, too," Tucker said with a yawn.

Kris let go of her toes and searched her bag until she found some jerky and dried berries. Ethan was sitting in Laurie's lap, so she called Tucker over.

"We're going to sleep cuddled up tonight," she said.

"Dad won't get mad?"

"No, Dad will be happy we are keeping each other warm." She held up the blankets and patted the hides.

Tucker came over, bringing the blankets that had surrounded him to add to the pile.

"You aren't putting the hides over you?" Janene asked from the next fire over.

"Two on bottom is better than one on top is the saying. The frozen ground will suck out your heat. Do you have enough to put some on the bottom?"

"Yes, we each have a hide. Thank you for the tip."

Kris smiled and then turned back to her son, who

was scarfing down his food. She nibbled some as well.

"We'll stay here until Dad gets back, right?" Tucker asked.

"That's up to Arland, Sweetie, and I'm sure it will depend on when he returns."

"If he does," said one of the boys whose dad was out there with Blake as he made his way back to their fire with his arms laden with blankets.

Tucker shot up. "My dad always returns to us."

The boy stopped and stared almost blankly at Tucker. His eyebrows furrowed, and his shoulders fell. "Until he doesn't."

"Your dad will, too. They'll all be back," Tucker said.

Kris tugged on Tucker's coat, urging him to sit. "It's okay, Sweetie."

"John's not my real dad. My real dad didn't return." The boy turned away and slumped off to where his mom and sister cuddled near the fire.

Kris's heart dropped. That poor boy. She wanted to bring him into a hug but knew the kid tried to play it tough. These kids have been through too much.

"Dad will return to us. He promised, and he always keeps his promise." Tucker's lower lip trembled. He looked into her eyes and whispered, "Besides, I saw it, Mommy. He returns."

"I know, Sweetie. He will. That boy has been through a lot of heartache, and that's where he's speaking from."

Tucker stuffed the last piece of jerky into his mouth and drew the blankets up. "What if I squash sister?"

"You won't squash sister, and besides, you know she'll let you know if you do."

Tucker grinned. "She does have a really loud screech. I have never heard that from her before."

"Me neither. I think you were right. I think she saved us by calling out to you."

"One of many times, Mom. One of many." Tucker pulled the wrap back, kissed his sister's head, and then lay down and wrapped up in the blankets.

Kris lay down next to him, seeing Ethan already back asleep too. Laurie met her eyes and smiled. Kris wanted to talk with her friend, dissect the day, and share how incredible their children were and the resiliency of their community. Yet her eyes felt heavy, and her tongue slow.

Arland stepped quietly up to them. Laurie's attention drew away from Kris and to him, so Kris slowly lowered her eyelids.

"Hannah wants to sleep with Tyler so he can keep her warm," Arland said with a huge sigh.

"It's hard to watch our children grow. She's an adult now. You have to trust her and let her make her own decisions," Laurie counseled.

"I know," his voice sounded defeated.

"Come," Laurie said. "Ethan and I will keep you warm."

Kris didn't mean to eavesdrop, but they were right there, sharing their fire. She was happy for Arland and Laurie. They would make a great couple when they were both ready to move on with their lives. A single tear ran down her cheek. She missed Blake. It had been a long time since she had to sleep without him. His warmth and security had spoiled her. Without it, she felt the burdens of keeping her family safe and warm.

To divert her thoughts, she wondered about

Mercy. Tucker had the gift of sight; did Mercy have a gift, too? Tucker had mentioned many times before about his sister saving them all. What had he seen that he hadn't shared? A shiver ran through her as she wrapped her arms around her children. What heavy burdens her children carried, and where would they take them?

~7~

Blake eased into position, the cold from the snow seeping into his body. Laying on his belly would give him the best cover and shot. Thankfully, he had on his good winter gear so he only felt the cold and not the wet. He turned to his right and saw Butler in a similar position, except all he had on for protection was Arland's hand-me-down coat.

To his left, his other two men hid in the boulders. They held the best position possible, and though they wouldn't be able to hold off an army, he hoped he could change Meyers's mind and send the men back the way they came.

His body tensed, and he evened his breath as the first few men came into view. They stood in the area they had stomped down, searching for tracks. Blake narrowed his vision and focused on the rifle one of them held lazily. With a deep held breath, he pulled the trigger and heard the resounding twang of metal on metal a half-second before the startled man screamed and dropped the gun into the snow.

Three more shots went off with three more twangs and three more men dropping their guns and cursing.

"What's going on?" a man asked as he joined the other four who stared at each other and into the woods as if they hadn't a clue.

Blake shot the speaker's gun out of his hand. Instead of screaming and staring around in shock, he yelled, "We're under fire. Take cover!"

The men scrambled to squat behind trees along the trail.

"What's going on up there?" Blake instantly recognized Meyers' booming voice from farther down the trail.

"We're under fire, sir," the other hollered back.

"How many casualties?"

"None, sir. They targeted our guns."

Blake could hear murmurs and discussion. He licked his lips. Should he speak up now or wait to see how Meyers would play this.

"Send in another five men," Meyers shouted.

Blake tensed and breathed deep as he readied to take two shots. These men didn't seem so confident. Their guns shook in their hands as they swung them left and right. The fifth man actually got in a couple shots before his gun was taken out, and he ran with the others back toward cover.

He heard Meyers curse, and then quiet resumed in the forest. Blake eased his back and stretched, never taking his eyes off the trail. Could they be trying to come around the side? Even with snow constantly falling, he would hear footsteps squeaking on the fresh snow.

Finally, after Blake thought he'd be frozen to the ground, Meyers's voice boomed out.

"I appreciate you not killing my men. Well, at least these ones. The problem is, though, you killed my lead scout. Brutally, if I do say so. How can I let that go?"

Blake glanced at Butler, who watched him intensely. Blake knew all he had to do was nod, and Butler would stand and walk back into that army, facing certain consequences for him and his family.

He blew out a breath and sucked it back in.

"What you should be asking yourself is, how will you keep your men alive in the forest during a snowstorm all night?" Blake called out in his strongest tone.

Would it work? Did Meyers have enough common sense to know that they would freeze without preparation in this storm?

"Anything can last a night," Meyers called back.

Blake's hands clenched and unclenched around his rifle. He had to think. Smart. How did this guy think?

"Even if the snow covered your tracks and you lost your way back? How will you keep your men alive then?"

Blake heard the hissing argument that ensued and couldn't stop the wry, one-sided grin his lips pushed into. Dissension in the group. They were held together loosely and by only one motivation: surviving. Staying out in the frozen forest would seem impossible to a group of city people, a death trap.

Cold seeped into Blake as the sky darkened. The sun had set. True cold was about to set in. How long would these men last when they felt the deep freeze of a mountain storm?

"Our camp back there has firewood, strong shelters with comfortable beds, and lots of food. Why don't you go back and get warm. It's yours. We don't need it anymore." Blake hoped his ploy worked.

Those men had to be freezing. He was, and he was a mountain boy decked out in snow gear. With the idea of warmth and food, the men wouldn't want to keep going.

People started stirring, and Blake could see a good number fading off through the forest, following their half-filled tracks back to camp. He hadn't heard the command or another word from Meyers and didn't trust them, so he settled back in even though his body stiffened with cold.

Sure enough, sometime later, more men stirred and made their way back the way they had come. Blake still gave it another twenty minutes or so. It was long enough that his stiff muscles didn't want to budge as he rolled over and pushed to his feet. Cautiously, he peered through the darkening forest.

When he felt sure that no one from the marauders had stayed behind, he signaled to the others. A few groans carried through the thick blanket of snow as his comrades shadowy forms filtered in from the forest. He clasped hands with Kevin and John and then glanced toward where Butler walked toward them, a smile spreading his lips.

"I can't express enough gratitude…Chantry!" Butler shouted as a twig cracked from the direction Meyers and his men had fled.

Butler took a flying leap toward Blake, knocking them both to the ground as a shot echoed across them. Two more shots fired, and Blake heard a grunt as a body fell close by.

"Sir?" Kevin asked as he and John pulled Butler's limp body off him.

Butler lay unmoving. Blake gasped as he tried to get to Butler. His side burned with white-hot fire. He looked down at the snow turning dark with blood. Blake pushed through the pain and raised on his knees to check Butler, whose own side was dark with blood.

"You're both hit?" John asked.

"There was only one shot," Kevin said.

Blake looked back at the body his men had put down. One of them kicked him over to ensure he was no longer a threat. He knew that face. It was the other scout.

"Quick, get the first aid kit from my pack." Blake painfully shrugged out of his backpack and let the men rummage through it. "We have to stop the bleeding."

"On him or you?" Kevin asked.

"Butler. I'm fine." As he said it, he touched the blood that seeped from his own wound. It came slowly, though, not pumping like Butler's.

He handed his machete to John. "Get a travois ready for him."

With the solid thwack-thwack of his blade chopping down saplings, Blake worked quickly, slowing the bleeding from the man that had saved his life.

"A life for a life," Butler rasped out as Blake shoved another wad of gauze into the man's wound.

"Stop going all fatalistic on me, Butler." Blake rolled him over gently to make sure he was right about the exit wound.

"It went straight through him and into you," Kevin said as he took a blanket from his pack to wrap around the poles John cut.

Blake ignored the comment and wrapped the bandages tight around Butler. He knew a bit about medical aid, but it wasn't his top skill. In the dark, he had no idea how to go about stitching him up. They needed Laurie, and they needed light.

A wave of dizziness made his head swim. After Butler was as ready as he could be for travel, Blake pulled up his shirt and tried to examine his wound in the dark. He reached around behind, and his hand came back clean.

Blake squeezed his eyes shut and growled low and deep.

"What is it?" John stopped chopping the poles and came back over with his machete.

"Nothing."

John reached for his shirt to look at the wound. Blake slapped his hand away and grabbed the machete from him. "Let's go."

"What if they follow our tracks?" Kevin asked.

"If they want to be foolish enough to follow us into a snowstorm, let them. We'll pick them off one by one." He turned back toward the camp and shouted, "Did you hear that? Follow us and you'll all die!"

They did their best to strap Butler to the travois and took turns pulling the groaning man through the woods. The snow fell heavily upon them as they pushed through the foot of snow that had piled up in the last several hours.

The eerie snow-lit darkness played with Blake's mind. He did his best to follow the path, but with the heavy snow and no light, it was virtually impossible to see what direction it went. He stopped under a large, thick fir tree with branches hanging down in the snow. Pushing his way under its snow-ladened curtain, he found the ground around the trunk bare of snow and virtually dry.

"We stopping?" John asked.

Blake reached over and felt Butler's pulse. The weak beat of life felt slow compared to Blake's racing heart. He fell to his knees and began digging into the duff at the base of the trunk.

"Has he lost it?" John asked.

"I don't know, but he's losing too much blood," Kevin said.

"Sir, maybe we should leave this traitor and hurry you back to Laurie." John moved to do just that.

Blake shot a look of pure hatred toward them. "You know we don't leave a man behind."

"But, sir, it could cost you your life," John argued.

Blake gave him a dirty look and then shrugged off his backpack, choking on the gasp of pain that wanted to escape. Digging through his pack, he found his fire starter and a precious piece of tinder. He cleared an area and lit a fire.

"Get me a branch for a torch," he commanded.

Kevin pushed through the curtain of snow-covered branches and returned a few moments later with a wet piece of wood. Blake ripped off a section of the blanket on the travois and wrapped it around the end of the wood.

With his knife, he dug into the trunk until sap oozed out. He covered the blanket wrapped around the stick in the sticky substance. Without preamble, he dipped the torch into the little fire he had made until it lit with a glow. That one little beacon brought with it a sense of hope.

"Now, let's get back to our families." Blake grit his teeth while he pushed to a stand and protected the torch when ducking through the curtain of tree.

The torch didn't help him finding his location, but the fire brought warmth, light, and a sense of peace. He knew that if he pushed on, keeping the ridge to his left, he would eventually hit the road. Once there, they would find their people.

A deep longing for his family filled him. He

wanted to feel Kris's arms around him and see the love in her eyes. She saw something in him that no one else did, something that made him want to be the man she thought he was. He wanted to hoist Tucker up to his shoulders and listen to him ramble on about all the latest observations he's had. He wanted to nuzzle into his sweet-smelling daughter, hear her coo and reach for his bearded face.

Those images kept his feet plodding on until he reached the soft open clearing of the road. A sigh escaped his lips. "We're going to make it, boys. We're so close."

Blake turned up the road, losing himself in his memories of his family again. His reason for living. His reason for everything.

"Look! There, through the trees to the left. A fire glow." Kevin said, pointing into the forest.

Blake stopped, his vision blurring as he saw the orange glow coming through the trees. His body felt numb, his lips and cheeks tingled.

"Our men have returned," he heard a guard shout.

"We made it," Blake whispered and fell face first into the snow.

~*~

Mercy's crying woke Kris up. Next to her, Tucker lay still except his eyes, which were wide and searching. Kris leaned up, soothing Mercy with soft pats and murmurs. Tucker turned his attention to her.

"What's happening?" she asked, trying to push through the grogginess threatening to pull her back into sleep.

"I think Dad's back," he said, though his pale face

said more than his words.

"They're back!" a guard shouted. "Two injured."

"Tucker, you want to lie here next to Ethan?" Laurie asked as she rose and started grabbing her bag.

Arland had already taken off, his laces still untied. Kris bounced Mercy, who had settled into a whimper as she tugged on her boots.

"Are you okay with staying?" Kris asked him.

Tucker shook his head. "I want to see Dad."

"I'll stay with Ethan," the older boy who had lost his real father said. "My sister and I will." He nodded toward his sister sucking on her thumb. His mom had already run toward the commotion, as had Janene.

"Thank you, Nathan," Laurie told the boy. "One of us should be back soon."

The boy nodded and took his sister by the hand to the blanket where Ethan still slept soundly.

Tucker pulled on his boots and stuffed the laces down the sides. "Ready."

Kris stood with him and held out her hand. She warmed with the thought of being in her husband's arms, feeling his strength and comfort. Yet, her heart lurched as she saw Arland and the other men struggling with the bulk of a large and limp man.

"No!" Tucker yelled. He pulled his hand out of hers and ran toward his unconscious dad.

Kris's pulse pounded so loud she felt like it consumed her, and she lived in the constant whooshing of her heartbeat. He had to be alive. He couldn't have left them. She quickly followed her frantic son, catching Arland's eyes as she caught up with him.

"He's alive," he said gravely.

Kris bent over, bracing herself on her knees and

holding Mercy against her. A rush of emotion ran through her in a wave of heat and relief. He's alive. Tucker clung to her, his little cries bringing her out of her own emotional release.

"He's going to be okay," she whispered into his ear.

"I was so scared, Mommy," he said through quiet sobs.

Kris knelt down in front of him. "I know, Sweetie. I was, too." She wrapped her arms around him, sandwiching Mercy in the middle. She didn't mind, though. Her little whimpers turned into coos as she reached for her brother's face.

"Bubbu, bubbu," Mercy said.

Tucker pushed back and wiped at his eyes.

Mercy reached toward him again. "Bubbu, bubbu."

"She's calling me!" Tucker broke into a grin and covered his sister with kisses. "Yes, I'm your brother, your bubbu."

Another group of men passed them as they pulled a travois with Butler on it, blood covering his entire midsection. Kevin and John, though looking exhausted, didn't seem hurt and came behind them. Janene hung on Kevin's arm, tears running down her face and her free hand around her infant in the wrap that Kris had helped her make.

Kris reached out and touched Kevin. "What happened?"

"I'm so sorry. I begged him to leave the traitor so we could carry him, but he just kept pushing on."

"What happened?" she asked again.

"One of the marauders had hidden after everyone else left. He shot at Blake. The traitor jumped in front of the bullet, but it went through him and into Blake."

Kris stopped. Tucker tugged on her arm toward where they had taken Blake. She allowed him to pull her there, her mind trying to process what the man had said. Butler had tried to save Blake's life, but it ended up getting both of them.

Laurie had already set to work on Blake by the time they made it to his side. It had been hard enough to stitch him up after the bear attack, but seeing him bleeding and Laurie digging in for what she presumed to be the bullet made the blood drain from Kris's face, leaving her dizzy. She pulled Tuck into her, shielding his eyes.

Arland came and wrapped both of them in a protective hug. "Why don't we go get warm by the fire?"

Kris shook her head. She needed to stay with Blake, and Tucker must have felt the same way, for he wouldn't let go of her even when Arland proposed a game. With her arm around Tucker, she walked around the other side of Blake, keeping Tucker's eyes shielded from the work being done on him. Seeing David holding Blake down sent waves of nausea through her as she remembered being caught by Chuck and his men.

"If he's unconscious, why are you sitting on his arms?" Kris asked, feeling protective of her husband in such a vulnerable state. He would hate this.

"If he comes to and we aren't restraining him, someone is bound to get hurt." David nodded toward Laurie. "It's going to be okay, Kris. She did the same to Dillon, and he is recovering."

Laurie snuck a glance up at her and smiled, although it was weary and lacking the reassurance

Kris wanted.

"I got the bullet," she said as she sopped up more blood. "I'm pretty sure it didn't hit anything major."

Pretty sure. The words rang in Kris's ears. She trusted Laurie, but it was different with her husband under the knife. At this point, she probably wouldn't fully trust the top surgeon in the country.

"Is he going to be okay?" Tucker's voice quivered.

"As long as we can keep away the infection, yes, I believe so." Laurie went back to focusing on bandaging Blake up.

Kris reached for Blake's outstretched hand, letting hers warm his cold fingers. She focused on his face, seeing the scratches on his cheek and wondering what he had gone through to keep them all safe.

"Just about done." From her bag, Laurie pulled out a salve and heaped a teaspoon-size black dollop on the wound before she bandaged it up. She nodded toward David who took his weight off Blake.

Hannah ran over. "Laurie, we need your help with Butler. His pulse is weak. He's lost so much blood."

Laurie packed her things.

Kris reached over to grasp her arm. "Thank you."

"You're welcome. I have a feeling he'll pull through just fine. Probably just needs a forced sleep. I'll have the men bring over your hides and blankets. He needs to be warmed up."

"We can do that," Tucker said.

"I'm sure you will. I will check on him again after I see to his friend."

"Butler saved Blake's life," Kris said.

Laurie snapped her attention back to Kris.

"He jumped in front of the bullet that shot them both."

"I will do my best." Laurie nodded. "Hannah, I need you get the angelica root from our cart. You know the one. We need to get Butler's blood restored as quickly as possible."

Kris watched her head toward the next fire over where several people stood around Butler. She issued commands like a task force captain. No leader? She shook her head. Laurie was full of it; she led like a general in an army.

A few minutes later, David and another man brought over the hides, which they placed next to Blake, and the blankets, which they handed to Kris. After the hides were set, the men lifted Blake as gently as they could and lowered him to the makeshift bed. He grunted as his body hit the ground, but he didn't open his eyes.

She said her thank yous as Tucker cuddled up next to his dad. Kris situated the blankets and then joined him. After checking on Mercy, who had fallen asleep again, she curled herself around her son and husband. Soon warmth filled their little bed, and the frozen condition of Blake's skin thawed to a more normal temperature.

Tucker softly snored, and she had almost dozed herself when she felt Blake begin to stir. He didn't overreact or sit up straight, wondering where he was. He only tightened his arms around his family and breathed in deeply, letting out a soft murmur before falling back into a deep slumber.

That moment soothed Kris's fears. He would be okay. Having his love surround them eased the worry. They were still together, and together they would make it through anything.

~8~

Blake awoke to the feelings of pins and needles in his hands and an ache in his side. His calf burned when he moved, but it didn't throb as his side did. Warmth surrounded him. It distracted from his pain and made him want to stay there forever. The soft whisper of his family's deep breathing brought him a comfort he had never before experienced. He could stay here for the rest of his life.

He finally forced his eyes to open only to see his wife's beautiful blue eyes showering love on him.

"I made it back," he said, his voice gravelly and his throat raw.

"You did." He heard the emotion in her voice even as her lip trembled.

"It's okay, Krista," he whispered and drew her even closer, a feat made difficult by their boy between them clutching tight to his shirt and his daughter still in Kris's wrap. "It was bad?"

Her head bobbed before she nuzzled into him. "Laurie got the bullet out."

"Butler?" he asked, bracing himself to hear the worst.

"She went to work on him after you. I fell asleep before I heard anything."

He nodded, doing his best to remain stoic. "He saved my life."

"I know."

"I couldn't leave him."

"I would expect nothing less from you." Kris reached up and touched his cheek. When she pulled her hand off, it left a spot that felt bare and cold. She uncovered their beautiful daughter's face. In the firelight, her eyes looked as if they were turning green like his.

Mercy reached out toward him. "Dada, dada."

"Daddy's here, Sweetheart." He bent over to kiss her, his beard causing her to wrinkle her nose.

Tucker stirred then, his arm tightening on him. "Dad?"

"I'm here, Champ."

"We kept you warm enough?" Tucker rose on an elbow, wiping at his eyes and peering at him.

"You did."

"Do you have an infection?"

"I don't think so, Buddy."

"Good," he said solemnly and full of manliness.

Blake tried to push up, doing his best to swallow the groan of pain that burst through him.

"I think you should just rest." Kris planted a hand on his chest.

"I need to find out about Butler."

"Lie down and I will." Kris shivered as she drew the blankets off her and tucked them back around Tucker and him.

She scanned the camp, and he followed her eyes. Dawn barely lit the snow in a pink hue that covered the ground outside of the overhang. Most still slept on the dry ground in bundled blankets and hides. The fires were down low, some close to embers.

"You did well, Kris. Everyone made it?"

"Yes, everyone is now accounted for." Kris put a few sticks on the fire, and he immediately felt the increase in heat. "I'll be right back," she said before leaning down to plant a kiss on him.

Blake watched her go and then eased back, trying to find the most comfortable position for his side. Tucker snuggled in once he stopped moving.

"I prayed for you, Daddy. I'm so glad you are better."

It didn't pass Blake that Tucker had said Daddy rather than Dad. It tore through his heart that he had worried his family. Being back with them and knowing that they were safe made it all worth it.

"Thank you for praying for me, Champ." He kissed the top of his head and wrapped an arm around him. Maybe he should take a lesson from his son and pray for Butler.

Why had he put himself between a bullet meant for him? If Blake reversed the situation, would he have done the same to save Butler? Blake blew out a breath. Mind games did no one any good.

"The snow stopped," Tucker whispered, his head now lying on Blake's chest.

"It's like it came just to cover our tracks." Blake wondered if the storm, though rough, cold, and miserable, had been sent to save them. If he would have followed directly behind his people, would their tracks have been visible at all by the time the marauders had made it down and decided to follow them? They had to wait for Dillon, though, and events kept piling up reason after reason to stay behind.

"It did, Dad. It did," Tucker said reverently. "Did you know little sister saved us on the journey here?"

Blake realized then that, although he had told Kris she had done well, he had not asked how the whole trek went. Guilt twisted in his gut, and he promised himself he would ask Kris as soon as she returned.

"Tell me about it," he told his son.

There were times he thought Kris and Tucker saw too much behind coincidental circumstances. As Tucker told the story, he wondered if Mercy screaming at that moment had actually been the miraculous event they saw it as, or had she just happened to be upset right then? There was no way to know, and if believing that his sister had that special bond with him made Tucker happy and treasure his sister, then he saw no harm in it.

As Tucker finished the story, Kris came back and knelt down by them. She pulled Mercy out of the wrap, and she wiggled, kicked, waved, and squealed in delight. Tucker sat up and made a place for his sister in front of him between them.

"I was just telling Daddy about how you saved us again, Little Sister." Tucker let her wrap her hand around one of his fingers while he supported her sitting up. "Look, she's sitting!"

"She is," Kris said gently and then looked at Blake. "How are you doing? Can I get you anything?"

"I want to hear about your journey, but I am actually quite hungry," Blake said.

"You should eat then. You need your energy to heal," Laurie said as she kneeled next to Kris. "May I look at your wound?"

Kris pulled back the blanket, and Blake pulled up his shirt. He craned his neck to see the wound, never having the chance to check it out in the light. Laurie pulled off the bandage and cleaned off some black goop from his wound. It didn't look nearly as awful as he thought it would.

"No infection," Laurie said with a sigh of relief. She piled more black salve on it.

Blake sucked in a breath at the sting. "What is in that stuff?"

"Mainly activated charcoal." Laurie placed a fresh bandage on his side.

"You're putting charcoal in my wound?" Blake pulled his shirt back down, groaning as he tried to sit up.

"You should rest more, and yes, I am. Activated charcoal helps ward off infection. As does this tea." She handed a pouch to Kris. "This yarrow, nettle, and wild rose tea will also help restore your blood and help the existing cells carry more oxygen and thus faster healing."

"I'll take faster healing," Blake said, not liking how sore his side really was. He pulled up his leg then, feeling the burn in his calf.

"What was that?" Kris asked. "Are you hurt somewhere else?"

"Just a scratch."

"Where?" Kris said, crossing her arms.

He pulled out his leg and tugged his pants up. He couldn't see it from that angle, but by the look on the women's faces, it was more than just a scratch.

"Well, your *scratch* is infected. We need to irrigate it and put some of this salve on it," Laurie said as she rose. "I'll be right back."

"Do I need to do a full body check?" Kris asked, her lips thin and eyes stormy.

"My answer to that will always be a yes," he teased.

"That's not what I meant." Kris did her best to keep a straight face, but the corner of her mouth twitched.

"Besides the scratches on my cheek, which I'm sure you and Laurie would have said something about if they needed attention, I don't know of any more injuries." He watched her, enjoying the playful banter. It made him feel like they weren't fighting for their lives for once. The idea made him remember Butler, and his gut twisted. "You haven't mentioned Butler." Fear that he hadn't made it caused Blake to tense in preparation for the news.

"Laurie is doing her best. He's fighting, but he lost so much blood. Only time will tell."

Blake nodded. The news was better than he had expected. He squeezed his eyes shut, *God, help him heal. He saved my life.*

Kris rested a hand on his chest. "It was a very brave thing for him to do."

"It was." He opened his eyes. "I still don't understand it. He has a family, too."

"From the news traveling around," Laurie said as she returned, "he can't go back to his family without them receiving repercussions."

"I hadn't thought about that," Blake said. "We staged his death so he could leave the army without his family being mistreated because of it."

"Maybe once we are in New Forest Glen, Mr. Butler can bring his family back here. He said his baby is about the same age as Little Sister." Tucker took Mercy's hands. "You would like that, wouldn't you?"

"That's quite the journey, but not a bad idea. Things in the cities are treacherous." Blake thought about Tucker's idea. What would a few more mouths to feed cost? The man saved his life. The least he could do would be to offer his family a safe haven from the chaos that had taken over their world. If he healed enough to make the journey, that is.

~*~

Kris kept her gaze down, pretending to soothe her daughter as she quickly made her way back to where Blake rested. Maybe if she acted like she didn't hear the people calling to talk to her, she wouldn't have to stop. She glanced up long enough to make sure she still headed in the right direction and lowered her eyes just as Janene lifted her hand in greeting.

Finally, she made it to the fire area they shared with Arland and Laurie. Tucker and Ethan played on the blankets. She wondered how long those cars would last. Would they become relics that spoke of a different age? She refocused and met Blake's eyes.

"The council is meeting," she whispered.

"Then I need to move," he said, groaning as he pushed up to his hands and knees.

"Laurie said you should rest," Kris said, concern battling in her. She knew the council needed Blake, but at what cost to him?

Blake waved off her comment as he came to a standing position. His side throbbed, feeling like someone had used a meat pulverizer on it. His calf stung as well, but it was the dizziness that almost sent him back to his knees.

"I don't know, Blake." Kris grabbed his arm to steady him. "I can be your runner back and forth."

"I need to be there." The way he said it, Kris knew there would be no convincing him otherwise.

Hannah came over then, smiling as always. "Laurie asked me to watch the boys for a few."

"Thank you, Hannah," Kris said in relief. She didn't want Blake walking to the meeting by himself, but she also didn't want to miss out on the decisions being made today. After the trek here, she felt a responsibility to these people.

"Where you guys going?" Tucker asked, standing.

"To the council meeting," Blake told him quietly.

"Oh, I'm coming, too."

"Not yet, Sweetie. I have a feeling you will be on it when you are older, but right now, only grownups are allowed."

"Little Sister is going," he said, crossing his arms.

"Little Sister can't talk yet," Blake said. "Play. Take advantage of the time to just be a kid."

Kris turned to watch her husband. Had he really just said that?

"Come on, Tucker. Ethan and I are making a track in the dirt. We need your expertise with this tunnel." Hannah smiled up at him.

Tucker turned and knelt down next to Ethan. "Well, the first thing we need is a good foundation."

Kris touched Hannah's shoulder and mouthed her thanks. That girl had the art of distraction down. She would have made an excellent teacher. Still could, Kris thought.

Blake pulled her back to the present moment as he took his first step and nearly stumbled. She saw, as well as felt, the eyes of the others, so closely assembled, watching their fearless Survivalist struggle. Kris wrapped an arm around him lovingly and helped support his weight as they traveled to where the council was meeting at the farthest fire, away from the others.

It wasn't really a council, but that is what Kris

called it. They had no set of rules or voted-in leaders, but the group consisting of Arland, Blake, Laurie, Pastor Rob, Mitchel, David, and now herself had started meeting quietly before the community meetings to ensure they were all on the same page. To her, it was a council, and every community needed one.

When Laurie looked up and saw them, her eyes darkened and her lips thinned. "What are you doing up?"

"You think I would let you all decide the fate of the world without me?" Blake pushed forth a smile, though the crease in his brow gave away his pain.

"Since you're here, sit down." Arland nodded at the log someone had brought in. "We were discussing whether we should stay here for a few days to rest and recover."

"It's already close to midday," David said. "My family is tired, and their boots are still wet."

"Everyone is exhausted. Yesterday felt like a week," Mitchel added.

Kris thought a few days of rest would be good for Blake. He couldn't make a journey in his present condition, and she knew he would never submit to people pulling him in a travois. She watched as Blake stared out into the vast land of snow around them.

The birds had woken in birdsong as the sun had risen and the snow stopped. The land felt at peace, frozen in fresh, clean beauty. Yet, she had no idea of the danger that still lay out there.

"Are we still under threat?" she asked, though she looked at her husband as did everyone else.

"We won't know for sure without sending runners back," Blake said.

"Then that should be our first task." Arland nodded. "Do we all agree to stay at least until we have more information?"

Everyone nodded in agreement.

"So who should we send?" Arland asked.

"Dillon was our fastest runner," Mitchel said.

"He won't be running for some time." Laurie folded her arms.

Blake stiffened, and one look told Kris that he felt guilty for not asking about him. "He will be okay?"

"I don't think he'll have permanent damage, but really, I am no expert. Bullet removing is something outside my normal skill set," Laurie said with a small smile.

"Let's hope those days are behind us," Arland said.

Kris hoped so as well. Could they really find this Promised Land that Blake had shared with them and live undisturbed as their children grew?

"Keep moving," one of the guards, Declan, called out, interrupting everyone's thoughts.

Every head under the overhang looked up at the guard, who unceremoniously pushed the muzzle of his rifle into a person lost in an oversized jacket. The hood covered the person's downturned face, and the hands that were held up had holes in the gloves.

Arland immediately stood and strode over to the guard. "What is this?" he asked, his tone not his normal kindly voice.

"I've caught another one!" Declan cheered, looking around with glee glowing in his eyes.

"Has this person threatened you to be treated this way?" Arland asked, eyeing the gun.

"No, he has given no resistance." Declan shrugged. "I have a gun pointed at him."

"We will talk about protocol later." Arland rubbed a hand down his face. "Thank you, Declan. You may go back to your family now. Have John take over your shift."

Declan strutted into the overhang while everyone stared.

"Follow me," Arland said to the covered person as he made his way back to where the council sat.

"He should have at least checked for weapons," Blake growled beside Kris.

She agreed. Bringing someone into camp without ensuring they couldn't harm them was not the smartest response.

"Sit," Arland said calmly, nodding toward an open space between Pastor Rob and David.

"Are you armed?" David asked.

The person sat, reaching for the hood with trembling hands. A few council members gasped as a woman stared back at them. Her intelligent, almost black eyes watched them, seeming to observe and analyze everything.

"It would be foolish not to be," she responded with a hint of amusement. "Have no fear, I do not intend to attack."

Kris covered her mouth, trying to swallow the giggle that wanted to burst forth. She had no idea who this lady was, but she already liked her.

"Why are you here?" Arland asked, the corner of his mouth twitching.

"Hoping for sanctuary." She looked each of them squarely in the eye.

"From?" Blake asked.

"Meyers and his men."

"They have women with them?" Mitchel asked.

"Not many. Only when necessary."

"Why were you necessary to them?" Arland asked.

"I'm a dentist turned medic."

Laurie sat up straighter. Her hand landed on Arland's arm. Kris watched her friend analyze the woman before her as hope lit her eyes.

"How did you find us?" David looked out into the pristine snow.

"I had no idea if I would. I followed the paths of least resistance, and when I found the road, I had hope that it would lead to you, but," she said with a shrug, "I'm just glad it did."

"No one came with you?" Blake asked, his eyes narrowing.

"No." She looked down. "Two of us had planned on it, but he...didn't make it. I escaped last night while it still snowed."

"They could follow her tracks," David said.

She shook her head. "I made sure they couldn't. I took a cedar branch and covered my tracks for the first mile or so."

Blake sat back in his seat, his hand scratching at his beard. The woman impressed Kris, too.

"You weren't scared to come out into the woods in the middle of a snowstorm?" Blake asked.

"I grew up in Wyoming. Nothing about the woods scares me. I should have bugged out as soon as I had the chance," she said, looking down at her hands.

"What's your name?" Kris asked.

"Lexi. Lexi Yarrow."

"It's nice to meet you, Lexi," Arland said. "What are your intentions here?"

"As I said, sanctuary. I just can't tolerate being with Meyers anymore. The things they do are...inhuman. I'm hoping my skills will help me find a new community with you."

Kris could see the scrutiny while the others watched her. She knew she trusted easily, but something about this gal spoke to her, and Laurie practically bounced in her seat.

From across the overhang, Butler's moan caused all eyes to turn toward him.

"Is someone in need of medical assistance now? I would be happy to prove myself." Lexi met their eyes, almost pleading.

Laurie tugged on Arland's arm, and he looked toward Blake. "Blake, how do you feel about that?"

Kris watched Blake read the woman in front of them. Lexi held his gaze, not with rudeness, but an openness, a willingness for him to really see her. It made Kris like her even more.

Blake finally turned to Laurie. "You'll supervise her?"

Laurie bobbed her head vigorously.

Blake nodded at Arland, who said, "Okay, Laurie, see if Lexi can help our friend. Kris, why don't you go along...as backup?"

Part of Kris wanted to stay and hear what the council had to say, but she knew Blake would fill her in later. She rose and left the circle with Laurie and Lexi.

Everyone stared at them as they made their way toward the fire, where Butler slept fitfully.

"I'm guessing you don't have new people joining all the time?" Lexi said lightheartedly.

"Most of us are from the community those marauders you were with just took over. We were all neighbors," Laurie said.

"Oh," Lexi said, and for the first time, Kris heard hesitancy in the strong woman's voice.

"We're newcomers, though." Kris smiled with encouragement.

"The big guy is your husband?"

Kris laughed at the description. "Yeah, Blake. The people here call him The Survivalist. It's a long story."

"I hope I have long enough to hear it." She snuck a glance back at the council.

"I can't see them turning you out in the snow." Kris stopped in front of the fire where Butler moaned.

Lexi gasped and fell to Butler's side.

"You know him?" Laurie asked.

"Yes. He was one of the only men who treated me with respect in that group and would protect me when needed. I thought he was dead." Lexi touched his cheek, and Butler's eyes flew open. "Ben. It's Lexi."

Butler started to crawl away and looked frantically around.

"Chantry...," he whispered.

"Blake is okay, thanks to you. You're safe here. Laurie patched you up. Just rest," Kris said, pulling the blankets back up around him.

Once he settled, Kris eyed Laurie before they both turned to watch Lexi and the mixture of emotions that flooded her expression.

"He looked scared of me," Lexi said.

"Maybe seeing you made him think he was back with Meyers' group?" Kris said, but she would watch this woman closer. Butler's reaction wasn't what she had expected for the woman she had felt connected to so easily.

"That could be it." Lexi blinked rapidly. "What happened to him? How is he here? Meyers thought you guys threw him off a cliff."

Kris watched her warily. If the woman was a spy for Meyers, then she could give intel that would be a death sentence for the family he had tried to protect by faking his own death.

"He saved my husband's life," Kris said tentatively.

"Gunshot through his midsection," Laurie said. "I patched him up the best I could."

Lexi nodded. "I know that look. I understand that it will take awhile for you all to trust me. It is how I said, though." She looked down at Butler with a glow that Kris could only read as love or deep caring. "We had talked about escaping many times. When he…when I thought he had died, I decided to escape on my own."

"To the people who had killed him?" Laurie asked.

Lexi shrugged. "I knew your people were only protecting themselves. Besides, nothing could be worse than what I have seen this last year."

Kris chewed her lip. She couldn't imagine what she would have done in that situation.

"So, you already have a doctor." Lexi looked down at her gloved hands, holes showing her skin.

"I would call myself more of a healer. I am a midwife," Laurie said.

"She saved my daughter and me." Kris uncovered Mercy's face. Seeing her awake, she pulled her out of the wrap, and Mercy immediately started babbling.

Lexi started to reach a hand out, but she pulled it back to wipe the tears streaming down her face.

"Are you okay?" Kris asked.

"I'm sorry. I'm exhausted. Walking through the snow all night by myself and wondering if someone would find me…I just need a good sleep."

"What about Butler?" Laurie asked. "I really don't know what I'm doing with a wound like this."

Lexi looked up at her, gratitude keeping her eyes moist. "May I?" She pointed to Butler.

"Please," Laurie said.

Lexi lifted up Butler's shirt, gently touched around the bandage, and then did her best to look at the exit wound on his back.

"Seems to be holding up well. Time will tell, I guess." She lovingly tucked the blankets around Butler.

"Would you mind if I lay close to Ben? We could share warmth."

Kris hesitated. She looked to Laurie who shrugged. She couldn't help but trust the woman. Something about her seemed genuine. "Of course. It would be good to have someone keep an eye on him anyway."

"Thank you for your kindness." Lexi smiled before pulling out her blankets and setting them up alongside Butler.

"This world needs a lot more kindness these days. Get some rest." Kris rose with Laurie following.

"Thank you for looking at him," Laurie said.

"Thank you for saving him." Lexi smiled.

"I'm going to check on Tucker," Kris told Laurie.

"I'll be there in just a few. I need to persuade the council to let Lexi stay. We need someone with more medical experience than me," Laurie said quietly, for Kris's ears alone.

"I wish you luck, my friend," Kris said. With a glance at the council, she continued toward her son.

Tucker had pulled out a book from his bag and was reading it to Ethan and a few other kids. They sat mesmerized by the story. The scene gave her a little sense of normalcy. Kids lost in a book. Now that was something she understood.

"He's a terrific reader for being so young," Hannah said as Kris approached.

"He started at three. Surprised me. He hasn't stopped since."

"That's impressive. We need to keep that education going," she said, nudging Kris.

"Yes. Once we are settled, let's bring the idea to the council."

Hannah smiled at her. Then her gaze fell past her, and her smile deepened as a slight pink rose in her cheeks.

Kris glanced over her shoulder and saw Tyler looking at them. "Go on. I've got the kids."

"You sure?"

"I'm sure, Miss Lovebird."

"I really like him. He's kind and gentle, but protective and manly all at the same time."

"He's a good guy, Hannah. I'm happy to see life continuing even in the midst of this chaos."

"I don't think it could ever stop, Kris. Not with things like this." Hannah squeezed Kris's hand before walking past her toward Tyler.

Kris only watched for a second, but long enough that she longed for those sweet days when she fell in love with Blake. Would a relationship beginning in such turmoil last? Would it be stronger? Hers and Blake's certainly had become stronger, but the foundation had already been built.

She sighed as she sat down and let Mercy bounce

on her legs while she listened to her son read to the other kids. If she stopped thinking about how things used to be and focused on just the wonderful moments like these, she could almost feel at peace. She wondered how long it could last, for every moment had to end at some point.

~9~

Blake woke instantly, shooting to a sitting position before the pain in his side stopped him. The guttural scream sounded again. He pushed to his feet, following it in the ember-lit overhang. When he realized the sound emitted from Butler, he pushed through his pain and ran toward the man who saved his life.

A shadow loomed over his friend as light lit his cut-open stomach. The person sitting over Butler turned toward him and a headlamp blinded his vision. Blake threw up an arm and pushed toward the light, a growl emitting from his throat.

He grabbed both of the person's wrists until the bloody scalpel dropped to the ground.

"Please," a female voice cried out. "Let me fix him."

Blake tore off her headlamp, blinking his eyes until he could see Lexi's face through the dark spots. "What do you think you're doing?"

He heard the camp waking up around them, and soon Laurie and Arland stood next to him.

"He had internal bleeding," she pleaded. "Let me go and I'll show you. Please. The more blood he loses, the smaller the chance he survives."

Blake let go of her wrists, and she immediately went to work. He shined the light onto the slice she had made in Butler. Laurie kneeled next to her.

"See the discoloration here and here?" Lexi

pointed and looked at Laurie. "If I don't stitch it up, he'll die."

"Is your equipment sterilized?" Laurie asked.

"Yes, I still have medical supplies. One good thing about Meyers."

"Blake, give her back the headlamp. Arland, grab my medical bag. We need to get him to relax."

"I gave him a sedative."

"He screamed," Blake said through clenched teeth as he handed her the headlamp.

"There are some things that make it through these lightweight sedatives. If you want to help, you can hold him down."

Blake hated the idea of holding the man down, but if it meant he lived, it would be worth it. If he could trust the woman to save him. Kris had shared that Lexi and Butler had known each other, but how well and with what intentions he didn't know yet. He needed his comrade to wake up so he could clear the air.

It felt like forever while Lexi worked with practiced hands, and Laurie assisted. Every once in a while Laurie would meet his eyes and nod. If she approved of what the woman did to Butler, then maybe they could trust her.

Lexi sat back as Laurie gooped the black salve on all of Butler's wounds and then bandaged him up.

"Will he make it?" Arland asked.

"We'll know more tomorrow." Lexi looked up at him. "I'm sorry. I should have woken you before operating. I just got so scared. It needed to happen right away. I worried you wouldn't trust me to do it. That discussion might have taken too long."

"I didn't know," Laurie said, staring at Blake,

horror and guilt dancing like the flames from the fire reflected in her eyes.

"You did your best." Blake reached out a hand to her. "I appreciate that."

"My point has been made," Laurie said, her eyes now leveled on Arland. "We need her."

Arland glanced at Blake. "We give her a chance to prove herself, but no unnecessary intel."

"Thank you," Lexi said, her head lowering and body shaking. She reached out and caressed Butler's face.

Maybe Kris was right, but she trusted easily. If Butler made it out of this and he cleared Lexi, then he would give her a chance.

~*~

Kris adjusted Mercy as she took off her pack. The sun sank low in the sky, but Blake felt sure they were almost there. The people of the camp sat on the now snow-free ground to rest while he and several others went ahead to check. It had been a grueling two days of hiking, but they had prevailed. It had been a smart move to wait until most of the snow melted, at least in the lower elevations.

Tucker sat next to Ethan, chewing on a piece of jerky. He watched Butler with a curious expression. Kris would have to remember to ask him what he saw. When she turned her attention to Butler, she saw him settling against the tree, his face pale, but dark blue eyes light and happy.

After Lexi had performed emergency surgery, his recovery had become quite rapid. With a combination of the pharmaceuticals she had and the addition of

Laurie's herbs, he had been strong enough to make the journey not even a week later.

Lexi smiled at her before squatting next to Butler, giving him a drink of water. Kris could see the affection between them. She couldn't say love. Butler remained faithful to his wife, but the two had a bond that gave each other strength.

She thought about Blake out there, pushing through the exhaustion she knew overwhelmed him. He was still healing as well, not that he let that on to anyone. He had a drive, a mission to complete, so she understood his need to get there tonight if possible.

He had told her the other night that she gave him strength. Kris had almost laughed until she saw the seriousness lining his eyes. She nestled into him then, whispering that he was her strength, too. Having someone to lean on during these times could mean the difference between life and death. She saw that in her and Blake, in Arland and Laurie, in Butler and Lexi, and even in the newly budding Hannah and Tyler.

Kris hugged her daughter to her. She hoped that she and Tuck would find that person who helped them discover their own strength that lived inside. A breeze picked up, the birds chirped cheerily, and Kris closed her eyes to embrace the moment as peace filled her. She felt like home called.

A half-hour later, Blake strutted back into the rest place, a wide smile brightening her world. She hadn't seen him smile like that for such a long time. Immediately, a surge of happiness filled her. He had found New Forest Glen.

"Pack up, Tucker," she said, her voice lighter than she had heard it in months. "We're going home."

Blake brought her into his arms. "That's right, my love. We are going home."

~*~

Blake took Kris's hand and helped her up to the ridge. He had her leave the cart on the trail below where the others caught up. Tucker scrambled up to stand next to them. Blake wanted his family to see their new home from the best vantage point.

"Oh, wow," Kris whispered, her eyes scanning across the valley now bathed in an amber alpine glow.

Blake wrapped his arms around his family while he admired the view as well. The green foliage that covered the ground would provide fresh nutrients, the stream that passed on the far side would give them water for cooking and cleaning, the spring closer to the end of the valley would give them consistent drinking water, and the evergreens and deciduous trees would give them substance, shade, and shelter.

There was more than enough room for everyone to spread out or huddle close together, whatever they decided. As for them, he already had the location for their dwelling in mind.

"See that sloping ridge line there?" Blake pointed, showing his family.

Both Kris and Tucker nodded and Mercy cooed.

"That's where I would like to build our dwelling," Blake said.

"It's beautiful, Blake." Kris leaned into him.

"It's different than I thought." Tucker toed the ground.

"How, Champ?"

"I thought the ridges were higher that way, and the creek was bigger, and it ran through the middle and then down into a canyon out of camp."

Tucker explained in such detail that it sent a shiver through Blake, almost knocking out his great mood and confidence. His son's vision hadn't changed before. Why would it be so different now? Instead, Blake shook his head and focused on the moment.

"Sometimes, things look different in our minds, son. Are you not happy with this location?" Blake asked, sweeping his arm at the wide valley below them before resting it across his son's shoulders again.

Tucker squinted in the direction Blake had showed them for their dwelling. "It's great, Dad. I can see the tree where I'm going to build Mercy's swing."

"You're building her a swing?" Blake asked, steering them back down to where people started to gather on the trail.

"Yes. I have it engineered in my mind already. Ethan is going to help me. We won't be able to make the rope until spring when the grasses grow tall, but she will have it in time for her birthday."

Blake stopped walking to look at his son. "You are amazing, Tuck. Mercy is lucky to have you as a big brother."

"We are lucky to have her," Tucker said, looking at his little sister, who stretched out a hand from her wrap to him.

"Yes, we are." Blake brought them all into his arms. "We are so lucky."

"I agree," Kris said.

Blake led their people down the trail, through the narrow opening of the valley and into the wide open space just as the first star popped out. He stopped to point at the shining beacon of hope. Tucker's eyes squeezed shut as his lips moved in a silent wish. Blake closed his eyes to make his wish, too.

Looking at his family and the people milling around New Forest Glen, he realized that his wish had already come true. They had made it, found their sanctuary, and would have peace and abundance. God had led them to their promised land.

He would do his best to ensure none forgot the faith that it took to get them here.

****

I hope you enjoyed the Chantrys' trek into the wilderness to find the new location of New Forest Glen as they learned that survival was a team effort.

This is the conclusion of Part One of Grant Us Mercy. Part Two begins with Installment Six. New Forest Glen is supposed to be the Promised Land, yet the Chantrys and the community are faced with adversary after adversary. Will they survive together until winter releases its death grip on the community?

Find out by grabbing Part Two of Grant Us Mercy!

http://www.amazon.com/dp/B08YWX67LF

Keep reading for a sneak peek of Part Two.

[Join DC's Reader Team](https://mailchi.mp/16e5d6555ef6/dclittlereaderteam) for sneak peeks and specials!

https://mailchi.mp/16e5d6555ef6/dclittlereaderteam

Join DC Little on Facebook for survival tips and other fun posts.
www.facebook.com/groups/littlesthrivalists

Want to be the first to know when the next installment is released? Join DC's Reader Team HERE
https://mailchi.mp/16e5d6555ef6/dclittlereaderteam

Free Book!

[Join DC Little's Reader Team](#), and get a free book exclusive to her Thrivalist Team!

Blake had imparted some of his knowledge with the Arland in Installment One. In Installment Three, you saw a new side to Arland. Want to know what caused him to transform?
Read this exclusive story!

Grant Us Mercy:
Arland's Transformation

READ NOW!

https://mybookcave.com/d/d22b818b/

Next in Grant Us Mercy

Grant Us Mercy: Part TWO

Pushed into the wilderness in the dead of winter, one community attempts to survive without destroying themselves.

Grant Us Mercy returns with the Chantrys and their New Forest Glen community struggling for survival. They may have left Meyers and his marauders behinds them, for now, but their challenges have just begun.

Arriving at their new location in the dead of winter without all the stores they had prepared, leaves them in a predicament. Who do they listen to when decisions need to be made?

Record breaking snow storms, rushing frozen rivers, lack of food, and a community at the edge of collapse combine to make Blake wish he had never joined forces with Arland and his camp.

Will New Forest Glen become broken? Maybe Tucker's vision foretold of a location just for the Chantrys.

Join Blake and Kris on this action-packed Part Two of the hair-raising journey in the post-apocalyptic serial novel, Grant Us Mercy.

GRAB NOW!
http://www.amazon.com/dp/B08YWX67LF

SNEAK PEEK OF PART TWO
INSTALLMENT SIX – CHAPTER ONE

DATE: December 14   06:36

Blake should be relieved.
He sat atop the rocky outcropping overlooking the new camp as the end of his security shift came to a close. The foundation and map of structures were laid out a semicircle around the central fire, just as it had been in Arland's camp before. The conical bark dwellings had been voted the best shelter. The first people that lived in this area had survived for hundreds of years in bark dwellings. Why shouldn't they be good enough for them now?

As people awoke, they milled about greeting each other. Their happy voices traveled to him on the gentle breeze. Some didn't seem affected by their recent escape into the wilderness but just went about their daily activities with gratitude and optimism. Including his wife.

They were content and excited that their journey had come to an end and for the possibility of creating a haven for their families. Plans to do more than survive, but thrive, were underway as they talked about government, creating schools, and more of what normal societies would have. The people were genuinely happy and optimistic. Why wasn't he?

Something nagged at him. That unsettling sensation had started eating away at him the day they arrived when he proudly showed Kris and Tucker their new location. The location he had thought for sure would provide everything they needed.

There was protection not only from intruders but also from the elements as well. The little valley nestled in the midst of the ridges, kept the brunt of storms from unleashing upon them. The plant life had the majority of all they needed with only small treks to the medicinal plants that didn't grow here in the sheltered valley. An active creek ran through, and then there was the spring, their lifeblood of survival. Yes, it had everything they needed.

Yet, Blake saw the look in Tucker's eyes. This wasn't the land that he had seen in his visions. Blake did his best to push the thought out of his mind. The boy was just a child, and maybe his perception of the land in his vision wasn't accurate, or he hadn't seen as much as he thought, or they were just fanciful ideas.

He did his best to falsify any notion that this wasn't the perfect spot for the people, for his family.

His best wasn't enough. The uneasiness settled on him like an invisible cloak of responsibility. It weighed him down and left him unable to fully enjoy the present.

A twig broke behind him. Blake froze and cocked his head as he listened. Though the leaves and debris littered the forest floor like a moist carpet, the heavy steps were unmistakable.

An exasperated sigh drifted toward him, and the man stood directly behind him.

"You knew I was here...again."

"What kind of military leader would I be if I wasn't aware?" Blake asked as he rose to greet his friend. "You've done well, David. I would have heard a lesser man yards away. You got close...too close."

When he slapped David's back, he let his arm

drape around his friend's shoulders for a brief moment.

"Quite the place we are building, eh?" David said in an awe-filled voice.

"Yes. Yes, it is." Blake scanned the village again.

The community spread across most of the valley's width. Movement in the southeast corner caught his attention. Turning his head in that direction, he saw his son lift his hand while seemingly staring right at him. He lifted his hand as well, feeling the weight of responsibility pulling on his arm.

"You going to tell me what's been bothering you?" David asked, keeping his gaze on Tucker who had turned back to stacking rocks on the outline of their shelter.

"Nothing to tell."

"I still don't understand why you have the need to build your shelter so far from the encampment. Are we really that bad?"

Blake scrutinized his friend. Fine lines had etched around his eyes and mouth. He had always been a mite serious, but he had become contemplative and ever-observant since the exodus.

"No. It has nothing to do with you or anyone else." He shrugged and dropped his gaze to all the people working, laughing, and jostling each other. "I'm a solitary man. It's always been my way."

"We're keeping the structures more spaced this time. See?" David said, pointing to where his wife and children piled bark by the circle they dug out for their structure. "I'm even trying to come up with a way to section off the interior. For a little privacy." He winked at Blake.

"Yes, I hear you are trying for another baby."

"Why not? We have a midwife and now a medic. The fate of humankind might depend on us contributing more." He laughed and slapped Blake on the back.

Blake let the smile curl his lips, though the effect didn't reach his eyes or his heart. The idea of having more children, seeing his wife so close to death again, terrified him. The naïveté of the man, of most of the people in the camp, worried him. With the changes in their world, people would die more and from the simplest of things.

Besides, how could they think they were the only community trying to survive off the land as they were? True, the population would certainly be decreased. What had they said? Close to a ninety percent fatality rate.

The fate of mankind didn't sit solely on their shoulders, but their contribution certainly could make a difference. Maybe he stressed too much, as Kris told him. As long as they could provide for the increasing mouths to feed, why not encourage them to breed? The larger their village, the stronger they would be if ever attacked.

~*~

Kris watched Tucker wave at his dad. Once again, her husband sat on the rock outcropping that rose along the ridge. He had been withdrawn ever since they arrived at this place. She blew out a breath, watching the warmth of the air crystallize and fade away.

Cold seeped into her bones. Even with the sun shining down on them now, she couldn't shake the chill from the night. They needed to finish their shelter.

The spring gave them fresh drinking water, but at times like right now, Kris missed having to boil water for purification in the morning. The fire at least added warmth, even if it did use extra fuel. Wrapping the blanket tighter around her daughter held against her in the wrap, she bent over to continue digging out the circumference of their shelter.

Blake should be down here helping. His strength would make this job twice if not three times as fast. Yet, he sat up there moping, looking as if the fate of the world lay on his shoulders alone.

She stood again to stretch her back, her daughter cooing and reaching up to touch her cheek. Mercy. A smile tugged at the corners of her mouth.

"Dada," Mercy started and then continued in her babbling, telling Kris the secrets of the world. If only she could understand.

Yet, a peace filled her, and she looked once more upon her husband at his outpost. She felt his gaze caress her. He loved her and their family. Judging him for not being there every moment wasn't fair. He worked harder and longer than anyone. Besides, it had been his morning on duty.

A yearning ached within her. Why wouldn't he share his fear with her? Whatever bothered him seemed to be bothering their son as well. Tucker could be more easily distracted by the moment, especially when the other children came by to steal him away for a game of tag or rocks and sticks. Yet, times like now, when he worked silently and thought no one paid him any attention, he had the same crease between his eyebrows as his dad and the same heaviness bending his shoulders.

Kris pushed up off her knees and brushed at the dirt. Enough was enough.

"Tucker, time for a break. Come get something to eat and drink."

Working this much even before breakfast was new to them. That was one of the hardships of eating communally. You had to wait for everyone else.

The boy obeyed, taking the jerky she offered him and drinking long from his water bottle. He worked hard for a seven-year-old, with a determination that she hadn't seen in any other second-grader. Even now, she could hear several parents exasperatedly scolding their children who would rather throw dirt at each other than dig any more of it up.

"We won't get it up by tonight again, will we?" he asked, his gaze scanning their large shelter. "Maybe we should make it smaller."

Kris laughed. Just last night she had suggested the same thing to Blake. "You know your father has his reasons."

"No one else's structure is so large, though. Some of them will be sleeping warm tonight." He drew his hands into the sleeves of his jacket and wrapped his arms around himself.

"Maybe we could set up the tarp tonight to keep the heat in."

Tucker nodded.

"Is that's what's bothering you?" she asked her son, wanting to take the weight off his shoulders.

"Being cold?" he asked, not meeting her eyes.

"Yes," she said, watching him intently.

He shrugged. "Everyone thinks this place is perfect."

"And you don't?" She had heard his hesitation when Blake first showed them the overlook but passed it off as weariness or a disappointment in his own internal fantasy, but his face now told a more serious story.

"It has everything we need," he said, mimicking his dad's words whenever asked the same question.

"Tuck." She took his chin in her hand and turned his face until he finally met her eyes. "You have always told me everything. Don't change that now."

His gaze deepened as his eyes looked as if they lit on fire.

"It's not right."

"Tell me."

"The creek should be coming out of the cliffs with waterfalls and pools. The valley should be more of a triangle than a rectangle. The ridges are taller, the trees larger, and the spring should be trickling out of the wall of rock, not bubbling up from the ground."

"Oh, I see." She took a bite of jerky, contemplating his words. The color of his eyes had faded as he described the land as if he looked upon a memory. It was the same look that overcame him when he had visions.

"You don't, though. No one does. Why do I have to know these things? I don't want to. I don't want to know." He stood up, his fists clenched at his sides and his jaw set as his father's did when angry.

Kris's heart ached. She opened her arms, but he didn't enter them. Instead, he stormed out of the dugout beginnings of their dwelling. With an angry swing of his arm, he yanked up the not-quite empty bucket and stormed off toward the spring.

When had he stopped letting her comfort him?

It took all of her self-control to not follow him and bring him into her arms. If he needed space, she needed to respect that and let him have the independence that he fought for so hard.

Yet, it hurt. It hurt worse than if her own heart had been broken. Worse than if she were the one with the burden of knowing things that may happen in the future…a future impossible to change.

She scanned the village as it took form. Some structures now had their poles set and centered at the top.

The main fire's coals faintly glowed. She wished she could feel the warmth like the women who busily prepared breakfast at the fire. Today wasn't her day to cook, though, and there was still so much to do before they could raise their own poles and enclose their shelter. How they needed that shelter. A solid night's sleep untroubled by waking up shaking from cold was needed for all of them.

Maybe her boys would cheer up once their home had been completed. A warm dwelling full of laughter could do a spirit some good. They needed to have fun and time to see that, though this place may not be the place they will be forever, for now it was perfect.

****

I hope you enjoyed the sneak peak of Part Two.
Continue reading here:
http://www.amazon.com/dp/B08YWX67LF